THE MOON
and
THE GRYPHON

a novel

T.F. LONG

Copyrighted Material

This is a work of imagination—with places, characters, and events fictitious or are used fictively. Any resemblance to persons living or dead is completely coincidental.

THE MOON and THE GRYPHON

Copyright © 2023 by Thomas F. Long

All Rights Reserved
No part of this publication may be reproduced, stored in a retrieval system or transmitted, in any form or by any means—electronic, mechanical, photocopying, recording or otherwise—without prior written permission from the publisher, except for the inclusion of brief quotations in a review.

For information about this title
Contact the publisher:

NORTH HOUSE CREATIVE ARTS (N.C.A.)

northhouse.nca@earthlink.net

ISBN:
979-8-9888176-0-4 (hardcover)
979-8-9888176-1-1 (softcover)
979-8-9888176-2-8 (eBook)

Printed in the United States of America
First Edition

Cover and Interior design: 1106 Design

For D.L., A.L. and K.L.

CONTENTS

CODEX I
Suffolk England, 1940

Chapter One

A NARROW LANE STREWN WITH grey and white pebbles, and lined by ash and oak trees, rambled for some five hundred yards, finally reaching a courtyard before an enormous Georgian manor house called Cismontane. Extensive lawns fell away from the house, and below a nearby stable, bridle paths wound through tall groves toward a lake. The lovely acres might entice someone to midnight wander. Find a tranquil spot to haunt. Take stock of things.

So, one Autumnal evening, looking down from a rock outcropping, Marian Graves stood in quiet fascination, because below her, placid lake water reflected the night's canopy of glimmering stars. The ethereal jewels of light skipped about as a zephyr crossed the water's surface, but beyond, it was darkness that surrounded the lakeshore.

Stevan Romanov climbed up beside her and balanced himself by placing a large hand on her back. He peered at the shimmery water. "Ugh," he said, "I shouldn't have finished that bottle of Palo Cortado!"

"It's not the sherry, you sozzled sot!"

Stevan snorted with enough force to rustle his black handlebar moustache. It was a dark moustache, well-wrought, with ends that curled up upwards. It often gave his broad, square face an expression of casual amusement.

"It's the illusion," she said, "The stars seem to be below us."

"I see. It's an upside-down world."

"Stevan? I know you fear for your sister, your family. I know you worry."

"Um."

"Do you think we should go?"

"If I go, you shall remain here."

"I shall not!"

"As if I would put you into that kind of danger."

"*You* will not put *me* anywhere. I will go where you go. Stop trying to civilize me."

In the enfolding dark by the lake, Stevan may have been unable to view Marian's wavy, chestnut-red hair, and spooky green eyes, but he could smell her scent—a touch of patchouli. He smiled and considered what a wild woman she really was. He took in her earthy spice and nipped at her neck with tender intention. Then he straightened up and replied, "Not sure that is possible, in light of your upbringing!" He referred to her father, Charles Graves.

✦ ✦ ✦

"Romanov is a Russian name, not Montenegrin. I would have expected you to be a Petrovic or something," Graves said, dicing Stevan one evening at the dinner table after Marian had withdrawn—as was the custom for women of the day—leave the men to their cigars, port, and posturing.

Stevan gazed at the formidable Graves and said, "This is a question?"

"I'm questioning your ancestry."

Such an impolite way of asking, but Stevan said, "We are the Montenegrin Romanovs. Many, many years. Nothing to do with the Russians."

Graves nodded as if he had already known this. He continued, "And when your parents were killed after the Great War, you became the charge of some, half-couth—what? Magus, wizard . . . fellow?"

Another rude question. Stevan glanced at the ceiling. Hmm, scallop molding. He took his time, composing himself. His eyes were big and brown, and accustomed to observation. He looked back at Graves, and replied firmly, "Yes. I, and my sister Anastasija, became Herak's wards. You must know that Herak is a world-renowned philosopher."

Graves didn't miss a beat. "Who packed you off to England to study some god-awful fossilized language because he has a very odd notion about ancient books buried in the Oriental desert." He raised his eyebrows as if to say, Is that about it?

Stevan gazed at Graves, the angular face, the unflinching grey eyes, the hedge of white hair. Graves, known as Charlie to his close friends and relations, commanded the Air Ministry's Bawdsey Station. He also held a Senior Fellowship in Natural Sciences at Trinity College, as a physicist. Marian's father gave off an air of authority. But Stevan had a sudden insight—*Charles Graves is acquainted with Herak!* And he surmised Graves must know the true reason Herak sought the lost library, and it wasn't for the completion of his tome, *Gnostica*. No. What Herak sought, what he always wanted, were the Pachomian codices, books the stealthy monks had carried from their monastery early in the first millennium and buried in the desert . . . somewhere. Herak had claimed the codices contain tractates of poetic wisdom and revelation, yes, but also: words of power. But carrying the plot, Stevan replied simply, "Herak requires early millennia Coptic codices to finish his masterpiece, *Gnostica*. Now I have the knowledge and the capacity to seek such artifacts for him . . . except for this damn war."

As if irritated with Herak, with Stevan, Graves bellowed, "Montenegrins love war, war has been their chief occupation since the fourteenth century!" When Graves bellowed, the many creases in his gaunt face deepened. He looked like a three-dimensional woodcut. He lowered his voice in the manner of a conspirator and leaned forward. "You can disguise a Montenegrin with the bowler and birch of a Cambridge education, even have him study archaeology in London with Flinders Petrie—"

"Egyptology."

"But underneath it all, they're—"

Stevan smiled. He had an answer for Graves. One that would certainly give him something to bellow about . . .

+   +   +

Marian turned away from the lake. She nudged Stevan. "What are you thinking?" she demanded.

"I was thinking of how your father never finished telling me what Montenegrins are, underneath it all."

"Well, did you cut his sentence short?"

"I told him that on Tuesday, we'd gone down to Bury St. Edmunds and got married, and that he would not want to say anything nasty to me, his novice son-in-law."

Marian frowned. She whispered, "But . . . I was trying to find a way to tell him." She became quiet. Stared into the shimmery void below her. Suddenly, she turned and cried, "Dammit! Now you've told him. Dammit!"

Stevan stepped back. He almost lost his balance.

"So, then . . . what happened? What? What did he say?"

Stevan reached out, held her hands, "He said he already knew, and did I really think anything could get by him?"

+   +   +

On a late, gloomy, fall afternoon, Graves parked his Bentley near the mansion's front steps, strode down from the car, opened the boot, and pulled out a box containing a CRT. He had decided to allow his freshly minted son-in-law to test the experimental, very experimental, Bilateral Antenna Transmitter, the earliest form of aircraft-mounted radar. The CRT would provide the screen on which the operator could read the Doppler blips.

Carrying the box, he navigated wet, fallen leaves as he climbed the steps to click the latch and push the front door open with his elbow, as a waiter elbows through a kitchen door while holding a large tray, and tramped into a spacious hall. The harlequin marble floor rang with the sound of his footsteps. A butler appeared on a balcony at the far end.

"One moment, sir. I will assist you."

"Ah, no. No. Good God, no! No, no, now I've got it, Smythe." Graves kicked the door and it slammed shut.

Smythe disappeared from the balcony and reappeared a half minute later on the staircase. He was light on his feet and, in fact, held not a small resemblance to Fred Astaire. But quick as he was, he did not catch up to Graves until the red drawing room, where Graves had set the box on the Aubusson rug.

Graves knelt beside the box and pulled at the packing material. A fire had been lit in the south fireplace, and his face glinted in the firelight. "Smythe, put on the lights."

"What have you got, sir? You should have allowed me to assist."

"Oh, this? This is a CRT. Compliments of my bloody, damn pest son-in-law who had SOME roommate at Cambridge who has SOME influence with SOME damn SOMEBODY or other . . . to get me this damn CRT. You see, Smythe?"

"Yes, sir."

"And now we can screw the BAT into the Curtiss and see what we can see, you see?"

"Yes, sir."

"Smythe!"

"Sir?"

"Where is my son-in-law? Send him to me." Since Graves had, with a dose of umbrage, accepted the marriage of his daughter to Stevan, détente ruled between the two new in-laws. Well, it should rule, Graves had decided, because rather than the boy traveling weekends from Cambridge to guest at Cismontane, where he had intended to woo Marian as it turned out, and to bang on engine parts in the boat house, the lad—now married to Marian—damn-well should reside with her in the East wing of Cismontane. After all, where else would they go?

"Sir. Mr. Romanov has not yet arrived."

"I see. What about our guests?"

"Sir. Maria Felicita and Lili Sandor won't arrive until the séance next week. Remember, they are bringing the spirit medium, Logie."

"Well! Where is Marian?"

"Right here, Father."

Graves stood up. He glanced at the Queen Anne wing chair turned towards the fire. "Well, goodness, Marian, you're like a ghost. I didn't see you there, dear. Smythe, for god's sake, put on the lights!"

"Oh, well, Father, I was silent as a mouse, anyway. But you'll see plenty of me on the flying boat," Marian replied. She knew she had to constantly reinforce the idea that she was going on the test flight, or her father would exclude her. He would claim it too dangerous a pursuit for his daughter.

"Bloody hell!" He put his purple look on, his angry face. He couldn't abide his daughter running roughshod over him, especially in matters of her own safety. After all, he'd promised her mother, before she died, to bring their daughter up as best he could.

"You agreed to my being copilot."

"Marian, I agreed to no such damn irritating thing!"

"Father, your airing of the King's English is atrocious."

"Oh, so now you have the audacity to play school mistress with me?"

"Well, you decidedly play cage master with me."

"Blooming . . . bally-ruddy!"

"Father, do you recall our great ancestor, the Wolly?" She knew he did. On the morning of November 13, 1793, the Old Progenitor had inadvertently injured twelve church parishioners, and killed a horse, two hounds, and a fox. It seems he had at a raging gallop, led the hunt vanguard through the open doors of a local church while it was in service.

"I've got the Wolly in me. And I want to fly. You'll never keep me off that aeroplane, just as you would never have kept him from the fox hunt."

"Smythe!"

"Sir?" Smythe hadn't moved an inch, remaining quietly in the doorway during the row. He rather enjoyed observing a good and healthy quarrel. At Cismontane, he was able to observe many of them, because Graves had a brawling personality.

"Smythe, this pip-squeak, as the Americans say, is the keeper of the Wolly."

"The keeper?"

"So, she avows."

"Good heavens, sir."

"Quite."

"Laugh at me if you wish," Marian said calmly. She stood up, straightened her brown tweed skirt. Her hair flamed around her head.

"But Monday is August twenty-fourth. Mark it on your calendar. That's the day I fly." She stalked out of the room.

"Marian. Come back here." Graves started after her, but he immediately banged his knee against a sturdy fifteenth-century oak table. "Smythe!" he bellowed. "You blackguard! *Put. On. The. Lights!*"

*   *   *

As Marian took her leave, she thought of her ancestor—Wolly Wogganbogg Graves. She thought of his final foxhunt. Her father had told her the story of the Wolly's greatest fiasco, but instead of engendering prudence in her, as it was supposed to do, the tale sometimes made her crack a secret little grin. She understood that the Wolly's behavior had been appalling, and yet . . .

The very fox which the Wolly hunted that day in February was known among common folk of the time as Old Four Legs, because he was alleged to be the cagiest English creature on four legs. Indeed, Old Four Legs had used a church gambit with success on two previous occasions. The minister often ordered the church's massive double doors be kept open a crack, even on the chilliest days, so that the congregation would be disinclined to wander their attention during his detailed sermons. Twice before, on the run, Old Four Legs had boldly slipped through the crack, virtually unnoticed. And when the hounds bayed at the door, the deacon had slammed it shut. Old Four Legs simply lay down in a dark corner and licked his paws as if he owned the place. Outside, the hunters ultimately withdrew. At the conclusion of service, Old Four Legs crept away following the parishioners. Only Crowther, the gardener, was ever aware of the fox's antics.

But Old Four Legs attempted this maneuver one time too many, and in the wrong weather. Late November had been oddly mild that year. On the fateful Sunday, the massive double doors stood open wide to the bare trees and muddy lanes—this because the November air had the feel of a fine spring day.

A blast from a hunting horn rent the gentle air. Baying hounds flew across a ditch. Hooves shocked the ground. Reverend Michael Fowler paused in his sermon about sin and damnation and hell and such. Something had caught his eye. He glanced over his flock and through the open doorway. His brow wrinkled. His protruding ears reddened. He saw Old Four Legs bound up the lane, all in a panic, a fury of hounds nipping at his tail, the horses and riders close behind. The fox jumped the stone wall into the churchyard and made a run up the gravel path to the flagstone steps of the church. Fiery hounds and frothing horses surged after him.

Reverend Fowler shouted, 'The blighters are coming right inside!'

This was an alarming revelation for the people seated in the rear pew, including Deacon Axton-Smith. Axton-Smith had been snoozing, or daydreaming, at any rate, paying no attention either to Reverend Fowler's sermon, or to the familiar, jolting sounds of an approaching fox hunt. But when Reverend Fowler shouted uncharacteristically about some 'blighters,' Axton-Smith woke up. He turned. He saw. He, too, shouted alarm. He leapt to his feet and, striding, surmounted the pew in an attempt for the massive double doors. If he could just manage to close one, perhaps the onslaught would turn aside.

Axton-Smith was a thin, long-legged man of about fifty years, who always stood with his legs spread wide apart, his toes pointed outward. No matter where he was sighted—pub, town square, church or field, the legs forged an astonishing apex. That day, Old Four Legs took the apex to be an invitation. As Axton-Smith tried to pull the heavy door shut, the fox, a flash of red, ran right underneath the deacon and into the church.

The hot, pursuing hounds took the deacon down. They didn't mean it, they were simply intent on getting the fox, and the apex, remarkable as it was, simply could not accommodate the snarling pack. When the hounds took his legs out from under him, Axton-Smith toppled like an old lightning-struck steeple.

Still at a canter, the Wolly, riding a mighty steed named Apogee, charged the open doors, followed by his huntsman, Reggie, and his whipper-in Jacques. Wild, crazed, were their countenances, as if they were chasing the Red Devil himself. Foam flecked the Wolly's pink coat. The Frenchman, Jacques, wore a sneer on his face, while the stout Reggie displayed a placid expression, yet was flushed red as a winter beet. They all stopped just short of riding roughshod over Axton-Smith, who still wallowed on the stone floor, the hounds having trampled him thoroughly, their muddy paw prints covering his Sunday suit, a nice Harris tweed.

Old Four Legs had run straight down the aisle towards the pulpit but turned aside when the Reverend Fowler zipped forward like Saint Bernard the Crusader and, unthinking, threw a hymn book with impressive force at the fox. The shot missed the pointed snout by a mere inch. The fox desperately scrambled amongst the teeming parishioners, panicky skirts and trousers flying in all directions. There must be a hole, a place to hide! There! An opening climbed upwards. Old Four Legs didn't hesitate. Up he ran!

Six more riders plunged into the church, blocking the front door. The cornerstone itself shook with the abuse of man and beast.

Old Four Legs' dash up the staircase did not escape the Wolly. 'Stand aside!' he commanded to the immediate throng.

"On to him!" cried Reggie to the hounds, but confused by the commotion, they had lost the scent. Responding like a brigadier, the Wolly lashed his steed onward, almost trampling the ancient Bryer sisters, and he forced the horse into the stairwell. Up the wooden staircase climbed the Wolly astride the valiant horse, Apogee, hooves seeking purchase on the worn carpet-treads. Two hounds followed close behind.

As mentioned, Apogee was a massive stallion, some eighteen-and-a-half hands high, weighing some 122 stone. When he reached the balcony, the structural timbers yawned, as if awaking from an ancient spell, and Apogee shook his great head, ears back, wild eyed. At the far end, Old Four Legs whirled in circles. The two hounds—Locket, a stubby bitch, and Billy Bones, a ragged yet aggressive dog—were on to the scent now. Together, roaring like a deadly torrent, they plunged between the steed's mighty legs. The horse, already spooked, reared. When he landed, the balcony gave way. Horse, rider, fox, and hounds tumbled down with the crushing timber and rock, and the catastrophic collapse injured a dozen hapless church goers caught below.

Although sadly his horse broke two legs and had to be put down, the Wolly endured. His miraculous trajectory—two arcing somersaults over his horse's head—caused him to land directly on his backside, atop Old Four Legs. The impact killed the fox instantly . . . and made a considerable mess on the old church floor, but the Wolly came out of it with nothing more than a bruised backside.

Thus, the Wolly collected his prize, the smartest fox that had ever lived. In celebration, he nailed the fox-brush to the front door of the great house, "Cismontane." However, in the year hence, the townsfolk could only look upon the man with ill will, and they shunned him and treated him like a leper and refused to work in his fields.

The behavior of this notorious ancestor, the Wolly, played no small part in shaping Marian's character. When she made up her mind about something, she would always carry it through to the end—as did the Wolly in his foxhunt. Marian would consider, *good lord. The man had no limits. Is this why I am so stubborn? but well . . . perhaps I've got a bit of the chaos in my blood!*

Chapter Two

According to the luminous, radium dial on Stevan's new Longines-Weems watch—a wedding present from Marian—the early morning hour of 02:43 was the hour of hectoring thoughts. Some nights, the hour of hectoring came earlier or later but either way, Stevan was unable to sleep the night through.

Stevan stole a quiet glance at Marian as she slumbered beside him. He'd been trying not to disturb her sleep by tossing and turning, but he'd had it with being immobile. Because she seemed peaceful enough, he took the moment to slide out from under the duvet, grab his turtleneck, pants, and brogues, and soft toe across the rug to the bedroom door. He opened it quietly to slip through. He padded in his socks down the stairs and through the harlequin hall to the front door, where he dressed, and then stepped out onto the darkened grounds of Cismontane.

Stevan had been engaging in this behavior twice a week since early September. Now the gambit had become more frequent as the nights went on. He'd make his way down to the boathouse to work until an hour after the birds had begun to chirp. Then, if he wasn't up to his elbows in oil and grease, he'd head back to the house for breakfast.

Marian might already be at the table, or she may be coming down later. When she saw him, she might ask him what the hell he thought he was doing—going off in the middle of the night. At first, his intentions were largely purposeless—just to endure another sleepless night. But then a plan had come to him, one so wonderfully outrageous it had become an obsession. An obsession, but he wasn't ready to express to Marian, or to anyone, what he had in mind.

Occasionally, when wandering after midnight, Stevan would be surprised by Dick McBride—Charles Graves' close friend and master mechanic. That night, when Stevan opened the door to the boathouse, he bumped straight into Dick, who was hauling a tangle of camouflage nets under the glow of soft lights.

Dick said, "What are you doin' down here nocturnal, lad? Like the last time, the only creatures up and about should be the bugs, the bats, and the watchmen."

Dick was a short Irishman with round, ruddy face. His face became even rounder as it broke into a crescent grin. When he moved, he exposed a noticeable limp.

"Hello Dick. And you? After all, you're here too." Since Dick didn't reply, Stevan went on, "Well, I've figured out a fix for those sticky float valves. I don't want to forget my idea."

Dick had been dragging the nets to a side door. He dropped the ends and said, "Alright then. But I've always thought workin' on engines is what daytime is for." He peered at Stevan.

Stevan crossed the plank floor to stand near a worktable. His nights of obsessive behavior must stop, he knew, and he must admit to someone, his anxieties, and his plan to overcome them. Dick's gentle manner, Stevan recognized, had made way for an act of confession. In the moment, he decided to unburden himself. He smiled at the roly-poly man and said, "I don't sleep at night. I don't know what sleep is anymore."

Dick wrinkled his brow. Then he went to a cabinet to pull a bottle of Irish from a shelf. He grabbed a couple of pottery mugs and carrying, brought the lot to the worktable. He poured a double for each of them, folded his arms and said, "Well. You've got the bugbear. I see the bags under your eyes. What's tormenting you, lad?"

Stevan picked up a lag bolt from the worktable and stared at it for a moment. Did he want to tell Dick more than what he'd told Marian? Deciding, he tossed the link back. It rattled on the table. He said, "It's about my family. About my young sister, Anastasija. A long time ago, when she and I were orphaned, I made a vow to Anastasija: in times of duress, I would protect her! So, I may not be able to protect my little sister from the ravages of invasion—perhaps no one or nothing could—yet, for her, I must return to the high karst. But there is no transport. No route through France and Italy to my home. I've asked Mr. Graves—he has no ideas."

Dick picked up his mug of whiskey and said, "To Saint Christopher, the patron saint of long journeys."

Stevan nodded, raised his mug, and then took a healthy swig.

Dick observed, "And now. You're down here workin' on the aeroplane more and more, night and day. I think you are gettin' the idea of a plan. Aren't ya?" Dick put his mug down and walked over to the F2A flying boat. He reached up to put a hand on the lower wing.

Stevan said, "If . . . If the engines were hardened and fitted with electric start . . . If the wings were modified and strengthened, if the carburetors were made more reliable . . ."

Dick held up a hand, "Stop. Don't tell me any more. In a moment, you'll be crossin' Charlie Graves. And Marian."

"She knows I must go."

"And does she know ya plan to nick this aeroplane we've been restoring?"

Stevan looked down at his brogues. They needed a shine. He looked up, "I will tell her. This plan has come to me . . ."

"You intend to leave her?"

Stevan walked over to stand a few feet from Dick. He said, "Never. I wouldn't have it. She wouldn't have it."

"And how would Charlie have it?"

"So, I haven't worked that out. I haven't even talked it over with Marian yet. But if I could convince Mr. Graves I've made this aeroplane air-worthy for such a trip . . ."

"Well, to make the F2A prime, you'd be needin' a bit of help. And with Charlie, you'd be needin' more help. So, maybe your plan is just a bit of madness. You better figure out if it is. You've a lot of thinkin' to do, laddie."

Stevan took another swallow of Irish.

Dick returned to the worktable to finish his mug. He put it back in the cabinet, turned and said, "Goodnight now," and was gone a second after he opened the door.

Alone, Stevan poured himself another few ounces and sat on the bench to ponder his immediate future.

✦　✦　✦

One morning in early October, Marian had endured a sinking feeling, an inexact, imprecise feeling of . . . losing it. Losing what? She didn't know. The mood, an emotional vertigo, had come upon her quickly after she awoke. At least that's when she had become conscious of it, though it likely had assailed her all night in her sleep; she had a wispy memory of uneasy dreams, of something red, something deep. A dark pit! The sound of a bell. So, she had reached over for Stevan, and Stevan wasn't there.

God! She had felt immediate aggravation. He'd been removing himself from her. Begging off. Being elsewhere. Being silent, inattentive, distracted, neglectful. What terrible thing had she done? Why did he have to sneak away in the falling dark, leaving her alone with her down-spinning thoughts? She suspected that Stevan's intention was to remove himself from her. Then, it might hurt them less when they parted, when he set out for his homeland. The idiot! She'd already insisted she'd go with him! She could join his clan militia, or the Royal Montenegrin Guard, or . . . whatever!

For a while, she lay in bed listening to birds yelp and snap and screech shrilly from the treetops. She hated them. They squabbled over territory like lunatic despots.

She moped out of bed, moving slowly, slouching. The morning was cold. In a fog, she reached for her cashmere robe and wrapped herself up, hoping for sudden warmth but not getting it. She shuffled to the window to pull back the imposing drapery, a floral chintz, and she accomplished this with a single, practiced motion.

But there was no sun. Clouds as thick as Tolstoy spread across the sky. War and Peace (but not Anna K) and where would Marian end today? She didn't know, but it didn't feel good. It didn't seem auspicious. From her window, she could just see the lake and the boathouse. That's where her phantom husband was spending all his time these days. Buried in the boathouse, as they called it, although it was really an aeroplane hangar. He spent most of his time with Dick, the little, roly-poly master mechanic from Ireland, banging on Rolls Royce engine parts and smoking foul-smelling cigars and probably nipping on the side too.

Lately, he'd been drinking. After dinner. Port or whisky with her father. Her father! Considering the Wolly and the "vile chromosomes" and the "lost cousins," her father had never overindulged. Yet suddenly with Stevan, he seemed to want to prove something. God knows what. Moreover, it appeared to Marian, that Stevan was instigating the practice. And Stevan didn't stop there. He had begun pubbing with

Dick. That was no good because Dick could hold a barrel of whisky. He had a genuine affinity for "a drop of the craythur," as he referred to it in that absurd, wonderful language of his. He could drink Stevan under the table nightly if he wanted to.

As she stood at the window staring down towards the boathouse, she reasoned that if Stevan wanted to work on his hobby, that was fine. But the drink. The neglect. That was cruel. Why should he exclude her? After all, she loved aeroplanes too. She could fly! She had been up many times with her father, although, not in an untested aeroplane like the Flying Boat. But so what? She could be part of it, its reconstruction.

She turned from the window. The room was awash with daylight now; the shrimp-colored walls glowed. She crossed the room to stand before the mirror that hung on the opposite wall, a large, gilt-framed, seventeenth-century Florentine. It was a pool of light. She looked into the pool at her image, and her image stared back: chestnut-red hair, narrow nose, smooth cheekbones, slightly mischievous lips turned just a smidge upwards at the corners, green eyes . . . Even newly awake and just out of bed, hair a muss, eyes sandy, she was a striking woman. But today the frown ruled, and her mind turned only on Stevan. A rather short honeymoon, she thought. The melancholy came again in waves. In all her twenty-two years, she'd never been like this. Ever.

Talking to herself, aloud, she muttered in a mocking tone, "O folly! What is love! And where is it?" After a moment, she asked, "Did I make that up or am I quoting somebody? Yes. It's a line. From whom? Probably Keats." She thought, Is that why he's a poet of renown? Because he wrote down what every schoolgirl knows, but what I couldn't glean until I blasted got married?

"Love is an eternally setting sun,
always
going

down . . .

and out."

She turned and glared at the pillow, Stevan's vacant pillow. There! I made up *those* lines, you bloody Sod. She shuffled over to the armoire, cast open the doors, and began selecting in the following order: a pair of grey wool knee socks, a grey wool skirt, a grey-and-white Fair Isle sweater, a grey cotton turtleneck . . .

Today I shall wear grey. To match the Tolstoy sky.

◆ ◆ ◆

She had no time to mope. On her seventeenth birthday, her father had given her heavy responsibility. Henceforth, he had informed her, she was to run the household. What with his governmental duties pressing in on him, his work at Bawdsey, and his various business dealings, he couldn't be bothered with running the estate. He would teach her to oversee both the domestic help and the farmhands at Cismontane. And she was to administer the estate budget. It's like running a medium-sized corporation, he explained, and you've got to stay on top of it. Having no experience with running a medium-sized corporation, Marian didn't get the analogy. Yet, after a certain amount of brouhaha between her and her father, she had learned enough to keep things afloat. Now, she was quite expert at it. But it was demanding. And she had no time to mope.

Once dressed, she flung open the door of her room so that it banged on the doorstop with authority. She could hear a satisfactory echo in the hall. The harlequin marble floor was excellent for that—for producing either satisfying echoes or annoying concussions that racked the brain, depending on how the brain was faring that morning. Sound waves bounced eagerly from the floor to the ceiling and from the sky-blue lacquered walls to the floor and so on. Everyone always said the acoustics of the Harlequin Hall were remarkable and should be written up by the British Architectural Society, and that technicians with electrical metering devices should take careful measurements of the sound and fury for scientific study. Marian always politely agreed that it must be done. She didn't mean it, though. She liked her echo just the way it was: unquantified.

She descended the stairs, idly inspecting all the ancestral portraits on the way, thinking: Mother, father, grandmother, grandfather, even the Wolly . . . each at one time or other endured love! Else, why am I here?

Smythe, who had carefully noted her smash and crash, met her at the bottom of the staircase.

"Would you be taking breakfast this morning, Madame?"

"Thank you, no, Smythe."

"There is excellent kippered herring this morning."

"Kippered husband is quite enough."

"Coffee then, Madame?" He knew she often rejected the offer of tea in the morning.

"I am spending the day alone in the sitting room, and I don't wish to be disturbed, but yes . . . coffee . . . would be lovely."

The sitting room was light and airy. It had leafy wallpaper and floor-to-ceiling windows and a couch covered with Chinese-influenced chintz. Near the north window stood a drop-leaf Regency table that, with one side extended, served as a writing desk. She sat down before it, wondering if she could immerse herself in estate matters that day or if she would prefer to stare blankly through the window. And the hell with everything.

Smythe entered, carrying a tray loaded with a sterling coffee service, a large plate of kippers and sausage and toast and butter and jam and marmalade, several Irish linen napkins, and silver knives and forks and spoons. He placed it before her on the desk.

She glared at it, wordlessly. Smythe withdrew.

No sooner had she decided to taste the kippers and had lifted a forkful to her lips, than she heard a commotion in the hall.

"No! We did NOT order those!"

"Oh, but ye did, sir."

"We did NOT order a lorry load of . . . !?"

"Daffodil bulbs, sir."

"Daffodil bulbs!"

"Shall I just leave them in the courtyard?"

"I would advise you not, if you wish to live to see tomorrow."

"Ye missus wants um. I don't care where I leaves um as long as I get paid."

"Madame will pay you in spades! . . . WITH SPADES!"

Marian looked at the morsel of kippered herring she had speared with her fork. It smelled good. She stuffed it into her mouth and put the fork down with a clatter. Umm. It was remarkably good. Chewing, she arose purposefully, smoothed her skirt, and strode towards the hall where the fracas had taken on the weight of a great, poetic epic. What with the extraordinary acoustics of the Harlequin Hall, the combatant's voices rose and fell like thunder. Or they sounded like Titans clashing somewhere out beyond Arcadian fields.

"Ye damn well not speak to me like that, sir."

"I shall not speak at all. I shall simply boot."

"Smythe! What in the name of Heaven is going on here?"

Marian entered the hall grandly, calm and stern, her presence instantly imparting the weight of civilization upon the quarrelsome fellows.

"Why, Mr. Hawkins," she continued upon spying the hefty feed-and-grain man, "I'm surprised at you. What is this . . . shouting?" She intoned the word *shouting* as if she were forced to name a rudi-mentary, disgusting nastiness beyond rational description. It had the proper effect on Hawkins, who squinted and looked down at his feet in embarrassment.

Smythe said, "Madame. This. Man. Insists that you ordered a lorryload of—"

"Daffodil bulbs."

Smythe glared at Hawkins. "Yes, Genus Narcissus."

"A lorry . . . load?"

Hawkins gained a little courage. "Didn't ye say for me t' bring all the bulbs I could find, missus?"

Marian raised her eyebrows. She put her hands on her hips. "Well, yes."

Hawkins shrugged as if to say, Well, that's what I did. I brought you all I could find.

"But Mr. Hawkins, you had informed me that you would not be stocking any—"

"Daffodil bulbs."

Marian and Smythe exchanged a quick glance. Smythe was clearly saying, I told you so!

Marian turned to Hawkins. "Daffodil bulbs. You said you would be hard pressed to find me a DOZEN."

Hawkins suddenly became animated. He held his tweed cap in his hand; it flopped about as he waved his chubby arms.

He said, "Well, you see missus, I had a little luck when Jasper, umm, you know Jasper, he's down near Faring Cross. Well, he stopped by Tuesday on the way to London. And I says, 'Where are ye going with all them blasted bulbs, Jasper?' Because I could see his lorry was jammed packed with um. And he says he's going to sell um in market. I says, 'Well Jasper, I'll save you a trip. And I bought um all, missus, for the word of a Graves is always good, and everyone knows it. Even the Wolly got that fox, that crafty Four Legs, when he did warrant it. And he 'bout killed my grand-grandfather, too, doing it, but that's all water under the dam, or is it over the bridge? And so, when ye said ye want me to acquire ye all the daffodils I can find, well, I found all I can find. And it cost me a lot, and I'm out of purse and pocket, but I knew ye to be good for it, missus."

Marian turned to Smythe. She said, "My God! Smythe, these crafty tradespeople shall be our RUIN. They shall roast us alive and eat us. When they're done, they shall belch in satisfaction and then pick over our skinny bones until there's naught left . . . even for the birds." She turned to Hawkins. He was grinning, despite himself. "Well, come on," she said, "let's see what you've brought."

In the driveway stood a common dump truck, its bed filled to the brim with daffodil bulbs. Marian high-stepped up on the back platform. She reached over the gate and grabbed two bulbs, inspecting them. "Well, Mr. Hawkins, are they all like this? Or did you just put the good ones on top?"

Hawkins shrugged innocently, "I did scan each and every one of them, missus, and I guarantee they all to be of quality."

Smythe snorted, eyebrows raised. Hawkins shot him a dark glare.

Marian jumped from the platform. She was quite agile. "And how much are you hoping to be paid?"

"I tell ye God's truth, missus. Because ye were surprised with such a load, which I didn't know would do, I give ye bottom price straightaway."

"How much?"

"Sixty guinea."

"I deal in pounds sterling, Mr. Hawkins."

"Oh. Knock the shilling."

Marian shook her head. She muttered an aside to Smythe, which Hawkins could easily overhear: "You'd bloody well think he was dealing Dutch tulips." She folded her arms and glared at Hawkins. Hawkins shifted around on his feet but said nothing.

"Mr. Hawkins, I will give you twenty-five pounds for the lot."

Hawkins's eyebrows shot up. "Zounds, Missus! Now who is cooking who?"

"Sir. I cannot allot our entire fall seeding budget to daffodils."

"But ye said ye wanted all I could find."

"Please don't take me for a fool."

"Fifty pounds is low as I can go, missus," Hawkins said sincerely, pursing his lips and nodding like a parson.

Hand on hips: "Thirty pounds is my absolute limit."

"You'll have me out of pocket!"

Marian turned. She walked brusquely towards the front door. At the threshold she stopped. "Mr. Hawkins. Thirty-five pounds."

Hawkins thrust his hands deep into his pockets. His brow thickened. He looked dejected. "What can I do?" he grumbled. "Thirty-five pounds it is."

Marian nodded.

Hawkins turned towards the bounteous truck, the lovely lorry. With a little grin, he ambled to the cab. He wanted to skip, feel airy on his feet, but was determined to keep his dignity. He climbed inside. It wasn't all he'd hoped for, but by God, it was profit!

Marian took two steps into the driveway. "Crowther's waiting for you at the conservatory. He'll show you where to heap the bulbs."

Hawkins nodded through the window of the cab. He glanced away. Then he looked back at Marian.

"Missus? Crowther's awaitin' for me, ye say?"

"Well, he is our gardener."

Hawkins nodded again. "I know, missus."

"Goodbye, Mr. Hawkins. You drive a hard bargain."

Hawkins slowly grinned. He had a bit of the snaggle-tooth. "Ye knew all along ye were a goin' t'buy um."

Marian folded her arms across her chest.

Hawkins grinned. He put the truck in gear. "Ye are a good one, missus," he said, shouting over the engine noise. He headed down the lane to the conservatory.

Chapter 3

THE GALLERY AT CISMONTANE was a grandiose room. It stretched some ninety feet—half the length of the sprawling mansion. Before the long, opposing walls stood pedestals displaying marble busts of philosophers. Above them, the vast walls exhibited many frescos, medallions, and Pompeian grotesques, thoughts of metaphysicians as it were. The twenty-foot-high ceiling was heavily compartmented, with a color scheme of Pompeian red, pink, and gold on a blue background. A large demilune by Guido Reni loomed over twin doors that stood on the interior wall at the gallery center. A bronze statue of Diana, the Huntress, abided beneath a leaded-glass window. At the south end of the gallery, a chess table of Mexican mahogany and onyx was enshrined between two immense, German, elk-horn chairs. On diagonal corners of the table, twenty-one-year-old Scotch whisky swayed in the bottom third of Irish crystal tumblers. It swayed because Graves had bumped the table when he made his move.

"King's bishop to king's bishop four," he cackled. He reclined against the skillfully wrought elk-horn splat of his Black Forest chair and looked across the table at Stevan—a look of "What are you going to do about that?"

They had been playing for about an hour. Graves had suggested a game after dinner that evening, and with the claret and port at dinner, and the Waterford Crystal tumblers of whisky now, they were getting somewhat drunk.

Stevan had decided to broach the idea of his return to Montenegro; test the waters again. He grasped his tumbler. He swirled the scotch twice, took a swig and then replaced the tumbler at the corner of the table. He said, "You understand, I've got to return to Montenegro."

Graves frowned. He replied, "Hitler intends to storm our beaches. What's Montenegro got to do with it? I'll get you a Spitfire. God knows the RAF can use you."

Stevan smiled as he captured his opponent's piece. "Rook takes rook."

"Montenegro!" Graves muttered, now casting his frown at the chess board.

"Do you think the Cvetković-Maček agreement will last in Yugoslavia? No, sir, the Serbs and the Croats are always at odds. And Prince Regent Paul is flirting with the Tripartite Pact. When we replace his pro-Axis government with Britain's friend, young King Peter II, then Hitler will be snarling at our borders too."

"Dammit!" Graves said. He looked around himself while patting the folds of his charcoal-grey, worsted wool jacket. "What did I do with that cigar? You bloody well know we need you to attend to the war effort here. It will help your country in the end."

Stevan shook his head. "You don't need me here, sir. The RAF can do very well without me. They have the best pilots I've ever seen. But Montenegro! There I am needed."

Graves appraised Stevan. And how would the silly boy find passage to Montenegro? Enemy U-Boats patrolled the Irish sea and the channel, and Messerschmitts fighters contested the air. Graves pushed his chair back, got up, and stalked over to the fireplace, where a box of cigars sat on the mantel. He grabbed three Havanas in his right hand, carelessly, the way a monkey might grab a bunch of crayons, and then picked out another, a Hoyo De Monterrey, with his left, carefully, like a nun picking a rose, and tossed it to Stevan.

Stevan grunted, but he was aware of the treasure he'd just received.

Graves sat back down in his chair. He pulled a cigar cutter from his vest pocket and snipped the end of his Havana, then tossed it over to Stevan. He asked, "What the hell do you think you could accomplish by returning to the Adriatic now?"

Stevan snipped the end of the Hoyo De Monterrey. He struck a match and held the flame about an inch beneath the open end of the cigar, lighting it with the heat only. He puffed. A cloud of aromatic smoke billowed upwards.

He looked across the chess board at Charles Graves, fixing upon him with a gaze, and said, "The people of Yugoslavia are not unified the way you are in Britain. We have the capitalists, the royalists, the communists, the pro-Germans, the pro-British, the pro-Austrians, the pro-Italians, the pro-Turks, the pro-Albanians. Then we have the Ustashi Croatian terrorist organization, which exists mainly to attack the Serbs; the Serbian Chetnik organization, which dates back to Turkish occupation and exists to attack any invaders, according to their definition; and the Black Hand revolutionary faction that wants to kill the Austrians. There are those with ties to the Eastern Orthodox Church, to the Bogomils, the Gnostics, and the agnostics; there are the clan chieftains who follow the old ways and the young peasants and students who clamor for a new Yugoslavia—"

"Good God, what a mess," Graves muttered.

"And now, so soon, the Nazis will try to use our differences to make us their slaves. If only that energy could be harnessed for our defense!"

"Quite impossible."

"It can be harnessed, sir, but we need leaders. I have that capacity."

"You have that capacity? What? To lead a bunch of savages around that barren wilderness you call Montenegro?" Graves leaned forward. "And WHAT about YOUR WIFE?"

Stevan swallowed hard and replied, "She can stay here until I return. The war can't last six weeks if we stand up to Hitler now."

"Do I, per chance, hear the voice of experience?" Graves said, his voice dripping with sarcasm. "What in the world allows you to think you will return at all? If you're not killed outright, you'll spend the rest of your life sniffing around moldy tombs in distant wastelands. You think I don't know of your Montenegrin Gnostic philosopher, Herak? His associate, Thoth? Their quest for ancient incantations, words of power? They sent you here so I would look after you while you find out, up at Cambridge, how to do a dig!"

Stevan squinted at his new father-in-law and exclaimed, "I suspected you knew Herak! Why didn't you tell me? What was all that 'charlatan, wizard fellow' guff?"

Graves replied, "You imagined I was just looking for an aeroplane hobbyist to help with the F2A? That's how we met? No. Herak asked me to look after you, but let you think you were on your own. And how you repay me! You'll not be faithful to your English wife. I'm beginning to think you regard this marriage of yours as a joke, some sowing of your wild oats while larking in England . . ."

Stevan withdrew his cigar from his mouth. He leaned forward, his hand on the table. He replied, "If that's the way YOU acted in your youth, fine. But don't judge the rest of the world by YOUR sorry standards."

Graves appeared to not have heard Stevan. He said, "And your English wife is MY DAUGHTER! I suggest you contemplate, very carefully, your actions, my friend."

Stevan pointed a finger at Graves. "I will tell you this once. I love your daughter. She is everything to me. But there are forces in the world that are now beyond our control."

"Oh, spare me."

"Already, I am the leader of my clan. And I am educated. They need me. You see my duty is to return home."

Graves tossed down his whisky. "I see nothing of the sort. Educated! For what? You are an archeologist! Are you going to dig up a curse for the Germans? Toss a bunch of old bones in their path?"

Stevan stood up, his face crimson with anger. "That is completely uncalled for, sir!"

Graves also stood up. He said, "Your place is here, with your wife, boy. You are a married man. You have responsibilities now. Yugoslavia doesn't need you. Montenegro doesn't need you. What they need now are born killers supplied with American arms. Diggers of the past won't do them a damn bit of good at all." He turned and stalked from the vast, echoing gallery.

Stevan stood still, watching him go. His eyes slowly shifted to his own large hands. He lifted them chest high. They were opening and closing involuntarily.

✦ ✦ ✦

Late morning, three days on, Graves summoned Crowther via the intercom. "Bring around the Ariel, would you?"

Stevan looked up from reading the paper.

Graves said, "Come on, Stevan, let's go down to the boathouse, see if Dick has set the BAT in the proper location."

That was all Stevan had to hear. He jumped up, hunted for a jacket, and headed to the front door. Opening it, he immediately heard a pleasing roar. Crowther approached, piloting an Ariel Square four-cylinder motorcycle with sidecar. When Graves appeared at the door, Crowther cut the engine and dismounted the beast.

"Thank you, Crowther. Jump into the sidecar, Stevan." Graves walked around to the other side, put his left hand on the left handlebar.

Stevan looked at the sidecar, looked at Graves, and laughed. The two of them had, the past week, reached a suspension of hostilities, mostly by laying off the whisky, not by reaching a state of accord, but they were at least affable now.

"I can't squeeze into that!"

"No tighter than the cockpit of the F2A."

"Umm, not sure that is correct."

Graves jumped the motorcycle to an instant start. "Into the sidecar, Stevan."

Stevan looked at Graves quizzically. He said, "I can't jam myself into that thimble."

Graves said, "It's designed to fit any soldier. Do you fear the pace?"

Stevan darted his eyes left and right, shoved his hands deep into his coat pockets, and grinned. He had doubts about Graves' cycle skills. He said, "Your Lawrence of Arabia wrote the *Seven Pillars of Wisdom* before he met his end on a motorcycle . . . I have yet to pick up the pen."

"Lawrence was unhinged a bit—the war, you know—hop in."

"You were in that war, sir."

"You know, it's time you call me what everybody else does: Charlie."

"Yes, sir . . . Charlie." Stevan stuffed himself into the sidecar, grumbling, "I'd rather fly."

They bumped crazily down a narrow path that fell and climbed over rolling lawn, and wove, alarmingly, through tight trees in a manicured forest. Stevan had trekked this path many times, but in the sidecar of the Ariel, with Graves charging along at speed, well, good God! Finally, they arrived at the large wooden hangar. It stood covered in camouflage nets by the edge of the lake. Stevan extricated himself from the sidecar.

"Ah, that was fun," Graves said.

"Umm—" Stevan replied, cutting short whatever else he was going to say, and shook his head, as if clearing cobwebs. Graves ducked through a rear door, Stevan following. At the other end of the hangar, overhead doors opened wide to the lake filling the building with sunlight. Two flying boats sat over the water on mechanical platforms, a 1917 Felixstowe F2A, an aircraft derived by J.C. Porte from the Curtiss-built America, and a Sopwith Bat Boat circa 1914, powered by a 100-horsepower Green engine. The latter had a pusher air screw, a completely open tail section with descending rudder, and a pilot's compartment that looked to Stevan like a wide Eskimo kayak suspended from the wings, a truly strange machine.

"Dick! Dick!" Graves called out. There came a rustling from the far side of the F2A, then a tool dropped to the platform with a clang.

"Lord have mercy! I was thinkin' I was alone with me self," said a voice.

"Well, Dick, look to our guest."

During the previous two weeks, Stevan and Dick had reached an understanding. Dick—ever the romantic adventurer—had chosen to help Stevan modernize the flying boat, and to assist in dealing with Charles Graves. And so, Dick wasn't above touting Stevan's prowess as a mechanic:

Dick came into view and said, "Our guest? I'm sure to thinkin' we've turned into HIS guest, being he's fussin' down here all hours and days."

"Just been working on those engines. Have I got them tuned to spec?"

"You know a bit better than that, Stevan. If there's a man with a finer understandin' of metal to metal, of pistons and cylinders, pumps, float chambers, compound nozzles . . . If there's a man with a finer understandin' of the way things work, why he'd have t' be one of the holy saints!"

Stevan and Graves laughed. Stevan said, "So, you wonder where to find such a man? On the wall is a mirror. Take a look!"

Dick gave a snort. Now it was time for him to laud his own gifts as an engineer: "A holy saint I am not. Now come with me so that I can show off the spankin' new riggin' in this craft. By clever technique I've lessened the resistance by reducin' the interplane riggin'. I've changed to a high-lift wing section, decreasin' the span and area. You, Charlie, bein' a physicist and a gentleman, therefore know the speed, efficiency, and lifting capacity have thus all been greatly increased. And Stevan, it now has all virgin spars, new wires greased or painted, the latest in turnbuckles, split pins, sockets, and fittings." Stevan and Graves followed Dick around the F2A.

"The spars and struts are perfectly straight and symmetrical with good, clear-grain wood well varnished; the wires are at their proper tension, like the bride and bridegroom on the weddin' night, just enough to keep the framework rigid without bein' too tight," he said with a wink. "See up there? I've established fore, mid, and three-quarter aft cockpits all armed with Lewis 303 machine guns. The control cables are just so . . . Go up and try the levers."

Stevan climbed up to the pilot's cockpit, stuck his arm over the side, and manipulated the joystick, moving the ailerons and the elevator. Then he climbed in, crammed into the seat, and moved the rudder bar with his feet; there was no perceptible snatch or lag. "The way you have it rigged, Dick, I believe this aeroplane would fly itself," Stevan shouted from the cockpit.

"Aye. And you, Stevan, have spec'd the engines way past stock. A fine job."

"Why thank you, Dick."

Graves said, "Well, I'm glad you men have had fun restoring this old machine. I certainly enjoyed adding my sweat and tears to the project. I presume the BAT is operational now, Dick."

"I was gettin' to that, sure enough," Dick replied, "and it is ready, except for the actual test and demonstration. If we find out it works, then, sure enough, it's ready!"

"Thank you for that clarification, Dick," Graves said, then added, "Climb down here, Stevan, there is something we must discuss."

Stevan climbed down carefully, being sure not to mar any surface of the aeroplane and stood beside the two men on the platform.

Graves handed Stevan a dispatch.

"What's this?"

"Read it."

Stevan unfolded the cable addressed to Charles Graves. It read, "Fly Stevan South." Stevan observed that his mentor Herak had sent the message. Did Charlie have a method of transport? He looked up at Graves.

Graves could only frown. He had agreed to assist, at once, if Herak, suddenly urgent, were ever to send for Stevan. So now, Graves knew he must not oppose. Yet he wished to oppose!

"As you know," Graves said, "this is against my very core, to give you a method to return home . . . now!" He looked steadily at Stevan. "We're fighting for our very existence here in England. The Nazis want most to clear the RAF out of the skies over the channel so they can launch an attack against our shores. They think we'll fold like the Continent did. The Royal Navy would have a most difficult time with unprotected skies over its bow. Every modern aircraft is ready to engage in this battle. Our ships are standing by in anticipation of a Nazi invasion."

Graves glanced at Dick and continued, "You know how I feel, that there is every damn reason for you to remain here where you, by your own impetuous, and yes, selfish actions, have an obligation to remain."

Stevan couldn't let that pass. He replied, "Sir. . . . Charlie . . . My sister Anastasija is there, my Uncle Joko, my family . . ."

"Your family now resides in more than one place, son."

In the silence, Dick cleared his throat.

"There is a way," Graves finally said, and sighed. "But I do not condone it. In fact, I know nothing about it." He started towards the rear door, "Ah, Dick knows something about it. I've got to get back to the house . . . meeting with Sir John Slebbor, commander-in-chief of RAF coastal command." He receded through the door. "Carry on, Dick," he called out. In just a few moments, the Ariel fired up and shifted through the gears as it departed.

Stevan regarded the flying boat and said, "This craft could fly all the way to the Pillars of Hercules without touching land or sea. And from Gibraltar it's . . . "

"It's a little jaunt down the Med, around the Boot, and on to your little valley."

Stevan glanced at Dick; he didn't smile. With dead serious intention, he said, "That's the plan—to fly this old hundred-mile-an-hour aeroplane, open cockpits, a ceiling limit of ten thousand feet, to fly it past the Luftwaffe now in France with their 354 mph Messerschmitt BF 109Es, then, if I make it to Gibraltar to go on past the fascists in Italy . . ." Stevan looked at the F2A, such an alien craft in his present world.

Alien craft . . . the phrase echoed in his mind, the craft of gnosis: *the knowledge of the bright world beyond the cosmos.* The metaphysics his parents, Lazo and Yasoda, had taught him, and the gnosis from Herak . . . it all came to Stevan in a rush of thoughts: *This cosmos is overcome by the dark flames of the demiurge, and we stumble, trapped.* He considered: The Pillars of Hercules! This would be an act so far outside the enclosure of this world that a path would appear before us, we would breach the iron wall which bars the way, break the watchtowers, and penetrate terror's empty space, fly invisible through time, our Alien Souls!

"One catch, young Stevan."

Stevan raised his eyebrows and said, "I will clear it with Charlie. I'm not going to pirate his aeroplane. I'll ask him if I may borrow it."

At that, Dick guffawed. Then, he said, "But you're a goin't steal his daughter."

"She . . ."

"Now listen, Stevan. I've learned that Charlie will allow her away with you under one condition."

"Condition?"

"I must join you on the journey."

"You?"

"This is the only way it works, lad. I've been talkin' to Charlie. It's the missive from Herak—*Fly Sevan South*— that put Charlie over the top where your plan is concerned."

Stevan frowned, "Charlie knows?"

Yes, nothing gets by Charlie. He'd already sussed out your plan. He brought it up to me before I'd even said a word."

Stevan hesitated for a moment.

"Stevan? Are you with me, man? You can fly this aeroplane. But I'm comin' with."

And bring Marian on this perilous journey? But in his mind, Stevan could hear Marian say, *Try, impudent fool. Try to stop me!* Stevan nodded and said, "Oh yes, I will pilot this flying boat home."

✦　✦　✦

Marian had a horse. She liked her horse, Peter. Peter only liked her. Anyone else approaching within a yard was in danger of being nipped by Peter's strong jaws, his sharp teeth. If you got nipped, it hurt like hell. Stevan knew this, still had the mark on his shoulder to prove it. But feeling as himself again, and fairly bursting with cheer because of his plan, he had tracked his young wife down to the barn while she was washing and grooming her steed. When Peter saw Stevan, he lay his ears back, cocked his large head, gave Stevan the evil eye. Stevan took care to stand off a bit.

"You look most radiant."

"I'm washing the horse. Grooming the horse."

"Hmm. Probably showing off for him."

"He certainly pays me more attention."

"Well, still, you are quite darling."

"Hand me that sea sponge, would you?"

"Sea sponge? Where?"

She gave a disgusted little snort and pointed. "In the bucket."

Stevan walked over to the galvanized pail and pulled out a soaking wet sea sponge larger than one of his large hands. He crossed over to her, keeping a careful eye on "the teeth," and distractedly handed her the dripping sponge; then he receded a step out of Peter's nipping range.

"Thank you," she said. At once, she reared back and threw the sponge directly into Stevan's face with some force, a trailing-water overhead shot, as if she were bowling a cricket ball—really the best approach to a tall man, she'd determined. He never saw it coming since he was still very wary of Peter, who had been shaking his head in a manner that was causing Stevan concern. The sponge sopped him, face, hair, shirt, coat. A satisfying look of surprise and confusion crossed Stevan's face, Marian observed, just the effect she had intended.

"Damn you," she said, "You think you can treat me this way?"

Stevan sneezed, wiped his face with his sleeve with little positive result, the water dripping off him and puddling on the stone floor. "I . . . I, what? What did I do?"

"Don't play the fool, fool."

"But—"

"I haven't seen you for days. You get up in the middle of the night and disappear, you ignore me, you go off drinking with Dick—with my father, for God's sake! When you are about, you can't seem to put two words together, you mope, you brood, your head is elsewhere, you make me mope and brood, and I, I am not like that! In short, you are the worst companion a woman could have!"

"OK. OK . . . we'll see." He walked over to the bucket, picked it up as if it were full of seashore crabs, peered into it, wrinkled his nose. "Ah, still an alarming bit of water in here."

"What?" she said, "What do you think you are doing?"

"I think it's time the Keeper of The Wolly had a bath."

"Oh no. Don't you dare!"

Stevan raised the pail, sloshed it around, and took aim, but Marian ducked under Peter's neck and around the other side of the horse. Peter danced on his hooves just enough to cause Stevan to step back, then the horse raised his tail and had what must certainly have been a very satisfying bowel movement! The rounded balls struck the floor with a gentle plop.

With absolutely no hesitation, Marian took a gliding step, bent down behind the horse, scooped up a *road apple*—as her American friends would call it—and threw it at Stevan. She had a good, accurate arm, already proven by the sopping sponge incident a moment ago, and she struck Stevan's neck so that some of the poo snuck under his collar and down his shirt.

"Why, you! You!" was all he could manage to say. He flung the contents of the pail at Marian.

She ducked, but the horse-water soaked her back, and she cried, "Damn that's bloody cold!"

Stevan took the moment of her distraction, to brave Peter, scoop up several errant road apples and tossed a barrage at his lovely wife. Well, he thought, she's not the only one with the ability to hit the mark. Yes, he hit his mark, for there was a shriek, and Marian's left side was covered in exploded road apples.

But Marian was a quick thinker. It was just three elephant steps back to the feed bin, where she grabbed a scoop of bran mash, ran towards Stevan, and like a jai alai player, slung the mash at her darling husband. The mash struck Stevan in all his wet places so that it stuck or found its way through his shirt.

"Hey!" he cried. He felt most uncomfortable. It itched.

They both stopped and looked at each other. Marian cracked a grin. Stevan couldn't help himself, he started laughing. "Good God, woman! I give up. I'll be a good husband. I promise!"

"Well, you . . . you! I've been so angry at your behavior!"

"Marian, my love—I have something quite important to tell you. I have a plan. It, involves you. But first. We can't go back to the house like this." He looked around. The Ariel Square sat in an alcove near the heavy double doors.

"Snatch some towels, blankets. We're going to jump in the lake."

Marian stood with her hands on her hips. "What do the Americans say? Nuts? Are you nuts?"

"We are covered in earthly wretchedness. Time for a bath after all." He strode to the end of the barn to pull out the motorcycle. "Come on."

Marian unlatched Peter's lead line from his halter. Peter, evidently satisfied with his marriage counseling, swung his head around to look at Marian, and then clopped off to his large, comfortable stall, mucked out and strewn with fresh straw.

Peter knew a mixture of oats and bran mash awaited him in his feed bin. Could life get any better? Oh, yes it could! For Marian followed him. He entered the stall and turned around to look at his mistress. She shut and latched the lower half of the Dutch door, pulled a lovely carrot from her pocket, presented it to Peter, he who loved carrots! He took a little bite. Bit off a quarter. She smiled and held it out. Peter took another quarter, chewed thoughtfully.

"Good boy, you are!" Marian cooed.

Peter gently took the rest of the yummy carrot. Then he turned towards his feed bin, because, yes, he was hungry.

"Marian," called Stevan, growing impatient. He kick-started the Ariel.

"Right with you." She looked about for the towel and blanket footlocker, found it shoved behind a couple of hay bales, and removed several warming items. Arriving, she tossed them into the sidecar and climbed onto the motorcycle behind Stevan.

The stable drive met up with the boathouse drive after about three hundred yards. Stevan followed it until another path veered off to the left, a narrow lane that lay between tall grass and occasional whitethorn shrubs, this, the path that led to the swim beach and diving dock. Stevan cut the motor to glide down the last few meters. They dismounted. They glanced here and there and all around themselves, marveling at the wonderous fall afternoon.

As they walked out onto the dock, the late afternoon sun reflected longwave rays off fair-weather clouds making a kind of intrinsic glow of rose color all around them—alpenglow. The still water was not water. It was substance of gentle light. It seemed to rise up around them. Characteristically, Marian didn't hesitate, she stepped onto the ladder and slid silently into this light, this glow of lake water, making nary a ripple. Stevan, a fast learner, did the same, so that in a moment their heads bobbed in the firmament. They swam around each other, meeting eyes, assessing: who is this other? Do I know? Do I trust? What is this journey, this impact on our very souls?

Marian said, "According to the Countess of Blessington, love matches are formed by people who pay for a month of honey with a life of vinegar."

Stevan's lips formed a trace of a smile. Then words came tumbling out of him: "Oh, we are way beyond that. Yes, when I see you, I am attracted to you. But your loveliness starts with your eyes, pours into your mind and through your heart on into your memory, backward and forward . . . you know me, Marian, you have known me for many, many lives, my love!"

She squinted at him.

He continued, "Our emotions are in sympathy, our interests intersect. Intellectually, we understand each other, but you disagree with me at times! Yet this is good, is it not, as we counter check each other so that we find the right path? And in spirit, we are very alike! So, I say again, and again, and again: I take you to be my wife."

Marian slowly smiled, swam towards Stevan. "I take you to be my husband." They treaded water, almost floating, and then drifted towards the shallows, where feet touched a stone bottom, rounded pebbles, gentle on toes. Each shed clinging clothing, and, carrying such, emerged from the mysticality onto the twilight shore, their beautiful, naked bodies aglow, yet . . .

All over the world, bodies young, bodies old, were being rent by invasion, resistance, cannon, bombs, machine guns, tanks, opposing forces, assault, no peace, no tranquility, but rather, the illusion of political order, which brought nothing but chaos and destruction. Yet . . .

In between the raindrops, as it were, exist moments. For Marian and Steven these moments were soon to pass, but not yet . . .

"I'm freezing!" Marian cried; she tossed her wet things onto the rocks and made for the dry towels and blankets, Stevan right behind her.

Marian and Stevan lay on the towels, under the blankets, hugging each other, shivering, until . . . Well, what may happen between lovers, naked in their warming cocoon?

Chapter Four

A_{T QUARTER TO SIX} on a slightly misty morning in late October 1940, an antique but modified aeroplane flew up from a lake in Suffolk, circled twice over Cismontane, and headed southwest for the Bristol Channel. On the craft's tail were freshly stenciled call letters: ALN-S0U1. Just enough light from the promise of dawn illuminated the roll of the countryside and the small, sleeping communities below. Hideous craters pocked fields where enemy aircraft had jettisoned bombs, trying to escape Spitfires by easing their load and making a run for the North Sea. Spectral hulks of wrecked, gutted aircraft pierced the mud below.

Stevan piloted the F2A, its engines pounding out a smooth rhythm, Marian beside him as copilot, and Dick up forward acting as navigator. Passing through fair-weather clouds every now and then, they flew over county shires north of London.

Breaking into the prevailing quiet on the intercom, Dick shouted, "Aye, the kit's workin' fine; there now! The start of the Bristol Channel, and that mark there, that's Bristol." Dick was peering into the cathode-ray tube he'd connected to the BAT, the experimental, aircraft-mounted radar, and the screen displayed the radar's information.

Marian looked from the open cockpit for the shattered city and thought of the ruthless Nazi bombing that had come after Hitler announced he intended to raze every British city to the ground, to destroy Great Britain's population. She thought of her older brother who had been wing commander of 11 Group at West Malling in Kent, and of his death when the Luftwaffe attacked the aerodrome.

But Stevan did not fly over Bristol and instead met the Channel over Gloucestershire and loped along the Channel's southern coast. He met the north coasts of Devon and Cornwall and continued to Land's End and on, crossing over the Isles of Scilly.

They were flying at low altitude, about two thousand feet, and the three of them waved to a man and a sheltie walking in a field near Hugh Town. It was 8:30 a.m., still with intermittent clouds.

As they cleared the islands, the last vestiges of land, Dick looked down at the ocean, cold undulations almost hypnotic in effect, and a wave more formidable, fear, washed over him. The F2A could become lost out here. "Ah but must we stray so far off that French coast?" he said into the mike.

Stevan answered, "The 109Es may be up north, but they've got secondary craft that will run rings around us. I'm taking her up—we need a little operating room."

As they climbed 4,500 feet in ten minutes, Stevan mentally reviewed the equipment on the aeroplane: four machine guns; twelve ammunition boxes; three Colt revolvers with twenty-eight rounds of ammunition each; one bomb sight and four bombs for U-boats; a mushroom anchor and twenty-five fathoms of line; a parachute sea anchor; 479 gallons of fuel stowed in five tanks, 100 extra gallons stowed in the aft gunner's cockpit and along the mid and rear fuselage; a hand gas pump and a windmill pump; thirty gallons of oil carried in two tanks, one rear of each engine; a bilge pump, discharge and suction hoses with strainer; fire extinguishers, tool kit, canvas bail bucket, first aid kit, parachutes, life raft, drinking water and rations . . . Damn, thought Stevan. "I forgot the wine," he said out loud.

"Well, now that we know what your mind worries about, you'll be pleased to hear that I was rememberin' the spirits. It will take more than a blessing to keep us happy if we are forced to put down upon these waters." Dick stood up in the forward cockpit, was blasted by a rush of wind, and sighted back with a pair of binoculars to the fading Isles of Scilly. "Do ya think the wind, the one you Montenegrins call 'Rade,' sweeps about the ocean now and then? We're driftin' to the east."

"How far?"

"Well now, let me draw a line or two." Dick sat back down out of the wind and pulled out a chart and compass, fooled around with a triangle of velocities and said: "Seven degrees."

Stevan corrected his compass heading. He said, "Our dead reckoning navigation is over, we're out of landmarks."

"We've got flares and smoke canisters," said Marian, "I'll drop one every hour and we'll check for drift."

Stevan smiled. Marian seemed to have a mind that allowed her to enter an alien world and quickly comprehend the system that ruled it. Navigation over trackless ocean from an antique aeroplane? Easy! All the esoteric supplies he'd packed away on the craft? She knew how to use them, from machine guns to bomb sights. She could operate the BAT if she had to. She'd known nothing of warcraft until the last few weeks, but at a point she began living it, not studying it, but living it. From the time of their swimming in the alpenglow until their goodbye circle over Cismontane, it had been exactly three weeks.

"I mean to say, we have the courage to carry through," Marian continued after the pause during which Stevan appeared to be stupidly smiling. "Our intellect tells us we're in danger of being lost at sea, yet we feel we can find Gibraltar . . . Stevan, our intellect is a scribe, not a master . . . we bend it to follow our courage."

"Spoken like a true Celt," Dick said. He had overheard the conversation on his earphones.

Anger seared through Marian; she thought she had been speaking to Stevan alone—she had forgotten that the intercom was hooked up three ways.

Stevan said, "How lucky I am to have the both of you."

Which made Marian shake her head and whisper, "You . . . are a clod."

They were now flying at about seven thousand feet a hundred and fifty miles west of Brest, France. They were flying through clouds every minute or so.

"Hello," said Dick, "What's this? A whale? Or something a bit more sinister, a U-boat? Twenty-five miles ahead on course . . . and in the air! Voyagers? We've got company both down and up!"

"The aircraft bearing?"

"Directly ahead, man."

"Altitude?"

"About three thousand feet."

"Well, at least we're above it."

"I've a feeling it's a rendezvous, a kind of transport droppin' supplies to a U-boat."

Stevan began to climb. "We'll keep this cloud layer between us and them and look through the patches."

"Don't you think we should hie out for the rim?" Dick said. "Skirt the thing? This aeroplane is no match for modern aircraft."

"It's a match for the Focke-Wulf 200 which the Hun uses for transport and for a reconnaissance-bomber. It's a true flying snail and not acrobatic like we are with our biwings."

"If that's what it is," Dick replied.

Marian piped in: "Just a little peek, they'll not know we're here."

Stevan smiled. "Aye, Dick! Just a little peek!"

Dick knew his courage was different from Stevan's and, evidentially, Marian's. He had courage in the internal war against himself and his doubts, courage against the illusion of limits, but he saw acts of murder and mayhem, called battle during war, as yet another tally for the negative principle of man. To him, killing could be an act of courage, yet more often just an act of lust or fear.

"I'll bring us around a bit to the south so the sun will be on our tail in case they should look up through the patches," Stevan said.

"Check the forward guns," Marian advised. "We're going to get one for my brother and the Eleventh Group!"

The 11 Group, young Charlie. As he grew up at Cismontane, Dick and big Charlie taught young Charlie many things, including how to fly all manner of aircraft. Dick felt perhaps it was his fault that Charlie's only son, young Charlie, had eventually become a wing commander, only to be killed at West Malling.

"Ahh, I should have been teachin' him how to fish!"

"What's that, Dick?

"Oh . . . Sorry, Stevan, was I talkin' out loud?" He felt something cold and brittle pass over him. He could recognize battle lust, theirs, and, he admitted to himself, his own. He no longer wanted to protest, and now things began to move too fast.

He grabbed his binoculars and held the enemy aircraft in the lenses. In a rush of words, he shouted, "It's a transport! Droppin' odious supplies to the U-boat. Some of the crew's paddlin' about in a dinghy, picking packages."

"We'll go for the transport first—the U-boat won't dive without her crew . . . I hope."

"I'll go mount the aft gun," said Marian.

"No!"

She unfastened her seatbelt and began to remove her headset.

Stevan grabbed her arm. "Look, if I get hit, you'll have to take the controls."

She looked at him with a smile. "How am I going to drag your grandness and volume from out of there?"

"You'll just have to."

"You will just have to be the best pilot up here." She climbed out of her seat and, grabbing handholds, made her way to the aft gunner's cockpit, just behind the wings, squeezing in beside a fuel canister.

Dick heard the discussion. Once more, he wavered. "Stevan! Turn. Let's go on!"

Silence on the com.

"Stevan, she's right, if you are hit, no one else can get at the controls to fly the plane."

More silence on the com.

Then, "OK. The hell with it!" Stevan began to bank to the west.

"Stevan! What the hell are you doing?" Marian cried. "We are going to take this U-boat!"

"We're getting out of here!" Stevan said.

"Dammit, Stevan," Marian said, getting ready to lay into him.

"We've been spotted!" Dick yelled into his mic. Sure enough, the Focke-Wulf 200 had turned and seemed to be lumbering towards them, probably feeling superior to the World War I biplane. The curtain fell on their argument, the moment passed, the battle was on.

Stevan rounded the F2A and put it into a dive towards the Nazi aircraft. The sun was at the flying boat's tail, blazing through a patch in the clouds. At four-hundred yards Dick opened up with the twin Lewis machine guns.

The Wulf began firing too. Tracer bullets marred the air. Suddenly the Wulf banked and dived to its right, the pilot probably blinded by the sun. It was a ponderous turn, though, and Stevan was on it in seconds in the much more agile F2A.

Airspeed from the dive up to 145 mph, Stevan saw Dick pepper it broadside and he pulled back on the stick to rise rapidly over the Wulf, which disappeared in a tremendous explosion and ball of flame, its shock waves buffeting the flying boat. In the explosion's glow, the puffy clouds transmogrified into reddish spectral shapes of ghostly, phantasmagoric horror all around them. The shockwave added to the lift on the ascending F2A, but then seemed to suck it downward with a loss of pilot control.

By the time Stevan recovered control of the aeroplane, it had descended to a thousand feet. The crew of the U-boat fired vigorously at them, but the choppy sea rocked the boat erratically, fouling their aim. The sailors in the dinghy had paddled back to the U-boat and were disappearing down a hatch; the abandoned dinghy bobbed in the swells.

"I think she's goin' down t' Davy," shouted Dick.

"Yes, I see the gunners breaking for the hatch." Stevan banked the F2A hard to the left, circling an updraft to gain altitude; Dick adjusted the bomb sight. They ran at the sub at about 1,500 feet.

"Now," Dick ordered.

Marian, remaining in the rear gunner's cockpit, was the only one who could release the bombs, since that's where the release levers were situated. She pulled two. She smiled. Before the bombs had been loaded onto the F2A, she had painted, in a nice calligraphy onto the side of the ordnance, "Greetings from The Wolly." Both bombs missed but rocked the sub with their explosions.

"Damn! I thought we had 'er dead to rights."

"One more run. I'll bring us in at a steeper angle."

The F2A climbed to 1,600 feet, then dove at the U-boat, its decks awash, disappearing under the ocean swells.

"Bomb sights ready, bomber?"

"Copy!"

"Altitude?"

Dick read the dial: "Fourteen, thirteen five, twelve five, one thousand, nine hundred, eight—"

"Now!"

Marian pulled a third lever. A bomb released. Stevan banked into the wind. Explosion. Smell of cordite.

"The U-boat went under as we were in our dive," Marian said.

"Did we pound the evil thing?"

"I don't know." Stevan circled around the foam and froth of the battle area. He could see an oil slick and shreds from the dinghy; that was all.

"We'll not know for sure," said Dick with a bit of disappointment in his voice.

Marian noticed a change in the patches of clouds, many now knitted together to form a thick ceiling at about seven thousand feet. "Look upward, crew, we've got a cap," she said.

"We'd best get our bearings."

"Aye, Stevan. It'd be nice to squat upon the swells and take a reading of the sun from a fixed position, but I could not see through the hurly-burly above us. Can we poke through?"

"I don't want to land on the chop anyway." Stevan pulled back on the stick, so the F2A climbed to the clouds.

"Here we go," he said, keeping an eye on the gyroscope acting as an artificial horizon and the rate-of-climb indicator. He knew a pilot's worst fear should be of becoming disoriented in the vague leviathan of cloud, dimensions unknown, until he has no remembrance of which way is up, down, or sideways, a wraith-cloud impenetrable . . .

They climbed two hundred, three hundred, five hundred, nine hundred feet . . .

"A thousand feet of cloud?"

Then Dick: "We're through!"

They saw they were on the edge of a vast thunderhead rising perhaps forty-thousand feet in the air, chasms and pinnacles, perimeters white, depths dark as unraveled myth, other immense atmospheric specters in the west, stretching north and south, moving east.

"Look! Little cloud patches have all blown east as if to run away from their larger selves," Marian observed.

"We must run with them," Stevan warned. "This is a heavy front and a severe test for our flying boat." He altered the course a bit to the east. "Well, there's this, Dick, we won't fly hopelessly out to sea if we run before the storm—it's blowing east."

"But we dare not land on the shores of Vichy."

"Do you agree we were about twelve degrees west?"

"A good guess, I imagine."

"We're probably about ten west now. I'll try to hold her as close to the incoming front as I dare. We should make the coast of Spain, or if we're lucky, Portugal."

Eight minutes later a break in the clouds appeared below them.

"I'll drop a smoker," said Marian. "We must try to figure the drift."

They watched the trail of smoke from the marker tossing in the waves as they traveled rapidly southeast from it.

"Airspeed?"

"One-oh-five."

"The wind's blowin' at forty mph from a hundred and forty degrees behind." A pause. Our ground speed's one hundred thirty-one mph, give or take a mile." They flew on at speed.

✦　✦　✦

It had been two-and-a-half hours since the smoke reading. Stevan knew this due to the luminous watch Marian had given him, and he'd glanced at the dial twenty times in that span. "I'm stiff," he said to Marian. She had made her way back to the pilot's cockpit shortly after the discovery of the approaching front.

"But a half hour more should be bringin' us to the coast of Portugal," Dick said hopefully.

Sure enough, about a half hour later, Dick said, "I think I see landmass in the distance, through the haze." They had outrun the front a little, but it loomed to the right and behind them.

"My God, Stevan, engine two is very hot!"

"What? What's that, Marian?" asked Dick.

Stevan glanced at the water-temperature gauge. He saw the needle point above two hundred degrees Fahrenheit, so he immediately shut the engine down. The F2A still handled well enough with one engine, but her airspeed fell off to sixty-five mph. They continued to limp along like that, about fifteen mph over stalling speed, until the number one engine began to lose power. Stevan could see no apparent cause for the trouble until he tried to give it some throttle and met with no response.

"Dammit! The wire's come loose and the throttle's jarred closed . . . We're going down." He pushed the stick forward, nosing the plane down to gain airspeed, then turned into the wind to glide into the vicious chop whipped up by the approaching storm. The flying boat hit hard but remained upright, plowing a liquid furrow in the sea. Stevan looked at his watch again—2:00 P.M., Greenwich time. The looming storm's grey mass would soon engulf them.

"Dick, toss over the chute so the drag will keep us headed into the wind. Marian, pull out the cockpit covers. Dick, we've got to repair at least one of these engines to have some control when we blow near the coast."

"Aye. Even if we fix the both of them, we'll not get off in this sea."

Dick tossed over the sea anchor and then climbed the lower wing to engine two, while Stevan inspected engine one.

"You wouldn't believe it," shouted Dick, "machine gun bullets lodged in the radiator . . . the water leaked out slow and sure." Stevan pointed to his temple, then shrugged and refastened the throttle cable.

When the storm hit, the three of them huddled under the pilot's cockpit cover. They were rocked on the waters, but the sea-anchor worked well, keeping the craft headed into the wind. They took turns keeping watch for the shore, poking out from underneath the sopping cover.

Marian, hair soaked, eyes blinking away rain and sea water, cried, "I can't see much of anything! But I don't hear waves crashing on the shore."

Stevan said, "What, Marian? I can't hear you."

"What?" said Marian.

Dick said, "I'm going to open a bottle of sherry."

He pulled the cork, took a swig and tapped the bottle against Marian's leg.

She dropped back under the cover. "It's a tempest in a sea pot." In the dim light, she saw the bottle, grabbed it and took a warming drink of the sherry, then handed it to Stevan.

"Look here," he said, "I've got some cheese and salami, and for dessert, some of Mr. Graves's . . . er, Charlie's cigars!"

Marian, quite sure her father would not have given up a handful of his Havanas, exclaimed, "Well, you robber!"

Stevan grinned and replied, "Why, you tart!"

Dick, observing the little flirt-fest, remarked, "So now we've got tarts and robbers. Sounds like an Irish costume party down in the old town, Dublin."

Stevan grinned. He said, "So. You were a wild Irish costume partier back in Dublin?"

At first, Dick returned the grin; but then a shadow crossed his face. Memories flashed. He looked away and said, "Before the Great War, perhaps. But a conflict like that can change a man."

Marian, picking up on his sudden mood, asked, "Will you ever go back, Dick? After all, you are ordained in the Church of Ireland."

"Ah, Marian, of course, of course. Maybe down to Kildare, pray to the Lady, Saint Brigid."

Stevan passed treats out to each of them and then handed the sherry bottle to Dick.

Dick remarked, "She's a saint worth praying to, and the opposite of some of the beings now roaming the earth. Like your demiurge? You say Gnostics regard the demiurge as a blind god, a fool, a child of chaos?"

Stevan answered, "Some believe the demiurge is modeled on the god of the Old Testament, but we see him as akin to the Greek notion of a capricious god interfering in human affairs. His end game is to rule over humankind."

Dick said, "As has done before, has he not?"

Stevan replied, "Just so. Name the empire and he was there, wielding misguided influence. He only brings misery."

Dick said, "So we agree, the Gnostic demiurge is not the supreme God."

Marian said, "Of course not, Dick!"

Dick continued, "Because we Christians believe there is only one God, not two."

"However," Stevan observed, "Catholicism is, on the other hand, infused with pagan influences, the birth of Christ changed to December when all the sun gods were born, all those pagan deities made into saints."

"Ah now, what are ya goin' on about, young Stevan?"

Stevan took the sherry bottle from Dick for a swig and said, "Like Saint Brigid, Dick."

Dick grunted, reached for the sherry bottle.

Stevan added, "Christ returned the love principle to religion . . . There are Gnostic influences in your Catholicism."

Dick replied, "Not a position the Church ascribes to most exegeses of Gnosticism."

Stevan replied, "It is how we think about it, Dick, you'll see."

An alarming gust, force seven, whirled under the F2A's wings. The flying boat rose in the air, facing the wind, straining against the sea anchor, then relanded to bound over the waves.

Dick, completely unconcerned about the aeroplane's antics, changed tone and reflected, "As I said, I am devoted to the shrine of Saint Brigid, our goddess on the dour but emerald isle. She's a sure descendant of the Tuatha-de-Danann, a race that knew Simon the Druid."

Marian and Stevan squinted at each other in the half light. "Simon the Druid?" they said in unison.

"Why, yes, the famed Irish magician who fought a magical battle with St. Peter. Remember?"

"Remind us, Dick, we always want to hear about a bloomin' Irish magician."

"Well, Marian, Simon made a magic wheel which enabled him to fly, and he did fly, but St. Peter somehow brought Simon crashing to the ground, where the poor sod died."

Stevan said, "I think it's a variation of the legend of Simon Magus the Samaritan, who helped conceive Gnosticism. Another legend says he had himself buried alive for a week to prove he could rise from the dead, but no one saw him after that! I think the Church made sure to cast him as a foolish magician with these legends. Bad press as it were."

"Maybe such occurred," Dick replied, "but please be rememberin', that no doubt, a lot of foolish types in those days were claimin' to be deity."

Stevan was quiet for a moment, then asked Dick, "How do you put up with the notions of Herak's Gnostic circle, and with me, and with Charlie's esoterica? Even with Marian, who is . . . versed in Gnosis?"

Dick took a swig from the bottle. He said, "Going back to the Great War, Charlie and I are the finest of friends. The woman sittin' next to you—as I told you, she's like my own daughter. Are you rememberin' why I'm with you on this journey?"

At that, Marian smiled at Dick, grabbed his hand and said, just over the din of the raging storm, "Thank you! I'm so grateful!"

Dick winked at her. He turned to Stevan. "As for you? She loves you. That's good enough for me. Well, that and also, you're a tip-top mechanic and pub hopper."

"Why, I think the same of you, Dick."

Dick continued, "Meanwhile, with your man Herak? I'll be seein' what I can see."

Marian, now annoyed, exclaimed, "You two shall damn well add me as a tip-top pub hopper, if there were any pubs."

Stevan grinned and said, "The Wolly keeper should hop all the pubs, as she wishes."

A bottle-and-a-half of sherry later, Stevan pulled out a cigar, snipped it, lit it, handed it to Dick. Dick gave it to Marian.

Marian took a puff. "Ugh! How do you smoke these things?"

Stevan replied, "I thought you are the keeper of the Wolly. According to legend, he loved them. So does your father."

She gave the stogie back to Dick. "Here, make yourself unwell. I have to get a breath of sea water." She rose to slip her head from under the cover, out into the storm and rage. With her head in the air, she began to discern the low thunder of waves attacking the shore. She peered past the tail section, but could see nothing; yet, it was there: landmass. "Land ahoy!"

"What? Marian, we can't hear you."

"About three hundred yards."

"Dick, what did she say?"

"I'm not knowin' cause I'm not hearin'."

"Uh, this sherry has done me no good. It's inhuman to drink this much sherry at one time."

"Hey! I said, land ahoy!"

"Had I brought the whiskey instead, we'd a been a sight better off."

"Agreed! Whisky is a much purer spirit."

"I recommend the Powers Irish whiskey—a distinguished blend."

"Hey! Mariners! Land ahoy!"

"I think Irish is too astringent. I prefer the smooth elixir of highland malt."

Suddenly, the two of them were deluged by rain and sea. Marian had ripped off the cockpit cover. She shouted: "Land. Fucking. Bleeding. Ho!"

She had finally commanded their attention. In a flash, they were all sopping wet, scattering bottles, bits of cheese, sausage, and half-smoked cigars about their feet.

Stevan pulled out the chokes and fired up first the starboard, then the port engine, feeling smug that he had fitted them with modern electric start. Number two would run for a time in the wind and driving rain before overheating, which was fortunate, because they would need horsepower to maneuver in the storm. Stevan throttled forward enough to keep the flying boat drifting offshore and to the south. Presently the landmass faded its roar to the left. In response, he eased off in order to follow the contour of the shoreline. The land began to intercede between the F2A and the storm; they slowly drifted behind the leeward side of . . . what? An island?

Then Marian noticed they had stopped moving at all in relation the roar of the shore behind them. "Hey!" she shouted. "The chute's gone balls up. It's gone too deep and it's snagged on something!"

"Marian! You are starting to sound like your father!"

"Because I'm angry at a pair of sozzled sots!"

She clamored forward. Every few moments, the flying boat's nose submerged under waves, so that a deluge flowed into the cockpit, causing her to grab on to built-in grasps. Dick reached for the bilge pump, fitted the strainer and hoses, and began pumping out the wash that streamed past the scuppers to come aft.

Stevan increased the power, moving the F2A forward into the chop.

Marian ferried line while the flying boat sliced up-current from the chute—the sea anchor—and it came free. She pulled the trip line to collapse the chute and hauled the sea anchor aboard. Then Stevan allowed the flying boat to drift back into the lee.

At that point, Dick spotted an inlet glinting in dim light emanating from a high cliff. Cliffs rose on either side. Overheating forced Stevan to shut down number two engine again, but the shelter of the inlet allowed the aeroplane to be maneuvered easily with only one engine running.

Sliding it up on a strip of sand, Stevan shouted for Marian to wedge their heavy mushroom anchor among some rocks. From the forward cockpit, she wrestled the anchor over the side, then using the anchor line for hand holds, went over also. She landed on the beach, dragged the anchor through the sand, and lifted it just enough to secure it behind a small outcrop.

In the meantime, Stevan kept the F2A from being blown back off the beach by feathering the throttle. Dick went forward to pull the anchor line taut, securing the flying boat against tide and wind.

The tasks completed, Marian exclaimed she felt bone weary, as she shuffled back to the flying boat. Stevan climbed out on the lower wing to help her back up. In less than two minutes, the three of them had crawled further back into the fuselage, where they huddled, cold and wet, pounding rain just outside all around them.

✦　✦　✦

Chapter Five

A GENTLE, DRY, MORNING BREEZE rustled the fabric of the flying boat, whispered away the early morning mist, leaving a clarity to the sky and beyond . . . or so the Honorable Festus Griveaux thought. Albeit early, he was already attired in his blue business suit. He stood at least six-one, counting his handmade, stacked shoes. The look of his features, his countenance, seemed to vary almost moment to moment, perhaps depending on the wisp of his thoughts. In age, he looked to be, as Coco Chanel put it, *"It's difficult to say how old he is, darling—pick a number—anywhere from thirty to a thousand."* In the moment, Festus felt dapper, but as his shadow fell across the aeroplane from the cliff above, he realized a twinge of discomfort. He read the large, stenciled letters on the tail section:

ALN-S0U1

A, L, N, dash S, Zero, U, One, he said to himself. I can't decipher these call letters. An absurd biwinged boat abuses my shore in the calm of the morning, after a night of the finest of tempests! *What shall I do about this?* he thought.

I think I shall frame it as a rescue. And perhaps it is!

Hastening from his clifftop piazza, he wound his way down cliff-carved stairs to a garage, which housed several military-style trucks and rovers. He called to several of what he referred to as personal assistants, Athuro and Erimacho, who were always well armed, and bade them to engage one of the four-wheel-drive personnel carriers to take him down to the beach. He desired to get this over with, one way or the other, for he had other obligations that day, and every day of the waning autumn season.

His negotiations with the Portuguese, Spanish, Italians, and Germans—about the establishment of his polity, *The Independent Republic of Suebi*—presently required most of his attention. He planned to establish an exclusive jurisdiction on the Iberian Atlantic shore, of banking, gaming, intermingling, and relaxation for the elite of those, and perhaps other nations. Legitimate Suebian passports would become available, for a price, allowing concealment of undesirable identities, thus allowing travel of those identities to previously unavailable locales. All it would take for these and other agreeable things to occur would be a substantial buy-in from each member nation, off-book. Perhaps he could even entice Coco Chanel to become involved, lend her glamour, amoral ethics, and business acumen to the project.

How had he gotten so far? How had he acquired so many followers? Well, he thought, while bumping down the track to the beach, I am a mystical entity, and I am comprised of mysteries that imbue me with power, power over minds and desires!

The truck arrived at the driftwood-strewn beach, where it wasn't hampered by the flotsam, but rather crunched over every storm-driven obstacle, pounding broken tree limbs, sea logs, horseshoe crabs, dinghy boards, wine bottles, starfish, etc. into the sand. The truck came to a halt within twenty-five yards of the biplane.

The Honorable Festus motioned for Athuro and Erimacho to take up crossfire vectors aimed at the craft, then he walked up to within thirty feet of the aeroplane and said in a loud voice, "The ruler is not androgynous. He is the father!"

After a moment, from inside the flying boat came two voices in unison, "The Romanov command—We eke victory to great deeds!"

The Honorable Festus Griveaux was startled for just a trice, but for that moment, time did not proceed. Everything slowed to a halt. Something had disturbed him. He took a second and third look. Strange encounter! He gave a cautious snort and said in a pleasant voice, "A very good morning to you. Would you care to join me for breakfast?"

Stevan looked at his watch. Six forty-five. He shrugged at Marian and poked Dick, who was relaxing in sherry slumber.

"Delighted," came what the Honorable Festus Griveaux considered to be a rather slow reply, and this time a male voice alone spoke. Good, he thought, I've caught it napping. He licked his lips.

Stevan appeared in the pilot's cockpit. He said, "Good morning!"

Poor fellow's a rumpled mess, thought the Honorable Festus. "Indeed, it is! Terrible night last night. It appears you've had just a modicum of difficulty."

Having taken in the crossfire positions further up the beach and wondering what the deuce they had gotten themselves into, Stevan replied, "Yes, sir, I hope you can forgive us for taking shelter in your magnificent cove."

Marian climbed into the cockpit beside Stevan. She was carrying a small suitcase, which she handed to him. Dick emerged just after her.

Dick said, "Well, now, a beach of some beauty, a sky for an airman, and a host of consideration and culture. Good morning to you, sir."

The Honorable Festus replied, "Is that all of you, then?

No reply.

A little touch of a frown crossed the Honorable Festus's forehead, but it was hidden beneath his weird salt-and-pepper forelock.

He said, "My name is the Honorable Festus Griveaux, President of the Independent Republic of Suebi. You will be my guests. Come, you've obviously experienced a dreadful night. You may revive in the comfort of my dwelling." He pointed to a white mansion on the cliff overlooking the cove.

"Why, thank you," Stevan said. He helped Marian climb onto the lower biwing, just for show, since she was better at disembarking the aeroplane than he was, then climbed out himself, followed by Dick. Once they stood on the beach, the Honorable Festus motioned for them to advance to the truck; however, the crossfire gunmen maintained their positions. Stevan noticed and thought, By the time we arrive at the truck, I could probably get them to crossfire each other.

*   *   *

The great house was not magnificent, due to its badly executed Mediterranean architecture and its opulent but vulgar neomodern furnishings, the interior theme done in greys and blacks. The pile had likely been a private dwelling at one time, before clueless entrepreneurs had acquired it in the twenties and turned it into a posh hotel, with bad updating, but added amenities. It fell out of favor with discerning good-timers, and now the President of the Independent Republic of Suebi had acquired it? The rooms were many and large, but instead of the lovely, dark polished wood of Cismontane, this southern mansion was all of stone and stucco. No doubt such materials, aided by large doors and windows that had been redesigned to capture the ocean breezes, now kept the interior cool in the hot months.

"Please, refresh yourselves, Phloxopha will show you to your rooms upstairs." The Honorable Festus motioned to a blank doorway; out came a woman, who from a certain distance looked quite young, until upon closer viewing looked much, much older, her hair not blond, but greyish white, her eyes fiery. In all, she had a rather overheated look. "Then come down for, well, let's call it brunch, in about an hour. You must tell me why in the world you are adventuring about in that . . . most unusual aircraft and how you ended up in our cove."

When they arrived downstairs, they were shown, again by Phloxopha, to the terrace, or as the locals called it, the piazza, since it was very large. It overlooked the cove and the Atlantic Ocean. From the piazza, one could see storms approaching at a great distance, and when the sun set, the various shades and hues of red and pink could be almost alarming, until shortly, darkness came to bring its own flashes, bursts of bedazzlement, electricity in the looming clouds rendering an astonishing vision, one marked by appalling, earsplitting thunderclaps and distant rumbles, leaving in its wake disquietude.

But in the quiet after the previous night's gale, a long cypress table, likely used outdoors for its resistance to rainstorms, was set with a spread of ocean delicacies. In addition, breads, cheeses, and all manner of jams, sweets, and pastries enriched the food offerings, and various bottles of local wine, labeled of Suebian origin, stood at intervals down the length of the table. Dick strolled towards the enticing spread. He had just reached out for a lovely shrimp when a uniformed waiter quickly intervened.

"No, sir! This buffet is set for a business meeting taking place shortly. If you and your friends would follow me, sir, I will show you to your table."

Dick and Marian raised eyebrows at each other. Stevan, preoccupied, gazed down at the flying boat, small, lonely, and forlorn—considering how to fasten it more securely to shore.

Their table sat around a corner in an alcove, out of the way of the main piazza. Once there, they could no longer view the forthcoming business meeting, but the table did have its charms, since it was spread with scrambled eggs, rashers, toast, butter and jam, tea, coffee, cream, and sugar. Just as they arrived, from around the opposite corner, the Honorable Festus appeared with a smile.

"I have often observed English-speaking folk prefer a hearty English breakfast to our southern European breakfast fare. No?"

"You are very kind to us, sir," Marian said. "We are most fortunate to have made your acquaintance on this beautiful but isolated seashore."

"While your companions are still a rumpled mess, I see that you are wearing a very nice little cocktail dress. Do you always think ahead, Miss—"

"Mrs. Romanov."

"While I can't possibly have the others appear at our meeting, why, you, you would be most welcome. Why don't you join us?"

"I think not."

"But I could show you that we are not isolated. Oh, no! We are a nascent but soon-to-be bustling independent republic where many will wish to work, and visit, too, as tourists! In fact, our meeting this morning is with important stakeholders who understand the potential of our little country. Why, we will become a grander banking center than Lichtenstein!"

"Very impressive," replied Dick. "Just the kind of thing the world be needin' down here."

The Honorable Festus had an ear attuned to the suggestion of sarcasm. He stepped closer to Dick and said, "I advise you will explain to me exactly what you are doing, flying around in that . . . thing"—he nodded towards the beach where the F2A was tethered—"invading my country." Perhaps trying to project an air of power and menace, Festus stared rudely at Dick.

Dick, wondering what was suddenly going on, squinted up at Festus but he couldn't quite track the fluid expression on Griveaux's face. Then, in an abrupt turnabout, the Honorable Festus Griveaux shifted his glance to Marian and Stevan, and at once reared back and laughed.

Stevan raised an eyebrow, looked at Marian and Dick and then back at Festus, who was now wiping a tear from his eye and grinning back at them. They all regarded each other. At once, as if everyone finally got the joke, they all laughed.

Dick said with a chuckle, "Ah, I'm sure your army was terribly intimidated by our feathery craft."

Just then, the Honorable Festus's personal secretary, Ororotohos, a short, buxom woman with an icy stare, walked up and announced, "Your Excellency, your guests are arriving."

"Please," said the Honorable Festus, addressing the travelers, "have your breakfast before it gets cold. We will meet again this evening for dinner." With that, he abruptly turned and marched off. Immediately, Ororotohos signaled to a man in a window. A door flew open and twelve-foot-high barriers were wheeled from within to be set across the expanse, in order to block off, from approach or view, the main piazza.

"That was odd," Marian remarked.

"Marian, something is amiss here, darling. We might want to self-stamp our exit visas. I'm going to check on the F2A."

"I'll be comin' with," Dick said.

"I'm going to explore this dwelling. Check the exits."

"Well, then, Dick, go with her. I think this is a dangerous place for a woman to be walking the hallways alone."

Marian said, "Before I go anywhere, dammit, I'm having breakfast. I'm hungry!"

And so, they did have their repast, and found it most satisfying. They even ordered up extra rashers, toast, and mugs of coffee.

Down at the beach, Stevan found that the flying boat had been disturbed, inspected, violated. Mucky boot prints marred a wing, and a support cable was snapped. But the gun magazines had not yet been removed, and the single bomb that remained was still in its compartment under a wing. Nobody had molested the BAT radar. He found the tools, repaired the broken cable, and then began working on the bullet-riddled number two engine.

Above, as Marian and Dick explored the mansion, they often encountered uniformed staff, to whom they nodded with deference, as they didn't want to appear to be a problem or to be guests that needed monitoring. They found many rooms and hallways of the mansion to be locked, blocked, or under construction. Where they could enter, the upper floors revealed sheer drops to the sea from either balconies or windows, but rather than being beautiful with endless views, these interiors felt forbidding.

"Let us change course, Dick, head down to the depths, see what's under the main living quarters."

"Why, sure! Amazin', the folks unaware of the wonders that lie beneath Cismontane! Goodness knows what's to find under this monstrosity."

Devising a circuitous route, they wound down various stairways. They faded into alcoves or behind corners or into doorways when footsteps approached, being averse to exposure while snooping in the nether regions of the headquarters of the President of the Independent Republic of Suebi. The man seemed a bit unstable. Who knows how he would react if he were to be informed of this endeavor? Trekking down a descending hallway of stone and stucco, lit only by the occasional dim yellow lightbulb, they came to a door marked Garage. About ten yards further ahead, a passageway veered off to the left and down, but eventually came to a dead end.

"It's dark down here! I can't see a damn thing. Have you a match, Dick?"

"The thing about a cigar smoker, well, he's always got a pocket full of matches. Here ya go."

Marian struck a match to give a feeble illumination to their surroundings.

"Look into that nook. Is that a candle?"

"A bat, I'd be wagerin'!"

She lit another match, closed the distance to the alcove. "It's a candle."

She burned her finger, dropped the match, and lit another. Dick grabbed the candle and held it out so she could put flame to the wick.

When they could see much better—the candle having the effect of a flood light compared to the near total darkness they had encountered—Dick, after taking it all in, said, "I've seen this before. Would you be knowin' many a cathedral has secret passages and hidden doorways? I'm a bit familiar with this sort of deception."

Marian squinted at him. "What. Are. You. Going on about?"

With his fingers, Dick felt around a subtle depression in the wall about three feet above the stone floor. Satisfied, he stepped back, lifted his right foot, and with the heel of his boot, shoved the lower corner of the stone block. With reluctance, the block moved just a little. Then abruptly, it pivoted forty-five degrees. At that moment they heard the click of a latch being released. In the dust rising from their efforts, they saw the subtle outline of a doorway in the stone.

"I'd wager this door hasn't moved in fifty years."

"It is a door, isn't it? Dick, you're like Sherlock."

He smiled. "Did ya ever hear of Houdini?"

"Do you think this is a passageway? Where do you imagine it goes?"

"Down, I'd be thinkin. Down t' Davy."

"Down to the beach?"

"Perhaps it would be beneficial t' have a peek and a gander."

Together they pushed at the outline in the stone, first, on one side to no avail, but then on the other side, which, with what they were sure was too much racket, transmuted it from impenetrable wall to open portal.

"Ugg, that's a dank odor."

"I hope they weren't usin' this to toss in dead bodies, God bless us!"

"Don't be so morbid. If you are right, it stinks because it hasn't been opened in fifty years."

"When we are descendin', if the flame flutters and goes out, it will mean there is no air, and we'd be a gaspin. So, let me go down first to check the atmosphere."

"I have the candle."

Dick held out his hand.

She moved away. "Oh, no! I'll not be put off!"

"Oh, good God, Joseph, and Mother Mary. What will Stevan think of me?"

"He will think WE are brilliant when WE confirm this is a passage to the sea."

"Well, WE better go look before WE be missing upstairs."

Cobwebs. Many. Carved stone steps, narrow. They ran twenty at a time, each flight turning at a ninety-degree angle, first one way, then the other. There seemed to be many flights going down, down, down. The air held and, became sweeter as they descended, soon giving the distinct scent of salt spray. The ocean!

Dick glanced at Marian. "I think we get the gist. This was an escape passage to the sea. Surely, we would find an opening to the beach at the bottom. Best to turn around now, go back up—we soon are losing the candle."

"Oh, come now, we've gone this far. We must confirm the exit."

"Marian, I have a hankerin' for lookin', but I don't think even I have enough matches to get us out of here. Too far to go down, too far to go up!"

"But—"

"Like your father always says, 'Some things require a leap of faith,' and I believe the door is down there, waiting for us . . . Houdinis."

"First of all, my father never said such a thing. He said, Some things require a leap of faith after six days to Sunday of research and preparation.'"

"Please, my girl—once upon a time, you listened to me!"

Marian turned, held out the candle to see Dick, his wan smile. Something stirred in her, old memories of his ever kindness, good humor, good advice, and perhaps even wisdom, since she was a little girl. She looked down at her feet, a momentary act of contrition, and in doing so noticed her abused designer flats splashed with candlewax and her wrinkled, dusty cocktail dress.

"Dammit! What will I wear for dinner!"

"Well, at least you can wear a smile with your gunnysack, for we've found an alternate route out of here, though we may not need it. But I think we've done the research and preparation of which your father would be approvin'."

She glanced at the candle, shrunken to the size of half a cornichon. "You are right. We better climb."

"Right you are!"

Fifteen minutes later, they were back at the entrance, trying to figure out how to close the portal door.

"If you pull the edge, you'll likely crush your fingers, Dick."

"There must have been somethin', somethin' I'm not seein'."

Searching the space with the tiny nub they still called candle, Marian's designer flat stepped on a pointed object.

"Ow!"

"Marian?"

"I've stepped on something rather mean. It poked me." She bent down. "It's a boot pull."

"I'll have a look." Dick took it, turned it in his hand. "This is ancient, and a time in the past it was modified in shape. I think I know what to do with this."

"The wax is actually welding to my fingers!" Marian declared, "I must rid myself of this thing."

"Can you just bring it to the portal? I've an idea how this works."

Quickly, she crossed to the opening, held out the tiny flame.

"Ah, I see here. Look a little closer—here is a little hole right where a doorknob would be. See, the boot-pull fits." He pulled gently at first, but with increasing pressure, until the heavy stone door swung in on what must have been stout hinges. As the door closed, it caused a draft, which blew out what was left of the candle flame.

Marian laughed. She said, "I think our work here is done."

Chapter Six

T HE INDEPENDENT REPUBLIC OF Suebi experienced a calm, pleasant evening, the temperature about seventy-six degrees Fahrenheit, with fair-weather clouds turning into soft rosy hues slowly drifting overhead. Phloxopha met the three dinner guests at the bottom of the stairs and ushered them to a beautiful table setting outside on the piazza.

"His Excellency will be with you shortly. Please help yourselves to a glass of sangria."

"Sangria! A drink unknown at Cismontane!" Marian exclaimed. She had revived her dress and pumps, doing quite a bit of work on them so that one would never realize she had spelunked in them. Besides, her chestnut-red hair and green eyes enabled her to get away with all kinds of nonsense; her striking mien allowed her to breeze through a social faux pas with a turn of her head, a pleasantry and a laugh.

"Peach-basil white sangria," Phloxopha revealed. She seemed proud of it. Perhaps she had made it herself. "For dinner we have salt cod cakes with arroz de Braga, shrimp in hot pepper sauce, and beef stew with red potatoes, sweet potatoes, and green beans."

"Well, now you've got my attention, madam," Dick confessed.

"An Irishman always celebrates a good serving of potatoes," Stevan announced tactlessly.

"Was a time, we were ever lucky to have potatoes."

"So, there was, Dick." Hearing their host make this observation, they turned to see him approach. He appeared wearing a grey suit, white shirt, light grey tie, and shiny black stacked shoes. "I always laugh . . . in dismay at the story of that dreadful potato blight."

"Thank you, sir? It was a trial for my people, it was indeed."

When they were settled in their seats, the Honorable Festus at the table head, Marian to his left, Dick to his right, and Stevan seated opposite his host, Marian asked, "And was your business meeting a success?"

"Everything I hoped for and more! I have almighty powers of persuasion it seems, such as my ability to make my investors understand their self-interest and how their interest coincides with mine! And now, already my country has a new name to express its true nature."

Stevan, "Well, that was quick."

"We still, as a group, must dot the i's and cross the t's, but I will soon fill a hole in the political order."

Stevan, "Political order? What order? The world is aflame, you just don't know it yet."

"Not here in the soon-to-be designated Independent Autocratic Republic of Suebi, where all citizens will be happy."

"How will you ensure that?"

"Why, with uniformity of economic outcome for everyone! It takes a strong central government to control the economy—this is my forte."

Dick asked, "Will religion be permitted in your republic?"

"Never, Dick. Religion is the root of all evil."

Marian quaffed the remainder of her glass of sangria and poured another from the icy pitcher. She could see where this was going.

The Honorable Festus went on, "Discriminating nation-states will give our Autocratic Republic succor and assistance, both financial and military, because we will be a fellow traveler on the map. Like minds, simpatico systems of rule and belief. And here, everyone will be happy. Why? Because of the planned level of our society! We will chop off the head of anyone who pokes their noggin above our baseline! Except for the politicians, the ones who make it all work. The people know they need us, so we will live as I do here."

Stevan said, "So, there will be politicians at the top tier of society . . ."

"Naturally! As I said, if anyone from the hoi polloi gets too uppity, we will deal with him. As for us leaders, we will be there to keep everyone smiling. The people will want for nothing."

Marian said, "But you could not sustain this vision without constant infusion of funds from outside sources, these investors you spoke of. Your system doesn't actually produce anything to create the kind of wealth that would fund your schemes. What is the interest of these donor states?"

"You see, my dear, in a little country like ours, this totalitarian approach can work. I can monitor every last gardener, truck driver, fisherman, soldier, etc., make sure everyone is a living contributor to the state. And if you are not part of the solution, as they say, you are part of the problem! There is no exit for you, you must bend to the will of the state. It's for your own good! But in a much larger country, well, you can't do that—catalogue all the night ramblers, magicians, bacchants, maenads, mystics, wizards, and the haunters of misty hollows. In a large country, our level of unification is impossible to enforce. Too many outliers, independent folk. That is why large autocratic governments eventually exhibit societal decay. But you know," he mused, thinking it over, "if large countries were able to gather and quantify all the facts, compile dossiers about each and every individual in the population, keep it all up to date . . . then the sizable states, too, could have sustained autocratic success! Can't be done, though. Too much information to track!"

Dick smiled at the Honorable Festus's description of the people who would oppose his system. He said, "As Marian has already asked, why do these larger states deign to support you?"

"Because I give the illusion that the system works! Then the true believers have a north star to point to. Me! Who knows? Perhaps one day, my classism will succeed, and at least for a time we wield all the power! First, we create the myth. We display our tribal superiority, our passion, our successful statism!"

Stevan observed, "You will succeed only until you run out of financial infusions from your fellow autocrats, and they will soon get tired of bankrolling you."

"Ah, true enough, I'm afraid. Everything ends, eventually. But it's a bit of an experiment—do this, try that, a fluid approach, do whatever it takes to upend the old order. That is why we will never have a constitution, basic principles and laws written down. That would only hinder us—we have to be free to try anything."

"But why upend the old order, the order that provides laws and protections for the most people?" Marian asked.

"Putting aside the war for a moment, they've got it, we want it."

Dick observed, "Then they will have it and we will want it!"

"Yes! War and strife forever! Chaos! It's the way of humanity, always has been."

Stevan said, "I think you are quite reactionary. You propose birthing a republic by establishing a kind of government that has oppressed people for thousands of years. These governments are nothing more than criminal endeavors clothed in sanctimonious claptrap or pseudo-psychological dialectic, autocracies that exist for the rulers and their narrow tribe at the top."

"Well, you are young, full of hot blood and vigor! Everything is so black and white to you, but you do not understand."

"Sir. Do not patronize me. I would point out the political and economic systems you propose to overthrow, our liberal democracies and largely free-market economies, have brought more people out of poverty in the last one hundred years than any other system ever devised by man or god."

"I ask you, why should I wish to bring them out of poverty? It just makes them harder to control. Just a moment ago, your friend was lamenting the war, strife, and chaos in the world. Control is what we need! Keep them wanting and needing. Promise a lot and give them a little. Just enough. You see?"

Marian said, "That is not economics, that is politics."

"Now you catch on to the game! It's all political!"

"We can do better. We have done better."

"When the autocracies win this war, and I count myself among them, we'll show you better! Well, have we had enough to drink? Oh, dear, I think the stew has lost its warmth. Phloxopha! Bring a new pot of stew. You've let this one go cold!"

Marian, halfway through her third glass of icy sangria, felt a little tipsy. She tried a spicy shrimp. "Jesus, Lord, Michael, and Mary, this shrimp is like Hades itself. Positively scorching!" She gulped the other half of her third glass.

"Marian, what can I do for you?" Stevan asked. "Come," he said, getting up, "Let us go for a little stroll on the terrace."

Marian looked up at him, deciding.

"Please," the Honorable Festus said, "sometimes a stroll is just the thing after a first taste of our spicy Portuguese shrimp!"

Stevan held out his hand. Marian nodded and arose. They walked together arm in arm, far across the expanse of the piazza.

Dick and the Honorable Festus remained at the table, quietly sizing each other up. Phloxopha returned with the fresh pot of stew, a properly steaming pot, and set it down between the two diners.

"Now, Dick, this is a dish a man like you can admire."

"I've always enjoyed a hearty stew, sir."

Phloxopha ladled stew into a bowl for each of them and then withdrew.

"Tell me, why were you so interested in knowing the details of our stance on religion?"

Ignoring the question, Dick said, "I don't suppose ya have any whiskey? I seem to have limits regarding sangria."

The Honorable Festus signaled with his left hand. Phloxopha reappeared.

"Please bring a flight of whiskies."

"Why, most hospitable of you, sir!" Dick exclaimed. Remembering his encounter with Festus at breakfast, though, something now in his host's manner seemed in a similar way askew. Wary, Dick said, "Why do you ask?"

"Just because I would ban religion in our little republic doesn't mean I'm not a religious man," the Honorable Festus said. "But religion for the people simply gets in the way of my political philosophy, surely you can see that?"

"Then what is your religious view?" Dick asked, evading the question. He knew his host loved the sound of his own voice and would state his philosophy with gusto.

"Take this war," the Honorable Festus said. "I see this war as the only way for man to atone for his sins and purify his soul. Now, great armies are being commanded by leaders who act as unifying priest-deities, leading their people through fire! Fire eliminates in sacrifice the spiritual scalawags among us."

Dick noted, "A most unusual theory, and a bit startlin', I might add, for I don't see the war as the alpha and omega for mankind … it is not the five loaves and two fishes spreadin' comfort and sustenance among the miserable masses."

"I know of nothing more holy than sacred slaughter. In the name of Jehovah, read Joshua!" said The Honorable Festus. He began to quote: "'So Joshua defeated the whole land, the hill country and the Negeb and the lowlands and the slopes and all their kings. He left none remaining, but utterly destroyed all that breathed as the Lord God of Israel commanded!'"

No longer wary, Dick replied, "But ya must read further, man! You are imaginin' a world without the concept of Christ. As you observed, mankind has been maimin' and slaughterin' since things got organized before written time. Sacrifice? The kind to which you refer? Blood has flowed from the veins of bulls, goats, chickens, lambs, children, virgins, kings, substitutes for kings, and many times, with love! Sacrifice a son for the love of the Lord. Sacrifice a stranger and plant him in the ground with love, for the pagan harvest. But don't ya see, man, Christ has transcended bloody sacrifices. No more! No more because of his horrible, painful, humiliatin' death. A human can experience no horror unexperienced by Jesus. His murder has moved wanton sacrifice into the realm of the symbolic. Try to understand: the Eucharist."

Just then Stevan and Marian reappeared from their stroll on the piazza. They had overheard some of the conversation. Stevan said, "The war has no meaning other than it is being nurtured by a foolish blind god of this low sphere called earth!" Dick looked up at Stevan and shook his head, but too late.

The Honorable Festus grinned and thought to himself, *Well, he stepped into that one!* Time and experience had turned Festus into a patient entity. He was now subject only to an occasional lapse, and besides, he was gaining his objective by goading these impetuous guests into revealing their gnostic affiliations. He said, "H was a hunter and hunted a buck."

Dick looked up, shrugged. Stevan rolled his eyes.

But Marian knew the rhyme and answered, "G was a gamester who had but ill luck."

The Honorable Festus shot her a stabbing glance.

◆　◆　◆

Phloxopha returned with the flight of whiskies, various scotches, bourbons, and an Irish. As she set the tray down, they all reached for a decanter and poured themselves a glass. It seemed the best thing to do.

But the Honorable Festus frowned behind his salt-and-pepper forelock. He said to Phloxopha, "Bring me the sword."

The three guests looked up quizzically; Stevan and Marian had caught on to Dick's disquietude. The three of them clinked glasses. Marian took a sip of her whisky, a nice Glenmorangie, but Stevan and Dick each quaffed their respective shots of Four Roses and Powers.

The Honorable Festus leaned back in his chair, grinning at them. The thought of the sword, a prize antiquity in his "library," had improved his mood.

"Did you suspect? I am a collector. I keep, right here in this very villa, an accumulation of books, everything from first-edition novels, to reference books like, say, *Industrie-Compass 1939*,"—lowering his voice, the Honorable Festus leaned in conspiratorially—"which, my friends, the Germans, would rather I not have, and they would really be alarmed if it fell into enemy possession, since it would expose bombing targets,"—he leaned back into his chair again—"to ancient scrolls from the ancient desert, artifacts from antiquity, chain mail, armor, clubs, spears, and, oh, yes, swords of all kinds. I have a sword, Stevan, I believe will be of some interest to you. I could take you up to my . . . library but, well, Phloxopha will bring it. She can do everything, you know.

"Now, believe it or not, Lisbon has been a cornucopia for an artifact hunter. All manner of spies snoop around that 'neutral' city, yes—it's a place where the Axis and the Allies exist in an uneasy truce— but also, what shall I call the other prowlers? Collectors? No. Let's say *accumulators*! Accumulating items for those in the know . . . seizing special items for me!"

"You will establish a museum? Culture for the new republic?"

"Yes! That's it, Marian. Culture!" The Honorable Festus caught a whiff of Marian's sarcasm, but chose to ignore it. "A museum! What a wonderful notion."

Stevan poured himself another shot of Four Roses bourbon. "How do you acquire this bourbon, these days?"

The Honorable Festus gazed at Stevan. "You'd be amazed at what I have acquired." He glanced at the approaching Phloxopha, who was cradling a sword almost three feet in length.

"You see, when I first arrived at your strange little aircraft down at the beach, I thought, Well, this can't be an invasion! How inept that would have been. No, I decided that I was performing a rescue operation. Yet, I felt it essential that whoever was in that aircraft, they must be made aware of who commands this region, this Fatherland. So, I informed you. Your reply turned out to be most curious. You said, and I quote, 'The Romanov Command. We eke victory to great deeds!'" The Honorable Festus took the sword from Phloxopha, held it almost tenderly for a moment, and then tossed it with a clatter onto the table in front of Stevan. The toss displaced a decanter of whiskey; it teetered at the table's edge, a pending disaster, but Dick, a long-time whiskey man, observed and caught the vessel in his left hand. He placed it back on the tabletop. Stevan frowned at his host.

"Go ahead, pick it up, feel it, be sure to read the runes of victory inscribed on the blade. I know who you are, and I know you can read Saxon runes."

Stevan held his gaze with the Honorable Festus. At length he said, "I don't appreciate your behavior."

The Honorable Festus replied, "Oh, I do apologize, in that, at times I favor the dramatic gesture, forgetting such behavior is not always enjoyed by my companions."

Stevan held his gaze for several more moments, but then shifted his glance to the sword lying on the table. It was quite exquisite, in a remarkable state of preservation. Holding it by the hilt, he withdrew it from the scabbard. The hilt was decorated in silver, depicting flowers, leaves, and foliage designs; the twenty-eight-inch bifacial blade was etched with Saxon runes. Stevan turned it, held it up to the light so that he could read the etchings.

"So, what does it say, my friend?"

Stevan looked again at the Honorable Festus and slowly grinned. "It says what you have heard before. It says, 'We eke victory to great deeds.'"

"Yes! When I heard you, the two of you, say that phrase down at the beach, I took it as a sign. I made inquiries about who you are. I know! You were a ward and student of Herak! You think I don't know of Herak, the Montenegrin Gnostic philosopher? I always hated him and his pretentions of gnostic power! Do you know how I obtained this sword? This fount of mystic power? I stole it from him, the only one in known existence!"

Stevan leaned back in his chair, poured another shot of bourbon, picked up the glass, turning it in his hand. He said, "I'm tired. I'm going to bed."

Marian rose and said, "I also."

Dick said, "I ate so much of your delicious stew, and drank so much of your fine spirits, I can't keep my eyes open."

The Honorable Festus said, "But, my friends! The night is still young. We have much to discuss!"

Flashing her green eyes, Marian said, "Tomorrow is another day. See you at breakfast." They casually took their leave.

✦ ✦ ✦

"Where did Dick go?"

"Directly to bed—he really was tired. But he wants to leave this sinkhole tomorrow."

"Stevan, what did Festus mean, that he took the sword from Herak? How could that have been possible?"

"Only one way. Herak wanted him to have it."

"What? Why?"

"I wonder. Did the presence of Herak's sword draw us here to this obscure cove in the middle of a tempest? Did Herak plant the sword so that I would meet Festus Griveaux? Assess him? I believe I detect a byzantine structure at work—a design from Herak."

Marian wrinkled her brow and massaged her temples. She was having trouble concentrating. She finally observed, "As we know, it was Herak who set us on this journey south."

Stevan nodded. He said, "A cryptic cable from Herak convinced your father to let us go, to give us the flying boat."

She questioned, "Should we depart tonight?"

Stevan alighted from the bed where he was sitting; he strolled over to the double doors and stepped out onto the balcony. A demi-lune shone in the southwest, casting bright moonglow over the calm water. "Perhaps we could, if we were able to elude the staff and get to the beach unnoticed."

At this, she perked up for a moment and said, "Stevan! We didn't have a chance to tell you. We discovered a clandestine passage to the beach. Really! I thought of the passageways beneath Cismontane, and it occurred to me, well, these old piles all have them, don't they? So, Dick and I took a little excursion underneath, so to speak."

Stevan, who was standing in the balcony doorway, crossed into the room, and sat back down on the bed. He smiled. "Go on."

She related the circumstances of the discovery at length.

"We have a way, then. Time to wake up Dick? I don't trust our host's benevolence after the sword theatrics. When a despot starts with that behavior, it only continues to escalate."

Marian ran her fingers through her hair, then shook her head, rearranging her locks and waves. She felt frazzled. She groaned and said, "I forgot one thing pertaining to our exit.

"Oh. What's that?"

"Um, me."

Stevan turned, looked into her eyes, and grinned. "You're still a bit of a sozzled sot!"

She said, "Ugh, whisky on top of sangria. Not my brightest pub hop. I'm afraid I would put our departure at risk: as in trip, turn an ankle, make too much noise—all the female cliches."

Stevan replied, "You know, I might not be much better tonight."

She said, "Listen, Stevan, I have a startling amount of experience with a despot—my dear old father—and I can tell you that by tomorrow morning our President of the Autocratic Independent Republic of Suebi, having had his amusement, will likely be more accommodating and helpful, at least for a time. We may have an opportunity to take our leave peacefully and avoid any unpleasantness all the way around."

Stevan held Marian's gaze. He turned the idea over in is mind as an engineer might attack a vexing fitment problem. "If we stay the night, which would allow our exhausted Éireann friend to get a good night's sleep, and then we pack up our meager belongings tomorrow, bring them with us to breakfast, point out we must take advantage of the present fair-weather pattern—"

"Did you repair the number two engine?"

"Oh, indeed, both engines are ready to deliver maximum power."

She gazed into his big brown eyes. "Oh, are they?"

Chapter Seven

THE NEXT MORNING, AGAIN calm, warm, pleasant, the smell of wild roses, birds of paradise and other seaside flowers wafting through open windows and doors, the chirps, the whistles of songbirds, and the buzz of honeybees among the flowers, the gentle lap of wavelets striking the sand beach of the cove, a zephyr fluttering the gossamer lace window curtains, fluttering a few locks of Marian's chestnut hair as she lay asleep, her head on the pillow beside Stevan: *What a day!* he thought. *What a day! I almost forgot where we are and who our host is.*

He gazed at his wife, marveling at the happiness she brought him simply by being asleep in bed beside him. "You are beautiful! I love you more than the number of red hairs on your stubborn little head!"

Marian opened an eye. "I heard that!"

"So, do you love me too?"

She stretched, arms up over her head, yawned expansively, then lay back on the pillow. She coyly pulled the sheet up under her chin. Glancing up at him, she smiled and replied, "As long as you keep your engines tuned."

After a time, when they weren't ravishing each other, they realized the moment had come for them to put their exit plan in action: pack up their scant belongings, appear at breakfast, and then try to take their leave.

Downstairs at their table they found Dick already stuffing in bangers and biscuits and gravy.

"I wouldn't call that an English breakfast."

"Well, Marian, I guess"—he glanced at his watch—"it's really more like lunch." He winked. "I've already been talkin' a blue storm with our host, preparin' him to be amenable to our imminent departure. I've been explainin' about prevailin' weather patterns on the Atlantic, how they usually blow westerly, so we're needin' calm to keep from bein' blown over the edge of the earth and sea as we continue south on our adventure, so to speak."

"You are a Celtic speaking marvel, aren't you?" Marian said.

"I speak only in the plainest of tongues—you know this of me."

Phloxopha came with their usual breakfast, placed the toast, eggs and rashers, coffee and cream on the table, and took a quiet leave. While they ate what would be their last satisfying meal for a while, Stevan repeatedly pushed his chair back and got up to look over the wall at the F2A. Each time he looked, the flying boat still seemed alright, shipshape, in Bristol condition, so, he'd return to the table, sit down with a thump, and pick up another crispy rasher to snap in half with his teeth.

From the far end of the piazza approached the Honorable Festus Griveaux, President of the Independent Autocratic Republic of Suebi. He wore a tunic embroidered with what must have been his coat-of-arms, a sort of flaming sword, a sword that looked to depict Herak's stolen broadsword, now mysteriously held in the Honorable Festus's possession. On his head sat an old-style officer's peaked field cap, also adorned with the sword insignia. Accompanying him, dressed in olive cotton, tropical uniforms came Athuro and Erimacho, the "personal assistants" who had set up the beach crossfire vectors, plus several other soldiers in similar uniforms. They all carried Lugers in canvas holsters, the holster's flaps also displaying the sword logo.

Dick, the first to notice, said, "He's changed his accoutrements."

Stevan and Marian looked up to see the approaching squad. She said, "Basing his behavior on my father's may have been a miscalculation."

"I never thought your father was so offensive, just a father looking out for his daughter," Stevan confided. She flashed him a smile.

The formation tramped up to the table. The Honorable Festus observed, "I see you have enjoyed your breakfast once more, but now that you are finished, we have other business."

"Yes," Dick said, "as we'd been discussin', we'll be packin' up and biddin' Your Honor a fond farewell."

"That is correct! Please accompany me to the garages where we have transportation to the beach."

Stevan ate the other half of his rasher and, crunching, said, "We weren't expecting such a formal send off."

"Well now, a fellow traveler in esoterica deserves special attention. Please gather your things, we must go now."

They wound down the cliff-carved steps to the garages—Athuro and Erimacho leading the way, the Honorable Festus and his armed guard following, the three guests sandwiched in the middle. When they reached the building, the soldiers herded the "guests" past the waiting personnel carriers, around a corner, and into a room with a barred window.

"What the hell is going on?" questioned Stevan in a Sergeant Major voice.

"Oh, just a little delay. We have people coming to ask you a few questions about a submarine and some sort of aircraft that went down in the Atlantic off the French coast," the Honorable Festus replied with what was clearly a smirk. When he and his guard walked out of the cell, Athuro and Erimacho blocked the exit, barring the travelers from also leaving.

Dick and Stevan exchanged a glance and without hesitation, together rushed Athuro and Erimacho, knocking them hard against the wall.

Stunned by this brash and unanticipated act, the pair hardly resisted when Marian removed the Lugers from their holsters, gave one to Stevan and pointed the other at the Honorable Festus. His guards, returning the favor, pointed their pistols into the room, Festus's two assistants now experiencing the wrong end of a crossfire vortex between Stevan and Marian and the soldiers outside the door.

The Honorable Festus said, "Oh, come now! Up until this moment we have had an amiable relationship. Why taint it and make us forget all our lovely evenings and the stimulating conversations in which we have engaged?"

Stevan replied, "Most humorous. Instruct your guards to lay down their weapons."

Ignoring Stevan, the Honorable Festus said, "Oh, Phloxopha! I summon you. Would you please join us?" Then commenting to no one in particular, he said, "She can do everything, you know."

In the half light of the garage, Phloxopha seemed to materialize as she often did, out of the ether, her white hair glinting. She didn't need any further instruction by her superior; she simply stood next to Festus and began speaking in an unknown tongue, perhaps an ancient language from before recorded time, perhaps something else, but the words flowed into the cell and around the ears of Marian, Stevan, and Dick, inducing an indistinct haze to swirl around them, fogging their perceptions of reality by impairing their eyesight, their hearing, and their vocal ability, as if they were enveloped by a sort of haboob, hot and dry, which enclosed them in a netherworld where they stood alone and helpless. Time, unquantifiable, passed for the three captives, signifying nothing: a minute? a day? a month? a year? No markers, clocks, calendars, no rising or setting sun, march of the planets or turn of the galaxies . . . nothing save emptiness. Who would be the first to stir? The first to shake off the heaviness of dark matter, of connected particles, remnants of excess atoms?

External time had continued, though they didn't know it. It was Stevan who saw something: a flaming pyre, hot, oppressive, smothering; he thought he could barely withstand the heat, but then saw Phloxopha standing within the swirling flames fanning them, and then he knew. He had known this, perhaps subconsciously, all along, but refused to accept it. Phloxopha: a demon in service of the Honorable Festus. As soon as he realized the truth of this, he remembered the teachings of Herak. He remembered to remember a contra-spell, a spell of opposition. He forced his dry tongue to move, his baked lips to part. Invoking Sarapis, he said,

"From stary heavens, I have flown,
My wings—the earth surround;
The water of the seas: my blood!
My glance of lightning flash astound;
Hear my voice of rolling thunder . . .
Echo in the hills and vales,
And beware, O foolish hunter!"

At once Phloxopha shrank back, and with her withdrawal, the suddenly waning fire diminished to oblivion. Slowly, the others began to stir.

Marian found herself sitting on the floor cross-legged, the Luger she had taken from Athuro, gone. She felt confused as to her state of being: how had she ended up on the floor, what had happened to her?

Over in the corner, up against the wall, Dick began to sing:

"And Louie was the King of France
Before the rev-o-lu-shy-on
Way, haul away, we'll haul away Joe!
And then he got his head chopped off
It spoiled his cons-to-tu-shy-on,
Way haul away, we'll haul away Joe!"
Way, haul away, we'll hope for better weather,
Way, haul away, we'll haul away Joe!"

Stevan looked at Dick, his dishevelment, and roared with laughter. He thought, *The man voices a rather nice Irish tenor for these ridiculously appropriate lyrics!* With that, Stevan felt the last remnants of the oppressive miasma, the demon malediction, lift from his shoulders. He crossed to Marian and pulled her off the floor, wrapped her in his arms.

She shivered and sighed. She said, trying to keep her chin up, "That was most disconcerting!"

Stevan glanced through the barred window, night already falling, though it had been midday when they were forced into confinement. He said, "I know what we are dealing with now. We can't linger here in this damn cell."

"Well, Stevan, call the bell captain," Marian said.

Ignoring her gibe, Stevan said, "Let's rouse Dick."

Dick got a hold of himself with a pull from his beaten-silver hip-flask. He passed it around for each of them to take a swig of sherry, but instead they tasted Powers. "Yes, I dumped the sherry and nicked a bit of Irish from the lovely decanter that almost fell off the dinner table. Seemed only fair!"

Marian took another sip, shrugged and pointed at the lock.

Dick bent down, and peered through the keyhole. "Well, now! The key's still sittin' in it, pretty as you please. All you have to do is give me two of your hairpins and somethin' to slide under the door."

They looked around the cell, but found nothing useful until Marian, from her meager belongings, removed her sheer black cocktail dress. "I think I can slide this out under the door because, as James Cagney probably said, 'I cotton onto your plans.'"

Dick took the two bobby pins and pushed the key easily from the lock.

They heard a clunk rather than a ping, which meant the key had landed on the dress, not the bare floor, and Marian gently pulled the dress back under the door with the key perched precariously at the edge of the garment.

"Easy as a day at Punchestown," Dick said. With the key in hand, he unlocked the door to peer through, hoping to not see Phloxopha glaring back at him. The garage appeared to be quite empty.

They made plans quickly.

Stevan said, "It seems, Marian, your little exploration underground will be of benefit. You say the passage is adjacent to this garage?

"I believe so. As we navigated the shaft, we passed a door that identified this location. From there you continue down the dim shaft to an unlit branch, which leads to our escape."

In the garage, Stevan found the closet he needed: Brooms, etc. He broke off two handles, then grabbed shop rags. He tied and tacked rags tightly around the broken handle ends. Diesel fuel in a jerrycan provided the rest of the torch ingredients, except for Charles Graves's matches. He gave Dick and Marian each an unlit torch as they walked the far wall looking for the tunnel door.

"Should we be makin' further use of that abundant diesel fuel?" Dick wondered.

"Yes, it is tempting to light this place up. But I have found fires are most unpredictable and often cause you more harm than good. I might favor a clandestine departure."

"I've found it," Marian said. She pushed the door open, then noticed her distracted husband scanning the garage, perhaps still contemplating an arson event. Mimicking her father's voice, she ordered, "Stevan! Jump in the sidecar!"

That got his attention, the memory of Charles Graves's ridiculous motorcycle attachment and his order for Stevan to climb in. It had become a joke at Cismontane. Stevan laughed and crossed quickly over to the door.

As she led them down the passage, dim light from an occasional bulb became almost useless. Dick lit a torch. They started down the branch passage leading to the escape tunnel.

Suddenly, Stevan said, "You go ahead—leave me a torch. There's something I must do."

"No, Stevan! We go now! You will not leave us!"

"Marian, what I must do is crucial to our escape. Please find the exit at the bottom. I'll be with you in a flash." Without further argument, he turned and jogged up the tunnel.

"I could kill him!" Marian fumed.

"I'd be guessin' you'd have to get in line. But instead of murderin' the poor sod, the thing to do is write him an ode: An Ode to the Exasperatin', Infuriatin' Husband."

She cracked a grin. "God, the man *is* infuriating!"

"Funny, the man says the same about you. Come on, luv, before this torch runs out of life."

Chapter Eight

THE DESTINATION: THE HONORABLE Festus's library, located on his very private fourth floor. Stevan considered that no one would expect him to be wandering free within the mansion. Certainly, they would not expect him to breach the fourth-floor redoubt and the private library. He climbed the tunnel stairs to the first floor. Since it was dinner time on a balmy evening, the president and his business guests would be out on the piazza. He stood at the edge of the hall, assessing. Yes, a large party had convened outside.

At once, a man carrying an accordion startled Stevan. The man continued by, followed by others carrying instruments. He let them clear, and then with his glance sweeping left and right, crossed over to climb the main staircase. He wanted to avoid any staff, but had to consider the entropy of time. Yes, time, an arrow flying in one direction, present—to lost opportunity.

I mustn't waste time, thought Stevan. It occurred to him that the staff may not have been aware of his incarceration, and if he were to encounter one of them, well, he would simply be a guest, as always! On the way up, he met no staff, hosts, or guests. How nice. He made good time up to the fourth floor, where he immediately found the prize doorway—elaborate, framed with imitation Spartan temple columns.

As he stepped inside, the view of the holdings in the "library" looked to Stevan impressive—at first. A vast room spread out before him. Long refectory tables crouched under displays of *objets d' art:* stone carvings, ivory carvings, statuettes, exquisite snuff boxes, along with beautiful table clocks, jeweled enamel boxes, watches, tapestries, menorahs both silver and gold, paintings . . . Stevan stepped forward: Was that a Chagall? His mind began to spin. A thought began to dawn on him. Could this collection be assembled from so-called degenerate art that had been confiscated by the Nazis? He had heard about this from fellow academics at Cambridge, and his father-in-law had concurred. If so, how had the Honorable Festus acquired this vast collection? It was anybody's guess, but to Stevan, the amassing of these stolen personal items only spoke of horror. Though he felt nauseous, Stevan still had a job to do. He turned and glanced here and there, searching.

To the left, on a dark cypress wall, hung the ancient implements of war that the Suebi president had referred to at dinner before tossing the broadsword onto the table in front of Stevan. That sword was what Stevan now sought. It wasn't difficult to locate. It was displayed horizontally in a place of honor in the middle of the wall, nothing near or crowding it, so that it commanded the room. The scabbard sat on a display table directly underneath the sword. Quickly, Stevan crossed the room to Herak's stolen treasure, grabbed the hilt, pulled it down off the wall, grasped the scabbard in his other hand, and sheathed the weapon. Then he attached it to his belt so that it hung down beside his right leg. He exited the room in quick strides, frowning at the thought of what he had just viewed.

He descended the stairs at a more casual pace, seeing what he could see. At the top of the second-floor staircase he heard the clinking of ice cubes from below—likely sangria being poured into empty tumblers. Talk interspersed with chuckles. Just as he hesitated, considering his options, a staff member ascended the staircase carrying a satchel. He saw Stevan, gave a friendly nod. Stevan returned the greeting and casually descended the remaining stairs to the hall. As he tried to unobtrusively proceed across the hall, an attractive, dark-haired woman wearing what could only be described as a little black satin dress, bumped into him accidentally on purpose and shoved a drink into his hand.

"It's alright," she said in French, "I have two." Sure enough, she held another icy drink in her left hand. "What is your name?" she asked.

"Stevan," he said with maximum economy.

"I am Coco," she replied in English with a winsome smile.

"I . . . you are Coco? Coco . . . ?"

"We don't use full names around here unless we know to whom we are speaking." She glanced over the gathering and said, "I don't know if I like these people." She appraised his rumpled aviator outfit, the sword hanging at his side, wrinkled her nose and said, "You are not of these people. Who are you?"

"If only we had met sooner. But I apologize, I must go. I have a car waiting. Au revoir!"

As he turned away, she said, "Don't be like the rest of them, darling."

He looked back over his shoulder at her, held her gaze for a moment and nodded. Then he performed a fraudulent exit out the main door, marked time until he could no longer feel her eyes cast in his direction, reentered the mansion, avoiding any eye contact, and ducked into the partially concealed tunnel entrance. He made his way to the passage, where his torch stood waiting for a match. With the lit torch casting an eerie illumination, Stevan advanced down the tunnel to the open stone door. He wanted to inspect its design and construction, wondering at the hinges and fasteners that could sustain such weight for years on end, but that arrow of time flew into the past, and he was pressing onward. So, after entering, with finality, he pushed the heavy door shut behind him.

Down the stone carved steps into the darkness, where his light could not yet reach, he went, taking care not to misstep on the steep staircase. The atmosphere was dank, like a cellar, but after many steps, he caught a hint of salt air—he must be more than halfway to the bottom, he thought. He stopped and listened intently for any telltale sound of friend or foe, but only heard a ghostly moan of sea air working its way through cracks and fissures in the surrounding bedrock. After two dozen more steps, the burning wrap at the top of his torch broke off, hit the steps below him, bounced, rolled, and extinguished itself. It had burned through the broom handle.

"Ah, for the love of . . ." Stevan growled, not finishing the thought. After all, words have power.

Then he heard a friendly voice say, "Ah, for the love of the library, it's bloody well about time you got here!"

"Marian! I can't see a damn thing, but I love to hear the sound of your voice!"

She lit a match, "Now. You are literally five feet from me, you see?" Stevan descended the remaining steps.

The match tried to burn Marian's fingers, but she dropped it, and in the darkness she felt Stevan's arms wrap her in a hug. She also felt the sword hanging at his side.

"What the hell have you been doing?" she asked. "Have you lost the plot? What, you've stolen back the sword?"

"Herak's sword. We will need it, I promise you. Where is Dick?"

"We found the exit to the beach. He's at the portal keeping watch." She grabbed his hand and led him through the darkness to the narrow opening where Dick stood observing the putative path to their flying boat.

In the dim light finding its way through the cliff opening from the mansion above them, Dick saw Stevan being pulled near. Without preamble he noted, "It appears to be a clear path, but I can't determine if there's a lurker behind that overturned dory halfway up the beach on the left."

Stevan surveyed the theater of operation. Moonlight mingled with the mansion's electric lights to illumine the beach, yet he could not discover if guards were about. He could hear the babble and boisterousness of the party taking place above, and he remembered observing men with musical instruments making their way through the hall towards the piazza, carrying various horns, a drum set, two accordion-like keyboards, a flute, one of those gypsy guitars so popular in the region . . . "I think the band is about to play," he said.

Marian replied, "In more ways than one."

Dick questioned, "How are we to be crossin' that one hundred yards to our craft? There's too much moonlight, and those yards are seemin' like a mile."

"I have a plan," Stevan said. "Marian, you and Dick slink along the cliff to the right. I will go left, above the dory. Either it is clear, or I will deal with anyone there. You must sever the anchor line."

"Too dangerous, Stevan. You'll not bring a sword to a gunfight, as they say."

"Marian, this is our chance. You know we cannot stay here. Escape and freedom, our only aim!"

She touched his arm. "I know."

"Marian, no matter what happens as we attempt this, don't think of the past or the consequences for the future. Don't think of victory or defeat or pain and death. Empty your mind, just be aware of the enemy and yourself. Be aware of your abilities."

Marian allowed Stevan's words to flow through her, and she nodded. She and Dick crept through the opening, made their way along the cliff, near the anchor. On exit, it was a tight fit for Stevan, he being the much larger of the three; he could barely squeeze through, and tore a hole in the shoulder of his flight shirt.

When he reached a position above the dory, he saw no one, so he quietly advanced on the target and found many empty bottles of familiar-looking sherry, and cigarette butts strewn in the sand. As he peered around the area, he heard someone snoring, clearly, quite distinctly, but could see nobody about. Then he realized the discordant racket was coming from underneath the dory. It seems the guard—was it several guards?—had decided to take a very urgent nap out of sight. Stevan waved to the other two to cut the anchor line as he retraced his steps under the cliff face. Above, the band began to play some awful, martial marching music, if it could be called music, and proceeded to make quite a racket in the horseshoe bay, sound bouncing from cliff to treetop.

No longer taking care, Stevan walked across the beach to where the anchor was wedged in a rock formation. He said, "Well, you haven't cut the line."

"It seems you are possessin' the only blade."

"I think it's just as well. Let's not jettison our good anchor if we needn't."

Marian remarked, "You carry it this time, gentlemen, I've had my fill."

So Stevan and Dick each took ahold of the heavy bell and they all walked the hundred yards to the F2A Flying Boat, Marian wrangling the anchor line as they went. The gentlemen wrestled the kedge anchor back into its compartment in the bow of the flying boat. They climbed back down to the beach.

"We've got to give her a good push," Dick said, adding, "she's not so heavy with nary a passenger aboard."

Stevan said, "Especially unladen—I think we have been relieved of our case of Palo Cortado!"

Marian lamented, "They've stolen our sherry?"

"Many empty bottles up by the dory. Be thankful—that is why the guards now sleep so soundly."

The three of them pushed hard but the F2A was reluctant to move. At last Dick suggested, "Marian, climb in the aft—jump up and down."

She turned her head towards Dick. "Aye, Aye, Cap," she said, annoyed at being ordered about. Nevertheless, she climbed up onto the lower wing, up into the cockpit, and worked her way aft.

There, as she jumped and landed, the bow would lift just enough for Dick and Stevan to move the craft bit by bit until at last it floated free. They climbed in.

Above, on the piazza, the band played on, but thankfully had switched to Hungarian gypsy music, the musicians still attaining an impressive, ear-vexing volume in the cove.

Stevan scrambled into the cockpit, stashed the broadsword, then sat and latched his seat belt. Marian took the three-quarters aft gunner's seat, and Dick went forward to check the BAT radar set.

Light ocean breeze, flowing through the inlet where cliffs rose on either side, began to weathercock the flying boat. It turned away from the beach and slowly pivoted about 90 degrees. They needed 180 to take off into the wind.

When they had drifted about twenty yards offshore, they suddenly heard voices on the beach. Two men had overturned the dory and were trotting towards the aeroplane. One, grabbing the other's arm, stopped; then he raised his rifle.

"The drunkards woke up," Stevan muttered. Just as he pressed the switch to fire the port-side engine to assist the F2A in its turn towards the inlet—towards freedom—he heard an explosion of machine-gun fire from the rear of the flying boat. Both men spun and fell to the beach.

When the F2A had turned about 160 degrees, Stevan hit engine two. The aeroplane motored out into the horseshoe bay. Spotlights beamed down from the piazza and from the cliffs above the inlet. Dick began firing towards the cliffs on the left at the mouth of the inlet. Stevan glanced at the oil pressure gauge. Pressure good enough. A speedboat knifed towards them from the far side of the bay, machine-gun fire coming from its forward deck, Marian returning fire from the aft gunner's seat. Stevan opened the throttles on his twin Rolls Royce engines, trusting they wouldn't die—oil pressure was OK, but the engines were not properly warmed up. Still, the speedboat fell behind.

The F2A hit the mouth of the inlet at seventy miles an hour, withering fire exploding from the cliffs above, Marian and Dick returning heavy bursts of .303 caliber ordnance and streaming tracers. Stevan heard Marian's machine guns go silent. Must've jammed, he thought. The flying boat cleared the inlet, climbing seven feet per second.

Dick glanced back to see the mansion and the bay lit with electric lights, the confusion of the enemy below, and wondered if the band still played.

Stevan said, "Check on Marian, I think her cannon jammed."

Dick climbed aft past Stevan and though the hull until he found Marian slumped in her seat, holding her side.

"Ah, sweet Jesus," he breathed. "What happened, lady?"

Marian gave him a ragged smile. "I'll be alright."

Dick saw her bleeding wound. The first aid kit was only a few feet forward. He grabbed it. "Snuggle over a bit now, so I can dress this—what have you got, Marian? Look at this, a bit of a bullet hole!"

She gave him a sideways grin. "I guess I'm baptized."

"And that's what the Horrific Festus would say, but that is wrong, this is not sacrament, I assure you, it is the opposite."

"Festus," she said. "I think we have a present for him. Tell Stevan."

Dick didn't comprehend at first. He looked at her. She shifted her glance to the bomb release lever. The light dawned. Dick said, "What? We can't be going back there. Are you daft?"

"I am the descendent of the Wolly. Chaos is in my blood."

Dick glanced at her bloody clothes. "You look a little wan, dear, we mustn't detour on the way to Gibraltar where you can get proper care."

"Dammit, Dick," she said. She picked up the intercom headset and put it on. "Stevan, are you there?"

"Yes! I'm there. I couldn't raise you. What happened?"

"I got baptized." She shook her head as she said this so that Dick would see she didn't mean it. "We have a bomb. Let's drop it on our erstwhile host."

"Is that what the Wolly would do?"

"I suggest to you, it is indeed."

Stevan banked the F2A to gain altitude—he thought he might circle a few times to do so.

Dick went forward. "She's havin' a bullet hole in her side, Stevan. Hie on to Gibraltar where she can get care."

"I can hear her on the com. She's made up her mind—I can be quick about it."

"I'm believin' you want it more than she, and I don't approve. If you love her as you profess, you turn this aeroplane to the south now! I've known this woman since freckles and pigtails—she might as well be my daughter, and I surely love her like a daughter!"

Stevan was sure he'd never seen Dick's face crease into out-and-out fury.

Dick leaned his face an inch from Stevan's and added, "Or was Charlie the soothsayer when he suggested that perhaps for you, Marian is just a dalliance!"

"Dammit!" Stevan shouted back, "Don't you dare say such non-sense!" He looked away, was silent for a moment, then said, "But, you are right! We must go now! I don't know what came over me!"

Through her earphones, Marian could hear the shouting. She shouted back, "We've got a sigil to deliver to Festus, it just might seal his fate."

Stevan muttered to himself, "Yes, I do know."

He looked at the altimeter: 8,500 feet. Just above the aeroplane intermittent, fair-weather clouds drifted in the moonlight; but as he turned to bank away from the mansion, he saw a strange formation in the air directly ahead, a cloud that was not a cloud.

"Dick! Do you see what I see?"

"No . . . What? It couldn't be . . . "

A gaseous form flowed in strands towards the flying boat. Stevan banked to the right, into the breeze, but the flow was not deterred; rather it seemed to increase speed in pursuit of the aircraft.

"What in the name of heaven is this?" Dick shouted as he ducked through the passage to the forward cockpit.

"It's not heaven, Dick, it's Phloxopha . . . " Stevan decided to climb up into another layer of air pressure—perhaps the gaseous formation couldn't follow. The maneuver failed, and as the tendrils of gas encircled the aeroplane, the crew began to hear the strange chant, the flow of incomprehensible words, that had overcome them in the garage cell.

"Stevan," he heard Marian call to him over the com, "Didn't you say you had an exorcism that worked last time?"

He banked the F2A downwind, thinking perhaps that would work, but the tendrils followed easily. "This is different, that's all I can say right now." He began to experience a sluggishness of thought; he was losing contact with the more obvious aspects of reality. What would the F2A do if he pushed the stick forward? The aeroplane went into a dive.

Up forward Dick shouted, "Goin' down t' Davy!" then gave a kind of odd cackle. The tendrils followed the F2A, as did the rush of strange words.

"Stevan!" Marian shouted over the com, "Pull up! You are losing the aircraft!" She felt faint; she tried again, "You said we would need Herak's broadsword! Why?" The F2A went into a slow but alarming 40-degree downward spin. If it kept up, they would shatter on the cliff below the piazza.

"Stevan!" Marian kept shouting over the com, "What the hell are you doing? The sword, Stevan, the sword is the answer!"

Because of Marian's annoying insistence, and despite the fog in his mind, Stevan remembered. Herak's broadsword lay next to his right leg. He had taken it off when he first climbed into the aeroplane and had wedged it beside him in the cockpit. Now he pulled it free. With his left hand he withdrew the blade from the sheath, shifted the hilt to his right hand, and hung the blade over the edge of the open cockpit. Holding it steady, braced against a stanchion, he ran the blade through the air, through the tendrils. Still, the blade had no actual effect since the slashed tendrils immediately recombined. But it was then Stevan realized that the fog was not fog. Stevan shook his head, looked closer. Good God! The cloud tendrils were made up of what must have been a billion elementals, creatures, demons, all linked together by atomic tethers, and all screaming at the top of their microscopic lungs—screaming the mind befogging chant of Phloxopha! The horror, the demon mass, had become visible to Stevan because of the apparent wonders and effects of Herak's sword. As Stevan clutched the sword, he could see what he could not have seen, and hear what he could not have heard, and an incantation—a Herak teaching—entered his mind, a specific sequencing of vowel sounds, and he knew what he must do: He sang "AAAA AAAA OOOO

AAAAEEE O AA A . . ." From his baying came an effect: the sword subtly vibrated in his hand as if animated by an electric current.

As the flying boat continued its downward spin, the now-animated blade sundered the flow of encircling tendrils and words. All kinds of odd screeching and bits of matter like something collected on the bottom of a fish tank spun away as the broadsword sliced through the demonic strands. It seemed Phloxopha's malediction could not withstand Herak's sword, but the manifestation she had conjured was massive and it appeared to tear at the flying boat's wings and rudder; the craft still spun out of control. But Stevan's mind had cleared. He grasped the mad urgency and existential peril that confronted them. With effort, with all the knowledge he had gained over the years of studying aeronautics and having hands-on experience with many kinds of aircraft, Stevan slowly, but not too slowly, gained control of the flying boat. He saw the roiling mass of infernal strands begin to fold in on itself and vanish, and he pulled up, aided by cliff updraft. The implosion of the strands released the crew of the flying boat from their thrall.

"Up and over, nice as you please!" said Dick on the forward com.

Before Stevan could comment with a bit of sarcasm he'd saved up, he felt the F2A suddenly lighten and ascend.

Over the com: "Bombs away!" Marian had released the final bomb. "Greetings from the Wolly!"

Looking down, amazed at the lack of machine-gun fire coming at them, they realized that the party guests and the band had scattered, run for their lives, disappeared. But more significant, the soldiers had vanished too.

Since their altitude was low, about five hundred feet above the mansion, the release of the bomb put the F2A in jeopardy from the blast. In seconds, the bomb hit, crashing through the north piazza, which was constructed over the garage. They could hear the crash of the bomb tearing out heavy beams, shattering stone and stucco, but there was no explosion. Stevan gained altitude and circled.

"I don't believe it!" Marian said.

Stevan wondered, "How are the British going to win the war?"

✦   ✦   ✦

The crew of the F2A flying boat followed the Portuguese and Spanish coasts until they landed in the harbor at the fortress of Gibraltar at 6:30 a.m. Soldiers filing out of morning mess stared in amazement as the slow flying boat lumbered in for a landing, skimming across the slick calm of the harbor. They knew the RAF needed aircraft in the Mediterranean, but this was ridiculous. The biwing flying boat drew quite a crowd at the dock.

Dick called for medics while Stevan attended to Marian, whom they'd laid out on blankets and flight jackets in the midfuselage.

When the medics climbed into the flying boat, they cast about wide-eyed, having never seen such a contraption. What a sight! Then they secured Marian to a stretcher and carted her off like a queen to the infirmary, where the inexperienced staff gave her the best care they could muster.

While they attended to her, Marian told stories of home, including the Wolly fox-hunting fiasco, the great daffodil incident, and—involving Peter the horse—the road-apple fight with Stevan. Told with much vivacity and mirth, these anecdotes and gags of hers were to the lads like loving missives sent from family and fireside. When she'd had just enough repair to body and soul, Marian said goodbye to the lads, all friends now, and bid everyone luck. Once aboard the F2A, she discovered that men from the depot had resupplied the flying boat with provisions.

Dick had decided to remain at the garrison—the troops sorely needed a mechanic of his caliber. He wouldn't see Stevan and Marian again until 1943, while bringing supplies for the resistance.

Stevan and Marian flew past the dangers of Sicily and the heel of Italy, to come 'round Lovćen and land in a small lake near Njeguši, Montenegro. But it was no better there. Like a Phloxopha malediction, the war had reached out to enlace the Balkans. As planned, Stevan and Marian joined the resistance, and were successful until, in 1945--just at the end of the war--they lost. But what they lost was not a skirmish, not a battle, not the war. Oh no. What they lost was each other.

CODEX II

Egypt, December 1945

Chapter Owway   -1-

Amon-Ra took a sip of tea but didn't swallow. Instead, worry lines crisscrossed his forehead, whorls appeared on his cheeks, and ditches ran from his nose to the corners of his downturned mouth. He spat into the dirt outside the bungalow. Aged by the desert sun, he looked much older than a man of twenty. Yet twenty he was. "The cup is cold," he said loudly.

From inside, the mother shouted, "There is no fire for warming tea. If you had a job and got us money for cooking straw, if your lazy brother dried and stacked the dung like he should, maybe we'd be warm when the days are cold."

"I had a job. We had a felucca. Manu burned it." Amon-Ra, who spoke in bitter tones, adjusted his white turban as if his mind were elsewhere, as if those words had been said that way many times before. He squatted, his feet pulled under him, toes pointing outward from under his robes, and then leaned back against the whitewashed stone of the bungalow, the inside of his elbows on his knees, his right hand still holding the cup.

"They murdered him!" the mother shouted.

"Manu burned father and the boat too. Now we have no way to work."

Perched on the stone seat outside the door, Amon-Ra's younger brother, Dodi, pressed his long, bony fingers to his temples. "She doesn't keep it straight. She doesn't remember the boat."

The mother stepped into the doorway, scowling, black skirts swaying about her, wild gray hair exploding from under her black cap, knobby hands clutching the casement. "Then burn Manu." Her whisper was like gas escaping from a hot ember.

Amon-Ra threw down his rough pottery cup. She'd hit a nerve. His eyes shifted left and right, yet he did not care if the neighbors heard him. He shouted, "I'm sick of it! Father shot the thief, the thief's brother killed him. That's the end of it! Manu's run away."

Taking Amon-Ra's side, Dodi said to the mother: "It's what happens when you take a job guarding the irrigation equipment. Everyone wants it. Father should have kept working the boat with us."

The mother snorted with contempt.

Amon-Ra stood up to glare at the mother. Croaking like a raven, he said, "You know we have sought Manu. His family hides him. They sent him away. Maybe to Cairo. If we could find him, we would kill him."

The angry words broke through the early morning din of clinking pots and cups, of sneezes, of banging doors and muffled footsteps, of squeaking chimney grates, and of water sloshing into the street. The angry words attracted the villagers. Whether or not the brothers would avenge the murder—and when, and how they would do it—was speculation for the whole town. Neighbors stepped into their doorways; few were the secrets in the dusty, Egyptian hamlet of al-Tasr on the Nile.

Amon-Ra turned, aware. From across the street the cousin, Sharky, glowered at him, but it was the new red-and-white striped shirt and white linen trousers Sharky wore that gave Amon-Ra a start. Then he remembered. Last week Sharky had found a talisman from the old days and had sold it to a junk dealer in Nag Hammadi. It was in the city he got the money and bought the clothes. With a backward flick of his knuckles, Amon-Ra tapped Dodi's arm. "Come on." The brothers started towards the door of the bungalow, but the mother would not budge. "Hey!" Amon-Ra said, "We're going out back."

Though the whole street was staring, and the mother wore no veil, she stood her ground, her bird-like face purple with rage. "Avenge your father. KILL Manu! Burn him! Stab him! Poison him!

Behind Amon-Ra the street agreed, and Sharky's voice in particular rang out clearly: "Avenge your father, cowards!"

The brothers pushed aside the old mother and ran through the house to the camel pen in back.

"How do they expect us to find him?" Amon-Ra said.

"If the village wants blood, everyone should help us," observed Dodi.

"But they don't help. They just harp."

"And they're sleepy. Manu could steal the fountain from the square before anyone'd notice."

As the brothers entered the backyard pen, Dodi stepped in camel dung. He wished he hadn't. It squished up over his sandal and between his toes. *The camels*, thought Dodi, *they always want to shit!*

Three months before the alleged killer, Manu, threw the petrol bomb to murder the boys' father and burn the boat, the father, Ali, had haggled a side job penning camels for the local nabob—Ilyas. Never one to resist a good deal, Ilyas would sometimes acquire too many of the dromedaries, and then the Bey would need an extra camel corral until he could sell the beasts. For providing a pen, the family got to keep the camel's milk if a cow happened to be lactating, but lately, none were. Still, it was Amon-Ra's charge to watch over the camels, milk them, if necessary, and feed them from the meager amount of straw grudgingly provided by Ilyas's tightfisted camel driver. Meanwhile, father had deemed Dodi the less responsible brother, so he was given a different job, a job he hated and would shirk whenever he could.

Despite a black mood, Amon-Ra laughed. He said, "If you had been drying and stacking the shit like you're supposed to, we'd have had fuel for the fire, and the old one would never have put the shit on us out in the street."

"It's Manu who's put the shit on us," Dodi replied.

"Come," Amon-Ra said, "We're taking these camels for a ride."

Dodi had never been allowed to ride the Ilyas camels. He grinned. "Can we? Ilyas might not like it!"

From the mounting block, Amon-Ra began tacking up one of the beasts. "Ilyas doesn't have to know."

Dodi hesitated, but then decided to do the same. When he finished rigging the saddle, he asked, "Where are we going, Amon-Ra?"

With the motion of a boxer's jab to the gut, Amon-Ra shoved the reins he was holding into his brother's passive hand, wheeled quickly around, broke into a run, and then ducked back into the house, emerging seconds later with a prized possession, his knife. Long as the beak of the King Crane, curved like the early December moon, shiny like the sad desert stars, it was hand-hammered of Damascus steel and had belonged to his father until the day he died. Amon-Ra tucked the camel hide sheath under his belt. He grabbed the reins from Dodi. The younger brother was then compelled to quit picking at his bemired toes, command his camel's attention, and follow Amon-Ra from the compound.

Leading their camels, they turned down a path that curved by the river. Amon-Ra shuffled along quickly. His brother hopped after him.

"Where are we going?" he managed to shout to Amon-Ra, who was well ahead on the path.

Amon-Ra stopped and waited for Dodi to catch up. When he was just a yard or two away, Amon-Ra said, "Did you see Sharky and his new shirt? The pants? Eh?"

Dodi nodded his head to say that he had seen all.

"Well, you know he's been grave robbing."

Dodi, who was an innocent, widened his eyes. "Oh, they arrest you for that!"

"They don't have to know."

Dodi shook his head in disagreement.

"Everyone does it," Amon-Ra said. "I've been doing it for years but never with any luck. And now I'm telling you: When I say I go to Nag Hammadi, I really go grave robbing. I've looked everywhere. Still, there's one place I haven't tried in a while." When Dodi seemed doubtful, Amon-Ra pointed to tools he had brought in a canvas sack. "Don't worry! If anyone questions, we say we dig sebakh for the garden."

With grubby fingers, Amon-Ra rubbed his moustache. Then, reaching up, he grasped the stirrup straps he'd rigged and climbed several rope steps onto the saddle. Dodi shrugged and climbed up his own rigged straps. The brothers thought the rig was easy enough to use, since these camels were old and achy and were reluctant to kneel. Ilyas probably wanted to sell them for their meat.

In a few hours the brothers approached Jabal al-Tarif, where the ascetics had once lived, an area of high cliffs overlooking the Nile. Amon-Ra knew thieves had robbed the lower caves and tombs long ago, nevertheless, after tethering his camel, he climbed a pile of boulders that had fallen from the cliff face.

It was not a hot, strenuous climb, the temperature only sixty-five degrees Fahrenheit that day, and Amon-Ra felt comfortable wrapped in his robe. Yet his mind was uneasy. This day, a mist floated in the air, a cloud thick enough to partially blot out the sun. Strange, he thought, because in December, one never encounters such a vapor at the cliffs. He called to Dodi, "Come on!"

They crept into four lower caves but found only red letters painted on rocks and cave walls, inscriptions written long ago by monks: Old Testament psalms and foretokens of Sarapis:

I am Jupiter, Isis, Aesculapius the healer;

The whole world I embrace;

You may see

The falling moon, the rising sun,

Yet, not see me!

For I am the Invisible One . . .

"There's nothing here in these lower holes. We've got to climb!"

"You climb," Dodi said. "I watch."

Amon-Ra scowled. "You climb a little."

They went higher. Shortly, Dodi stopped and would go no further. Amon-Ra went much higher, his sandals slung over his shoulder, his bare toes probing notches in the rock. As Dodi watched, Amon-Ra inched along a thin ledge towards caves to the north, until the swirling mist turned him into an indistinct, phantom-like form hugging the cliff. Then he disappeared.

Heart pounding with excitement, he entered a high cell—indeed, he had never climbed this high before—only to discover it contained but one footprint slightly etched in the rock floor. After continuing along the ledge, Amon-Ra found a cave above his head, and he pulled himself up into the enclosure—deeper than the others, the recesses musty and dim. Gnostic inscriptions covered the walls:

"I am the wife and the virgin.

I am the mother and the daughter.

I am the members of my mother.

I am the barren one and many are her sons.

I am she whose wedding is great, and I
have not taken a husband.
Why, you who hate me, do you love me,
and you hate those who love me?
You who deny me, confess me,
and you who confess me deny me.
I am the bride and the bridegroom
and it is my husband who begot me.
I am the mother of my father
and the sister of my husband
and he is my offspring."

The writings would have disturbed Amon-Ra, had he been able to read them, because he would have found them confusing, yet suggestive of his feelings for the mother. For she is barren who has sons who do not avenge her slain husband. She is unloved who has no lover, yet she is loved and hated by her sons she doesn't have. And she is like her mother, and her mother's mother, and like her father, and like her husband, for surely things they have said and done are things she has said and done, and it goes on the way it always has, the mother, the dead father, the sons, the blood revenge . . .

Peering into the cave's dark recesses, Amon-Ra grew uneasy, for its depths were unexpected, the way the mist had been unexpected. Although he had been able to overcome his earlier fear of the wafting vapor, it was when that fear combined with this newly discovered fear of deep, moaning caverns, that the day became too much for him and he decided to give up the idea of grave robbing altogether. For all he knew, some dreadful spirit had lived in those shadows for centuries. And still lived there now.

He backed away, but too quickly. His bare heel struck a carved stone pomegranate protruding from the wall, and he tripped headlong through the mouth of the cell. His robe caught on a jagged crease in the rock face, tearing spiral-like as he tumbled down the wall. The tear suddenly arrested, where the material was sewn with heavy thread at the armpit, suspending him abruptly one meter from the ground, battered, alive, swinging like a pendulum. When the material gave way, the now-naked Amon-Ra landed on talus tailings and rolled to the foot of a large boulder. He lay there for a time trying to ascertain if he was still in one piece, until Dodi, came bounding down the pile, chanting and screeching.

Discovering Amon-Ra fairly sound but naked, Dodi laughed uproariously.

In reply, Amon-Ra picked up a rock to heave at the mocking brother but instead spotted where the rock had been, a glint of pottery.

"My brother, look here," Amon-Ra said softly, with reverence, and he began throwing aside small stones. Dodi joined him. "No, no!" Amon-Ra shouted, "Get the tools!" He continued digging with his hands.

Even with the tools, it took the brothers the afternoon to uncover the artifact because it was encased by dense soil and solid rock. It had lain there for many, many generations. As they worked, Amon-Ra swooned several times from having knocked his head and bruised his bones in the fall from the cliff, but each time he recovered to return to digging. Often the brothers would glance up at the colossal, menacing boulder overhanging them, for fear their excavation would cause it to tumble forward and crush them. It proved steady, however. At length they unearthed a large pottery jar, covered at the mouth with a shallow bowl and sealed with bitumen.

"Look at the color, it is red! This is old!" Amon-Ra cried. His battered hands grasped two of the small handles near the top. He set the meter-tall jar upright on the ground.

Immediately, Dodi jumped back. "I saw it move!"

"Yes, you saw it move, fool," Amon-Ra said, "I moved it."

"After that, after that!"

Amon-Ra ran his fingers through his moustache and then adjusted his white turban, which miraculously still covered his head. As he aligned the cotton folds, his fingers brushed the gash over his left eye, and from faintness, he had to squat upon a nearby rock. Dodi strode quickly over, offering his brother water from a bag. Recovering momentarily, Amon-Ra shifted his glance back and forth between the jar and Dodi, finally settling on the latter with a brief look of inquiry.

"Amon-Ra! Be careful," Dodi said in response. He pointed at the jar. "Watch for jinn trapped inside."

Amon-Ra hammered his left fist into his right hand. "There is treasure inside!"

"Treasure, Amon-Ra? It is common for a jinni to be trapped in a big jar like that. Three years ago, what befell al-Majd when he smashed a jar? A jinni picked him up and dropped him eight kilometers downriver, right in the middle. Twelve men saw it. They launched a dory, but al-Majd was gone."

"What jinni? It was a whirlwind. Be sensible."

"Don't open it, Amon-Ra."

Though his head ached, Amon-Ra shuffled to a large rock where the tools lay and wrapped his hands around the worn wooden handle of Dodi's mattock. "Perhaps not a jinni. Perhaps ancient hashish or a bag of spells, eh?"

He approached the jar and raised the tool. His brother backed away. With a sharp, downward plunge, Amon-Ra smashed the side of the vessel. Immediately, golden powder burst from the hole. It glittered and swirled around him, confusing him, and he even thought he saw something otherworldly. Squint-eyed, he peered into the dust, shook his head and peered again.

Indeed, something otherworldly floated in the midst of the swirling gold, but it wasn't a jinni. It was a jinniyah! Her garments were sky colored and befangled with golden stars; her right hand held a trumpet of beaten gold, and her left arm a bundle of leather-bound papyri.

Because of a good head start, his brother was already well away when Amon-Ra tried to run. The jinniyah pointed the trumpet at him, which bound his will to move. Standing before her with his clothes cast off, he was like a mystes purified.

The jinniyah said:

"This day, this day, this, this
The Royal wedding is.
Art thou thereto by birth inclin'd
And unto joy of God design'd
Then may'st thou to these letters tend
Where all is all from end to end.
Keep watch and ward
Thy self-regard
Thy self with diligence thou bathe
The bridal chamber shall be yours
And luck be with you all your days."

Just at the finish of the incantation, a wind scattered the swirl of gold fragments; the jinniyah within shapeshifted and disappeared.

When Amon-Ra finally recovered his wit, he knelt down for a look inside the jar but found the opening still too small to glimpse its contents. He grabbed the mattock, widened the opening, and discovered his prize. The treasure was neither hashish, nor gold, nor magical bone of mummies. It was neither a bag of spells, nor jewels, nor mystical horn of rhinoceros. Instead, ancient books filled the jar.

Books! What kind of treasure was this? Who would buy old books? He sat idle for a moment. Then, much like a burglar preparing to crack a safe, he blew on his fingertips. After a quick, cat-like glance behind him, he plunged his arms through the hole in the jar. However, once his hands were touching the dry, brittle plunder, he moved slowly; with care he removed one volume after another, placing each by the other on the dusty ground or atop flat places on nearby boulders, until the jar was empty. He called out for his brother, "Dodi. Look here!" But frightened by the jinniyah, Dodi had already jumped on his camel and abandoned Amon-Ra at al-Tarif.

Amon-Ra squatted before his library, meticulously counting the number of books: fifteen. After untying the thong of the nearest volume, he squinted at it, estimating it was about seventeen centimeters wide by twenty-eight high. He pulled back the cover to find yellow pages, thick, rough, as if hand pressed, scrawled with strange writing like that in the cave. In examining the other volumes, he found them to be the same and wondered: Who would buy old books you can't even read?

Shadows grew long about him. He found his sandals lying nearby and put them on. Then he glanced up at what was left of his tattered robe, still jammed in a crevice high above him. He could not retrieve it, as he was too broken from his fall to climb up again. He yanked at the part he could still reach, but the robe remained ensnared. Luckily, on the ground under the robe, he found his knife. With a weary gesture, like a field laborer grabbing the last bale, he tugged at the nearby canvas sack. Next, he squatted down and stuffed the books into the sack, stood up, and stumbling, stubbed his toe. He yelped with pain and annoyance and then, limping, carried the bundle to the camel. There, he hoisted the pack over the saddle and lashed it tight with string, and he was able to secure the knife to the saddle. Remembering himself, he removed the turban from his head. To prepare for the tiresome journey back to al-Tasr, he slowly wrapped the dirty, blood-flecked cotton around his naked haunches.

The sun lay for a moment, smoldering, abandoned on the horizon. Cadaverous fingers of dark, iron-red flames spread narrowly, stretching eastward towards the cliffs. In the last flare of sunset Amon-Ra saw his father. He saw a felucca, burning. And he thought of Manu, the man with the petrol bomb. He thought of the fearful spirits that surely haunt a killer, forever.

With squinting gaze and downturned head, he guided his camel along the treacherous path through the fallen talus and dirt. He was aware that these thoughts of death and spirits were not good to dwell upon—especially while walking the cliffs alone at dusk—yet he continued to think of such things. The shadowy boulders looked like skulls and carcasses of nightmare creatures. Startled, he glanced up. He craned his neck to look behind himself. Could Manu be lurking? When he had started for the cliffs that morning, Amon-Ra had thought there was such a chance, for the cliffs attract men and spirits alike, all kinds from the highest to the lowest.

Once he'd overheard the Coptic priest from the village talking with a Cairo stranger about these cliffs of Jabal al-Tarif. The Copt had told the stranger what all the village children knew, what Amon-Ra had known as a boy: that over the centuries the red-dirt path had been trod by the human parade, complete with attending daemons, starting with the majestic Pharaoh, his army, his countless slaves and captives of war, and continuing with: the gods of the dead, Anubis and Osiris; also pagan priests and their overseer, Idi, governor, hereditary prince and vizier; and Christian monastics, Coptic monks, Sufis, Islamic prophets, unaffiliated mystical ascetics, Gnostics, wanderers, hermits, saints, misanthropes, and mendicant friars; enlightened teachers, yogis, magicians, wizards, phantoms, philosophers, charlatans, pilgrims and jinn; conquering gods and their armies, howling sphinxes, Greek democrats, the goddess Isis, Roman fascists, mad caliphs, palace guards; unmarried pregnant girls, wandering Jews, traders, policemen, goat farmers, runaway lovers, devils, water carriers, hunters, wild dogs, mourners of the dead and official members of funeral processions; shades, thieves, rock snakes, desert jackals, Sun Kings, maze farmers, Gryphons, jewelers, boatmen, spirits, stone cutters, artisans, desperate men and . . . grave robbers.

Amon-Ra knew all this. What he didn't know for sure was whether murderers trod there, too, and that's what bothered him. Yet, often a murderer is also a desperate man. Amon-Ra had reasoned this. That's why he had half expected to stumble across a trace of Manu in the caves: his prayer rug, his lantern, or his molasses jar, or perhaps even the craven fugitive himself, hiding like the coward he was. Not unreasonable, this expectation, for Manu's family lived in Hamarah Dum, the town below the cliffs. The police had first sought him there (perhaps without warning), and maybe Manu scurried out the back door, like a cur, and made for the tombs of Idu and Thauti. Amon-Ra had even brought his knife, just in case he discovered the murderer cringing in the shadows like a bat. Fighting him to the death, Amon-Ra would have either been a hero in his village, or dead himself and a martyr. But no. His luck was bad. He could tell by his treasure of books.

He stopped where the talus became rolling instead of steep, and the path less treacherous. Strewn over the flats on either side of him were pits from the secret, illegal excavations of Abasi Siefar, of Hamrah Dum, whose clan needed money to buy automatic weapons for blood feuds. The clan knew a go-between in Nag Hammadi willing to purchase whatever they could find—if it had the look of age about it—so the Siefar clan had dug many holes. Occasionally, Amon-Ra had spied them at work. In his melancholy mood that evening he saw the pits as mournful shadows and thought of them as trap doors to the underworld through which, even now, untold spirits climbed to cavort far and wide over the haunted night talus, chasing down the wicked and the lost.

He shivered. No wonder Manu wasn't to be found at the caves. The nights were hell up there. He wished he had his robe to wrap about himself, and he cursed Dodi for having run off, leaving him with nothing to borrow. At least he could have wrapped his brother's black turban about his naked shoulders. His left shoulder was stiff and sore because it had been wrenched in the fall, and his armpit ached where the robe had pulled against him before it ripped away. His head hurt, and his fingers were sore. But he could ride now that the path was safe. He grabbed hold of the stirrup straps with his right arm, and with some difficulty, climbed up into the saddle. Riding stiffly, he turned south on a dirt road that ran about two hundred meters out from the foot of the talus. To the east of him lay farmland, to the west, desert and the looming cliffs of Jabal al-Tarif. After a half hour he could see the lights of Izbat al-Busah. He considered begging refuge for the night from his acquaintance, al-Sayyid, but quickly thought better of it, not knowing how to explain his naked, battered condition. Besides, he couldn't wait to get his hands around Dodi's throat.

After skirting a gravel quarry to the southeast, he followed the road along an elevated irrigation dike, crossed a railroad track and highway running from Nag Hammadi, and turned south with the bend in the river. The evening dampness filling his nostrils, he rode through the fertile lands of his clan and village and so passed all the places where he had played as a boy: the tree by the rock wall, the little inlet, the knobby hill, the herder's shack, the ditch with the long grass.

Ahead a few village lights guided him to the familiar streets of his recent humiliation. Soon he rode into the courtyard behind his house (Dodi's camel was munching straw), dumped the canvas bag of books by the outdoor oven, unsaddled his camel and fed the beast, taking straw from his brother's camel. Aching, he crept into the house, aching not only in his bones but in his mind too—for revenge.

In the dim light, he could just make out images on the table: a darkened lantern, a bag of biscuits, half a dozen beer bottles. So! While he, Amon-Ra, had been struggling to return with a treasure for the family, struggling while naked, cold, thirsty, hungry, wounded, and pressed by darkness and underworld shadows, spirits and jinn, his brother, Dodi, had been relaxing with bottles of beer! Where did Dodi get the beer? From Sharky, no doubt! Obviously, little brother had been gossiping with cousin about the treasure! Amon-Ra's hand closed around the neck of the nearest bottle. With his left hand he pushed off his sandals to walk softly up the jerry-built stairs to the makeshift loft, to Dodi's bedding mat. There, Dodi snored like a decrepit hog; his exhalation soured the room and curdled the cat's milk at the bottom of the stairs, his head lolled to the side, his legs were splayed, one foot still shod in the dung sandal.

Scowling, boiling with rage, Amon-Ra raised the bottle to give his brother a backhand smash across the forehead. Yet, looking at the snoring, snuffling pig, his hand froze; he could not bring himself to do it. Dodi was a fool, but the brothers faced many predicaments from the outside: how to find hated Manu and what to do if they cornered him; how to dispose of the strange, useless books, avoid the police and end up with a profit; and how to overcome the searing scorn of the townspeople. They must forget their differences and bind together against the common enemy. Though Amon-Ra was still enraged and would have enjoyed giving his brother a good bash on his thick skull, he instead shattered the bottle against the wall near the pillow Dodi lay on, the boy not even stirring, and then crossed the room to his own mat, wrapped himself in a blanket, and immediately fell asleep.

+ + +

Chapter Esnav   -2-

IN AMON-RA'S DREAMS, THE jinniyah of the red jar came to him as a swirl of gold fragments—to tell him again to keep watch and ward his self-regard and to tend to the letters from end to end that she had given him. He tossed in his sleep, banged his head against the wall, but did not awaken. In the morning he crawled downstairs, aching from head to foot, to find Dodi sitting at the table with the bag of books on the floor and several volumes open before him.

"You miserable bastard son," Amon-Ra said for a greeting.

Dodi looked up. An amused expression crossed his face. "This is the treasure?"

"More than you."

"But tell me, brother, what happened there by the great rock? How did you escape the jinni?"

"Jinniyah! She gave me these books."

"What?"

"Yes, and commanded me to watch over them."

"That is all? Did she not scoop you up? Did she not suck the brain from your ear? Did she not pull you down through the tombs of Idu to the well of death and cover your fingers with golden serpent rings and—"

"She could have!" Amon-Ra cried, raising his voice, "for all of your help, you faintheart!"

"Amon-Ra! You . . . she . . . what could I have done against a jinniyah? One of us had to live to care for the mother. It was my duty to run."

"I lived. You die!"

"My brother."

"You left me naked at the cliffs."

"I'm sorry."

"I was cold and battered, and you abandoned me."

"I thought you were gone. Most certainly dead. Not many live when they encounter a jinni. But you'll feel better when we trade the books for gold."

Amon-Ra sat down on a stool across from Dodi and stared at him. "We cannot sell these books. We must watch over them or the jinniyah will return and we WILL die. She commanded me."

"You, my brother. You are the keeper."

"Oh, no! She saw you, too, running like a dog."

"She did?"

"Yes."

Dodi looked grim.

"What is it?" Amon-Ra demanded.

"There has already been . . . an accident."

"Accident?" Amon-Ra's eyes shifted from his brother to the books on the table and then to the bag on the floor. "There are fifteen books. They better all be here!" He pulled open the bag to remove the rest of the books, two and three at a time, placing them on the table with the others and counting them all carefully. "The books are here, but some covers are missing, and some pages have been torn out." He glowered at Dodi. "What's going on?"

"It wasn't me!"

Amon-Ra knew fragments of last night's rage still flew aimlessly in the deep places of his mind, waiting for an attraction to gather them together again—for an unholy explosion. His hands tightened around the tabletop, whitening the knuckles.

Dodi, sensing a certain menace in the air, quickly explained what had happened that morning. He'd awakened with a dreadful sinking feeling because beer does not agree with him and he'd drunk some beer the night before, so sick with worry over his brother he was. The first thing upon waking, he put his hand in a smattering of broken glass near his pillow, and the glass cut him. He didn't know how it got there, but supposed he'd dropped a bottle before retiring, because he'd been so tired.

Next, he went downstairs looking for a rag to wrap his hand with, to stop the flow of blood, but upon stepping into the big room, he smelled an odor that he hadn't smelled around the house for a long time: that of fresh bread baking in an oven. He peered out the front door and down the street, assuming that the smell was drifting in from a neighbor's kitchen; however, out there the odor diminished rather than increased. No one was in the street. There was no smoke and no one selling bread. The only thing he could notice out of place was a new wooden sign, displaying a family name, next to the cousin's door across the way. Back in the house, standing next to the table, sniffing and musing, he forgot why he'd come downstairs in the first place. A drop of blood landing on his leg reminded him that he needed a bandage of some sort for his hand, and he remembered a rag that the mother had left by the back window several days ago, a rag she was saving for one of her crafts. There, reaching for it, he glimpsed through the window a sight so unexpected that it sent him back to the bright days of his childhood. The mother was standing by the clay oven in the courtyard, smoke billowing out above her, dough table next to her. And that's where the odor had come from. From the mother. She was baking bread again!

He'd run outside to give her a hug, a thing he hadn't done in years, and she'd accepted it begrudgingly before bending down to put more fuel in the oven. As he stood watching her, he was beset by the feeling that something was out of place. He went over it: the smell of bread baking, the billowing smoke, the heat of the oven . . . That was it: the hot oven. Fuel! Where did the mother get fuel? On the ground where she used to keep the dry chips for burning, there sat Amon-Ra's canvas sack, and out of the mouth of the sack spewed some old books. It was suddenly clear the mother had been ripping pages out of the books and tossing them into the oven. Then, with her knife, she had hacked up a leather cover and tossed that on top of the burning pages!

Hearing this, Amon-Ra cried out to the prophets, but almost immediately stopped himself for fear the jinniyah might hear him and learn of his bad job, so far, of guarding the books.

Continuing with his explanation, Dodi said he had asked the mother where she'd found the books. She'd replied that last night, her GOOD son, Amon-Ra, had brought her the fuel. Realizing that he had to act fast, Dodi ran across the street and stole the new wooden sign the cousin, Sharky, had hammered up next to his door, a sign with the cousin's name on it. Anyway, it was most certainly a snotty idea he'd picked up in the city. Dodi said he had chopped it up and traded it to the mother for the books. And that's how he'd saved them and why they were sitting there on the table instead of flying all over al-Tasr in the form of smoke and ashes.

Amon-Ra thought back to last night when he had almost smashed a beer bottle over his brother's head; had he done that, Dodi might not have arisen early enough to save the books. He might not have gotten up at all. "You have done well, my brother. I praise you. You are worthy of guarding the books with me."

Dodi smiled broadly. "Then you forgive me."

"Forgive you?"

"For leaving you yesterday."

Shaking his brother's shoulder with his good right arm, Amon-Ra said, "It is completely forgotten."

Dodi nodded happily. He said, "We must hide the books now, before Sharky comes looking for his sign. He's bound to suspect us."

The brothers hid the books in a hole under loose floorboards beneath the bench by the front window, vowing solemnly to keep them a secret, just between themselves, and, of course, the mother.

Chapter Shomt   *-3-*

A DRY, HOT WIND PULLED dust and sand from the courtyard. Sand spattered against the bungalow's whitewashed stone; fine, light-brown dust filled the air. Distracted, Amon-Ra cursed and wiped his nose with his sleeve. It had been a week since the jinniyah had given him the books. Earlier in the morning Dodi had laid out dung to cure, and with the wind and the heat, it hadn't taken long. Now Amon-Ra stacked the chips under the roof overhang near the camel pen. Dodi had made it his duty to keep the mother supplied with fuel; he had discovered that if he did his part, the mother continued baking.

Sometimes Amon-Ra lent a hand, as now, but usually he was busy at his fish-cleaning job down by the river. Several fishermen had come to the bungalow door three days after he had found the red-jar books. They had knocked on the door and asked if he wanted a job. What luck! It was hard to get a job these days, and they'd come looking for him! Yes, he had said, and he was hired on the spot.

He glanced at the sun. Almost time for work. He slapped a black fly that had landed on the back of his neck for refuge and a meal. Just then an awful commotion on the rear path startled him: sounds of grunting and swearing, banging, the grating noise of a heavy object being dragged across stone, snapping wood. He spun around.

Pulling a great load of tightly bundled chopped straw for the oven, lashed to a drag board, Dodi struggled and grunted up to the gate. But he was having trouble getting through. First, he opened it wide and tried to force the load into the gap before the wind slammed the gate shut, but the wind was faster than he, and the gate banged against a tender area of his body where it had no right to bang. Next, he stacked and wedged several large rocks between the gate's bottom struts and the ground, only to have the drag board catch in the holes where the rocks had been, making it impossible to budge. So, he picked up the back of the drag board, to leverage it forward, but got the thing stuck between the gate posts. In a fury, he tried to loosen it by jerking his arms up and down like a Cairo steam hammer. The drag board whined and groaned against the posts but didn't really budge, and its stubbornness sucked some of the breath out of him. Then, after carefully bracing his sandals against a rock, he pulled back with all his might—grunting like a wild boar—and promptly dropped the board on his toes.

For an instant he threw his head back, face to the sky. His expression seemed to say, *Avenging Jinn! My poor toes! Always in trouble. If only I owned boots instead of sandals!* But immediately he cried out horribly, and hopped with crazy lurches on his heels. While veering off beam, he dislodged one of the stop rocks. This was enough for the relentless wind. With tremendous force it blew the gate forward, not shutting it completely, but rather jamming it on top of the drag board and the straw, pinning the load tightly to the ground. When Dodi stopped hopping and howling, he looked back at the damage, the jammed load, the stuck gate. He shook his head and collapsed on the dirt.

"It might have to stay there till the river floods it out!" Amon-Ra shouted against the wind. "Where did you get that chaff?"

Dodi, close to tears, looked up. He turned red, realizing Amon-Ra had witnessed the drag board antics. He said, "It fell off a cart. It's for the oven, not the camels. Now, help!"

Amon-Ra gave in, ignoring the cart comment. "All right, but I've got to get down to the river." He prized up the gate with a thick pole and tied it open with twine. Together the brothers pulled the load to a pile of burning-straw near the outdoor oven.

"A job well done," Amon-Ra said without irony.

Dodi grinned. Whenever he grinned, his long thin face had a decidedly upward arch to it; the high cheekbones rose higher, the eyebrows climbed, the edges of the mouth leapt like flames, teeth flashed white lightning.

"Come on," Amon-Ra said with fondness, "You can walk with me."

Tracking dust and straw in their wake, they stomped through the bungalow. The wind on the front street was no better, howling like some depraved creature from the White Nile. Heads down, the brothers almost bumped into their neighbor, the village Coptic priest. A round, pleasant man with a fat face, he greeted them warmly.

"This is a rare wind," he shouted, "You should be inside."

"Hello, al-Qummus, the fishing boats are in. I have to go to work."

"They must have scooped up lots of fish today, enough for the multitudes, so fast were they sailing." He observed pieces of straw shooting from Dodi's sleeves flying down the street like arrows. "What have you been doing, Dodi?"

"This morning I brought a big load of burning-straw home to the mother."

"Did you, Dodi? Well, bless you. The whole town is talking about the change in you brothers. For the better! Come. Step into my doorway."

The brothers followed the priest into the sheltering vestibule. There, they could hear each other better and didn't have to shout.

"Such a change," the priest said. He squinted at them, marking them. "Did you get a sign?"

The brothers glanced at each other.

"I thought so," the priest exclaimed. "It doesn't matter, Copt, Muslim, when you get a sign, you change for the better." He fixed each brother in turn with his watery brown eyes, first Dodi, then Amon-Ra. "What was the sign?"

"Eh? A sign?" stuttered Amon-Ra, not wanting to talk about the books or the jinniyah, yet, floundering under the gaze of the nosy priest.

Dodi stepped in. He flashed white teeth, "Oh, yes, al-Qummus! He took the cousin's sign right off the doorway. It was wooden. The cousin bought it in Nag Hammadi and—"

"Now, slow down, Dodi! What cousin? Who took it?"

"Manu. He stole the cousin's sign. Our cousin, Sharky."

The priest smiled wryly. "You brothers don't still think of killing Manu, do you?"

"Oh, yes, al-Qummus."

The priest became angry. "I don't know what you are talking about with the cousin and the wooden sign, but you two have had a sign from God! Don't go against it with killing."

"It is a clan matter, al-Qummus," Amon-Ra said gravely, no longer stuttering.

"But what if he is innocent? Have you thought of that?"

"We found his staff and a petrol can but a hundred yards from the boat."

"But why would he leave those behind?"

"I don't know, al-Qummus, perhaps someone saw him. Perhaps he was afraid. After killing Father, he knew we'd get him."

"Look, you brothers, some enemy of Manu could have planted his staff by the boat, along with the petrol can. The al-Siefar deny he had anything to do with it."

"Then, why has he run away?"

"But he hasn't. My nephew, Andarawus, saw him just yesterday on the road from Hamrah Dum. He was selling molasses."

"How strange!" Dodi said.

"Yes," Amon-Ra agreed, "It is strange. Come, Dodi, I must go to work. I will think about this, al-Qummus."

"Please, please do, before there is more killing—and of an innocent too." The priest stared at them for a moment to make his admonition felt and then ducked inside his house. The brothers made their way through the blasts of dust, down the street and around the corner, towards the river.

Chapter Eftoo   -4-

"I'LL TAKE THESE THREE oranges and this packet of tea."

"And the sugar, Amon-Ra, don't forget the sugar."

"And this small tin of sugar."

Dodi turned and pointed. "Look there, Amon-Ra, shopping at the brass merchant, Sharky and his brothers."

Amon-Ra didn't glance up from digging through his purse. Now that he cleaned fish, he had money, and anyway, he thought Sharky was a bandit—though he didn't say so. Ignoring Dodi, he said to the merchant, "These oranges are soft. I'll give you quarter price."

"Mister, they are soft because they are filled with juice. They are Cretan oranges, brought here at great expense."

"Yes, but look! What are these black spots? No one would pay full price for spotted oranges."

The merchant's eyes shifted up to the right. "They are leopard oranges. It is the way they grow, they are special. Grown that way to please the King of Crete, who has a leopard. Three quarters price."

"I met a Cretan once. I didn't like him. He was spotted too. Half price."

The merchant nodded.

Amon-Ra started in on the poorness of the tea packet, how battered and cracked the package was.

Still observing the cousins six stalls away, Dodi said, "Sharky has big money to spend today." He waved until the cousin saw him.

Sharky nodded briefly at Dodi, but it didn't distract him from firing rapid instructions to the brass merchant, nor from shoving money into his hand. Then he motioned for his four brothers to follow, and together they made their way through the merchant stalls of the weekly bazaar, the rugs spread with goods: oranges, grapes, figs, sacks of wheat and maize, dried meats, and freshly baked bread; the peg posts cascading with cloth: jellabiyas, Egyptian cotton shirts, turbans, headdresses, frocks; other peg posts trimmed with hammered brass and tinware, heavy pots, ladles, pans and plates; and rugs spread with little tin boxes and hashish pipes. Between the stalls, townspeople jammed the bazaar's makeshift avenues, not just people from al-Tasr but also from other towns of the region, Hamrah Dum, Faw Qibli, Izbat al-Busah, Dishna.

Amon-Ra had finished with the tea packet and was warming up for the sugar tin when Sharky slashed his way through the crowd and tapped him on the shoulder.

Sharky was stocky, wide shouldered, thick necked. His brothers did whatever he said. "Amon-Ra! Cousin! We are proud of you! You and Dodi are the talk of the town, the way you hold your heads high." He looked at Amon-Ra's purse. "And you have money now! You don't need to borrow from me."

"It wasn't so long ago that you were broke too," Amon-Ra replied acidly.

"We all have money now!" Sharky replied. He put his arm around Amon-Ra's shoulder, the bad one. Amon-Ra made sure not to wince. "I won't tell you where I get mine, but I do want to tell you—ha!—we have had our differences, just so, but we respect you. We will help you find Manu. We will go to Cairo if we must. Then when we all kill him, you will be a hero!"

Amon-Ra shrugged. Sharky let him go. Gathering up his brothers, he formed a phalanx and they marched off towards the mineral-water stall. He called back over his shoulder, "Don't worry, Amon-Ra, we will help!"

When they had gone, Dodi asked, "But do we want his help?" Amon-Ra didn't reply; he seemed to be musing. Dodi said, "I wonder where he gets his money."

After a long pause Amon-Ra said, "He's a bandit." He laughed. "And a grave robber like us. But he knows people in Nag Hammadi, maybe even Cairo. What his brothers dig up or rob, he knows how to sell. Then there's also what he steals himself."

◆　◆　◆

Just as Amon-Ra cut the bread for supper, Dodi came bounding through the bungalow door like a gazelle. The mother frowned.

Amon-Ra looked up from the cutting board. "You are late again," he said.

"Amon-Ra! Mother! Ilyas wants me to drive a camel for him! Look!" Already Dodi was shouting like a camel driver. He pulled an Egyptian pound from his pocket.

The mother's face beamed when she saw the money. She said, "Oh! How our luck has changed. Good! Good!"

"How did it happen?" Amon-Ra asked.

"I was having tea at the Ka Ba—"

"Tea? In a café?"

"Yes Amon-Ra. Abbas invited me. He paid. He said that I was worth having as a friend since I was going to kill Manu when the coward came out of hiding, and since I was so responsible now and helped the mother, and since I had a responsible brother that did fish work."

"Praise the Ibis!" the mother cried. She beamed at her sons. They stared at her openmouthed, shocked at her sudden pagan outburst.

Dodi continued, "We were sitting by the street, when suddenly comes a great racket of hooves. I look up to see five camels rushing towards us with no driver. Well, I am a fast thinker. You know this." At that, Amon-Ra lifted his head and rolled his eyes. "I grab the shiny brass teapot, jump into the street, and swing it round my head. The camels stop in their tracks and just stand there looking at me. Up comes Ilyas . . . and his driver. When they see I have stopped the runaways, they thank me and buy me more tea and sugar. Before I know it, I have a job with Ilyas!"

In the month that followed, Dodi ran up a large tab at the Café Ka Ba. The owner, Wadi, had agreed to give Dodi a line of credit to hang himself with, since after a week the boy hadn't been fired and had even gained a modicum of community respect. Dodi took immediate advantage.

When leaving the mosque, or strolling the square in the evening, or sitting by the fountain, Dodi would slap neighbor A on the back, or hoot to cousin B, or perhaps encourage camel driver X to come and have tea with him.

"Come on, Labib, let's take tea down at the Ka Ba, and you can tell me what happened with the soothsayer in Nag Hammadi. No, no, don't worry, for such information, I'm buying."

Though Wadi let it go on for a while, eventually he became concerned about payment. One evening, grunting and shuffling his giant feet, Wadi asked Dodi to settle up. The timing could not have been worse. Dodi had that day invited his boss, Ilyas, for coffee the next evening, along with Ilyas's father, several brothers, and a cousin or two. He wanted to tell them his ideas about the camel business.

Whether they'd listen to his suggestions he didn't know—few ever had before—but it was essential that he show off his management skill by being able to pay the bill. How badly it would reflect on him if Wadi cut off his credit!

"Wadi, you know I have money, lots of it—"

"Then settle up!"

"Sure, as soon as I get paid."

Wadi shook his head. "They'd have to pay you till harvest to make a dent in this bill. No more credit until you pay up."

"But, Wadi—"

"No!"

"Wadi?"

"I said no."

"What if I had something of value to trade to you for credit, something from antiquity worth a fortune?"

"That would be different."

"It would?"

"Well, it depends."

"Tomorrow, after the noon hour, I will bring you something very valuable."

"We shall see, Dodi."

✦ ✦ ✦

The next day at about noon, the mother, seeking water from the fountain, carried a bucket to the square. Amon-Ra left for the fish works shortly afterward. When Dodi came home at midday, the bungalow was empty. Perfect! After one last glance through the window, looking up the street and down the street and then up the street again, Dodi bent low, arms and legs jutting, spiderlike. He didn't want anyone chancing to see him.

First, he pulled the bench away from the wall. Next, using a bottle cap, he pried up the loose floorboards, grimacing at their loud squeaks. He found the canvas sack and reached blindly inside, feeling around with his fingers, finally removing the top volume and leaving the others alone. He ceded the sack to its hole, hidden again with the floorboards and the bench, stood up for a glance out the window, and then wrapped his prize in an old cloth. With no time to waste, he went whistling out the door—to the café.

As he entered the café, Dodi observed Wadi peek with interest at the package before quickly altering his expression to something distant and noncommittal. Dodi, a young man who enjoyed drama, removed the cloth with a flourish and a grin, started to place the treasure gently on the counter, but at once pulled it back, held it to his chest, and said, "Maybe . . . maybe not a good idea. I'll go."

Wadi was hooked. Dodi had hooked him like one of those ugly fish Amon-Ra had to clean down at the river. But Wadi knew how to dicker. "What is that? An old book? Here, let me see."

As if a reluctant participant, Dodi lay the ancient book on the counter. Wadi squinted at it, opened it, examined it carefully. He said, "Look, the letters are no good, you can't even read them." He did not waste his applied skepticism for a minute. This was business. He screwed his big face into a scowl, his massive white eyebrows flaring wide.

Dodi said, "This book is very ancient. Look at the gazelle-hide cover, eh? Look at the spiral on the front."

"I don't know. Where would I sell it?"

Dodi looked startled. "You'd have to keep it quiet. Thieves would love to have it. You'd best take it to Nag Hammadi."

"Well, to whom? I don't want to get arrested for trafficking in antiquities. I don't know who to trust."

Dodi flashed his white teeth. "I know someone who knows. I will ask. In the meantime, give me credit for tonight."

Wadi snorted out a derisive laugh. "I don't think so."

"Please, Wadi, it's my big chance tonight. I've invited my employer."

"Well, I'll give you . . . I'll give you these oranges." He reached for a basket and put it on the counter.

"Come on, Wadi, this book is worth at least five, ten pounds Egyptian."

Wadi made a noise through his teeth. "I'll give you four pounds, and that's my final offer.

Dodi's heart leapt. He didn't argue. When he'd walked in, he hadn't figured the book to be worth even the fruit. Then he said, "And the oranges."

Wadi pushed the basket across the counter and put the book under his arm.

✦ ✦ ✦

At noon six days later, when Dodi came home from his camel-driving job intent on taking a snooze, while Amon-Ra was sitting at the table eating bread and goat cheese, having not yet left for the fish works, and as the mother gossiped in the front window with a neighbor, one of Sharky's brothers clamored through the bungalow doorway. Loose floorboards by the window creaked when he entered, and he glanced at them. Sweat covered his face. He spoke with heavy gasps, as if he'd been fast running: "Grab your weapons quickly. We have found Manu, he's alone."

Breadcrumbs bouncing down his chest from the mouthful he had just taken, Amon-Ra leapt to his feet, knocking his chair over backward with a crash. He stood, trembling slightly, like a startled dog. The moment of fate had come, and now he wasn't sure what to do.

Dodi didn't get it at all. "What?" he said.

"Bahiyah saw Manu down by the pump house . . ."

"Here? In al-Tasr?"

"Yes, Dodi, he's fallen asleep by the side of the road, his molasses jar beside him."

Due to the Coptic priest's earlier admonishment, both Dodi and Amon-Ra had begun to entertain doubts. Perhaps Manu was, indeed, innocent. And now Amon-Ra thought it odd that a guilty Manu would fall asleep in al-Tasr. Maybe the sleeper wasn't really Manu. Perhaps Bahiyah was mistaken. "How does Bahiyah know the face of Manu?" Amon-Ra asked.

The messenger shrugged. "Who doesn't know the thirteenth son of the sheriff? It was the twelfth son your father killed. And everyone buys molasses. All know him."

It was so, the brothers agreed. Everyone in the village had at one time or other bought molasses from Manu. With the jar on his back, he would roam far and wide crying, "Sweet molasses, black molasses," over and over until the day's end, often trekking from Hamrah Dum to the country near Nag Hammadi. There, he would spend the night in a goat shed before plodding back to his village.

But where had he been during the past weeks? No one had seen him. Amon-Ra concluded just as he had many times before, that Manu had run away and hidden himself. Why? Because he was the murderer. What else could Amon-Ra think? He nodded. Dodi stood up.

By the window the mother turned. She had ignored the inconsequential nephew who had come running into the bungalow; yet after she'd heard the name *Manu*, not once but twice, even three times, she abandoned her tattling and demanded, "Who has found Manu?"

Dodi replied indirectly: "He is at the pump house."

The mother's unblinking eyes hovered above her black veil; she looked like a raven. "Are your mattocks sharp?" she asked, although it was not really a question. "Get them." Without a word, the brothers ducked through the back door, their cousin in tow, and crossed directly to a lean-to where the tools were kept.

"Here, Dodi, you take mine," Amon-Ra directed, reaching inside, "it is sharper than yours. I'll bring Father's. If Manu is guilty, is it not fitting?" Amon-Ra tossed his mattock into the air and Dodi grabbed the upper handle in midflight. One end of the steel head was pointed like a pickaxe, the other was broad and sharp as a knife. "We must talk to Manu. Look into his eyes. That's where we will find the guilt or innocence."

The cousin said, "What does it matter if he's guilty or not? One of them did it. If we cannot discover who, the kin shall pay at random."

Amon-Ra scowled. He knew this was the law of the land, the guiding principle of the family feud: someone must pay—if not the criminal himself, his kith and kin. Whether it was right or wrong, Amon-Ra didn't know, but he had thought a lot about it lately. In the end, he didn't want to go against the unwritten law. He picked up his father's mattock, pulled open the gate, and ran down the path towards the pump house, his brother and cousin close behind.

Even as the brothers and cousin dashed away, the mother shuffled into the yard, dust puffing out from under her black jellabiya. The mother crossed over to the lean-to, her steps unwavering, determined. She pulled out Dodi's mattock, weighed it in her hands, feeling its heft. Carrying it like a baby, she hurried back through the bungalow, crossed the front threshold, and marched down the street, towards the pump house, nodding a greeting when she saw neighbors in the windows. There were many neighbors in many windows, for the news had spread quickly: the time had come—blood revenge!

◆　◆　◆

The priest, al-Qummus, scurried through the great hall in the monastery of Saint Palamon. He had spent the morning cleaning icons, a job he could have given to a servant, but he preferred to do it himself as an act of devotion. He had dusted and shined the statue of the black Virgin, restored the carving of the Mother and Child, rubbing it with sesame oil; cleaned and rehung the paintings of the saints and of the Dove and the Fish; changed the water in the bowl and the lilies in the vase of the Virgin; and seen that the coffins were swept clean. Now he was late for lunch.

He came to a heavy door at the end of the hall, pulled it open with a grunt, and shut it again with a bang that caused reverberations inside and out. In the garden, a monk, Pachomius, was blocking the path with a weed cart, and he wouldn't move it quickly. Though hefty, al-Qummus was light on his feet. He danced around the cart by threading through the bushes, skipping over seedlings on the balls of his feet, robes flying, humming to himself. Not wanting to be late, he squeezed through a gap in the wall rather than maintaining dignity by using the main gate. After all, he was taking his son-in-law, Andarawus, to lunch.

While charging down the road, arms swinging furiously, he noticed something strange near the pump house: a group of men standing in the hot sun. They had formed a semicircle around another man who seemed to be asleep, head between his knees, a molasses jar at his side. One man held a raised mattock over the sleeping man's head. Oh, dear God, al-Qummus thought, that's Amon-Ra and the others. They've found Manu.

Chapter Etyoo   -5-

THE PUMP HOUSE WAS a simple stone hut standing in tall grass by the side of the road. It held the main pump for the irrigation network; machinery that droned hypnotically through the window and the wall cracks. When Amon-Ra had arrived there, shortly before al-Qummus, he had found the cousin Sharky waiting with an animated yet grotesque smirk on his face. Twelve steps away, Sharky's brothers stood guard over the oddly inert Manu.

"You see? I told you we'd find him!" Sharky whispered harshly.

Amon-Ra glared at Sharky but said nothing. "Come," Sharky whispered again, "You and your brother have the honors."

Sharky pulled him forward. Amon-Ra did not resist, yet moved slowly, all the while staring wide-eyed at his intended victim, the inert man. While laboring with the molasses jar on the hot, dusty road, Manu had probably been lulled by the pump-house din and had decided to rest in the shade; And look! There beside him, a hashish sack, and empty bottles of beer! From drinking the *hasis*-infused beer, he had fallen into a stupor. Now the soothing shadow had receded, causing his head and knees to roast in the sun's glare, his stark silhouette falling beneath him. Yet Manu did not stir. Amon-Ra felt that hot sun on the back of his own neck, and he noticed there was no wind. Gliding overhead, a single raven croaked.

Sharky pushed Amon-Ra into place directly before the bent figure. Dodi stood on Amon-Ra's left, Sharky on his right, the others filling in on either side, seven men altogether waiting to kill Manu. Amon-Ra imagined he was in a dream. He wondered if it was Manu's dream of his own death. He looked at the others. They made him feel helpless, as though he were in the grip of a sphinx or some other large monster. It was like the time he fell into the river.

When Amon-Ra was a boy, his job had been to pull empty nets into his father's felucca. One morning a net had snagged on something floating in the river and pulled him overboard. He felt the line slip through his fingers as he plunged underwater, but he was a good swimmer for a boy his age, so he wasn't worried, he would just swim to the rudder and climb up the rudder steps. When he burst to the surface and blinked the water from his eyes, he found he was already ten yards from the boat, the heavy current rapidly sweeping him northward. He could see his father and the deck hand stringing out nets on the far side of the boat; it seemed they hadn't noticed what had happened. Good, Amon-Ra thought, I'll be back before they can tease me. He went into his efficient side stroke; ten repetitions would bring him alongside, but when he looked up, he was twenty yards away and drifting towards an eddy. He swam overhand, hard, kicking powerfully with his feet. He fought the great Nile with all his strength, but it kept bearing him away, its grasp too tight. He fell into eddies and vicious whirlpools, which pulled him under. Though he slashed his way to the surface each time, it took a lot out of him and he thought he might drown. Then the back of his head hit something hard. A hand had grabbed him by the hair to keep him aside a boat. He had thrown his arms over the gunwale of a dory, and half from being pulled, half from climbing, had scrambled into the boat. While lying on the floorboards gasping for breath, he had looked up into the eyes of an old fisherman.

Amon-Ra felt an elbow in his ribs. Sharky was glaring at him. Even Dodi glanced at him, a bit impatient. Riveting his eyes on the back of Manu's skull, almost in a trance, he raised his father's mattock up over his head.

"Amon-Ra!"

He heard the cry and looked. Was it the old fisherman, the one who had pulled him away from the inexorable grasp of destiny that day so long ago? No, Amon-Ra realized, snapping out of his stupor. Instead, stirring up a virtual dust storm, al-Qummus was running towards the group, shaking his fists, shouting again and again, "No, Amon-Ra!"

Amon-Ra stood frozen, but only for a moment. Almost at once, he lowered the mattock to his side and dropped it. As he did so, a surge of energy filled his veins. The grim pull of the unwritten law still wrenched at him, the insatiable jaws of the blood feud still sought him; their combined strength was akin to the Nile's inexorable grip, and yet, perhaps for the first time in his life, he felt something different—his own power.

Al-Qummus had closed to within fifty feet of the men. Manu began to twitch.

Sharky said, "I'll kill him!" With a grunt he raised his mattock high.

Such was the power Amon-Ra felt in his mind and body, he could have jumped into the Nile and swam seven miles upstream. He could have run through the caves of Jabal-al-Tarif, chasing shadows and jinn and spirits back into the ground. He could have put a new roof on the bungalow, dug a garden, sown a field. His right arm shot out just as Sharky started the death blow, and he blocked it, grabbing the cousin's forearm in a vise-like grasp.

"What?" Sharky shouted in a fury. "Let go!" He wrenched his arms left and right trying to pull free from Amon-Ra. One of the other cousins stepped forward to help Sharky but Dodi stopped him, saying, "It is between the two."

Up to the group the priest ran, puffing so hard he was unable to speak. Amon-Ra threw Sharky down, pulling the mattock from his grasp. As Sharky fell, he struck the molasses jar, upsetting it, spilling its sun-warmed contents on the ground around Manu. It flowed out in a rush, the fiery sunlight glinting off the dark liquid.

With a soft rustle, like a breeze crossing a room, the mother stepped through the semicircle and in one motion buried the point of her mattock deep in Manu's brain. None of the men had seen her arrive, and none had known she was there until she struck. Blood splattered over all of them. The moment before she lashed out, Manu had lifted his head from his knees, but he was driven to the ground by her blow. Blood and molasses intermingled with the dirt beneath him. The mother cried the name of her dead husband three times:

"Ali! Ali! Ali!"

The blow struck with the grim sound of cracking bone and crushed flesh, and one terrible gasp escaped from Manu's mouth. At the sound, Sharky whooped and cheered. Al-Qummus stared at his priestly robes, now blood splattered; amazed, he fell to his knees and cried. The cousins, smiling and laughing, yanked Sharky to his feet. Dodi stood still, first staring at the mother, and then at Amon-Ra.

Amon-Ra bent down to place the hard-won mattock on the ground next to his own. Like a drop of falling light, courage had come to him; now it was gone. It had come like a radiance, as if through a fury of thunderheads—a thin, ethereal shaft penetrating the dark tempest, an illumination, inspiring, but all too brief to really matter.

Sharky leaned over, grabbed the mattock, turned, and with two blows of the sharp end, hacked off Manu's right arm.

"For God's sake, stop!" al-Qummus shouted.

Sharky dropped the mattock and grabbed the priest by his robe. He said, "Do not interfere again. If a wise man wants to make himself useful, he can bury the remains when we're done." With that, he picked up his weapon and began working on Manu's right leg, hacking through the thigh. His brothers joined in until Manu was completely dismembered, and they were all covered with blood.

Still kneeling in the road, eyes closed, praying, al-Qummus felt something touch his leg. He looked down in horror to see Manu's severed head, which had rolled up against him. In a fury, the priest grabbed the head by the hair and held it up as if for Salome. He shouted, "Another martyr?"

Lurching, Sharky grabbed the head from al-Qummus. "Get out of here, priest! This is a clan matter!" Sharky glared, then threw the battered head at the priest—the bulging eyes, the pallid skin, the bloody gray lips twisted into a silent scream; it hit al-Qummus in the chest and he grunted. So, there was no reasoning with Sharky when he was in such a state of blood lust. Al-Qummus frowned, turned, and walked away.

Sharky pulled the knife from Amon-Ra's belt. "You can let me borrow this fine weapon of my uncle's, eh? That way you, too, can take part in the revenge," he said.

Amon-Ra didn't move other than to push his feet into the sand like a child.

Sharky laughed and flipped the knife to his right hand. He plunged it into Manu's chest, cutting it open. He pulled out the dead man's heart. Like a gourmet chef, he carefully but quickly sliced it into seven pieces, and handed each man his share. "Do not worry, Amon-Ra," Sharky said, "When you join us in eating of this heart you join us completely in the ultimate blood revenge!"

They all ate. Amon-Ra swallowed his piece quickly, without chewing; it smelled of death and was bitter, bitter.

The mother would not join the men in their ritual. In her mind, she had avenged her dead husband. If the revenge required further action from the men of her clan, so be it. She would stay and watch, but that was all.

"There, Amon-Ra! You are a hero," Sharky concluded, slapping him on the back.

Amon-Ra stared at the grains of sand near his feet, counting them, musing on them. He crouched and scooped some grains into his hand. Today he had fought the desert. For a moment he had been a lion in the wind, unmoved. But the cunning desert had defeated him. With all its centuries of practice it was far too clever, too much of a match for one simple man with no method of wisdom. Wisdom. Such a word. He thought of the jinniyah. Perhaps that's what the books were: collected words of wisdom written down by some ancestor sage, words that explained a method of strength and courage and love, a method so strong that nothing could dim it; for surely, this, too, was nurtured in the desert lands: wisdom. All you had to do was read the strange letters. Amon-Ra looked up at the empty sky. So, who could read old letters like that? What good were such books?

Dodi, walking with the mother, stopped and took Amon-Ra's arm. "Come, brother. You cannot stay here. Come with us." The three of them walked together down the path.

Sharky and the cousins were already ahead of them, but Sharky stopped and grabbed Amon-Ra's free arm to walk alongside. "You are stronger than you look, Amon-Ra, you gave me quite a tussle."

Amon-Ra didn't respond.

"But the way it happened; it was meant to be. Manu got what he deserved, and our family is mighty again." He poked Amon-Ra in the ribs and whispered in his ear, "The mother is wondrous, is she not?" Then he addressed the three of them. "Now hear me. The sheriff will learn of this and come looking for weapons to prove we did it. Clean your mattocks well. And if you have a gun in the house, or any contraband, you'd better move it, or he can arrest all of you. Don't worry about the priest. After what he witnessed, he won't talk. Hold your heads up, eh?" With that, Sharky released Amon-Ra's arm, trotted ahead, and gathered his brothers into a phalanx to march as conquering heroes into town.

Passing the butcher shop with halting tread, Amon-Ra stopped dead at the sudden odor. Sweetly fragrant oranges, elaborate festoons of them, dangled baroquely from the butcher shop's roof beams. Between the festoons, skinned carcasses of sheep and goats hypnotically twisted and untwisted on their tethers, air drying. Preservative cloves pierced the oranges; the perfume of fruit and spice kept the black flies at bay, or so advised an ancient clan recipe, but today the fumes lacked potency, and Beelzebub swarmed to the meat. Though it did not exactly improve upon the meat's stench, the perfume altered it, making a different stench which passersby might mistake for something better, something pleasant. Amon-Ra made no such mistake. In his stomach, the piece of Manu's heart pumped and thumped and beat like a dragon—he was sure of it, and he bent double, almost retching in the street. Dodi and the mother had to pull him upright to maintain family dignity.

The eyes of the villagers watched without watching; villagers busied themselves by means of sudden errands that took them alongside Sharky and his brothers, and then past the mother and her sons, villagers intent on their business, yet with an errant glance here, a look there. Pick a melon from the stand, shake it, press the ends, look down the nose at it, slide a glance past it to the mother's garment, soiled to the stitching. See the son's jellabiya, darkly smeared, and look there at the mattock, sticky with blood and molasses.

◆　◆　◆

Soon, the villagers knew the sheriff, Husayn, would come swooping down from Hamrah Dum. Strong men from the Hawwarah would accompany him.

"Where is my thirteenth son?" he would ask. "Where is my beloved Manu?" After many questions, he would find that no one had seen anything, nothing could be told of, and nothing confirmed.

Yet, at last, someone would gossip, "As the sheriff knows, it has been whispered that Manu was a killer, that he killed Ali, and so cursed himself with the blood revenge."

Another villager would comment, "If it please the sheriff, you might find an old molasses jar by the side of the road. The wind whirls into the jar but discovers it empty, so it flees."

And another: "Why? Honorable Sheriff, it flees to search elsewhere. You can hear it moan through the hollow mouth, if it please the sheriff, as it goes on its way." Every villager would be interrogated:

"Your Honor, it searches for Manu! Is he not missing? Are you not looking?"

"I do not play games with you. Please do not nail me to a wheel. Please do not roll me off Jabal-al-Tarif."

"It is only gossip, Your Honor. I tell you all the rumor I know to try to help Your Honor."

"Do the sons of Ali know something? I could not say for sure, Your Honor."

◆　◆　◆

Back at the bungalow, Dodi and the mother gathered scrubbing brushes and cleaning powder. Dodi wrapped the blood-stained mattock in a burlap sack to carry with him. The mother filled a similar sack with their soiled, blood-stained clothes, and they set out for the river. At the river they would clean the mattock; if the stains would not come out of the clothes, they would tie up rocks inside the arms and throw the bundles from a boat—that was their job. To deal with the treasure was Amon-Ra's job.

Amon-Ra peered into the dark hole under the floorboards. So weak, so sick, such a fate. His mind was a cauldron, it boiled his body; sweat dripped from his eyebrows and the tip of his nose. It ran down his arms, his torso. I must pull myself together, he thought. Get rid of the books or the sheriff will have an excuse. You cannot give a man like that an excuse. He is deeply cruel, the cruelest man in all the desert. He would not hesitate to arrest the mother, too, along with Dodi and me, no matter how we reasoned with him. Take heed, the jinniyah had said to him, take heed and ward thy self-regard!

Amon-Ra knelt down. Crouching, with his left hand braced against the hole's edge—he dipped his still-sore left shoulder, stabbing out his right hand. Immediately, he found the canvas sack: wide open. From surprise (he was sure he had cinched it closed) he upset the books so that they fell sideways inside the sack, and some of them, the ones without thongs, opened. All the while, his stomach whirled from the leaning over. Perhaps al-Qummus will keep the books safe until the sheriff goes away, Amon-Ra thought. He pulled the wide-open sack upward but had to pin the near side of it against the floorboards because, involuntarily, his torso convulsed. Wretched, Amon-Ra heaved, and easily as could be, up came the piece of Manu's heart. Like a small fish, it flopped into the sack, coming to a rest inside one of the books. Amon-Ra didn't want to look. He yanked the sack completely out of the hole and resynched it.

Chapter So-oo   -6-

Tano's Shop

"Do I think Cairo is as cosmopolitan as Paris? Well, sir, why not? After all, the French have been here since Napoleon's invasion. Intellectual, artistic, and gastronomical possibilities abound. It is true of all Egypt, sir. There are interesting peasant dishes to be sampled in the Upper Nile Basin, and for the intellect, there are the monuments to visit. Also, what of the little things one can collect? Occasionally, a crafty peasant secrets away a treasure from antiquity—until he thinks he's outwitted the law and can sell it. Naturally, we . . . don't deal on the black market. You are interested in collecting antiquities?"

Tano's shop was small, elegant, from the delicate cut-glass window in the door to the Persian carpet running down the short, cypress-paneled hall. Ancient treasures sat atop mahogany chests. More lay hidden in drawers. Many of the objects had survived the rule of twenty Egyptian dynasties as well as the successive reigns of Alexander the Great, the Roman generals, the Turkish Beys, the

Fatimids, the Crusaders, the Mamelukes, the Ottoman Turks, the British diplomats, the Napoleonic French, and just lately, Rommel. A low chest supported a small sarcophagus. Finely carved divinities occupied its corners: Isis, Nephthys, Serket, and Neith. Anubis pranced at the center. On another chest sat a statue of Nut, the celestial cow. On others, a golden medallion of the phoenix, five red pottery jars, a red granite fragment from the enormous colossus of Ramesses II, a small stele of Ptolemy II and Arsinoe, and a piece of an obelisk of the Fourteenth Dynasty, with an emblem of the king's son, Nehesi.

There was a brass oil lamp that might have belonged to Aladdin, in that it was not one of those silly knockoffs, but rather, an ancient, exquisite piece. Beside it lay jewelry unearthed in Troy, perhaps jewels that once adorned Helen. On the leather-topped tables, ancient books lay open on stands, including Coverdale's Bible of 1535, the famous "Bug Bible," so-called because of a passage that reads, "Thou shalt not need to be afrayed for eny bugges by night," whereas the Authorized and Revised versions read, "Terror by night."

Next to it, open to the proper page, lay the "Wicked Bible," published in 1631 by Barker and Lucas, in which the Seventh Commandment reads, "Thou shall commit adultery," the printer having omitted the negation. Tano had acquired the two Bibles from an English lord in trade for two Ptolemaic sphinxes, entirely gilt.

The customer shrugged in answer to Tano's question. An idle tourist, Tano thought. He often charmed potential collectors, engaged them in subtle flattery, but it was well past noon, and this mention of gastronomical possibilities had fired his appetite. He decided to get rid of the man quickly. "Sir, I'm awfully sorry, but I have a luncheon date. Please come back at four." Tano ushered the man to the door.

The man scurried towards the door, suddenly intimidated by the stocky Cypriote. Perhaps it was the army medal Tano wore on his lapel. More likely, the dealer's jackhammer arms transmitted subtle threat.

In reaching out for the doorknob, Tano saw through the window a small, white-haired man occupying the vestibule. *So, he's heard about the codex,* Tano thought. With one arm he opened the door and shoved the customer out, and with the other welcomed the little man, bidding him to enter. Though Tano hadn't seen him in years, he couldn't mistake the man, the sharp facial features, the amber cat eyes. "Greetings, Thoth," Tano exclaimed.

Thoth simply replied, "Have you read any good books lately?"

"I only possess one," Tano confessed as he led Thoth into a back room where a steaming kettle sat on a coal-fired Aga. The hot stove warmed both the room and the shop, since Tano felt sixty-four degrees outside qualified as cold.

"Tea?"

"Thank you . . . But add some cold water to the cup as it is a bit warm in here."

Tano smiled and thought, *Such a particular sort of character.* He said, "Well, look, the Aga must either run all the time or not at all. I shut it down by April."

Thoth, not paying any attention to Tano, had crossed over to a sideboard, where sat a leather-bound codex. It had simple tooling of the ankh hieroglyph of life on the front.

"Be my guest, open it," Tano said, observing the little man with amusement. He had known the volume would be a magnet.

"What is this little piece of leather you have set beside this codex? I fail to see that it belongs."

"When I acquired this antiquity from a local peasant, upon examination, I found that piece of—what? It looks like a small fish. I found it inside the volume, haphazard. It had stained some of the papyrus pages. Yes, surely a recent addition, but I must maintain provenience, so I have included it with the codex."

Thoth carefully opened the book, examined it, appreciated the high aesthetic value of the fastidious lettering that adorned the papyrus pages. Most notable, the scribe had written the sacred text in Greek! That would indicate a very old volume, older than fragments unearthed elsewhere written in Coptic. Thoth closed the codex, turned and stared at Tano. "What is the price you seek?"

The cat eyes always gave Tano a vague feeling of anxiety. Hurriedly he said, "These days, I only deal in gold."

"Are there more?"

"As I said, I only have the one."

"Yes, but the peasant?"

A crafty look passed over Tano's face. He didn't want to reveal his source, for his idea was to revisit the peasant, this Amon-Ra, and wheedle the rest of the books from him. "I can't really say."

Thoth gave the ghost of a smile. "Try again."

"Honestly, Thoth, we must not pressure the source, or he will go underground."

"It will be worth your effort, Tano, I warrant that. You will have my assistance in acquiring great treasures in all their splendor."

Such a statement from Thoth. This, this would be worth much more than whatever he could get for the codex library! Over the years, whatever Thoth said happened. You could count on it. "We will need camels," Tano said.

✦ ✦ ✦

"If you arrive at al-Tasr in a motorcar, you might as well be the king of England," Tano had advised, "considering the attention you would draw. This kind of transaction—and the brothers and the mother would agree—needs to be hidden from snoopers and stool pigeons!"

"Stool pigeons," Thoth repeated, "ah, mobster talk."

Tano chuckled. He said, "Like Edward G. Robinson, and Bogart. William Powell in *The Thin Man*."

Thoth smiled. It occurred to him that mobster movies might give Tano insight into his chosen profession, that of a man dealing antiquities from a Cairo backstreet shop. How much film did Tano watch? Thoth wondered if Tano wished film would replace the deliberate sequencing of the alphabet, the written word. He considered: There are always new systems vying for attention. One fine day you watch a flock of cranes in flight and from each bird's place in the flock and the constantly changing angles and relationships to each other as they wheel through the air you invent the alphabet! Many things follow from that.

They rode comfortably on the well-behaved camels Tano had provided; the man knew his humped ruminants. Thoth rather enjoyed the view from that vantage, since usually his eye level was a mere five feet or so off the ground.

When they arrived at the bungalow, they found Dodi out stacking dry dung. He immediately recognized Tano and ushered the riders around to the rear of the house, where the mother was hanging a few shirts on a line to dry. There they tethered the camels. With a quick gesture of admission at the back door, the mother quickly faded inside.

When Thoth entered, the mother stared at him rather rudely, a bit transfixed.

Dodi entered with Tano. He said, "I just saw Amon-Ra. He will be here in a moment, but I have something to tell you." He addressed this to Tano.

"What is it, my boy?"

"Amon-Ra does not wish to sell the books. And he has been approached by another buyer, one who threatens. So, he has hidden the books where they will not be found."

"Oh, he will change his mind. Look at the money he earned for selling me the one book!"

Interrupting, Thoth asked, "Can you describe this other buyer?"

"A man with a flaming sword on his military hat. Very friendly, in a bad sort of way."

"He brought two soldiers with him," said Amon-Ra, who had just entered through the back door. "I didn't like them. The mother told them to get out."

The mother nodded and made a face.

Thoth said, "You have done the right thing." He looked at Amon-Ra. "Keep watch and ward thy self-regard. Do not let them take these books from you."

At that phrase, the very same admonishment the jinniyah had given him, Amon-Ra stepped back and stared at Thoth.

Thoth said, "I am here to help you."

Meanwhile, Tano began to perspire; he knew when you are with Thoth, things tend to veer in strange directions.

Amon-Ra said, "I know these books are sacred. I regret selling one."

At this, Dodi looked sheepish and felt sorry for selling one to Wadi at the café Ka Ba.

Thoth crossed over to Amon-Ra, touched his good right arm, and looked up at him with the cat eyes. He said, "Amon-Ra, the jinniyah does not scorn you. You have done the right thing. The codex—the book—is now with me as it should be. Soon, I must examine the others. I will assist you with this burden."

"The jinniyah? How do you know about the jinniyah?" He glared at Dodi, but Dodi shook his head.

Thoth did not reply. He just gazed up at Amon-Ra.

The mother cleared her throat. Amon-Ra looked over at her. Then he nodded and looked back at Thoth. He said, "Come back tomorrow, but late in the day, after supper time."

The next evening, Thoth and Tano, again riding their camels, returned to the bungalow. Knowing the routine, they continued around back, where they dismounted. But something was wrong, the air smelled of burning, but not of the usual fuel for the oven.

Tano walked over to the back door, peered inside, turned, and said, "There has been an incident."

Thoth approached, looked in and saw the charred interior, the table collapsed in ashes, and the disarray of household possessions—pottery smashed, lamps broken, drawers pulled out and tossed haphazardly.

"The house has been ransacked," Tano said.

"Search! Have they been killed?"

Tano tried the steep staircase, but it would not hold the big man's weight, and he backed off. Thoth, much more agile, quickly climbed up to the makeshift loft. He verified that no bodies could be found there.

They heard a bang from the front door being flung open and through it came a husky man followed by four young men. The man stopped, observed, and said, "Tano!"

With one look, Tano realized these men had been in some sort of violent altercation. Blood stained their clothes; bandages covered scratches and cuts. He said, "Sharky! What has happened here?"

Sharky stared at Thoth. "Who is this man?"

"He is Thoth, our friend, you can trust him."

Sharky continued to stare at Thoth, then decided and glanced away. He said, "They looked like officials, men from the government, perhaps from Cairo—who can say? They came to this bungalow and thumped on the door so hard I heard it from across the street. I saw about ten men in uniforms. When the mother opened the door, she didn't like what she saw and slammed it shut again. She must have barred it with the plank she keeps by the door because the men could not open it." Sharky stopped talking for a moment as if that was all he intended to say.

Tano, impatient, said, "And?"

Sharky somewhat reluctantly resumed. "I . . . know Amon-Ra has trade he found. I am sure of it—I've seen the extra money the brothers flash around. At first, I thought maybe these men were helping the sheriff because of the blood revenge and wanted to search the house. He can arrest all of them if he finds something illegal. But then again, this mob did not look like the sheriff's men."

"OK," Tano said, "So you became involved. I can see that. What did you do?"

"We grabbed whatever we could, planks, a crowbar,"—he looked at his brothers—"and ran across the street to distract the intruders while Nodi ran around back and persuaded the family to get away and bring the trade with them."

Thoth said, "But I see it didn't stop there."

Sharky nodded at Thoth. "Yes. One of the men began to go to the back of the house, so I banged him on the head with a plank." He smiled. "His companions didn't like that." Sharky's brothers sniggered at that comment. "We had a fight. They finally chased us away, but by then, the mother and the cousins were gone from the house."

Nodi, since he was the youngest brother, wasn't supposed to speak, but because his job had been perhaps the most important, spiriting away the aunt and the cousins, well, he thought he had a right to add to the narration. He said, "The men ran around back, but they didn't see me going around the other side."

A look from Sharky told Nodi that his narration was finished. Sharky said, "They broke into the house and smashed it up, looking for the trade, I guess. Watching from across the street, I could see they found nothing. Maybe for revenge, they set the house on fire."

Nodi, always a little troublemaker from Sharky's point of view, butted in and said, "As soon as they went away, we grabbed burlap soaked in water and beat out the fire."

"You have all done well," said Thoth, "That is clear. Now I want you to realize that I am here to aid Amon-Ra. Please tell me where he went."

Sharky sighed. "You seem to be alright. Still, I don't know if I trust either of you. You are dealers."

Tano said, "I am the dealer. He is the buyer."

"I don't see the difference," Sharky replied. "Anyway, trust me, you never know where Amon-Ra goes."

Thoth said, "I understand." He looked at Tano, "We must take our leave."

✦　✦　✦

Before riding to Amon-Ra's bungalow that evening, Thoth had journeyed to Nag Hammadi to send a cryptic telegram to Stevan Romanov of Montenegro. It was matter of extreme urgency, and the urgency took root because of codices written in Greek—a very rare find. If any of the texts contained words of power, it would be the Greek volumes.

But Thoth's plans had come to naught. It had become obvious that whatever part of the codex library Thoth could obtain, he must get the volumes out of Egypt, a locale that suddenly seemed to be crawling with malevolence. For this, Thoth had called for Stevan's assistance. But now, Amon-Ra had gone to ground along with Dodi and the mother. It might take time to find them because they would trust no outsider and no villager would give them away.

Chapter Shashf -7-

Njeguši, Montenegro, early spring, 1946. Stevan sat on a rock near the well he had been engineering and digging. The Fascists had thrown bodies into many of the old wells in the valley, contaminating them, so now, new wells were sorely needed.

From across the clearing, Stevan's Uncle Joko observed his nephew with concern. Stevan would at any time bury his head in his arms and essentially fall apart, shoulders shaking, strange sounds, moans and sobs sneaking out from under his arms. Yes, shatter and ruin ruled in the land. Yet a loss to Stevan's very soul is what shook him in this tumbled-down time.

✦ ✦ ✦

I say goodbye to my wife my love and almost all I am, Stevan had thought during that frozen December night. Through his shattered mind it came . . . *I say goodbye, God-be-with-you! She is lost. She is lost! Now there is only one miracle that could make me carry on. Only one! . . . only the survival of my new born child, Anastasia!*

✦ ✦ ✦

After Stevan and Marian had first arrived in Montenegro, and had united with Stevan's sister, Anastasija, and his uncle, Joko, they joined forces to establish a guard to protect the teenage Peter II from the Prince Regent and his Axis companions. But in March 1941, an Axis invasion forced the king and his representatives into exile. The king ordered Stevan, Joko, and the resistance to remain behind to prevent any enemy foothold in the mountains, and so the high karst where the Njeguši camped and roamed had remained virtually inviolable. During that time, Marian and Stevan were expecting their first child. But then, on December 22, 1945, Marian—Marian!—died after delivering their daughter, Anastasia. The complications from the wound she had received while escaping from the "Sham Republic of Suebi," as Stevan referred to it, had been more of a danger to her than anyone had realized.

Now, observing his nephew, Joko thought, Ah, times have taken their toll as they are wont to, taken Lazo and Yasoda, Herak, Marian . . . Now they lick at Stevan's boots, times do, to see if they like the taste. He was about to offer his nephew a slug of raki from a goat skin when a clansman trotted uphill carrying an envelope. The young man hesitated when he saw Stevan slouched on the rock.

Joko said, "Here, give it to me." The boy handed the envelope to Joko and retreated. Joko walked over to a nearby stump, sat down and waited, sipping from the bota, and smoking an evil-smelling French cigarette.

After a while, Stevan lifted his head and said, "What the hell is that noxious odor?"

"The Gauloises, the Gaul women!" Joko replied. "Want one?"

Stevan gazed at Joko, his eyes bloodshot, heavy lidded. He didn't say anything.

"Here," Joko said. He got up and crossed to where Stevan sat. "This came for you." He handed Stevan the envelope.

Stevan said, "Telegram." He opened it. It read:

03 05 46 ER32ZZQ65
TYE66 PD NAG HAMMADI EGYPT 500
STEVAN VOJVODA CRNA GORA
A FLIGHT OF CRANES AL-TASR ARRIVAL
THOTH
NNNN

Stevan stared at the message and realized his past was reaching out for him. He'd almost forgotten his ambition of six years ago, the archeological pursuit and discovery of ancient texts, his quest for mystical knowledge, his quest for Gnosis. He said, "Remember Herak, Joko?"

Joko snorted. When he was just a boy, Joko had witnessed an epic philosophical battle, a clash of chromosomes between his sister-in law, Yasoda, and the great esoteric philosopher, Herak. It had happened when Lazo had taken the clan to Herak's grotto, deep in the karst.

Stevan said, "When I studied with him, Herak told me that one day someone named Thoth would ask for my assistance, and when that happened, I must provide it."

Joko said, "I know."

With a raise of his eyebrows, Stevan handed the telegram to Joko.

Joko read it, nodded, and said, "I'll send a message to our English friend—"

"He's Irish."

"Irish but working with the English—"

"He's in Italy—"

"Naples."

"Napoli, working with English transport—"

"Probably sitting in some café, the limper, demanding Irish or stout."

+ + +

Four days later came a knock at the library door of the family manse, Vojvoda Lodge. Most of the structure, postwar, still stood, overlooking the Njeguši valley. Stevan was sitting before the fireplace cradling tenderly in his arms his infant daughter, Anastasia. He looked up but didn't move. Anastasija put down her book. The Anastasias: Stevan and Marian had agreed that when they birthed a girl, they would name the baby after Stevan's younger sister, Anastasija, but with an English spelling.

Anastasija strode across the room, pulled open the door to admit whoever had knocked. She beamed when she saw who stood in the doorway. The orb of Dick's face, the sun, shined back at her.

"Tired of the English, are you?" Stevan called out from the fireplace, without looking.

Anastasija winked, grabbed Dick's hand and pulled him in. He gave her hand a squeeze and limped over to the fireplace.

"Hello, ya wee darlin'," he said, taking baby Anastasia carefully from Stevan and holding her gently in his callused hands. She squealed and laughed. He squinted in the dark room; to him Stevan looked tired and distracted. The last time he had seen Stevan was during the funeral at Cismontane. Back then, King Peter II still had friends in Montenegro and had arranged an air transport for Stevan, which lay over in Italy to pick up Dick and then had flown them with the casket to England, to Cismontane. When they had arrived at the house, and delivered the casket, Dick had never seen any man in such a state of desolation as Stevan, and Dick had experienced plenty of his own anguish over the death of Marian, for he loved her as a daughter. The entire village and surrounding countryside turned out to pay their respects, for truly everyone loved or at least respected Marian, she who ran the estate for many of her young years. Hawkins, the tradesman, gave a heartfelt lament as he lay a great bundle of daffodil bulbs on the frozen ground by the Graves family mausoleum, but Marian's father, Charles Graves, had never emerged from his attic rooms, where he endured, punishing himself for allowing his only daughter to leave England with the Montenegrin devil, Stevan.

Stevan and Dick had not been allowed into the house, and in Graves's mind, they had been banished forever. Realize, at that time, he was unaware of his granddaughter's birth. Stevan had left word, but Graves had refused any communication.

Anastasija interrupted Dick's reminiscence. "Would you care for a taste of Irish?"

Dick, still hugging baby Anastasia, didn't seem to get it at first. Then the idea slowly registered in his mind: Irish whiskey. "I would. I would, indeed. Irish. On the entire continent of Italy, they haven't a drop, did ya know? All ya can get is the Poteen."

Anastasija gave a slight smile. "Joko knew."

"Did he now? And where is the affable bandit?" Dick replied.

"Carousing at the local, no doubt," Stevan said.

Anastasija crossed the room to an ornate rosewood cabinet; hand-carved images of roebuck, wolves, rabbits, and eagles adorned the two doors. She poured a double shot of Irish into a tumbler, turned, and found Dick standing behind her, a grin on his face.

Stevan, who had taken Anastasia back into his arms, cracked the first smile he'd managed in months. "The man is a shameless whiskey-hound."

"Says the pot to the kettle," Dick retorted.

Stevan shrugged; Dick had him there. He said, "You know, Anastasija, I believe I'll have one too. I mean, while you're pouring."

"I think I'll make it three," she said, and poured glasses for herself and her brother.

Two hours later the bottle stood almost empty. Anastasija had taken the baby to her crib some time ago and had retired herself. Outside, the wind howled and moaned at the windows, but the fire still crackled warm, and the chimney still drew well and did not puff smoke into the room.

Stevan said, "You know, Peter's royal government in exile was headquartered in Cairo for a time, in 1941."

"I did hear such a rumor," Dick noted. "Then he resided in London, but now I hear Peter's gone to Chicago."

"Tito put an end to him here."

"Aye, with fraudulent elections and purges."

"He convinced the Allies to back him."

"Tito fought the Axis in Yugoslavia with success. That's all the western generals wanted to hear about. They didn't care about his 'liberation committees' and trials of loyalists and Catholic prelates. And now, I don't know how safe we are here in these times, Dick, but as the man said, 'Frankly my dear, I don't give a damn.'"

"I'm understandin' you and your grief, my dear friend, but wonder if it's right to just be givin' in."

"Too late, my Irishman, we are a communist country now, like the Fascist Republic of Suebi, once Festus turns the coin over."

"Aye, the man is nothin' if not flexible. Why, he'll be turnin' the coin over with gusto, oilin' up to Stalin and Tito."

Stevan frowned. "And now this directive from Thoth."

"Directive?"

"Yes. I pledged long ago to Herak, that if I ever received an urgent message from a man named Thoth, I must offer him assistance as quickly as possible. This is something I am pledged to—it cannot be avoided or ignored."

"And what about Baby Anastasia?"

"My sister is aware of this possible circumstance, however unlikely it might have been, and now she must care for Baby Anna." At this, Stevan shook his head, drained his glass and slumped into a chair. "I will do this, somehow, and I will be back as quickly as possible."

"Doin' what? Ya don't even know."

"Somehow I've got to travel to Egypt, and there is no King Peter to help me with transport now."

Dick sat down on the other side of the fireplace. They sat in silence for a time, just listing to the crackle of the embers and the moan of the wind outside. At length, Dick raised a question. "Whatever did ya do with the flyin' boat?"

Stevan looked up. He said, "Well, it's been hidden for six years in a limestone grotto on a small lake called Naas. It's all disassembled and packed into crates, the engines packed in grease, the fuel canisters and lines purged of fuel. I thought one day I'd reassemble it and return it to Charles Graves, when the world wasn't so insane."

Dick didn't say anything at first. He stood up, crossed over to the cabinet and poured himself two fingers, and then drained his glass of "the créatúr." He said, "I'm thinkin' the flyin' boat was exactly made for a world that is actin' insane."

Chapter Eshmeen   -8-

THE F2A, REASSEMBLED, REFITTED, and now rechristened *Daffodil* in honor of Marian, flew up off the small lake called Naas. It soared over Vojvoda Lodge, dipping wings for Anastasija as she stood on the balcony off the tower room. With her left arm she held her niece Anastasia, and with her right, a red scarf clutched in hand, she waved adieu by forming a scarlet arc. "Fly by protection of the Celestial Rose," she cried, and, "Godspeed!" Then she stood watching the aeroplane slowly recede into the Adriatic mist.

The F2A followed the Ionian Islands down to the fingers of Greece and on along to Crete and its southern coast. At the end of the island they turned to the southwest, using the stars to guide them on target to Alexandria. They would follow the Nile up to Nag Hammadi and al-Tasr.

Time yawned by, stars rotated, a watch said the aeroplane was two-and-a-half hours past Crete. There! A glow on the horizon. Further. Lights! There lay the city named for the Macedonian god/king and conqueror: Al-Iskandariyah. Alexandria.

It was Stevan's idea to enter Egypt west of the seaport, flying over sparsely populated settlements and uninhabited desert to avoid encounter with any forms of authority, British or Egyptian. With no running lights, he would keep the glow of Nile settlements in view on the left from a height of almost ten thousand feet. The plan worked well all the way to Cairo, but past that point the riverbanks were dark. He was forced to fly directly over the Nile to distinguish it from the shadows of land.

As the stars began to fade within the diffused light that proceeds sunrise, Stevan abandoned the Nile to allow the F2A to drift over the eastern desert; but soon the Nile lay directly ahead: the river course had swung ninety degrees to the east and so marked their destination.

Below, fishermen launched feluccas, some with twin sails. They were jewels adorning the features of the river. The *Daffodil* came directly out of the rising sun, causing her to be invisible to the fishermen below yet audible by roar of her engines. She slapped the river's face with her smooth belly, sending quivers of anticipation along its length and breadth.

Within moments residents lined the shore to view the source of the commotion: the strange biwinged flying boat called the *Daffodil*, with its twin engines, sky-blue camouflage, cannon fore and aft, flowers painted on one side, a fin bomb painted on the other with the motto *Greetings From The Wolliyah!* Such an exotic sight!

From the deck of a steam-powered Nile riverboat, *Le Prince Aleksandar*, moored south of the Nag Hammadi swing bridge, the Honorable Festus Griveaux trained his binoculars on what seemed to him to be a very familiar aircraft landing on the river. He grinned. This is verification of my power, he thought. I have willed that we would meet again! Now it has come to pass! He called out, "Oh, Phloxopha! Come here, dear. Bring Ororotohos. See if the two of you can make it crash!" He pointed at the flying boat skimming across the water.

The fiery-eyed, platinum-haired woman appeared, pulling along a short buxom woman possessing an icy stare, Ororotohos. Phloxopha had been training Ororotohos in techniques of disruption. But it was too late. The flying boat had slowed and turned to motor gently towards the docks.

"Never mind, my dears. Instead, wake up our musketeers,"—Festus had come to enjoy referring to his henchmen as musketeers—"We've got reconnaissance to do!"

He was certain the crew of the flying boat had arrived for the same reason he had made this journey. Word of a possible codex library had spread in select esoteric circles across the globe. Even Stalin had heard about it from his minister of culture, Molotov. Festus chuckled to himself at the thought. He mused: Funny how the Ministry of Culture houses the Soviet Intelligence Service. Molotov has convinced Stalin the secret texts are a key to the occult, which neither of them believe in, yet they are funding me, Festus, to obtain the books! I guess "Comrade Index Card" is a man who leaves nothing to chance. Well, I leave nothing to chance either. I will ambush Stevan, his lovely wife, and the Irishman. They will pay for their escape. I will prosecute them with malice for the attempted bombing of my President's Mansion, for scattering my guests, ruining my gala! I lost funding due to those aerial creatures with their machine guns and bombs and . . . they stole Herak's sword! They used it against poor Phloxopha. She was so dejected after that . . . for days!

The musketeers clambered up on deck. Half of them looked to have been beaten black, blue, and bloody. Festus appraised them and thought, the Egyptian peasants made a mess of my guard on their visit to the book finder, Amon-Ra.

"Musketeers! You need to redeem yourselves." He gave them photographs of their quarry, which the Republic of Suebi staff photographer had taken years ago at the mansion. In gelatin-silver, black-and-white prints, Stevan and Dick appeared disheveled, but Marian looked smashing in her black cocktail dress.

"These aero-jockeys must be captured and brought to me. It should not be difficult. They will look a trifle older, but how can you miss them in this desert town?

"They seek the codex library just as we do. Perhaps they will lead you to the library hiding place, so follow and capture! Be vigilant! I shall remain here. My lieutenants will keep me informed on your progress. Do well, for I will grade your success or failure." Festus liked barking out this last order. Just like Stalin, he decided.

✦ ✦ ✦

Stevan, Dick, and Joko moored the F2A in a back current out of the way of boat traffic. They secured the aeroplane, locked down the armament and fuel as best they could, and took the inflatable dinghy to shore. There, they were greeted by the mayor of Nag Hammadi and met by a delegation appointed to welcome possible investors into the area. Perhaps the visitors were seeking to place orders at the sugar factory. Perhaps they wanted local aluminum ore. Stevan told them that there may well be a need for both products in his home country across the Mediterranean. Upon discovering that Stevan hailed from Montenegro, the mayor asked if he knew King Peter II.

"Yes, he is a friend," Stevan replied, repressing his emotions, "When my English wife died, he found us transport back to her homeland for the funeral. I am most grateful to him."

"We support his cause. He is a very fine young man," the mayor said. "Any friend of his is a friend of ours. You are most welcome to our oasis on the Nile!"

Stevan thanked the mayor and the delegation. He assured them that he would carry any price quotes back with him to the minister of trade.

Dick kept his mouth shut, for once perfectly happy to let Stevan do the talking. Joko, also quiet, glanced here and there—always wary in a foreign land.

The mayor said, "But if you haven't come to buy ore or sugar, what brings you to our bustling town?" He arched his left eyebrow while gazing at Stevan.

Stevan replied, "I am a scholar from Cambridge, specifically, an Egyptologist. These men are my colleagues who assist me on my travels. I am here to catalogue any recent local discoveries of antiquities."

The mayor grinned. He said, "There seems to be quite a few of you fellows visiting this region lately."

At this comment Stevan and Dick exchanged a worried glance. Stevan looked away, took a moment. He considered that Thoth may have arrived in the hamlet ahead of other seekers but not by much; then came the delay to ready the *Daffodil* for flight. Other interests have already caught up, Stevan surmised. And who was likely to be in the hunt? *H* was the hunter and hunted the buck. Festus! *Well,* Stevan thought, remembering Marian's retort, *We will see if we can make him G, the gamester, who had but ill luck.*

After thanking the mayor and the delegation for their hospitality, Stevan smiled, looked around, and said, "We've had a long journey and are a bit famished. Can anyone suggest a good restaurant for brunch?"

The mayor smiled at such a term. "Brunch," he said. "Well, I recommend the Fish Market, very good, very fresh . . . fish right from the boats." He swept his hand towards the feluccas with crews casting nets on the river and said, "I have business to attend to, but please enjoy your . . . brunch! Perhaps we can socialize another time."

The Fish Market, situated on pilings out over the river, proved to be a pleasant place to relax after a flight over sea and desert. From their table, the men could view feluccas sailing on the river as well as the *Daffodil* floating at its mooring. They ordered grilled local fish,

Egyptian style, with spicy tomato, onion, and pepper sauce. They drank fresh mango juice and had bottles of cool water. And they made plans.

Having discovered that Festus and his henchmen likely had been lurking on the shore, Dick became concerned about keeping the F2A secure. It was decided that both Dick and Joko would return to the aeroplane to keep watch, while Stevan remained in town to locate Thoth, though he was not sure how to do it.

Finished, Stevan paid the bill. Dick tossed an absurdly large tip onto the table, which made Joko give a muffled guffaw, and they strolled out onto the wharf. Seagulls eyed them with interest.

As they walked past a piling, Stevan felt a tug on his shirt. He looked down to see large, luminous black eyes gazing up from under a shock of dark hair. A boy of about twelve pulled on him and said, "Come."

Stevan looked at him quizzically.

The boy said, "I Nodi. Come now." The boy turned and took off at a trot.

Stevan shrugged and began to follow, but he called out over his shoulder, "This must be about Thoth. I'll meet you back at the boat." Then he turned and shouted to the boy, "Slow down, son." Stevan didn't want to run; he had decided the large feast of fish would prefer a calm seat in his stomach. The boy vanished around the corner of a narrow alley flanked by mud-brick buildings. "Hey," Stevan barked, "you don't speak English, do you?"

When Stevan finally caught up and turned the corner, a voice answered with heavy accent, "No, but I do." Stevan saw a husky Egyptian step out of an archway, the boy standing next to him.

Wondering what was next, Stevan halted and said, "So?"

"So," the man replied, "do you know any men of letters?"

Good, Stevan thought, it's a test. "I know of one."

The man stepped forward. He had a large knife under his belt. He said, "And?"

"Thoth."

The man gave a trace of a grin. He said, "I am Sharky. You already know my little brother, Nodi. We are friends. I will take you to Thoth."

CODEX III
California, March 1973

Chapter Unus   -1-

Anastasia Romanov

WHEN I FIRST GLANCED at this name of a student enrolled in one of my seminars, I thought, Why would anyone try to pass herself off as a namesake of a lost, most likely murdered, Russian princess? I wondered if it was a misguided attempt at glamour. Therefore, during the first seminar she attended, about twenty months ago, I think, I glanced over the new faces, trying to determine which was Anastasia Romanov's. It took only a moment. A young woman with pale complexion and raven hair sat three chairs down on the left, staring at me with eyes as dark as the depths of the universe, except . . . I looked closer. Was she cross-eyed? No! I thought. It must be a trick of the light. Still observing her, I moved my position to determine the state of her peeps. As I came out from behind my chair, I brought my clipboard and pen. Here's a tip: if you are getting yourself into hot water and can't pull out a cigarette for distraction, because you are not a smoking idiot, have your clipboard and a pen to use for misdirection and bamboozlement. I walked a little to the left of the class to achieve a new angle of light. Why was I pursuing this? Ah, yes, I could see I had been mistaken. She was not strabismic. If she were, it would have made it very difficult for her to work on the codex photographs. I noted she was wearing a dress, something unheard of for our female graduate students, a black-and-white patterned dress with short sleeves and modestly scooped neckline. It complemented her supple figure. Around her neck hung a single pearl on a thin, gold chain. Her left hand rested on her lap, but I could see that in it she held a fresh spring daisy.

Can you see the state of my mind? A spring flower! Until that moment I didn't know spring from an ink well. It was as though Anna Fearina, the Queen of Spring herself, had come to attend my vernal seminar. Thinking this, I felt foolish, so I examined my clipboard. I said, "Anastasia Romanov?"

She broke into a radiant smile. A charming, small gap showed between her front teeth.

"Yes, I am Anastasia Romanov, Professor MacRobbin."

Her English had a slight accent, Eastern European—Slavic, I would have said.

"Er, welcome to the seminar and to the institute."

"Thank you, Professor. I have long been fascinated with the tractates of the Nag Hammadi Library. I hope I can assist in some small way their accurate translation."

By now, my other grad students were eyeing us. Karl, a somewhat abrasive as well as smelly student from Luxembourg, began to smirk in an irritating way he has, that signaled he was about to deliver a remark he thought clever.

He turned to Anastasia and said, "Well, the Romanov princess lives! You've aged so well. So, tell us how you escaped the Bolshevik murderers, we'd all like to hear that one."

She shifted her (rather nice, I'd by now determined) eyes to Karl, staring at him but not speaking. Eventually the poor SOB turned red as a rose. She said, "My father was born in Montenegro, a once-free country that's located in what is now southern Yugoslavia. Romanov is a Slavic name. Like the Russians, we are Slavic people and Anastasia Romanov is a family name that goes back for generations, quite apart from the Russian lineage."

I smiled. I'd never seen Karl so completely, yet politely, put in his place.

The Institute for Antiquity stands on a quiet, tree-lined and shady street on the Claremont Graduate School campus, outside of Los Angeles. The building is not terribly large, but there is a garden in the back from where the breeze wafts through open windows. All in all, it's a rather contemplative, scholarly, pleasant place, an agreeable post from which to direct the English translation of the thirteen leather-bound Gnostic books.

I'll always remember the codices in their original form, before we cut the pages and preserved them between plexiglass. A craftsman had simply tooled the now-tattered covers with a cross or an ankh or a spiral. Inside, the papyrus pages, yellow and cracked with age—indeed, some flaked apart when handled—were inscribed with Coptic writings. That was a surprise! Many scholars would have expected, even hoped for, Greek, the language used for most ascetic Hellenistic literature. Although these works had been originally composed in Greek, this surviving set had been translated into Coptic. Coptic in this regard means Egyptian; the consonants CPT are akin to those in the word *Egyptian*, GPT. Coptic formed the era's Egyptian language, mostly written with the Greek alphabet.

Yes, although many scholars would have preferred Greek texts, the fact that they were Coptic translations was my ticket to ride, because

I am one of the few scholars capable of working in early Coptic, and that happenstance largely contributed to my sudden, ascending star.

The codices, buried in the fourth century near the town of Nag Hammadi, Egypt, survived against all wrath of authority. The Gnostics were besieged in those times. Agents of Bishop Athanasius of Alexandria would have destroyed the library and its scribes, had he found them. In response, the *monks* had learned to live occult lives, giving their knowledge carefully, for there were many who would murder their teachers and burn their works.

Conventional thought on the Gnostics assures us that they were a group of heretics of the early Christian Church, a few crazed, over-heated, underfed monks, or sometimes magicians and their lascivious women. But Anastasia has a different theory about the origin of Gnosticism, and that is the subject of her thesis. The circumstances surrounding the announcement of her thesis idea were quite droll; therefore, I related the incident to my Associate Director, Dr. Mortimer Littlejohn aka Dr. Moe, who has a singular appreciation for the telling of droll incidents.

"Dr. Moe," I said, as I burst through his door without knocking—rude, I suppose, but I always do so. "Where were you Friday night? Anastasia gave an impromptu party following her thesis request."

Dr. Moe was sitting on a window seat in his office, watching a chipmunk attempting to mount a bird feeder in the garden. He raised his wacky eyebrows. In my opinion, they needed barbering.

I continued, "I actually drank too much wine and dozed off under a monstrous, leafy plant in her greenhouse. Anastasia is not a graduate student who is starving in a garret. In fact, she has some intriguing things, antique chests, Dodson's coaching prints, Tiffany wine buckets. There is a rather nice seating arrangement in the greenhouse, so that Anastasia and I and Byah" (our executive secretary) "and Dr. Como" (teaches at the School of Theology at Claremont) "sat in a foursome.

But the last thing I remember, before waking up in a reclining chair to find a four-point Hudson's Bay blanket covering me, was Como waxing at length about the scroll, *Pesher Habakkuk*."

"I know of it," Dr. Moe replied noncommittally, lumbering across the room to the coffee pot. "May I offer you a cup? Drunkards require a gang of coffee in the morning, as Old Blue Eyes, Frank, likes to put it."

Though Dr. Moe is African American, he enjoys using his one musical reference, Sinatra, whenever he can. He thinks it makes him hip. Those who are aware of his admiration for Sinatra tend to wonder why he doesn't prefer Sammy Davis Jr., but you can't put Dr. Moe in a box. I said, "Yes, pour me a cup. Now, what perpetrated this impromptu bash is the following. Friday, as perhaps you know, was midsummer's day. In celebration, Anastasia had picked an array of delicate flowers, woven a garland for her neck and worn it to the biweekly seminar where the translation team presents the buds of their progress on the texts. She has the ability to get away with that kind of singularity, flowers adorning her throat, like a pagan priestess. After offering up her translation of *The Thunder Perfect Mind*, a rather fine, poetic translation, I might add, she requested the subject of her PhD dissertation: to argue that Gnosticism was, in one of its aspects, an effort to unite the Goddess religion with the God religion."

Was this an appropriate place for her to discuss her proposed dissertation? Of course! We are a liberal academic enclave. Dr. Moe handed me a cup of coffee. It was actually a teacup, some kind of bone china from Harrods. He couldn't repress a sort of delighted look at the description of Anastasia's proposal. Usually, his expression is noncommittal over such things.

"I was a bit shocked, as was everyone else, so I leaned back, tossed my pencil on our old, oak, leather-topped conference table, looked up and down at the graduate students and professors sitting with their eyeglasses on their noses or tossed on the table before them amongst scribbled notes, translation drafts, and tumblers of water, looked at their faces, some horrified, some amused, but all staring at Anastasia.

"I finally replied, 'But Anastasia, the Goddess religions had become aberrated by the time of the Abrahamic religions, although, its deities were often appropriated, renamed, and canonized into the patriarchal hierarchy.'

"She answered, 'I believe I can demonstrate the existence of a widely disseminated Goddess religion in the age you've mentioned. I will argue the Gnostics attempted to interpolate some of the old ideas into the canon of the prevailing religions. For example: some branches of Gnosticism taught that the spiritual and the sensual worlds are not hopelessly severed from one another. I will explain how Wisdom came to be combined in Gnostic thought with the Goddess "encompassing the whole scale from the highest to the lowest, from the most spiritual to the utterly sensual," as Jonas said . . .'

"I heard someone whisper 'sensual' none too softly, forcing me to clear my throat and glare around the table, where all eyes looked down at fingers or notes.

"'As expressed,' she continued, 'in the Gnostic combination *Sophia-Prunikos*, Wisdom the Whore.'

"At that point poor old Partridge knocked over his water glass." This information delighted Dr. Moe, who broke into a rather toothy grin; he hates Partridge.

"The contents streamed across the table, soaking notes of colleagues on the opposite side so that they accused old Partridge of getting excited. Meanwhile, Karl was hopping about holding up dripping notes while brushing water from his cavernous pants, if you can picture that, and complaining in that annoying voice of his, 'Anastasia! Do ya always have to disrupt dese meetings? Look at—'

"But Anastasia rolled right over him, continuing, 'In the Goddess religion, the priestess revealed the wisdom of the Great Mother. Part of that wisdom was knowledge of creation. That they gave the knowledge in an "utterly sensual" manner enraged the Levites, and others, who, in turn, called them whores. So,'—and here Anastasia looked around the table, but believe me, everyone was paying attention,—'this behavior can be traced all the way back to the Sumerians, if you recall to mind the *Gilgamesh Epic.*'

"'What do you mean?' demanded Professor Partridge.

"'I refer to Gilgamesh's friend Enkidu who was civilized through an encounter with a so-called prostitute.'

"At that point chairs creaked as the occupants shifted, and poor old Partridge waxed crimson.

"Anastasia continued, 'Attitude was all important. The priestesses made love to the initiates who had no thought of dominance or power. Instead, through gentleness and trust, the priestess and the initiate learned what creation is: reaching out, combining opposites, touching, going beyond language, connecting body, mind, and soul in innocence, shedding labels, so that all being feels life anew: Joy! Responsibility to live! The corrival cultures reduced such knowledge to an object of ridicule. But the Gnostics knew what had happened. *The Wisdom of the Whore* became a rallying phrase in Gnosticism, just as the insult *Yankee Doodle* became a term of defiance and pride for Americans during the revolution.'"

Picking it right up, as he does, Dr. Moe observed, "So, Anastasia suggested the Gnostics wished to teach this knowledge to the prevailing patriarchal hegemony."

I nodded. I said, "I'm telling you, Dr. Moe, it was a heated dissertation proposal. Anastasia salvaged the situation by inviting us all, especially Partridge, and even Karl, to her house that evening. Do you know, everyone accepted? She met us at the door with glasses of tasty wine that she said was from Montenegro, then waltzed us around the house and greenhouse, proudly showing off all manner of plants while talking about xylem and phloem and root systems and mites and such. She served grilled Northwest salmon for dinner, a delicious rice dish, and fresh, wild asparagus."

I detected a bit of snark when Dr. Moe commented, "It was all quite marvelous." Then, he asked, "And what did you have for dessert?"

I said, "Ah, poor Dr. Moe—living vicariously through me! One of the students had brought a plate of brownies."

"And you ate one?"

"The chocolate was quite good. I had two. I should have saved you one."

"You, Dr. MacRobbin, failed to read the memo I sent around to the staff, the one that warned not to eat from plates of student confections. And that is why you embarrassed yourself by falling asleep at a party. Clearly, the brownies were what they refer to as *magic brownies*. Mix that with wine, and a tired professor . . ."

"Hmm."

"So, you spent the night in a recliner. I bet the grads got a hearty laugh out of that! Who covered you with the four-point Hudson's Bay blanket?"

"It seemed like Anastasia's touch, but I don't know for sure since I was awakened by birds chirping just before dawn, and, except for a few grad students slumped on the couch, everyone had left. Anastasia had gone off to bed."

"You say that wistfully."

In reply, I grunted at Dr. Moe and turned toward the door. I'd had enough of this conversation. I left Dr. Moe with his chipmunk and returned to my office to get back to work.

So, rather than muse over brownies, tired professors (well, me), leather recliners, infatuations, Anastasia, etc., I tried to think of things, pressing things, like funding for example. There is no metaphysical defense against love, but if you get deeply enough into the funding problem—a concrete, down-to-earth conundrum such as who is going to pay the bills—your attention shifts for a time, so that perhaps love becomes distrait and goes elsewhere.

Our seed money comes from the Claremont Graduate School and the School of Theology at Claremont. However, those monies are not deep; they only buy the paper clips and the magnifying glasses, and perhaps Dr. Moe's rather nice bone china tea set. The real support is provided by private contributions and grants. Sometimes, along with the contributions come certain requests from the donors that, if within reason, we try to accommodate.

Once, as a favor, we invited to one of the digs at Faw Qibli a certain benefactor and his quite fetching mistress, Naomi. She soon became extremely popular with the male archaeologists and the diggers, the latter who had never seen anything quite like her. Before becoming the mistress of the benefactor (I won't name him) she had achieved minor fame as a stage actress. Out at the digs, perfectly in character, she would put on one-woman shows in the evening just to amuse herself, not to mention everyone else. It happened that word of the racy extravaganzas reached a newspaperman at Nag Hammadi, who, with a photographer, arrived on a sultry evening to get the story. The benefactor blanched at the idea of publicity because he was married, but Naomi decided such publicity, if it hit the Western magazines, would revive her sagging stage career, and so fanned the flames by exploiting both the benefactor and the male staff at the digs, putting them at odds, causing a general ruckus. The benefactor shortly abandoned her through dark of night, but already she had wound the newspaperman and photographer around her little finger, as they say. Within two weeks a lot of rude publicity hit the media. It eventually cost the benefactor a nasty divorce settlement; however, Naomi returned to the London stage in triumph.

We were willing, mostly, to suffer such lucrative funding activities if it meant the walls of scholarship would, for the nonce, delay tumbling down around our ears. But that was before we had discovered that suffering could rend as deeply as the pungent Karl.

Chapter Duo   -2-

T HE FOISTING OF KARL upon our academic enclave was my fault. It happened because of the persistence of a well-heeled European spiritual society that had been following the Institute's work on "the heretical books which evaded the burning of the library at Alexandria," as their undersecretary, weirdly named Roto, put it upon telephoning me on my private line one day in the depth of the winter. How she got the number I don't know, but I have my suspicions, which will become obvious in a moment. The under-secretary went on to explain that our work was valuable to them; yet she wouldn't elaborate other than mentioning their leader's appetite for collecting or at least learning the contents of "secret books." They were willing to contribute a large sum of money to the Institute, but there would be "certain favors" asked in return.

The woman's voice resonated with a most odd timbre. Furthermore, she was using my private line. I got my back up and I informed the undersecretary of this society, the Honorable Order of the Suebi, that I wished to know the name of their leader, because I intended to chastise him and his group for this insulting phone call. The undersecretary rudely replied that their leader's name would be revealed only when we had come to a mutual arrangement.

I hung up on her. I wanted nothing to do with the society or its money. I can't exactly say why, as it was a subjective decision. But I kept hanging up, or I was in conference, or I was gone to Egypt. They were irritatingly persistent. In time, economic realities weighed upon my shoulders. There were many worthy projects waiting to be funded, projects on the history of religion in the ancient Near East, the classical world of Greece and Rome in late antiquity, and the early biblical world. I had professors and graduate students clawing over each other to get at the golden goose. And so, one ill-begotten day when the secretary, weirdly named Loxo, as opposed to the undersecretary, Roto, called, I consented to speak to her. I trusted her voice would be less grating than that of her colleague.

The upshot of the call concerned a graduate student here at the School of Theology at Claremont, none other than good old Karl. I began to recall, as the secretary babbled on, that Karl had already applied to and been rejected by the Institute, I think solely on grounds that he stank horridly, both Dr. Moe and I had agreed. However, in consideration for a large grant from the Honorable Order of the Suebi, would I reconsider Karl's application to the Institute?

Apparently, Karl from Luxembourg was one of the society's would-be scholars. He had first attempted to infiltrate the Institute like a spy, not revealing his intentions or affiliations, if you can imagine such a thing. After all, we are not discussing nuclear triggers. I am not James Bond. This isn't HQ. But there have been difficulties, which I will elaborate upon later. I thought under the circumstances it might be advantageous to keep an eye on Karl, because he must be up to something. The best way to keep him in view was to take the funding from the Suebi Society and admit the smelly boy to the Institute as a member of the translation team on the Coptic Gnostic project. After all, to his credit, he was somewhat qualified in that ancient Coptic language.

That's how we became stuck with him. As I've noted, a peculiar odor always engulfed him, a unique fetor, which permeated his clothes and even lingered on the chairs he had occupied. I discussed it one day with Anastasia. We were huddled at the conference table, over a piecemeal tractate, when Karl burst in, fuming around us for a few minutes both literally and figuratively.

His accent invariably became heavy when he was agitated. He shouted, "Der fools! Sie use der black background! How ken vee reconstruct lacunae mit der black background?"

The translation team had been pouring over papyrus pages in an attempt to reconstruct *lacunae*—missing pieces. Actually, we had been working from photographs of pages, as the originals were kept locked in the Coptic Museum in Cairo. The problem is that it is difficult to reconstruct *lacunae* in the ancient pages while working from photographs with black backgrounds, because the dark letters blend in, and you can't tell what is a hole and what is a letter. The pages were photographed by the U.N. agency, UNESCO, against which Karl now railed with impertinent outburst. It's true that UNESCO had performed amateurish work, but I disliked agreeing with Karl, and so rebuked him harshly. Furthermore, it was crucial that I stifle any hint of dissension. There had been obstacles, and, indeed, mysterious deaths, that hindered translation of the Nag Hammadi manuscripts for more than twenty-five years after their discovery in 1945. The infighting among metaphysical professors with reputations to advance, combined with a tight wrap of government red tape in Egypt, had also proved to be a bothersome barrier.

In addition, it has been said that during the time of the library's unearthing, several codices (the technical word for books of bound papyrus) were smuggled from Faw Qibli via a World War I biwinged flying boat amidst bursts of machine-gun fire; however, that assertion has never been confirmed through the discipline of serious academic rigor. We know for certain a single codex was smuggled from the Nile basin, but the man who possessed it disappeared—rumor hinting of mysterious death, and the manuscript sank, perhaps into the clutches of a private collector.

A few sensational journalists suggested the unfortunate events stemmed from the Gnostic malediction, the so-called "Jesus Curse," inscribed near the end of one of the codices, the Apocryphon of John, in which Jesus says that anyone who would reveal his teachings in exchange for payments or gifts would be cursed.

Who am I to discount a malediction? After all, we've been cursed with Karl. After I had sent Karl away, I got up and opened five windows to get a gale blowing in the conference room.

Well, I suppose there's no need to go on about the superficial drawbacks of the clownish Karl, because I could have put up with his odors, his annoying proclivities. Rather, it was his affiliation with the Honorable Order of the Suebi that I found intolerable. I had discovered through a few well-placed phone calls, that international police had implicated "THOOTS" seven times in theft cases concerning priceless antiquities from the Near East; however, no convictions had resulted. My Interpol contact further informed me that the head of the Order, Festus Griveaux, had in the early 1940s attempted to establish a Luxembourg-size Grand Duchy on the coast of northern Portugal for the purpose of catering to the autocratic countries of the world, with gaming, private banking, purchased citizenship, etc., but when Portugal joined NATO in 1949, Festus and his elaborate plans were given the boot.

Clearly, the Honorable Order of the Suebi was unsavory. That I ought to have run a background check on it before jamming full our pockets with its possibly tainted money was an observation of useless hindsight, because I had already earmarked for research half the funds THOOTS had given us. I couldn't return the "gift" without bringing my own judgment into question. You see, I was still quite ambitious, and I didn't want to jeopardize my position for a questionable point of ethics.

Chapter Tres   -3-

Though I wrestled with this difficult ethical question concerning money, somehow Love did not become bored, take a boat to Santa Catalina, lounge on a surfside boardwalk, drink rum and coke, tan its legs . . . no.

Anastasia! She would knock on my office door and say, "Dr. MacRobbin, may I ask you three questions about tractate so and so?" It was as though she had just come from a refreshing shower; her thick, black hair smelled like an ocean breeze, her pale arms leaned on my desk as we bent over the translation; I couldn't think, but only listen, rapt, to her intelligent conversation, and I would wordlessly agree with her excellent insights.

I know anyone reading this would think that I was in pathetic form, a lovesick puppy, or a driveling schoolboy, and, so much for my previous years of propriety concerning grad students. So be it, but I didn't realize the shape I was in until one afternoon, just like many afternoons, with Anastasia leaning over my desk, her hair a tumble, the air around her smelling of flowers and ocean mist, and I said, "Anastasia, I must tell you that I—"

I was going to confess adoration, but I caught myself and stopped in midsentence. She peered at me, searching with those universe eyes (don't say *Oh, brother*, because if only you'd seen those eyes, you would know the depth I plumbed), but instead I said, "I, I'm in a most difficult, ethical fix. I wonder . . . if . . . wouldn't you give me your advice." Then I told her about the dilemma with the Honorable Order of the Suebi.

When, on the following afternoon, I related this information to Dr. Moe, my most trustworthy confidante, he gagged. Yes, I already knew I had committed a faux pas beyond all reason; thus, I could do without Dr. Moe's gurgling apoplexy, but still he chose to play the scene until I brought the curtain down in the form of a decanter of Powers Irish Whiskey. I offered him a short tumbler.

"A professor does not ask the advice of one of his twenty-five-year-old FEMALE graduate students," Dr. Moe persisted, having found his voice with a chug of whiskey. "No, no, no, no, no and Institute directors do not blab to such persons about INSTITUTE MONEY MATTERS!"

"Moe!" I cried, overlooking the sexism of his observation. "She's twenty-nine" (I'd looked it up in the records—she's really twenty-eight, close enough), "and this is love!"

"This," replied Dr. Moe, grabbing the Powers and pouring himself another short—a third full—in order to cast a theatrical toast at me, "This was a man!" He quoted from *Julius Caesar*, but with irony, I think. He drained his glass again.

"Fine. OK. Fine, Moe, but you see, there's more to this story than love. Oh yes. Because when I mentioned to Anastasia the Honorable Order of the Suebi, she turned *a shade of pale*, sort of like the song..."

"What song? What are you talking about?" Moe replied, irritated. He's so much older than me, he fails to catch musical references from the sixties. For him, it's Sinatra or nothing.

"She's aware of the Order of Suebi. She says the Suebi inner circle and what she referred to as 'her clan' have been bitter enemies for generations. Do you remember the rumor about codices being smuggled from Egypt in late 1945 or early 1946? Smuggled via a World War I flying boat? She claims her father flew that aircraft."

"Oh, good God," responded Dr. Moe, slumping into a leather wing chair. "Oh bejezus, you see what becomes of this? One of our prize graduate students is breaking under the strain of your attentions. She's having a nervous breakdown, inventing stories because she's under a crazed delusion such tales will impress you."

"They do impress me. I believe her. She took me to her house to show me a cablegram sent in 1946 from a man named Thoth in Nag Hammadi to her father in Montenegro. I saw it yesterday. As I held the fragile paper in my hands, Anastasia began to quietly weep. Well, that hammered me into the ground a few paces, the sight of this poised woman, this cool-under-fire Anastasia suddenly grieving in front of me, and like you, I considered she was, perhaps, in the midst of a nervous breakdown. Then she whispered, 'Thoth gave this to me a year ago when he told me the truth about my parents, about their deaths, how they were murdered by the people of the Suebi Order.'

"That was the cause of her sudden sadness. The cablegram had acted as a memory cue for her, bringing a mass of burdensome associations to the surface. She paused and sighed so plaintively that I reached out and held her hand. She continued in a flood of words, 'He may as well have opened a moldering trunk, and under the decaying clothes and chipped china, the blackening hand mirror from Sarajevo, the photograph of unrecognizable children, found letters stuffed inside a crane bag, each faded letter rewriting my history, so that memory is bogus, self-image suspect, and my parents, if they ever lived at all, are of a dream.'

"You see, Dr. Moe? She wasn't cracking from academic pressure or from the clatter of my beating heart . . . It's just that she'd discovered only a year ago that her parents had not died in the war, they had been murdered, and the Honorable Order of the Suebi, the THOOTS as I am starting to call them, was somehow involved in their deaths. So, when I let it spill that THOOTS, (or the THOOTSTERS?) are zeroing in on the Institute, she had good reason to be upset."

Moe grunted like a goat, which I took to be agreement, so I continued my narration.

"'Anastasia,' I said softly, 'what is it that you fear?'

'I asked him,' Anastasia replied, 'What is a child of a dream, Thoth? Another dream? There is a killer, Thoth told me, he said, Anastasia, there is a killer who wants your blood, just as he managed to kill your parents in the end. All that can help you is the myth, the story. Find where the ancestors gathered around the fire to speak their knowledge.'"

As I've said, one of the things I admire about Dr. Moe is that he's quick on the uptake. There are professors who couldn't find their way through Anastasia's story with a sealed beam headlight and a guide map. But Dr. Moe reached the other side in short order by noticing key words and following them as Nimrod followed blazes in the forest.

"That is an appalling yet electrifying story," Dr. Moe mused. "When a Southern European, even one a generation removed, speaks of clans, dreams, myths, ancestors, fire, and knowledge, there's a good chance he, or in this case, she, speaks of Gnosticism."

"Exactly my thoughts, Dr. Moe, as you shall see if you permit me to think aloud for a moment. Gnosticism certainly took root in Europe. Though it sprang up in the Near East, it spread along the Mediterranean coast, through Turkey and Greece and into what is now Yugoslavia."

"Right," muttered Dr. Moe, who had decided that I shouldn't face alone the task of thinking aloud, and so he cleared his throat to continue distinctly, "and even into France. The Bogomils and the Cathari were the two big movements, but there were a lot of little groups that didn't agree with anyone."

"Exactly," I said again, trying to assure Dr. Moe that we were thinking along the same lines. "Gnosticism was not a unified religion, like Christianity, but rather, it took different forms, espoused varying ideas. Yet it did have one unifying factor: it was a myth-laden mystery handed down through tales, spoken prose and poetry, from generation to generation. The precise content of a Gnostic's tale was less important that the manner in which it was composed and told. In a way, the Gnostics predated Marshall McLuhan by a few thousand years, in that their medium was their message. This technique of method was achieved through various mystical practices, sometimes ascetic, sometimes quite the opposite."

Dr. Moe refused to allow me to have all of this. He added, and quite rightly, "And what were those practices? Well, here's one I came across the other day in my research. The Gnostics avowed that anyone born of Eve had the right of direct knowledge of the divine, because, they said, the kingdom of God is here on earth, within each of us. They had a funny way to muse on this—"

And Dr. Moe chuckled because he was about to announce a word game. These things amuse him. I think he would have found the Oedipean Sphinx great company for a Sunday brunch in the faculty lounge. The two of them could have taken turns posing riddles, and then gnashed tooth when the other failed to solve.

"They would contemplate a statement such as: 'That which you have will save you if you bring it forth from yourselves. That which you do not have within you will kill you if you do not have it within you.'"

I threw my hands into the air. After all, aphorisms like that, if aphorisms is the word I want, can drive you up a wall, much less give you direct knowledge of the divine. I brought the conversation back down to earth by asserting, "Also, as we've seen, there were apocrypha (secret books) written down and hidden. They were filled with philosophic discussions of the origins of the universe, and the myths, magic, and mystical practices such as we have in the Coptic Gnostic Library."

Since Dr. Moe refrained from butting in at this juncture, I felt ready to form my preamble to the-coming-to-the-point of this . . . recapitulation of Gnostic culture. I said, "The Gnostics' freewheeling approach made them unpredictable to the authorities of the time. Those who are unpredictable are dangerous, aren't they, Dr. Moe? Therefore, the ruling powers assailed the Gnostics, driving them underground into loosely organized, secret clans. These clans have continued to exist over the centuries, unknown, except to a few poets and writers who occasionally impart such knowledge in their works. Wordsworth, for example, immortalized the Gnostic lament, 'The world is too much with us; late and soon, Getting and spending, we lay waste our powers.'"

This mention of *laying waste our powers* struck a deep chord within Dr. Moe. He began foraging in the cabinet for the Powers Whiskey. Upon being unable to discover the decanter (I'd hidden it by sleight of hand), he turned and said that we'd just given a fine thumbnail analysis of Gnosticism, but what the heck was I driving at anyway, and where's the blasted Powers?

"What am I driving at?" I repeated, booming like a stage actor. "I think that it was from one of these clans that Anastasia's parents sprang. Further, I think the Honorable Order of the Suebi is a society dedicated to destroying such clans."

I find it most effective to bring my colleague up short every now and again. It discourages him from dozing off in my presence. I'm not saying that I didn't actually believe my theory, which was spawned by what Anastasia had told me about the bloody actions of the

THOOTSTERS (OK, not her word, mine), but I would have had to admit there was no proof for her assertion. Officially, the THOOTS had been implicated in theft, but it is one thing to spirit away antiquities from the world market or from their official curators in order to make a big financial score, or even for the purpose of locking said treasures into a vault to privately drool over on occasion, but it is quite another thing to spawn a foul, murderous conspiracy.

I know what you are thinking: that we were going about this in an awfully deliberate, academic manner. After all, a girl, a beautiful, intelligent, highly cultured, intriguing, fascinating young woman, Anastasia, for whom, incidentally, I felt tenderness beyond rationality (I mean, we had hardly been intimate, although I had once slept under a monstrous leafy plant in her greenhouse), who possessed a mysterious background that both gave her strength and left her vulnerable, needed help, serious assistance, because, for God's sake, there were (might have been) murderers after her, and alas, we, Dr. Moe and I, sat chatting in my office, drinking large gulps of the best (cheap!) Irish Whiskey.

I imagine that had we been Sam Spade, or Mike Hammer, or Bogie himself, we would have: A) hauled Karl into the office and asked him outright what the hell he thought he was doing here and slapped him around the room a little bit and told him that we were on to his grubby little Society and that if anything happened to Anastasia we would personally dip his stinky torso into a vat of Chanel No. 5 head first and not remove him until the following April for a spring planting as a geranium, and B) flown to Europe without jet lag, found the hidden leader, this Festus, of THOOTS, in other words the head THOOTSTER, bounced him around hither and thither, then turned him over to the international police along with an air-tight case for the murder of Anastasia's parents.

However, the fact is we are not Sam Spade, but Men of Academe, the net result being that we have our own way of doing things, and though our methods may be less direct than Bogie's, nevertheless, they are, in the end, completely effective, I assure you.

At this point Dr. Moe and I agreed that we should meet with Anastasia, put all our cards on the table, encouraging her to do the same, and see where we stood. Evidence of her assertions would be most welcome, but we doubted she could provide any. Yet I still believed her tale, because she is not someone I could disbelieve. Does that make sense? If she lacked the evidence to convince the police to help her, no matter. We had a plan.

I asked our executive secretary, Byah, to call Anastasia at once for a 6:00 P.M. meeting, giving her about an hour and fifteen minutes to finish up whatever she was involved with. There was a good chance Dr. Moe and I would be sloshed by then if we kept laying waste our Powers, and so I chased Dr. Moe back to his research. Meanwhile, I sifted through notebooks of Jean and Marianne Doresse, the French scholars, who, in 1947, were the first Europeans to publish reports of the Nag Hammadi discovery. I was looking for mention of the smuggling incident that involved the World War I flying boat, purportedly commanded by Anastasia's father, but I had no luck.

Chapter Quattuor   -4-

BEFORE I KNEW IT, six o'clock had clattered down on me. That's how it is when you are involved with books—asleep to the banal ticking of clock and the trite braying of schedule. It was a euphonious knock on the door that wakened me from my research; assuredly, this wasn't the mundane that had come calling. Quite the opposite, this was Anastasia. I became somewhat nonplussed after she walked through the door, because she was wearing a Lycra cycling outfit such as the Olympic competitors wear, an outfit that looked as though it had been sprayed on by an airbrush. One look confirmed that my imagination had been completely correct about her lithe figure, for, indeed, she was a feminine yet athletic girl. As she pulled her hair aside, I could see perspiration beading the nape of her neck.

"Excuse my attire, Professor MacRobbin—"

"Call me Griffin."

She smiled that gap-toothed smile, making me feel more transparent than she was. "Griffin. I had been out for a ride and had cycled past the Institute when I heard Byah shouting my name. So, she'd been trying to reach me this afternoon by telephone—"

"Oh, yes," I affirmed, "Well, I thought it important to address this problem concerning the THOOTS."

She wrinkled her brow and said, "The—"

"Oh, that's what I am calling that ridiculous society now, the Honorable Order of the Suebi. But I don't mean to make light of it. Dr. Moe and I have discussed it and have developed a plan. Since the plan involves you, I thought you might like to hear it . . . but I do apologize for giving you such short notice."

As I spoke, her expression became serious. She sank into the leather wing chair so recently occupied by Dr. Moe. "You mean to help me?"

"Well, certainly! That's why you're here, isn't it? Or did you end up working on the Coptic Gnostic project by accident?" I mean, it was obvious to me that she had come to the Institute to reach out for help, an intellectual attempt, perhaps, but even so, she was seeking those of like mind, like interests, because she had an inexorable link to the Nag Hammadi Library, and that association portended danger for her.

"It's no accident."

"I thought not." I rang for Dr. Moe. No point in him missing this. Moe lumbered in at once; he must have been waiting with bated breath. How a man five foot six, weighing a hundred and thirty pounds, can lumber is a puzzle to me, but Dr. Moe Littlejohn achieves it. The only reaction he had to Anastasia's Lycra cycling suit was a slight elevation of his wacky eyebrows.

"Dr. Moe," I said by way of greeting, "Anastasia was just telling me that joining the Institute had been her ambition for a long time."

"Oh, was it because your family, or I think you said your clan, has a connection with the Nag Hammadi Library?" Dr. Moe questioned, getting right to the point.

"It's true."

Dr. Moe continued, "You've made a serious accusation against the Honorable Order of the Suebi. Have you proof that any of its members conspired to commit murder?"

Anastasia's cheeks and throat turned slightly red. "You don't understand," she whispered.

Dr. Moe and I exchanged a glance. I said, "No, Dr. Moe, you don't understand. That murder took place in . . . " I turned to Anastasia.

"In Montenegro, 1945, my mother, while giving birth to me, died of a wound inflicted by the one who commands the Suebi Order. In 1946, the same hand killed my father in Cairo at the original Persian Fortress. But there is no proof now,"—she sighed—"my parents are long gone. But if you heard their story, it might make a difference to you."

"Indeed, it might, Anastasia," Dr. Moe agreed.

I interrupted. "Look, Anastasia, I must ask you about the texts that your father took. Where are they now? Why hasn't your clan turned them over to the Coptic Museum? Wouldn't that assuage the Order of the Suebi?"

She hugged her arms and shivered, a slight tremor, causing me to recall that earlier I'd hung a cashmere sweater on the back of my desk chair. I offered it to her. Perhaps my questions had brought on the shiver, but I don't think so, because the late sun beamed at a low angle in the sky, and a breeze fanned the office, cooling it nicely.

She pulled the sweater over her head and replied, "The Coptic Museum could not protect the texts from the Suebi Order. Magical and mystical wonders are written down in them, and we can't allow the Suebi to have access to such writings. It would be dangerous. Also, the texts mention the existence of a Gnostic treasure, which I will never allow to fall under the shadow of the Suebi Order!"

This answer struck me as defiant and somewhat fanatical. I glanced again at Dr. Moe. What did we have here in Anastasia? Was she mad? An immensely gifted yet mad individual haunting our halls of learning? But what was this treasure she had mentioned? What were the magical writings that could be dangerous? You understand, I had experienced just enough of the hidden world, what with my esoteric theories, which had been proven in skiing competition, that I thought perhaps something new was presenting itself to me, the next step . . .

"Our plan, Anastasia," I confided, "involves recovering your father's hidden codices. I admit that there is a risk, because we would be exposing the books to the THOOTSTERS, but that is the point. We intend to use the codices to flush them out, to tempt their ill will."

Anastasia shook her head. "You don't comprehend the amount of power the Suebi Order wields, especially on the Continent. This plan would be extremely dangerous. They are like . . . the mafia, a kind of spiritual mafia."

Dr. Moe replied, "We have friends all over the world, Anastasia, those of intellect who recognize the contribution Dr. MacRobbin and the Institute have made to the world of scholarship. It is no secret that until Griffin MacRobbin came along, various scrolls, codices, and tablets lay unpublished for years because scholars couldn't decide who would get credit for what. Then Dr. MacRobbin said that he would publish the Gnostic texts in clear photographic reproductions so that scholars could make their own translations and publish their own interpretations. That got everyone's attention! It was a breath of fresh air in the dusty vaults of academe. When the first volumes of photographic reproductions were published last spring, a new standard was set for dealing with ancient writings."

"Yes," Anastasia agreed, "I know. I have long admired Dr. MacRobbin's work, as I've often said, and he is the reason I came here. But I don't wish to involve him or the Institute in such a dangerous course."

She admired me! She was here solely because of me! I could have died right there in my swivel desk chair and been reasonably happy.

Except that, for all appearances, it was but a Platonic admiration that she felt "for my work." No. I couldn't die yet. Not before discovering if our relationship could blossom.

I said, "Anastasia, I don't see that there is much choice. The police won't help you. Your clan doesn't seem to be able to protect you. The THOOTS henchmen know where you are. Furthermore, I'll wager the Society has been searching for your father's texts since 1947, and must, by now, be getting close."

Dr. Moe added, "I would point out that we are not doing this just for you. There are other motives. For example, if you could lead us to the hiding place of the Gnostic apocrypha, and we could salvage them, it would bring further renown to the Institute, and personally to Dr. MacRobbin and myself."

Anastasia's face clouded; suddenly she was angry. "I have told you that the Suebi must never see the tractates of magic and mysticism in those books! I will not allow them to be published!"

I felt that Dr. Moe's blunt approach had been crass, though typical of him. I let it go because I did want Anastasia to understand all our motives. In fact, I added, "While these codices may be great treasures of your clan, they also belong to the world at large. What will be their fate if we don't salvage them? The hoarding of these books only shrouds our human history. With such an attitude from scholars, other discoveries may never see the light of day! Isn't there a compromise we can reach?"

While I presented my side of the argument, Anastasia gazed openly at me. This was followed by a wan smile and the acknowledgment, "The two of you make a persuasive team." She said this and then became silent.

When a person becomes silent: Audible: just a susurration of breath; visible: the slight rise and fall of their chest under a cashmere sweater, their strange dark-green eyes looking but not seeing the credulous fools sitting opposite, but instead looking inward, and, as her face turns upward toward the ceiling—seeing what? A vast cavern? Great limestone pillars overlaid with cone shapes and long tubers that look as though they form a root system for a tangled ice forest above? Between the pillars arch the cavern ceilings, and even the furthest recesses sparkle diamond eyes! Yes! That must be it, I thought for some unknown reason, but that's what entered my head! Next time I'll sit on my hands.

She seemed to come back, as if climbing up from a cave, I decided, and leveled her gaze at Dr. Moe and me. She said, "So, I will make a bargain with you. You must grant me the final say on what can be published and what cannot from my father's small collection. I will not permit certain magical passages to be revealed, nor the description of the Gnostic treasure's hiding place. If necessary, I will destroy the relevant tractates. If you can agree to this, then I throw my lot in with you."

It can be an exquisite feeling, when after negotiations, human beings reach common ground. I stood up beaming, Dr. Moe and Anastasia followed. I walked around the desk, still beaming, and gave Anastasia a hug, whereas she returned the hug harder, so that I followed with a really good third hug, because I had never felt anything better, and Dr. Moe had to clear his throat to get us on another track.

I said, "For now, the only members of the Institute who will know of these plans will be the three of us."

"Loose lips sink ships," agreed Dr. Moe.

"The first step," Anastasia said, "will be to fly to New York to find Thoth, so that you can hear the story that he told me. The true story of my father's codices."

"Well, who is this Thoth?" Dr. Moe questioned.

She looked at me and then Dr. Moe with her immutable dark-green eyes. "Olympia Thoth was a great friend of my grandparents, Lazo and Yasoda, and of the philosopher, Herak—"

I interrupted, "Herak? The Montenegrin Gnostic?"

A smile flickered across Anastasia's face.

I said, "He taught at the university in Constantinople in the early nineteen hundreds."

Anastasia observed, "Do you just always know everything, Dr. MacRobbin?"

Why does she put me off my game? Because she's good at it? I get all shy and flummoxed for a trice, a nonce, a tiny, little span of time, yes, but then I recover in a flash! I replied, "Maybe."

Dr. Moe, the impertinent professor, looked at me and guffawed at the same time. I was shocked! I didn't think he could do two things at once. No more of my whiskey breaks for him! I said, "Well, how old is this Olympia Thoth? I mean, his pal Herak, had a professorship prior to the First World War."

Anastasia replied, "I . . ."—oddly, she hesitated as if she were considering what she would say next—"have no idea. He always looks the same to me, every time I see him. He spent time with me throughout childhood and beyond, overseeing my education, and it helps to explain why I am so good with languages, ancient and contemporary. He is a master of language, science, and magic."

At that last comment, I exchanged a glance with the impertinent Dr. Moe. Magic. I wondered if she uses the creepy spelling, *magick*, but then I regretted wondering it, because I haven't gotten where I am by being a closed-minded oaf. Dr. Moe raised his eyebrows as if to say, "See, she might be nuts."

Well, I . . . I know there are more wonders between heaven and earth than hath been dreamt of in your narrow philosophy, et cetera, et cetera, et cetera . . .

Chapter Quinque   -5-

WHOEVER SPECULATED THAT EYES are a mirror of the soul wasn't concerned with what he was letting *me* in for, because if that statement carries a modicum of truth, then Anastasia's soul is as deep and dark as her captivating eyes, and it follows to ask on many levels: Whom am I involved with?

I suggested, "It's a balmy evening. I feel like a walk. I'll walk you home, Anastasia."

"I would like that . . . Griffin."

Earlier, when she had arrived at the Institute, Anastasia had wheeled her bike into the reception room, where she had slung a down-turned handlebar over a table, using a copy of the journal *Symposia* as a buffer to scratches. Now she carefully retrieved the elegant machine, reared it up on its back wheel and rolled it forward through doorways and out into the calm night. It was a deep-red, hand-built Aero De Rosa, an Italian bicycle constructed from Columbus SL tubing, a strong but lightweight alloy steel. I'm sure the whole thing, including the top-of-the-line Campagnolo Nuovo-Record drilled-out components weighed no more than nineteen pounds. In California, the bike costs about two thousand dollars.

"Did you ever race?" I asked as I followed her down the steps.

"No, I just ride for the sheer joy of it. But this is a road racing bike. A friend in Italy sent it to me about a year ago."

"That's lucky. They're expensive little devils over here. I have a Mercian." A Mercian is a resident of the ancient kingdom of Mercia, England; however, it is also the name of an English racing bike made with Reynolds tubing, the English version of Columbus. Cycling aficionados are constantly arguing over which tubing is better.

"You have a Mercian? You ride?" She looked incredulous.

"Sure. Not as much as I used to about a hundred years ago, but I get out now and then," I said with a drip of false modesty. "I used to race in Colorado. It was an efficient way for us ski racers to keep in shape during the summer."

"Ski racers?"

I guess she wasn't aware of the sportsman side of my personality, just as my ex, Jennifer, hadn't truly been aware of the intellectual side. But, there was no reason Anastasia should have known I was more than an egghead, whereas Jennifer had failed in sixteen years of marriage to discover that I possessed any qualities other than that of a—what is the word used today? It used to be jock. What? Come memory. Hose? Hulk? Chunk? Hunk? That's it, that of a hunk.

"Come on, Anastasia, did you imagine that I was but a bookworm? My former wife thought I was merely a jock." I reverted to stammering "jock" because I couldn't get behind the word *hunk* as an identity noun.

Anastasia stopped short, leaned her bike against a tree, and placed her knuckles on her hips to project an actor's version of skepticism. "Well, no," she said, "I had never imagined that the famous Professor Griffin MacRobbin had raced through his university years on skis and bikes." Delivering this, she grinned. I cracked a grin too. She made it sound so . . . funny.

"Well, I did race around, and I was pretty good," I blurted like a seventeen-year-old. "And I still keep in fair shape, so if you want to have a race out on the Post Road, we could, I guess, but we should bring a picnic."

Anastasia laughed. She said, "Well I do like picnics." After retrieving her De Rosa, Anastasia hooked her free arm through mine. She wheeled and guided the bike with her right hand on the stem. We walked down the quiet, darkening sidewalk. She said, "I would like that, Griffin, we could ride together. And I'd like to see your Mercian."

This exchange between us about the bicycles was most fortuitous, because suddenly we had become three-dimensional human beings to each other, rather than a stretched canvass of "MacRobbin the wunderkind professor," and a frescoed wall, "Anastasia the beautiful and talented graduate student." What other facets our lives held for each other remained to be seen, but promise arose.

Our conversation drifted back to the Nag Hammadi manuscripts. I commented on the uses of Gnostic poetry versus prose.

"I love Gnostic poetic imagery," Anastasia exclaimed. "This for example, 'Justice created the beautiful Paradise. It is outside the circuit of the moon and the circuit of the sun, in the luxuriant earth, which is in the East in the midst of the stones. And desire is in the midst of the trees since they are beautiful and tall.'" She quoted from On the Origin of the World, a Nag Hammadi Library tractate.

Just then we strolled by the college conservatory, its windows illuminated from within. Through the glass we could see patrons walking under leafy trees, in jungle-like surroundings.

"Let's go in," Anastasia suggested. "I'm enchanted by such places, especially at night."

"I know you are. You're the only graduate student I know who keeps a pet greenhouse."

"But what will I do with my bike?"

"Bring it inside. Professor Herman Horvitz of the English Department handles the evening shift here, I think because horticulture is his second passion. Anyway, he won't object to our stashing your bike in his office."

Once inside, a moist, nurturing atmosphere bathed our senses; the smell of plants and soil filled our nostrils. Soft strains of classical music, "The Lark Ascending," played over the sound system. A contemplative quiet stole over us so that we found ourselves seeking out a serene stone bench that stood beneath nearly intertwining trees, a lignum vitae, with blue-and-white five-petal blossoms, and an Indian Bo tree.

For almost fifty minutes we were silent, yet glanced at each other occasionally, smiled naturally, irrepressibly, the way a man and a woman sometimes do when energy flames from one to the other and back and 'round.

Slowly at first, but gathering speed like a river falling into a stretch of rapids, a thousand thoughts coursed through my mind. I mused about my life, starting with my Boston upbringing, and continuing with my Colorado escape, to my snubbing Harvard for Yale, to my wunderkind professorship, to my marriage and divorce of Jennifer, to this rather sudden sitting in the garden with Anastasia. After a while, it occurred to me that the experience of musing wordlessly in a garden with Anastasia, this quiet contemplation over where I stood in the scheme of things, seemed religious in content.

The moment the thought struck me, something I could only describe as psychic energy empowered me, and my mind became filled with Gnostic Jesus sayings, those kinds of allegorical nuggets that delight Dr. Moe but usually nettle me because of their enigmatic character. I suppose I had read the sayings at one time or another, but certainly, I had not memorized them, and I could see no reason that I should, at once, be overtaken by such a charged dance of esoteric thought. It was a round dance of energy, dance the round all: graces pace the round. I will blow the pipe. He who knows the father and the mother will be called the son of a harlot. When you make the two one, you will become the sons of man, and when you say, Mountain, move away, it will move away. Show me the stone the builders have rejected. That one is the cornerstone. Graces pace the round. I will blow the pipe. Many are standing at the door, but it is the solitary who will enter the bridal chamber. He who is near me is near the fire. It is I who am the light, which is above them all, it is I who am the all. From me did the all come forth, and unto me did the all extend. Split a piece of wood, and I am there. Lift up a stone and you will find me there. Dance the round all. When you see your images, which came into being before you, and which neither die nor become manifest, how much you will have to bear! The angels and prophets will come to you and give to you those things you already have. And you, too, give them those things which you have and say to yourselves, When will they come and take what is theirs? I am not a divider, am I? If thou dancest, ponder what I do; to each and all it is given to dance. In thy drive towards wisdom, a mirror am I to thee who discernest me!

These sayings were dancing and blowing from a source within me: Q-R-S-T-U-V, I love you if you love me! You are excluded only if you exclude yourself, he says. Bird of Paradise, Rosebush thorn, Father Nork is Felix Korn. The secret doctrines and festivals of the Christian Church are an outgrowth of the ancient mysteries, he says. The symbol resolves the split between the sensuous and the spiritual world. Understand? Yes? No? Then dance. To each and all it is given to dance.

The music shifted to a Mozart Allegro, and before I was aware of it, I had arisen from the bench to perform an ecstatic little spin! When I realized what I was doing, I felt the same way a poor sap must feel after he has been hypnotized on stage and been instructed to act like a chicken, and just when he is making the biggest fool of himself, the mesmerist claps his hands and wakes the sap up. Thus revived, he looks around in confusion, much to the uproarious delight of the audience.

Yet it wasn't Anastasia who was my clamorous audience; she was part of my act. I knew this because she stood, gave me a kiss on the cheek, and joined me in a two-step. Rather, I noticed a noisy group of conservatory visitors led by a woman with teased brownish hair. They had been ignoring the monkey puzzle tree and the firewheel tree and had, evidently, been concentrating on Anastasia and me as we sat occasionally smiling at each other, occasionally ignoring each other, until disrupting, we had up and danced! No doubt, we were high on drugs or pagan mental gymnastics, unaware that the conservatory grounds are a public place.

"Lord God! In such a state," said a Leopard Lily (fingering her glasses) to a Lipstick Tree (who was digging through her purse for her compact), "they might take off their clothes and make love right here in the garden!"

I intended to steal another glance at this woman to ascertain if we had ever been introduced. Perhaps she was the wife of a financial contributor to the Institute and had found my cavorting with a graduate student unseemly. As I looked over Anastasia's shoulder, the Leopard Lily had arrived at the part about our possibly making love right there on the stone bench, and a murmur of shock upped and circled from the ladies' group.

Professor Herman Horvitz glanced around the conservatory. He had been leaning over a balcony railing, perhaps estimating the worth of the coins in the shallow wishing-pool below, and he noticed the disturbance occurring in the group. A large woman standing beneath a redhead powder puff, nodding red pompoms above her, massed crimson stamens among dark evergreen foliage, conversed rapidly with her companions. Ha! There! Dancing under the trees! For, indeed, Anastasia had enticed me to do a bit of a tango. She grabbed my hands and we both danced. Horvitz laughed. Splendid! I know Horvitz always wanted to dance or do something illicit among the sensuous growth, lie naked in the Baby's Tears thick by the waterfall. He let that slip once when we were having a few drops at the faculty picnic.

The Lipstick Tree heard Horvitz guffaw and saw him grinning down from his perch. She nudged Massed Crimson Stamen, who in turn shouted up to Horvitz, "Do something!"

Horvitz frowned but realized that it was his job to ensure the conservatory ran with a modicum of decorum. He descended the balcony ramp, but it led away from the dancers, that is, Anastasia and me. By the time he wove his way around to confront us disturbers, we were no longer in tango but had slowed to a gentle sway, the movement of palms by a sea. Horvitz said to Massed Crimson Stamen, "They aren't causing any harm, now, are they?"

"Harm?" she replied with utter distain. "They should be locked up. When a man refers to inward feelings and experiences, of which mankind at large are not conscious, as evidences of truth of any opinion—such a man I call a Mystic: and the grounding of any theory or belief on the accidents and anomalies of individual sensations or fancies, and the use of peculiar terms invented or perverted from their ordinary significations, for the purpose of expressing these idiosyncrasies and pretended facts of interior consciousness, I name Mysticism . . . a savage place! As holy and enchanted as e'er beneath a waning moon was haunted by woman wailing for her demon-lover!"

She was quoting Samuel Taylor Coleridge to Horvitz. Taken by surprise, he backed into a spineless yucca.

This Massed Crimson Stamen seemed to know she was formidable when quoting the English Romantics—crazed literati obviously inspired her to subvert their rantings into testimonials for snowy logic and icy order.

"I will speak to them," replied Horvitz, referring to us, but I saw him spy a large tag pinned above Massed Crimson Stamen's right breast. It said:

Woman's Literature Fellowship
Eighth Annual Symposium

He must have noticed the other ladies wore identical tags printed in identical fashion, and he moved away from the spineless yucca. When he reached the Copper Leaf Match-Me-If-You-Can, he performed what I would call a *Laurence Olivier dramatic turn* and spouted a bit of Keats:

"First the realm I'll pass
Of Flora, and old Pan; sleep in the grass,
Feed upon apples red, and strawberries,
And choose each pleasure that my fancy sees;
Catch the white-handed Nymphs in shady places,
To woo sweet kisses from averted faces."

Delighted by the Horvitz riposte, the women laughed, but Massed Crimson Stamen looked stunned. Horvitz had quoted from "Sleep and Poetry." Meanwhile Anastasia and I walked up another path and hid behind a silver birch but peered out between the leaves to see how Horvitz was doing. Just as he had been taken by surprise by Massed Crimson Stamen, so she had been taken by Horvitz, because he hardly looked like an English professor, dressed as he was in gardening clothes. Massed Crimson Stamen collected herself, narrowed her eyes and quoted:

"And can I ever bid these joys farewell?
Yes, I must pass them for a nobler life,
Where I may find the agonies, the strife
Of human hearts."

But Horvitz wasn't through, and I thought: This will be a *contest!* He tossed Coleridge back at Massed Crimson Stamen as she had tossed Keats back at him, yet, when he'd finished his offering, I'm sure it was Anastasia and I who were the most surprised:

"Beneath yon Birch with silver bark,
And boughs so pendulous and fair,
The brook falls scatter'd down the rock:
And all is mossy there!
And there upon the moss she sits,
The Dark Ladie in silent pain;
The heavy tear is in her eye,
And drops and swells again.
Three times she sends her little page
Up the castled mountain's breast,
If he might find the Knight that wears
The Griffin for his crest."

Horvitz! The devil had seen us duck under the birch and immediately latched upon appropriate verse. He probably regarded us as lovers. But clever as he was, he couldn't have known how close he had come to expressing our other truth, that if ever there had been a Dark Ladie in trouble, it was Anastasia, and, indeed, I had come to her aid.

Be that as it may, I did take Horvitz's choice of poetry as a sure sign that Anastasia and I were now romantically involved. Horvitz knew it with one look. I think Anastasia knew it, too, because when I turned and kissed her, her ardent response revealed her heart to me.

While Horvitz and Massed Crimson Stamen continued to banter, Anastasia held my hand and led me down a meandering path under the trees. The content of my mind was still mystical.

I think Anastasia was also in such a mood, for she spotted a flowering vine by a rivulet, bent down to it and remarked, "Look, Griffin, a passionflower. Filaments of the corona are supposed to number seventy-two, equaling the number of thorns on the crown of thorns."

"Well, let's see," I replied, stalling for a moment while I tried to recall mythology of numbers. "Nine is a Goddess number because it is three times three of the triple Goddess, and eight is a God number, the Ogdoad, and the number of the name of Jesus is eight hundred eighty-eight. And nine times eight equals seventy-two." I glanced at Anastasia diffidently to see if she thought I was being too much of an egghead, but she noted:

"The main canonical number of Stonehenge is seventy-two. A season, midsummer for example, lasts seventy-two days."

Not to be outdone, I added, "The vernal equinox shifts one degree every seventy-two years."

The spirit of the poetry contest between good old Horvitz and Massed Crimson Stamen must have been catching, because Anastasia topped me.

"The flower's five anthers symbolize Christ's five wounds, yet five is also a Goddess number, like the five-pointed star at the center of an apple. And five seasons of seventy-two days add up to three hundred sixty days in a year with five days left over."

"Our five senses belong to the Goddess," I said, "because as you stated, she is sensuous."

"The five wounds of Christ may be the five senses, because when he put on the beast, that is, when he appeared in human form, he had to take on the five senses, which can cause one to forget supersensory knowledge."

"Yet the wounds are glorified. There's a combining here . . ."

Meanwhile, as we continued our mythoreligious discussion, I could hear Massed Crimson Stamen abandon the Romantics to give Horvitz a Victorian salvo in an attempt to create sympathy for her position, as Horvitz had done his:

"I, Eve, sad mother

Of all who must live,

I, not another

Plucked bitterest fruit to give

My friend, husband, lover,

O wanton eyes run over!

Who but I should grieve?

Cain hath slain his brother,

Miserable Eve!"

But Horvitz, a true Romantic, countered:

"A thousand handicraftsmen wore the mask

Of Poesy, Ill-fated, impious race!"

A searing insult! She took it to heart. I could feel Horvitz's position grow stronger. He continued to dazzle Massed Crimson Stamen and the ladies:

"A drainless shower

Of light is poesy; 'tis the supreme of power . . ."

Anastasia said, "I think Gnosis is intuitive knowledge, poetic knowledge. It is synchronism in events, thoughts, symbols . . . like the coincidences we just discovered with the numbers seventy-two and five."

"But," I replied, always the wunderkind professor, "it's difficult to separate intuitive-poetic knowledge from mystification or madness."

"Yes, the blossom is hidden. That's why the apocrypha are so important. They can clear away the confusion, and guide one to Gnosis."

In this answer of hers, I again detected that touch of fanaticism . . . or madness. But after what I'd just experienced while sitting under the Tree of Life, well, I was in no position to be the skeptic. My mind was still whirling, and I decided it was time to depart. I guided Anastasia directly past Professor Horvitz and the women's group. They took no notice of us, for they had reached an understanding. Massed Crimson Stamen was quoting to Horvitz:

"Then let us clear away the choking thorns
From round its gentle stem, let the young fawns
Yeaned in after times, when we are flown,
Find a fresh sward beneath it, overgrown
With simple flowers . . ."
Upon reflection, I'd never seen Horvitz look so happy.

Chapter Sex   -6-

LEAVING THE CONSERVATORY, ANASTASIA and I walked silently side by side. The only sound in the quiet neighborhood came from the precise click of gears as Anastasia rolled her De Rosa over the sidewalk. I was preoccupied. Her suggestion—that Gnosis has a synchronistic character—made sense to me, and this worried me, because, after all, it's a theory that's almost impossible to prove.

It was startling to me that Horvitz had chosen verse that described our situation to a T, verse about the Dark Ladie and her knight with the griffin crest. Corny, but synchronistic. And it was extraordinary that Massed Crimson Stamen had recited verse that instructs us to clear away choking thorns from 'round a simple flower's gentle stem. This, just after Anastasia had suggested the blossom of knowledge is hidden, and only by using the secret books as a guide could one find a way through the thorns of confusion—in the world of maya.

Well, I don't know about the world of maya, but I can certainly attest there had been confusion in the world of scholarship over Gnosticism. Before the discovery of the Nag Hammadi Library, we possessed almost no first-hand information concerning the Gnostics.

We knew only the bits and pieces of their history that their enemies had written, and believe me, these enemies were disinclined to flatter. Now, with the translation project, we could see the error in some of our former conceptions about Gnosticism, about its unrelenting negativity. For example, Dr. Moe has already touched upon one of the most startlingly positive ideas to come from the Library: that heaven exists here on earth as a capacity within each and every human being. And much Gnostic mumbo-jumbo is naught but instruction on mystical ritual, devised to enable a practitioner to engage his admirable qualities.

The other startling idea to come from the Library was revealed to me in Anastasia's thesis proposal, that Gnosticism is an attempt to combine a Goddess religion with a God religion. Thus, it is an attempt to integrate the male and female principles within the human psyche. However, as I told Anastasia, proposing the theory is one thing, but academic proof of that theory is quite another thing. I had to admit, however, that—largely through my efforts and that of the Institute— the research material is now available to any competent scholar.

Yes, we already held in our Library a vast fund of mystical ideas that had been lost for some sixteen centuries. But it was the matter of the secret books, the apocrypha that Anastasia's father had removed from the Nag Hammadi collection, that grew more and more intriguing to me. Why had he chosen to take just two books, when he must have had his choice of the entire library? Was it due to the mention of treasure? Or was it because the two books were the key manuscripts of the collection in terms of Gnostic mysticism and magic, as Anastasia averred. If what she claimed was even partially true, I thought, then those books might reveal such secrets that the world at large had never known, the deepest secrets of Gnostic magical practice.

My interest was purely academic in that this discovery would be the first of its kind, comparable to a mountain climber bagging a never-before-climbed route up a major peak, or an adventurer mapping uncharted territory—such as the vast wilderness described in the novel *Green Mansions*. But I must admit that, at least on some subliminal level, I hoped to find a lost, forgotten secret of human existence. After all, isn't that what motivates many archaeologists and other scholars who delve into the past? Even the pragmatic Dr. Moe seeks an answer to the ultimate riddle: Why are we here?

I suppose it would strain credibility if I failed to add that an avid curiosity nettled me over the notion of buried treasure, for you see, I wouldn't have kicked much had a cache of priceless gems fallen into my hands. Think of the worthy projects such treasure could fund! But Anastasia had given me the distinct impression the treasure represented to her clan and herself a kind of Gnostic Grail, holy, sacred, not for the selling. My ex-wife Jennifer had always lived by the credo *diamonds are a girl's best friend*, but Anastasia is a different sort of woman altogether, the kind of woman that makes you remember what you were when your principles were pure, gleaming with hallowed youth, rather than what you are now, after all the years of unholy deals and manipulations that you've had to pull just to get through another day with head above water.

Well, to sell the treasure or not? We would cross that bejeweled bridge if and when we came to it, as the saying goes. For now, we were approaching, not a bridge, but the lovely grove where her house stood, darkened, a crescent moon glimmering through the leaves above. But when, wordless, she beckoned me to follow her, her gesture—and the nightscape itself—suddenly stopped me in my tracks. I felt an odd twinge of fear, this despite my most recent musing that Anastasia rendered a good influence on me.

I felt uneasy because the scene struck me with the memory of a story my great uncle John MacRobbin had always told at the death of the year. In the old days it was said by members of the Boston Irish that Great Uncle John was a warlock, and so everyone listened with awed fascination when he told his traditional New Year's Eve tale. I didn't believe in warlocks, even then, but certainly old MacRobbin was an enigmatic man. His aura of mystery imbued me with an interest in ancient lore, and he thus influenced my decision to become a scholar of antiquity.

Now, standing in Anastasia's grove, I could still remember every word of the story, though I hadn't thought of it in years, and I could recall old Uncle whirling around before the fire in the darkened room, spinning himself and the tale. He would begin by choosing an adolescent boy in the audience to be his confidante, as he did with me in my youth, like this.

"It was many years ago. I was just about your age, Griffin, and I had sailed around the Isles of Scilly with my father to hunt in Brittany. After a week in the woods with the hunting party, I decided I knew enough to venture out alone. I crossed a blue ridge to the forest beyond to hunt with my first hound, Gospa, whom I had trained a twelve-month. She was a fine strong hound, not as big as Novica but with just as much heart.

"The forest was dense with here and there a swath of fern where great decaying tree trunks lay fallen, creating an opening in the canopy of leaves, allowing a small amount of sun to shine through. I was on foot, having left my horse at the forest edge, the interior being too thick for a horse to pass. Gospa was on to a stag—I glimpsed him before he bolted. He wore a small rack with four points on his head.

"Gospa gave chase, baying, and I followed as quickly as I could, although in a short time I fell far behind. As the sun plunged westward, I could hear Gospa's voice near, then shortly it would fade into the distance, into nothing. I sat down by a thicket near a stream, and the fading sun shone on a tangle of trees across the water, the forest beyond, dark.

"I pulled my horn to call Gospa, because I did not wish to bed in those quiet woods. There were no birds, I saw no animals save in the beginning that one quick look at the stag, and I felt the pain of solitude.

"The sweet horn gave such a mournful music as I blew that if the snakes had been about, they'd have slithered down their holes. I blew and blew, but Gospa did not return. Instead, just at dusk came a swan, like a vision, to the edge of the dark wood. White against the trees, it began moving toward me, though it was still quite far away. As it came closer, I saw it wasn't a swan, but a maid dressed in sheer white cloth so delicate I knew not how it was woven.

"The maid came to the water's edge, arms up risen, the stream between us. When she spoke, I thought I heard the tinkling of bells. She said she knew I was lost but instructed me not to fear for she could guide me through the forest. Believing she could, I rose to my knees, and in reply she beckoned me. Although I was too astonished to speak, I crossed the stream and followed her into the raven wood, dark, dark, and yet I could see the path where she walked.

"More than once, I reached for her to hold her hand, but she was always out of my grasp. Finally, we stopped in front of what I took to be a wolf cave, bones lying about, and on the ground, she spread a Persian carpet decorated with images of bear, deer, falcon and black bird, and many varieties of flowers, all woven in rich, harmonious colors. After placing beautiful clay pots around me, one filled with cool water, another with fruit, another with corn, she brought forth a fish that had been broiled, and we feasted and sat there in ecstasy. Over her shoulder I spied the stag. Beyond him I saw the moon shining through the leaves.

"I began to speak. I found myself pleading with her, asking her to allow me to stay, so that we could rule the wood together. I was no longer content just to have her as my guide.

"She did not speak, but smiled upon me, then rose and disappeared into the wolf cave, while nearby the stag again bolted away. I crept into the cave, calling out after her, but instead toward me came a different being, older, partially hooded, with disheveled hair surrounding staring round eyes, crooked nose, and crooked teeth. A serpent ringed the being's waist.

"At once I felt tired and indifferent and it grabbed me by the arm with a claw-like hand. I felt pain where it held me, all my will seemed to ebb through the wound. The fiendish being dragged me westward until we came to a circle of stones in a pattern of eight-lobed leaves, within it a circular ditch as big around as nineteen men with their arms outstretched. The dreadful being threw me into the ditch before climbing a pedestal at the circle's center. Upon reaching the top, it devoured the moon and stars. In the pitch blackness I heard its voice mocking me, screaming and ranting:

"'You have lost your hound! The wolves have your horse! Haw, haw, haw! You are nothing! I can see right through you!'

"I crawled through the muck in the ditch, its sides too steep to surmount. I crawled in circles. The horrible being railed me and mocked me until I lay in motionless apathy and I began to think: I am nothing. I enjoy nothing. I accomplish nothing. I am apart and forever alone—my despair an alder-wood stake driven through me. I don't know how long I lay there, with the fiend, at random, screeching:

'You don't exist! I can see right through you!'

"But as I lay there in the muck, something stirred deep within me, an inspiration! I slowly stood up while wiping the muck off me. I said, 'You give me good tidings, ugly being.'

"'What? What's that you say?'

"'If you can see right through me, then I am not here. And if I am not here, you are mocking yourself.' It moaned, and I continued, 'You are the object of your own hatred.'

"The fiend screamed as though in agony. I said, 'If I am not here, I must be somewhere else!' Immediately came a great flapping of wings and intense rush of wind, like a storm from the Atlantic, and I was spinning in air. When I opened my eyes, I found myself in a clearing, with Gospa licking my face. In the light of dawn, I saw my horse ninety steps away."

Though I had stopped in my tracks to contemplate Great Uncle John's story, Anastasia had continued up the path. I could no longer see her, but I followed in the dark, like Great Uncle John creeping into the wolf cave after the Goddess. I suppose Jung would have rallied around this one; at the very least, he would have insisted that I feared falling in love again, and so was drawing upon morbid associations to keep myself at a distance from the woman in question. More likely though, the image of the dark cave would have held all manner of pregnant meaning for him.

Well, the hell with Jung. And Freud too. On some level this woman frightened me, that's all. And my previous musing about Gnostic coincidence made the sudden recollection of Uncle John's story seem like a warning against Anastasia, against her beckoning me into dark grove under crescent moon. She is a mysterious woman, I thought, one not motivated by the traditional perks of our society: money, fame and fortune. She has a strange past, a strange name, strange associates . . . a strange, monstrous plant in her greenhouse.

Scared and in love—that's me, I thought as I continued forward into blackness, hands out in front like a sleepwalker, to fend off obstructions, so that I wouldn't bump my nose. I was progressing nicely, pushing aside vines, ducking branches, when my hand brushed a softness, a smoothness, a warmth, and it occurred to me that this was not something to avoid. Instead, I slowly clasped the decidedly feminine sensuality to me, until I held in my arms Anastasia. But it was Anastasia free of the cashmere sweater and the Lycra cycling outfit . . . she was quite naked. All my questions, thoughts, and fears took flight. Great Uncle John would have to voice his warnings elsewhere, because in all the universe the only sound I heard now was Anastasia's quick breath.

✦ ✦ ✦

Above us the moon drifted toward the horizon. Anastasia had led me past the greenhouse to a willow tree, and we made love beneath it, the willow's tumbled branches our safeguard. Stars dotted openings between the leaves. That night, I might have been anywhere in the universe—it didn't matter, if I was with her. How long would it last, this romance? Another moment? A week? Sixteen years? It had been long since I made love. I found my emotions ragged and torn.

"Griffin, are you crying?"

"Only for mercy."

"No, Griffin, I feel a tear." She brushed my cheek.

"And desire is in the midst of the trees since they are beautiful and tall," I said.

"You can't hide from me, Griffin."

I raised up on one elbow so that she couldn't peer at my moonlit face. "I've nothing to hide."

"Do you think of her?"

"Who?"

"Who else?"

"Anastasia, sixteen years of marriage is a long time, and—"

"You still love her."

I drew my knees up, seeing if I could obtain the fetal position. "I try not to think of Jennifer except in the most shallow of terms."

Anastasia kneeled behind me and threw her arms around my neck. She said, "Husbands and wives think they can toss each other away and never look back, but they can't. They are attached to each other by love or by hatred. Thank God with you it's love."

Who was the professor here? Who was the student? In one evening, this woman had demolished—piece by piece—the emotional Hadrian's Wall I'd so carefully, painstakingly constructed around myself. How had she done it? With gardens. With psychic imposition. With mystical love. Surely, I was coming apart at the seams. But I'd never show it. I set my jaw.

The following morning, I felt stronger, and I called Byah at the office to cancel my appointments, classes, fund-raising commitments, interviews, seminars, etc., and then hung up so that Anastasia could call Byah right back to cancel all her appointments, teaching assignments, etc., the two separate phone calls assuring Byah that it was mere coincidence that both Anastasia and I were off on the same day. Having done that, we grinned at each other, knowing we had another twenty-four hours entirely to ourselves. We were just slipping back under the covers of Anastasia's four-poster canopy bed when the phone rang.

"Hello. Yes, this is Anastasia. Oh! Dr. Littlejohn . . . Oh, OK, I know, everyone calls you Dr. Moe. How are you, Dr. Moe? No, I haven't seen him. Yes, well, I have a slight fever this morning, I think I'd better rest in bed so that it doesn't get anyone else . . . No, ha ha, honestly, he's . . . Oh, hell, he's right here." She handed me the phone. I grunted into the mouthpiece.

"She's not the only one with a fever, I see," Dr. Moe remarked right off the bat.

"OK, Dr. Moe, so you caught us, 'Love and scandal are the best sweeteners of tea,' as old what's-her-name said."

"In that case we'll not need honey for a year. But I no longer care about your private life, God knows you deserve a girl like Anastasia."

A . . . woman . . . like Anastasia? How many are there?

"So have fun . . . err . . . love, but, I've got us tickets to New York. We're leaving this morning at 11:58!"

"But . . ." I looked at my clock: 9:07.

"Now, look, we're on the trail of those blasted texts. You can kiss Anastasia on the plane ride. We've got to talk to this Thoth character."

"Well, he doesn't even know we're coming." This produced a splendid pause on the other end of the line. "Dr. Moe? Are you with me?" I heard mumbles. "Moe?"

"Oh, bother, I knew I forgot something!"

"Never mind, Dr. Moe, I'll have Anastasia call New York right now. Pick us up on your way to the airport."

"Well, what are you going to do for clothes?"

"Good grief, I'll buy a toothbrush when I get there."

"OK. Sorry to have had to ah . . . disturb you. By the way, you don't mind if I tell Partridge, do you?"

"Moe!"

"Ha ha ha ha."

I hung up. At first, Anastasia balked at the idea of dressing, packing, and leaving for the airport within two hours, but then she charged ahead, her mood light. She called Thoth, arranged a meeting with him the following afternoon in his office at the Metropolitan Museum, called the Institute again to make sure Dr. Moe had rearranged her schedule, showered, dressed, packed, threw out the coffee that I had made in the meantime because my coffee tasted rather rude, made a new batch, sliced up pears, apples, and strawberries, spooned on yogurt, heated rolls, sat in the greenhouse with me, sipped her coffee, munched delicacies, and waited for Dr. Moe, seemingly having the time of her life.

I thought, My God, what an age for a woman. My expression must have revealed my thoughts because Anastasia smiled and said, "You're saving my life. The least I can do is show a little enthusiasm."

CODEX IV

Stevan's Story
As told by Thoth

Chapter i   -1-

OUR DESTINATION: NEW YORK. Since we were arriving from the west coast, Dr. Moe chose a flight that disembarks at LaGuardia, because the incoming plane overflies Manhattan for a spectacular view of the city and its skyscrapers; as a bonus from my perspective, the cab ride to the Carlyle is shorter than from Kennedy or Newark. I stay there since an old and very wealthy friend of mine, Joe Ridder, foots the bill. In return, we have dinner together in the restaurant, the Dumonet; I usually line my arteries with the delicious sole meuniere and then clear them out while we drink exceptional Riesling and discuss the state of the world, including the latest discoveries in the realm of antiquities. No Joe this time though. I guess he was damn busy with overseeing his vast media empire. Anyway, what could I possibly tell him about Anastasia's quest?

Dr. Moe was grumpy on the airplane even though it was a Pan Am 747 jumbo jet with the circular stairs that climb up to the first-class stand-up bar. God knows what happens up there. Dr. Moe, the cheapskate, had bought us coach fare. Very good, very good, saving Institute money; but I had told him to use my private credit card.

He thought our scheduled meeting at the Met qualified as Institute business. OK, but from now on, I'm footing the bill. At least we could smoke, if we would smoke, if we did smoke, but we don't smoke. What idiot would smoke?

Evidently, all the passengers fore, aft, and sideways. The only way to cope with the resulting noxious cloud that enveloped us was to order Bloody Marys. Dr. Moe said the third one upset his stomach. Geesh! Meanwhile, Anastasia only drank one. What a demure young woman.

How many did I have? You know, I don't quite recall, but enough to get me to squeeze into a disgusting yellow cab after we landed, with poor Anastasia stuffed in the middle, with her darling feet on the transmission hump and Dr. Moe on the other side, sniffing with allergies.

I brought no luggage. Dr. Moe carried a small but precision flight bag in which he, no doubt, had fastidiously stuffed enough supplies for a month of Sundays; but he was outdone by Anastasia who wheeled a monstrosity, a portmanteau so immense I had to name it: I called it "Great Huge!" If worse came to worse, we could live in the thing, have tea at four, and dinner at eight, etc.

Meanwhile, back in Claremont, Byah was packing and sending my safari clothes and boots to the hotel. My hopsack blazer is a good travel companion, but it wasn't going to cut it in Egypt, or wherever we were headed after we interviewed this estimable Thoth character in his mysterious office in the bowels of the Metropolitan Museum of Art. According to Anastasia, his office location is underneath the rooms housing the collection of Ancient Near Eastern Art—a curatorial department with which I am completely familiar, having offered my expert assistance to the staff from time to time.

I could tell you about my Carlyle suite, the same one I always stay in—perfect for Anastasia and me, with Dr. Moe residing on the same floor down the hall—I could go into all that, but who has time? In Manhattan there are only New York minutes.

We took the "complimentary" hotel limo to the Met. You tip the driver ten dollars, but shelling out is still preferable to squeezing into one of those gross cabs with the crazy drivers taking you all over the Upper East Side on a wild goose chase. We could have walked, but Dr. Moe was disinclined.

It was high noon, yet it felt like office hours—nine o'clock sharp, West Coast time. Anastasia wore a smart blue-and-white dress that adjourned about four inches above her shapely knees, a dress that said, "Let's meet again later!" She looked as if she owned large buildings on the Upper East Side. Dr. Moe looked like, well, Dr. Moe, and I looked like a professor, still in my all-purpose, go-anywhere blue hopsack blazer.

Thoth had instructed an assistant, Raghib, to await us at the museum's Fifth Avenue entrance. He spotted us before we were able to find him. After introducing himself, he led us to an almost-invisible door, which he unlocked with an enormous brass key, and ushered us down a drab hallway which took us to an elevator—not a groovy (is that a word?) wood-paneled Carlyle elevator, but rather, a large, industrial freight elevator, and we descended floor after floor. Evidently, Thoth's office was located somewhere in China.

When the machine decided it had reached the end of its narrow journey, it yowled to a jouncing stop. I looked over at Dr. Moe. He rolled his eyes.

Anastasia turned to Raghib and spoke to him in Coptic. Raghib smiled, nodded, and replied also in Coptic. It didn't throw either Dr. Moe or me for a loop; we understood every word. Raghib had been Thoth's assistant for only a century and a half. Again Dr. Moe and I exchanged a glance. Perhaps this was a Coptic dialect we had not yet encountered. Sometimes the idioms could be confusing.

Raghib led us down another drab hallway to what looked like the door to a broom closet. He knocked. The door swung inward; Raghib stepped aside. Past the doorway I could see a room illuminated with carefully placed lamps and sconces that yielded a mild, appealing light throughout the area.

A voice said, in perfect New England English, if that's not an oxymoron, "Won't you please come in?"

We entered a room approximately twenty-six feet wide by thirty-three feet in length, ceiling twelve feet high, the walls lined with white limestone such as can be acquired from the shore of the Nile. What astonished Dr. Moe and me, however, were the ancient writings carved into every stone surface. We were so taken by the display, we failed the greeting, and instead walked along the walls observing the linear syllabary of Ancient Western Greek, the syllabary of the Hittite from Anatolia, the cuneiform wedges of Akkadians and Babylonians, hieroglyphs of Egypt and unrelated hieroglyphs of Central American origin. There were elements that might have been Sanskrit or Indus writings. We could not identify all the carved alphabets.

"I see you recognize these rudiments of written language."

I turned, embarrassed. I saw a diminutive man, white hair, shocking yellow, feline eyes, observing me from in front of his nicely carved desk—old growth rosewood? Anastasia was standing beside him looking at me with a wry grin.

I said, "Forgive our rudeness, we were overcome by your superb display of ancient alphabets. I am Professor Griffin MacRobbin, Director of the Institute for Antiquity at Claremont"—I turned toward Dr. Moe, who was still ogling a wall—"and this is my colleague Dr. Moe Littlejohn." At this, Dr. Moe turned and walked swiftly over to extend his hand for a handshake. Since I am familiar with the inner workings of Dr. Moe's mind, I could see he was quite pleased to observe that he stood at least several inches taller than our host.

Thoth smiled, shook Dr. Moe's hand and replied to me, "I am Olympia Thoth. I'm so pleased to make your acquaintances. Anastasia, my godchild, has told me much about the efforts of the Institute and about you, Dr. MacRobbin."

My radar always flashes orange when someone says they've been told much about me, but since the source was Anastasia, I didn't feel besieged. I replied with the standard, "Nothing too awful, I trust."

"On the contrary, I admire your work."

Dr. Moe, impatient for his chance to butt in, said, "Anastasia has told us a disturbing story of a malevolent society called the Honorable Order of Suebi and has suggested this . . . society has threatened her life."

Thoth glanced at Anastasia.

Addressing him, she said, "I've told them all I know. Now, Ollie, It's up to you."

Ollie! You know, in the course of a day, some things you just love. Not only was Thoth's first name, Olympia, in the Greek feminine form, but his nickname was Ollie! I was starting to like the man.

Thoth said, "I'll have some refreshment brought in, and we can ensconce ourselves." He pointed to a comfortable seating arrangement of suede and leather couches and chairs, a round table in between. As we strolled over to the seating, gawking at the walls on the way, Raghib again appeared, this time carrying a tray of chocolate pots and Egyptian ceramic mugs, also plates of sliced bananas, mangos, pomegranates, and date and green-fig spread with yogurt, for the included flatbread. I wasn't hungry.

Thoth said, "I recommend the hot chocolate, Muisca—from Colombia, not entirely authentic, we sweeten ours."

Raghib poured us all a mug. I forced a sip. Actually, it was rather good—I felt like I should be wearing short pants and Buster Browns. Anastasia sat with me on a love seat, Dr. Moe settled into a too-large leather chair on my left, with his feet dangling; it made him look like a dwarf, and Thoth sat across the table from us looking elegant and composed. He did something with his left hand, and the lights dimmed but still illuminated the alphabet walls in a soft glow.

Thoth said, "I will tell you what happened in Egypt, 1946, when Anastasia's father, Stevan, and his friends and colleagues, Dick and Joko, assisted me in securing two vastly important codices that were written in ancient Linear B syllabary Greek."

What was this man, Thoth, talking about? I'd never heard of such a thing, a papyrus codex written such. At this, I elbowed Anastasia, but she just looked at me and nodded assurance. What is it when you watch outer-space movies, or attend a presentation of a Wagner opera? *The Ring* cycle? Ah, yes, *suspension of disbelief.* I was going to have to dial that in.

Thoth began, "As has been recorded, the codices were dug up by two Egyptian peasants, Amon-Ra and his brother Dodi. I learned of the discovery through a vast network I maintain throughout the Near East in order to monitor the unearthing of certain antiquities that then exhibit unusual oscillations and reciprocations, because by being dug up, by being pulled from their resting place, they have been forced from their state of equilibrium—"

Dr. Moe interrupted. "I'm not sure I understand. When you suggest inanimate objects, dug out of the desert sands of time, exhibit bizarre tremors or resonance, it sounds like you refer to mysticism or magic."

Thoth replied, "Not magic. I am a scientist. This alludes to reality on a quantum level."

"Quantum? Quantum physics? Planck's constant and all that?" Dr. Moe said.

"Why, yes, Dr. Moe, you've heard of Planck's constant?"

"Well . . ."

Thoth said, "Photons display both particle and wave properties. The constant measures a photon's energy level as it relates to the frequency of the wave that carries the photon. But never mind about that. Do you know, a photon is a thousand-billion-billion-billionth of the mass of an electron? And an electron has hardly any mass at all. The reason electrons and other leptons have any mass at all is because of the Higgs field that the electron moves through. It's this Higgs field that interests me."

"Thanks," said Dr. Moe, a bit snarky, "that clears it up."

Thoth laughed. He said, "When certain objects have been disturbed, after many centuries of preservation in the sands of time, as you say, the electrons in the object and other leptons—muons, tauons—begin to spin, you get neutrinos spinning anticlockwise and antineutrinos spinning clockwise . . . Very dangerous, or perhaps auspicious for some, this spinning of matter and antimatter."

My turn to butt in. I commented, "What objects of antiquity have ever done this? This sounds like a . . . " I wanted to say, Paul Bunyan tall tale, but with Anastasia sitting right beside me I was reminded to mind my manners. I said, "I mean, that archeological digs could be dangerous on a quantum level seems at best far-fetched and a very difficult assertion to validate." (Whenever I want to say, "Bullshit," but be polite, I say, "It's a difficult assertion to validate.")

Addressing Thoth, Dr. Moe joined in. "You are talking about subatomic particles. You would need a six-acre lab and an IBM supercomputer to detect such particle movement."

Thoth smiled. He said, "More hot chocolate?" and poured us all a second mug full. Anastasia put some of the fig yogurt stuff on a piece of flatbread and took a bite.

Thoth said, "It is the Higgs field that a very few human beings are able to affect with their minds. But only when they're in physical contact with certain objects of antiquity, objects which for them create a resonance. Time seems to be a component of this ability, the antiquity of the object, the interaction of present day—kind of a spacetime continuum."

I took another sip of cocoa; it was addictive. I was beginning to feel quite relaxed on the comfortable couch sitting hip to hip with Anastasia. Something about Thoth's voice was quite soothing. Or was it the cocoa?

Thoth continued, "But there is another component to the wielding of this power: the word—not spoken aloud, but only imagined, like a mantra. As you know, certain ancient orthographies have no vowels and only consist of consonants. But an alphabet the Gnostics used for what they called *magical formulas* consisted only of vowels. These vowel chants would create an inner resonance in the mind of the adept, and by manipulating the Higgs field with this resonance, an adept is able to exponentially increase the mass of an artifact's leptons. That is why, Dr. Littlejohn, the particle movement in a chosen artifact can be felt on a physical plane. Members of Anastasia's clan comprised adepts who knew how to do this, wisdom handed down to Herak, Lazo, Yasoda, Anastasia's father, Stevan . . . " Thoth paused, then said, "I'd like to show you something." He snapped his fingers, quite loud, I don't know how he did that, and a few minutes later Raghib arrived in front of us carrying a sword; it looked to be quite old but well preserved. Saxon, perhaps?

"This broadsword," Thoth said, "is one of those objects of which I speak. It belonged to Herak. He caused it to be stolen by Festus Griveaux, who is the leader of the Suebi order. It was recovered by Stevan and now resides in my care." Thoth stood, took the sword from Raghib, carried it over to Anastasia and handed it to her.

She took it with a stunning reverence, as if it were a holy object, a relic. Holding it in both hands, she examined it carefully, then she stood, and grasping the hilt, withdrew the sword from the sheath, feeling its heft and balance. She spied something etched onto the blade and held it up for a better look. She said, "Runes!"

I stood up next to her to take a look, and Dr. Moe jumped out of his high chair so that he could come over for a glimpse.

Anastasia said, "These runes look to be Germanic, Saxon perhaps . . . I think I can . . . yes, the script translates to *We eke victory to noble deeds*, or is it *great deeds*? Could be either one."

Thoth clapped his hands and said, "Very good, Anastasia, your father could not have done any better!"

She replied, "Ollie, you could not have taught me any better!"

Meanwhile, I don't know about Dr. Moe, but I was flat-out stunned. Germanic runes are not exactly in our wheelhouse at the Institute. I suppose I could have dug up a backroom professor or grad student who could give it a go, but really . . . I knew Anastasia was a gifted student, but I was still not fully aware of the levels of her gifts.

And then something very odd happened. I asked Anastasia if I could hold the broadsword for my own close inspection. She smiled and held it out to me, the flat blade in the palms of her hands. I took the hilt, and when I did, the sword seemed to be alive! It vibrated in my hand; a subtle but noticeable current ran through it. Surprised, I almost dropped it.

Dr. Moe noticed my behavior and gave me a sardonic glance. I wanted him to also experience the unusual oscillations and reciprocations emanating from the antiquated object, but by the time I thought of shoving it into his eager paws, the vibrations, the current, the whatever-it-was had ceased, and it had become a perfectly normal ancient Saxon weapon that ekes victory to great deeds.

Observing, Thoth said, "Research has found that when one partakes in the ingestion of a psychedelic substance, it is best to have the proper set and setting—the proper set means, what has the experimenter been involving himself with, what has taken up most of his thoughts over the recent weeks? Setting refers to the immediate physical surroundings. Usually you want a peaceful, secure location for this kind of exploration. Yet, I am not alluding to psychedelics here, but rather to Anastasia's mindset. From the time of her youth, she has been imbued with the teachings of the ancients of her clan, the difficult, long, arduous training of an adept. She earned her gift day after day, year after year. Now her mind has achieved a certain resonance, which interacts with an antiquity such as this broadsword. That interaction, Dr. MacRobbin, is what you felt when she handed the object to you, but once she no longer held the sword herself, the Higgs effect faded."

Anastasia put up with this third-person narration with patience and good humor. She put her hands on her hips, a gesture I have been familiar with, and shook her head, a wry smile on her lips. When he was finished, she said, goading him, "I wonder at the leptons which permeate this hot chocolate!"

And I wonder at Thoth's character. Is he a trickster? Or what? The Egyptian god Thoth is said to have invented the alphabet, writing, magic, and science, and to have a birdlike head, the ibis, or alternatively, to have the mug of a baboon. Our "Ollie" has neither, thank heavens, but he does flash disturbing amber cat eyes. And his obsessions are very similar to his ancient deified namesake.

Without bothering to take the sword in hand, since he'd had a good look at it anyway, Dr. Moe climbed back into his chair to dangle his feet and settle in as if he were a little kid waiting for the rest of the bedtime story. He must have been so cute when he was a tyke.

Thoth, seeming to take Dr. Moe's behavior as a cue, sat back down in his chair and waited for Anastasia to figure out what to do with the sword. She took it back from me and gently placed it on the round table in front of our loveseat, which we then reoccupied.

Chapter ii   -2-

Thoth said, "To return to my narrative, I, after a few days of search in the Nag Hammadi area, located a peasant named Sharky, a rather rough character whom I knew to be a cousin of Amon-Ra, the local who possessed the remainder of the Gnostic library. Amon-Ra had gone into hiding because other interests, namely the Suebi Order, but others, too, had attempted to wrest the books from him. I convinced Sharky that only I could extricate Amon-Ra from his predicament, the task of keeping watch over the library as commanded by a jinniyah. All manner of robbers, thieves, collectors, power brokers, obsessives, maladjusts, and other unsavory types were seeking Amon-Ra and would be perfectly happy to slit his throat and steal his prize. As it turned out, however, Amon-Ra remained steadfast, refusing to hand me or anyone else the entire library. He finally did accept a generous payment from me for the Greek codice he had not yet sold to Tano—yes, this I desired at any cost—but I left the thirteen remaining codices with him. A shame, really, because I could have easily dropped them all off at the Coptic Museum in old Cairo.

"As I have told you, Anastasia, I had previously sent a telegram to your father in Montenegro, directing him to come and assist me. You know the level of urgency I needed. Stevan, Joko, and Dick arrived in Nag Hammadi a day after I had located, with the help of Sharky, Amon-Ra and his brother Dodi. By then, however, the Suebi Order was crawling all over the area with many loutish henchmen lurking around every corner. Have you seen the movie *Casablanca*? Picture that, but with the Suebi order instead of the Nazis.

"To bring Stevan to me, I further employed Sharky. This character knew all the smuggling routes throughout the area, and he seemed to owe Amon-Ra a favor, so I decided he was the man for the job. Sharky and his little brother, Nodi, brought Stevan to the felucca, where I was waiting in the cabin with Amon-Ra, Dodi, and their mother. We were anchored offshore, drifting in the north-flowing current. But for the situation, it was really quite pleasant. I had supplied various teas from the far East and an ample sugar packet, along with treats they would like. Dodi produced a hookah, of all things, and they smoked what they referred to as local tobacco. This is how they had amused themselves during their self-imposed sequester.

I had known Stevan during his childhood, but I hadn't seen him for many years. When I was about, he was away in boarding school, or university; when he was about, I was chasing down some dig or other. As we greeted each other like old friends, I found him to be an impressive man, big, strong, but not overly so. Also, intelligent and with an understanding of . . . what I call science. So, we caught up, and then got down to business.

"I informed Stevan that an . . . entity who had been at odds with his guardian, Herak, now lurked with henchmen throughout these environs. When Stevan learned that Festus Griveaux and the Honorable Order of the Suebi had anchored a paddleboat on the river, he laughed. It was not a mirthful laugh. He said he already suspected Festus sought the codices.

"I asked him what he knew of this Festus. It was then, with raw emotion, that Stevan went on to tell me about the ghastly dealings he had experienced with this entity. When he had finished his account, he took a moment to collect himself and then glanced over at Sharky.

"Sharky had brought replenishments for the hookah and was now sampling the pipe. Stevan knelt down in front of Sharky, looked him in the eye. Stevan said, 'You know the aeroplane that landed on the river? It has flowers painted on the side?'

"'Sure,' Sharky replied, the *Daffodil*.'

"Stevan laughed. He said, 'Yes! Just so! I need you to deliver a message to my men. Tell them it is confirmed, a being named Festus is here and likely to attack. Tell them we are sailing down river now.'

"Something about Stevan's demeanor commanded attention. Sharky, one who liked to give orders, not take them, nodded, took one last puff of the hookah, jumped into the dinghy with Nodi, and was off on his mission.

"Stevan wanted to examine the satchel holding my two codices, assess if it was secure enough to withstand an errant dunk in the Nile. The waxed canvas bag passed his inspection.

"Amon-Ra and Dodi, having worked on fishing boats, were proficient sailors, and they quickly set the sails. By using the Nile's current and by tacking, they angled the boat into the strong north wind and released us from the mooring. Then they used the same technique to sail us northward. It took several hours to journey from near al-Tasr on the Nile to Nag Hammadi that day. The gusts were relentless and lateen-rigged vessels don't sail close to the wind.

"While we made way, I wrote a spell and placed it in a leather bag. I tied the bag to a line and ran it up the mast, where the wind blew this way and that. If and when Festus Griveaux drew near us, his mind would be tossed like the bag, leaving him confused.

"Stevan noticed my ploy. He said, 'A shame you can't put him in a jar and seal the top.'

"I replied that it is good enough the subtle things work, but when we try to escape with the codices, his concentration will become strong. He is more formidable now than when Herak and your parents drove him from Serbia, more capable than when you had previous encounters with him.

"Stevan squinted at me, looking skeptical.

"So, I added, 'As you experienced, his familiar spirit, Phloxopha, has powers, perhaps derived from antediluvian phonemes that I don't understand, and in addition, all four of his "personal assistants," Phloxopha, Ororotohos, Athuro, and Erimacho, are of the material, their essence is eternal—only their form can change. We must keep the codices from Festus. I believe the Gnosis in those volumes will provide our best means to resist him. Even a man who is lower than the ass he rides could learn power from these texts.'"

*   *   *

As we listened to Thoth, Anastasia rested her head against my shoulder, and I realized she needed emotional support. Thoth's narrative, true or not, affected her far differently than me, her connection to the events were personal, intense. In response, I put my arm around her as if to shield her from whatever was to come.

*   *   *

Thoth continued. "As we sailed northward, I later learned tragic events were taking place on the river near Nag Hammadi. Dick and Joko had taken up residence on the aeroplane and, because it was a flying boat, the *Daffodil* contained cabins that were comfortable enough for a time. Since landing in the river, the unusual craft had attracted the attention of the locals on shore, but now curiosity compelled many of the townsfolk to launch dories and skiffs to paddle out to the flying boat for a closer inspection.

"Surprised by the number of casual watercraft that had paddled out to the aeroplane, Dick became concerned when some of the townsfolk banged their boats into the fuselage. Later, in describing the incident, Joko mimicked Dick. 'Well, now! Hello, there. No, don't touch the hull! Uh, no,' Dick shouted, took a quick swig of raki, then coughed. Dick stood in the center pilot's cockpit. Joko ducked into the aft cockpit and pulled his hunting knife to finger. He said he guessed he looked old and fierce enough that the townsfolk would stay clear of the aft section, yet, he admitted, he enjoyed the jammer of the citizens, the splashing and the laughter.

"After a half hour of this cultural exchange, two foreign-looking men—definitely not of the region—pushed through to the front of the flotilla by bumping their dory into other boats. They ran alongside the *Daffodil* and bobbed in the water next to the aeroplane. These rowers shipped their oars, stood up in their wobbly dory, reached out, almost falling in the water, and pulled themselves up to climb onto the lower wing.

"Observing, Dick said, 'I know yer not sailors, that's obvious, but saints be praised! You'll damage the wing! Get! Get! Back to yer boat.' The men looked at Dick, faces sullen. Dick climbed from the cockpit onto the wing, making shooing gestures with his hand.

"Joko said he watched with amusement as Dick stood on the wing, raki in his left hand, confronting the interlopers. He heard Dick say, 'Back in the little boat now, little men, this is no camel, Sopwith or otherwise.'

"Then Joko saw the nearest man approach Dick. There was no warning. Joko saw a silver gleam in the sunlight. It disappeared into

Dick's belly. Dick groaned frightfully and slumped on the wing. Joko saw the knife again and saw the other man advancing towards Dick, malice in his eyes.

"Joko grabbed the machine gun. He was screaming. He fired as he swung the gun, bullets traced through the air. Joko knew the gun would not aim as far forward as the wing, he was just trying to make the men back off their attack. It worked. The two attackers jumped into the river, but the townsfolk shouted alarm when they realized a tragedy occurring—Joko's errant and unintended line of fire had struck five boaters, who a moment ago had been having fun, laughing, and gossiping. Now they were slammed into the river by stray bullets. In his haste to save Dick, Joko had miscalculated the aim of the machine gun—he had meant to fire overhead, but, for some unfathomable reason, it seemed, he had not.

"On shore, soon after the sound of the gunfire, townsfolk and farmers came running from the shops, houses, street corners, and fields. A police vehicle and an ambulance lurched into action. And less than a third of a league downriver, a malevolent force celebrated.

"Festus, Phloxopha, and Ororotohos did a little celebration dance on the deck of *Le Prince Aleksandar*. Although they hadn't achieved all they desired, their plan had still been a success! Festus later confirmed to me it was he who had sent the two henchmen to cause havoc. When they did, Festus and his two 'secretaries' used their occult powers to concentrate subtle whispers, suggestions, and mystifications against the people on the shoreline and against the crew of the aircraft. Chaos and tragedy ensued. The tragedy would be blamed on the enemy of the Honorable Order of the Suebi, Stevan and his clan! Festus felt he had dealt that clan a devastating blow. But as Festus scanned through his binoculars, he saw one man, Joko, still unharmed, and wondered why. The grand finale of the plan was to have been a giant explosion consuming the aircraft. Although the three of them had locked in—to mentally heat the fuel tanks until they exploded—something kept interfering with their concentration, and their ultimate plan failed. When Festus told me all this many years later, I still did not disclose the spell I had cast on him, the spell in the bag twisting in the wind. After all, I might need to use it on him again, hopefully with a spell more powerful.

"As I have noted, Amon-Ra and Dodi were expert sailors, and as we approached the *Daffodil* they spilled wind from the sails so that we gently drifted next to the aeroplane. Stevan and I easily crossed over to the wing, he shouldering the canvas sack of my codices, I just trying to keep balance.

"Stevan called out to Dick, 'Ahoy! You were supposed to fire up the engines!' But when we reached the access to pilot's cockpit, we found Dick slumped in the copilot's seat with Joko beside him trying to staunch a wound in Dick's abdomen.

"'What the hell!' Stevan shouted, and I sensed the flash of fear and loss that almost overcame him.

"'Your friend, Festus, eh?' Joko replied. He climbed down into the passageway that led to the bow cockpit so that we could enter the pilot's space.

"Stevan gave Joko the precious sack of books, knelt and gently touched Dick's shoulder. He said, 'I'm taking you to the hospital in Cairo,' then he looked away to hide his overwhelming grief.

"'An' Mother Mary protect me from the sinful pleasures of that sprawling burgh!'

"Stevan glanced back and saw Dick observing him. Stevan said, 'The sound of your voice is the sound of light.' He paused. 'Don't you leave me too . . . Don't ever leave me.'

"Joko said, 'Hey, we must go now! I don't like the look of the men on the shore.'

"I glanced at the shoreline. I told Joko that I thought some of them were members of the Suebi order.

"Stevan, trying to focus, looked at me and confirmed, 'You say Festus has a one-hundred-and-ten-foot paddleboat moored just north of us?'

"When I nodded, he reached for the binoculars. 'Yes,' he said, 'it is right in our takeoff path in front of the bridge. I will motor downwind to gain some distance before we turn back into the wind.'

"Joko warned, 'I see police on shore, they are launching a motorboat. A man you sent named Sharky rowed out here earlier and told me not to trust them, they've been paid off.'

"Stevan hit the starter switches. In the Nile valley heat, the engines would be warm by the time he turned upwind.

"Joko said, 'Stevan, I shot . . . I have injured some locals. I don't know how it happened . . .'

"Stevan looked at Joko and then me. I told them both I suspected a kind of hypnotic trance was used on Joko, a trance caused by the Order of the Suebi. You see, I have made a study of their tactics. In the moment, I don't think Joko accepted my explanation—even though he knew such things were possible.

"As Stevan eased the *Daffodil* upwind, Joko went forward to release the mooring, and then we turned out into the flow of the Nile. Stevan shouted for me to tend to Dick, but I already was doing so, speaking hypnotic phrases in the Irishman's ear. Soon he told me that he felt the pain ebb, and his bleeding subsided.

"'I'm going to take him directly to British Hospital if I can find it,' Stevan shouted to me over the din of the engines and wind noise.

"I put on a headset. 'If we take him there, we'll be bound up in government red tape.'

"Stevan replied, 'They're going to get us anyway . . . I've got to obtain aviation fuel in Cairo.' He piloted the flying boat downwind for five hundred yards. The police boat knifed toward us. Joko manned the forward cockpit, his machine gun locked and loaded, as they say. Increasing power to the engines, Stevan turned west, then north into the force-six wind and opened the throttles. The police boat did a dance-bizarre in the wind-swept chop, the lightweight craft bashed by the waves. The *Daffodil*, however, had enough purchase to plow a furrow and then skim the water with its flat belly, gaining speed, leaving the police boat in its wake.

"That's not to say it was an easy takeoff, no, as we lifted from the water, I had to hang on to Dick with one hand and the cockpit with the other to keep both of us from being launched by the buffeting of the wind. But once up to takeoff speed, the wind provided instant lift, and we were seven hundred feet in the air well ahead of the intersect with Festus's paddleboat, which loomed ahead.

"Stevan told Joko it was time to send Festus a message, but Joko, now gun-shy, hesitated. He didn't know where his aim might end up. So, instead of strafing the paddle boat, we continued northwest, out of gunfire range, and then navigated north toward Cairo.

"I suggested, rather than bring a wounded man to the British, who were already suspicious and on edge because of the Egyptian nationalists, we should take him to the complex near Abu Sarga, which is a Coptic church in Old Cairo. I insisted that the healers there would serve him far better than the doctors at British hospital.

"I then told Stevan to land at the southern end of Roda, that I had some friends on the waterfront who would temporarily make the aeroplane disappear.

"The *Daffodil* approached Cairo, fuel gauges on empty but engines still running strong. I saw Roda up ahead, and feeling some relief, pointed it out to Stevan.

"He admitted he was afraid we would have to land and float downriver the rest of the way, which would have been, at best, awkward.

"The sky-blue flying boat was not easy to see from the ground. Even Cairenes lounging along the river wouldn't have spotted us until we were quite low. After landing, our presence caused little commotion. Unlike al-Tasr, Cairo was uninterested in the *Daffodil*. I directed Stevan toward ramshackle buildings, dirty and waterlogged on the river's edge, where decaying wood covered with creepers and decomposing vegetable matter revealed that the structures were as old as innumerable seasons gone by. With the engines still running, but at idle, I began shouting and gesturing to men lounging in the dilapidated pergola constructed on a terrace overlooking the river. They recognized me. After a short time, vines and wood, which seemed to form a bulwark against the river, parted amidst loud creaking of hinges and pulleys. We, the crew of the *Daffodil*, saw revealed a large, dark warehouse with a floor of green river.

"Stevan piloted the flying boat, wingspan and all, into the enclosure. He said, 'Smuggled goods? A secret door for the Brotherhood and their terrorist activities? Well—it's a haven for the *Daffodil* now.' He shut down the engines.

"Echoes of water slapped the stone interior all around us as men carrying torches filed down the rough walkway and tossed lines to Joko and me. I spoke to them. In response, they made a stretcher with cloth and pole. Stevan and Joko placed Dick on the stretcher and maneuvered him to the walkway. We followed the men through a winding passageway which opened into an unkept garden, riotous growth unrestrained, a carnival of vegetation, and quite a contrast to the desert of al-Tasr. Stevan saw a cart standing empty by a gate in the garden wall and walked the front end of the stretcher toward it, Joko following behind. They placed their wounded friend, still on the stretcher, amongst the burlap in the cart. He was dazed and seemed unaware of his surroundings. Though it was hot, the Egyptians covered Dick with the coarse material for the journey through the streets of Old Cairo.

"The Egyptians wheeled the cart down narrow lanes between old brick buildings, Stevan and Joko striding alongside, me behind. As I walked, I smelled the pungent fragrance of Byzantine cookeries . . .

"'Why are we stopping here?' I heard Joko ask. I looked ahead. Though the street wasn't blocked, we had stopped in front of an ordinary-looking mass of buildings. One of the Egyptians accompanying us, an Arab named Gawhar, ran forward and began an awful row with a merchant selling brassware, which was so disrupting, even by Cairo standards, that those in the immediate area shifted all their attention to the disruption. In a moment, the remaining Egyptians motioned for Stevan and Joko to pick up Dick's stretcher, and I followed them all through a doorway and down steep steps into a tunnel. We emerged in what looked to be a Christian rectory, religious icons and screens placed about a comfortable series of rooms. I saw fine, ancient woodwork inlaid with ivory and ebony medallions, surrounded with Byzantine carvings.

"From an interior room came a Coptic priest whom I recognized, and I introduced Stevan and the others to him. He motioned for the wounded man to be brought into a room nearby. When we entered, I saw elderly women sitting on benches covered with dirty cloth. The priest sent one of them out for the healer, and we transferred Dick to a table covered with soft mats.

"The healer appeared shortly thereafter, dressed in black, with her face cloaked below her eyes. She examined Dick and immediately turned to the priest, saying something in hushed tones. The priest turned to me and said, 'You are the healer who has helped this man, are you not?' I nodded.

"The woman in black murmured to the priest. The priest said, 'The healer says you have helped him, but she will give him something to speed his recovery further.' The priest turned to the women on the bench and said, 'Bring hot water and soap, bring a white plate, a feather, and black ink.'

"Three women left to fetch the items while Stevan stood beside Dick, who lay motionless on the mats, his eyes unfocused. When the women returned, the healer spoke an incantation, then removed Dick's shirt and blood-soaked rag, which covered the wound. It was bleeding very slightly. She cleaned it with the hot water and soap. I could see the gash, about two inches wide. I saw the healer pick up the snow-white plate and the feather. She murmured to the priest.

"The priest announced, 'Healer says she use a feather because it is made with the hand of God, not hand of man.'

"She dipped the quill in the black ink and began writing an inscription on the plate. Shortly, she stopped and spoke to the priest again, who announced, 'She must know name of this man's mother.'

"Stevan looked at Joko. Joko shrugged. 'Brigid,' Stevan said.

"The healer pronounced her version of the name, then held the feather out to Stevan, indicating where he should write *Brigid*. After he had inscribed the name, she made Stevan hold Dick up. She poured water onto the plate, covering the inscription, dissolving the ink. She spoke to Dick while holding the plate to his lips, he drinking the water—the inscription. I heard her say, 'Alashtu, Sinyushta!' I heard her say in ancient Chaldean, 'For the sake of the just, heal the organs of the son of Brigid.' Then as a sop for the clergy, in Coptic, 'Parch the wound as the sea dried up for Moses and Mary and Jesus.'

"The healer arose. Quietly, she walked to the door, stopped, turned slowly, pointed a finger at Dick, spoke a phrase. At once, we heard a familiar voice: 'It's darker here than November on the Emerald Isle. It must be religion we're gettin' then!'"

Chapter iii   -3-

"LATER, I FOUND AN empty alcove to take Stevan aside. I told him I needed to speak to him about something I had discovered in the texts. Stevan looked over his shoulder to be sure we were alone, then turned to me, one eyebrow raised. Surprised, he wanted to know how much progress I'd made examining the codices. I told him they take time to translate, the condition of the papyri, not always good. I'd had time to study one codex, and found it sublime—its content of myth, story, religion, psychology, and words and formulas of power. It was the latter I wished to discuss.

"I told him that working late one evening in the cabin of Amon-Ra's 'borrowed' felucca, an oil lamp my only light, The Mother seated in a corner watching me as a dragon wards the gold, and outside, Amon-Ra and Dodi night fishing from the deck, I came upon words so shocking I'd grown short of breath. I hoped the observant Mother didn't notice my odd behavior. I read the lines again and again, checking my translation. The words always came out the same. A tractate entitled Hypsiphrone contained an oath so powerful it could destroy our greatest enemy.

"Stevan didn't really react to this assertion of mine. He finally said, 'Destroy Festus and his Suebi Order?'

"I confirmed this but added, 'Or at least create a force beyond his power. An opposing force. But there is a condition: Festus must order the oath into his world, our present world, otherwise it cannot enter. It is from beyond the cosmos.'

"'So, he must be tricked,' Stevan said, having gotten the gist.

"I then instructed him: 'The moment Festus insists on knowing the oath, you must reveal it to him. But, and this is essential, he must command that you reveal it.'

"A grin glimmered across Stevan's face and then was gone, but he mused, almost to himself, 'So, he asked for it, now he's going to get it.'

"'Not exactly now,' I said. I informed him that the incantation's effect takes place over time. The oath is the fulcrum that puts in motion a design that will come from beyond harmony, beyond creation—but when and how long it takes to play out—I shrugged, I could not say. It might be many years.

"Now Stevan wanted to understand one thing—How would this supracosmic design be carried out? I told him that according to the texts, when the incantation is delivered, it will set events in motion that will animate the mythical Stele of Fate, an object of power which can stop fate's wheel, and so destroy Festus's creations, even Festus himself. Where the Stele is hidden, I couldn't say. I hoped to find a location revealed in the texts. I told him I'd go immediately and resume my studies, but I feared it is not for me to know. 'And understand,' I said, 'the oath and the Stele are related, but not the same. If you can deliver the oath to Festus, that action will animate the Stele of Fate.'

"Stevan asked, 'Why does it matter where the Stele is located?'

"I hadn't made it clear—I explained the Stele of Fate is simply a tool, the most powerful tool in the cosmos, but it will have no efficacy until we find it. To wield the Stele, one must first animate it by delivering the oath to the Festus—the commander of the lower spheres of existence. Once that has been done, we must have the Stele in our possession to wield it, and so, it is vital to discover its location—who knows, perhaps by using ley-lines. However, only an adept chosen by the oath would be capable of commanding it. Festus could not, because it is from beyond his cosmos, but he could destroy it. We must find it. Festus must not. By employing the potency of the Stele, we can in the end defeat him.

"I turned to go, but Stevan reminded me I hadn't given him the magic formula, the oath to deliver to Festus. I shook my head, annoyed at my preoccupied mind. I told him to say: *When you meet the Lion, and the Eagle, in consort with the Queen of Spring, you will meet that which destroys you.*

"When I told him this, I thought Stevan's reaction a bit odd. He locked his eyes on mine—not many can do that! Then a slow grin crossed his face, and he said, 'Ah, I see.'

"I questioned him, 'What is it you see?' But he simply shook his head and would say no more, so I asked him to recite the incantation once more.

"Stevan repeated the oath, then he asked if I knew who or what are the Lion, the Eagle, and the Queen of Spring. Who or what could wield the Stele of Fate? And Festus? Was he aware of the Stele?

"I felt something going on between us. I said, 'Do you know?' But he just grinned at me and said nothing. Finally, I added, 'I don't know who or what the incantation refers to, Stevan. That is why I told you the oath may take time to reach its end. As for Festus, no, he is not yet aware of the Stele, but after the oath is delivered, Festus will madly search for these two texts. He'll realize that what's inside may be his only chance of survival.'"

✦ ✦ ✦

Abruptly, interrupting his narration, Thoth said to Anastasia, Dr. Moe, and me, "Next, I'll tell you the rest of the events of that night, as Gawhar later told me."

He suggested we take a break, freshen up, so to speak, take a little stroll, reconvene in twenty minutes. That was enough time for Anastasia to wander off in her direction, looking for the loo, no doubt, while Dr. Moe and I headed for the men's room, Thoth's private one, which he generously offered. Women always get the short shrift.

Once we were alone, Dr. Moe looked concerned. He said, "This is a tall tale, plain and not so simple."

I replied, "I agree with you, except . . ."

Dr. Moe: "Except?"

I: "Well, the sword. It vibrated, pulsed . . . something . . ."

Dr. Moe scoffed. "There was something all right . . . in the hot chocolate, something psychoactive. Or . . . I'd wager there is a battery compartment in that phony sword. Don't be a sucker!"

"Dr. Moe! I examined the sword. It is no phony. It is a genuine artifact."

Dr. Moe stared at me, finally shaking his head. He said, "I think the attractive woman sitting next to you on the love seat has something to do with your assessment of the proceedings."

I stared back at him and then laughed. I agreed, "Maybe so, but isn't she the reason we are here?"

"Yes," replied Dr. Moe, "and I'm beginning to wonder at her account of the danger she is in."

"As I said before, Dr. Moe, I believe her."

"Do you? It wasn't so long ago you thought she might be nuts."

I said, "Let's not pass judgment until we've heard the rest of the story, as Paul Harvey always says."

Dr. Moe replied, "Oh, I want to hear the rest. It's a good, apocryphal story. Wild horses couldn't keep me away. Incidentally, I'm probably the only person around here who would get your Paul Harvey reference. Certainly not your young love, Anastasia."

Chapter iiii   -4-

WHEN WE RETURNED TO the great room, Anastasia was sipping what looked like a sherry. Then I noticed several different bottles and glasses on a tray. I looked twice. Yes. A bottle of Powers. I poured Dr. Moe and myself a double. It could only help. Thoth arrived, sat back down, and immediately continued his narration.

"It would be a few days, perhaps longer, before Dick could be moved. The Irishman told Stevan and Joko to explore the 'unsavory allure of Cairo nights' in his stead. This they agreed to do. Stevan asked if the priest could recommend a guide. When the priest heard the request, he snorted and said, 'I send for Gawhar. He make fine dragoman.'"

Thoth paused, then said, "So now I give you an account of the night's tragedy, which I put together at length by interviewing both Joko and Gawhar, but also by consulting many other sources I maintained in the city. I will tell it from an omniscient point of view and so refer to myself in the third person."

I leaned over to glance at Dr. Moe, raising my whiskey glass in a toast. I knew he'd be happy with more story time on the menu. He returned my gesture before settling back in his chair to listen to Thoth, the mythmaker. Anastasia poked me in the ribs, trying to persuade me to settle down. So, I did. Thoth remained silent, waited patiently until I stopped clowning around, and then, satisfied with me, began:

Thoth's Chronicle

Gawhar came late in the afternoon to take the Montenegrins to a café amidst a succession of cafés under an arcade. Chairs crowded the pavement; it seemed every chair was occupied by an Arab or a Berber drinking either thick coffee or a liqueur and smoking foul-smelling cigarettes, talking loudly, gesturing wildly. Stevan and Joko felt right at home.

Gawhar found them a table. A waiter came.

"What will you have, Gawhar?" asked Stevan.

"Just coffee."

"Come now, Gawhar, tonight we celebrate!" Stevan exclaimed. He didn't care what it was they celebrated.

"Spirits are forbidden by the Prophet."

"Spirits?" Stevan glanced around to observe other Arabs drinking liquor and ale. Then he looked at Gawhar and raised his eyebrows.

Gawhar's face brightened. He was a handsome man; his obsidian eyes gleamed over the flash of an engaging smile—which his close-cropped dark, graying hair and beard only accentuated. When his face brightened, he could talk his companions into . . . things. "I will have mineral water."

Stevan and Joko gave him a look of disbelief.

"Yes, yes, mineral water."

They looked at him.

"You are buying, are you not?"

Joko replied, "We are."

"This mineral water is expensive."

"All right," Stevan said.

Gawhar addressed the waiter. "Large mineral water for me and my gentlemen."

The waiter appraised the situation and nodded.

Joko raised his hand in order to get the waiter's attention, but the waiter was a man who had no time to waste, and he disappeared into the café. "He didn't take our drink order," Joko complained.

Gawhar grinned. He said, "It be fine, you see."

Shortly, the waiter returned with a dark-green magnum bottle, uncorked it and set it on the table, along with narrow tumblers.

Gawhar poured each a glass of mineral water. He said, "Many bubbles, no? Means it is good mineral water."

Stevan and Joko exchanged a look. Each picked up his glass and took a swig. Stevan put his glass down and glanced at Joko.

Joko grinned. Turning to Gawhar, he said, "Very fine mineral water indeed!"

Gawhar looked at one, then the other, flashed his teeth and nodded. He picked up his own glass, held it out for a toast. He said, "To a grand evening in the great, modern city of Cairo!" They clinked glasses, drained the drink, which, if you haven't already guessed, was not exactly bubbly mineral water, but rather, bubbly champagne, and then refilled the glasses.

As they drank their "mineral water," smoked and talked, street musicians, mostly boys, wandered about playing popular melodies. Then a band of girls, looking decadent in comic opera costume, arrived to play loud music and drive the street musicians elsewhere. The three celebrants ate little dishes of meat and vegetables bought from hawkers. The moon rose in the sky.

Joko looked at the cork from the magnum. He said, "It is time, Gawhar, to see the more notorious quarters of this city."

Stevan nodded in agreement.

The Arab leaped up. "Be right back, you see!" He returned just as Stevan paid the bill. Gawhar said, "No, no, no! Too much!" He took the waiter aside, gesturing. "These are not tourists, these are my gentlemen." He went on, gaining the attention of a growing number of tables. Gawhar excelled at this approach, as he had demonstrated that afternoon during the row with the brass merchant. Soon, a tall, skinny man wearing a crimson fez closed in on the party. He seemed to be the manager. Gawhar took the manager aside to whisper in the man's ear. The manager nodded, and in a short time, the manager and the waiter came over to the table and, with curt smiles and conciliatory movements, they handed Stevan a new bill. Gawhar stood behind the *Brigade de cuisine* with his arms crossed. Stevan paid the bill, left an acceptable tip, and then he and Joko followed Gawhar through the maze of patrons to a cart in the street.

"We ride," said Gawhar, "too far to walk." They climbed into the cart. It was driven by a resident Greek, a descendent of Alexander the Great—at least, that's what the driver let them know during a chatty discussion about destination and fare. As they rolled along in their "Cairo chariot," they passed a group of British soldiers, drunk and raving.

"I thought they were to keep a low profile, what with the nationalist movement here," Stevan commented.

"They don't want to move to Suez," Gawhar answered, "British soldier like life in Cairo."

They rode down narrow lanes for a while, then turned onto a wide avenue, which briefly fronted a garden and a hotel and then disappeared into a lane again. As they continued, Stevan became quiet. Joko and Gawhar conversed for a time, then they, too, fell silent like the streets around them. The district—was it still Old Cairo?— seemed to be locked up tight.

Finally, Stevan broke his silence and asked Joko, "What did you see when you looked back at Nag Hammadi as we flew above the river?

Joko considered for a moment and then said, "Town. River. Police boat."

Stevan frowned. He turned his hand as if to say: "And?"

Joko thought for a moment more and then added, "A Citroen Traction Avant. It was unusual, often parked on shore near our mooring. As we flew, I saw that car cross the bridge. It seemed . . . Was it trying to chase us? I thought, ciao, goodbye."

Gawhar broke in, "Chase?"

Stevan answered, "We have an enemy, a society called the Order of the Suebi. This society seems to have property and influence in many countries—"

Just then the cart turned a corner to reveal a large park lit with hotels and theatres around its perimeter. Stevan and Joko turned to view it.

"Esbekiya Gardens," Gawhar said. The cart drove toward the eastern end, away from the major hotels. Soon they came to a street ablaze with electric lights. Gawhar jumped from the cart, bought three bottles of champagne from a nearby vender he knew, and climbed back in again, giving a bottle each to Stevan and Joko. He grinned and said, "So, you pay, right? This travel make us thirsty, yes?" They all uncorked and took swigs of the foamy liquid.

"It would seem we have found the temple priestesses," Joko said. He took a closer look around and then added, "But these women might not be women. Look at the flaming rouge on their faces!" he exclaimed.

Some men began pacing alongside the cart, saying, "You come! Good time! Cheap!" They addressed Stevan and Joko, ignoring Gawhar and the driver. The women joined the men and began to pull at Joko's clothes.

"They smell foul of breath!" Joko yelled, and then belched odor of champagne. Gawhar shouted at the flesh merchants and drove them away.

"Look," Joko said pointing ahead, "See those women with their legs thrust out of their gowns? Legs long and straight, the women are lithe—"

"Women of the sea," said Gawhar.

Neither Stevan nor Joko had much of an idea what Gawhar meant, but Joko liked what he saw, so he cried, "Stop the cart!" The driver pulled the reins slightly, and the donkey halted in his tracks, glad of a chance to doze. The three passengers vaulted to the ground.

Noticing this, two women sauntered forward to crowd Joko. They asked him what he was doing there, but Joko shrugged. He did not understand vernacular Egyptian. In response, the taller woman whispered something in his ear.

Joko said, "English." She whispered again, and he called out, "They want us to go inside." He drank some champagne and offered the bottle to the whisper woman.

Stevan also swigged champagne. He surveyed the street and then said, "This crossroad might make me forget Festus Griveaux and his foul Order of the Suebi!" Almost at once, he felt a sharp pull on his right arm; it seemed Gawhar wished to seize Stevan's full attention. Stevan, shifting his gaze away from a veiled woman who was approaching to join him, turned and glanced at his dragoman.

"Festus Griveaux?" Gawhar repeated.

Stevan stared at Gawhar. He replied, "Yes."

Gawhar stated with conviction, "Festus Griveaux. Just at the end of the war, a personage of this name obtained the ancient Cairo ruin, the Persian Fortress. It sits abandoned on a cliff overlooking both the city and the Nile."

Stevan repeated, "The Persian Fortress?"

Gawhar mused, "It is a ghastly place, even by day, bats as big as falcons infest the towers."

Joko finished his bottle of champagne, shouted for another.

Brushing past Gawhar, the veiled woman sauntered up to Stevan, and oddly, reaching, put her hand on his chest. When she did, Stevan glanced down at her, yet he did not smile, because he had the immediate sense of a haunting spirit. But then he realized. He knew; it wasn't she. It was his late wife, Marian, who had come to haunt him, the memory of her suddenly flooding his thoughts, his heart; he longed for her so! The strange woman of the street, with her hand on his chest, as if charmed, stirred emotions in Stevan that he had been actively excluding from his consciousness: overwhelming feelings of loss. He tried to turn his face into stone, but a tear escaped to run down his cheek.

The woman said, "So. You see."

He didn't know who this woman could be, what she was—a fortune teller? a sorceress? a jinniyah? Was she a medium channeling Marian? At once, he turned away, not afraid of her, but rather, it was Marian's spirit that seemed to be warning him, perhaps informing him of a different haunting: something . . . figure . . . something . . . the street of ill fame? the alcohol? They had failed to provide the insulation he'd hoped for. What was it that bedeviled him about the Citroen speeding down the road toward Cairo? And now, information about Festus and his Persian Fortress—Festus—who had killed Marian as surely as if he had shot her himself?

Then he knew. He cried, "Joko! He's here! He's in this city tonight!"

Joko, trying to create his own distractions so that he could forget, just for a moment, the townsfolk he had shot while trying to save Dick, pretended he didn't hear Stevan. Instead, he chuckled as the whisper woman tried to pull him toward a doorway. But since he was a bit tipsy and was leaning against the cart to steady himself, and since he was wondering if it would even be wise to move, the whisper woman couldn't budge him despite really bending her back into the effort. As he watched her antics in fascination, two more women joined the whisper woman to pitch and pull at Joko's arms. Joko thought this effort hilarious and burst into whoops of laughter. The women seemed to realize their exertions were somewhat ridiculous and began laughing too.

Exasperated with Joko's rollick, Stevan pushed his way into the cart, grabbing Gawhar by the collar as he went, thrusting him into the cart also. The driver, who usually ignored actions on the street, turned slightly, cocking an ear. Stevan said, "The Persian Fortress! Joko! Get in the cart!"

Joko realized Stevan was wild about something, but . . . for the love of—

"Drive!" Stevan yelled. The driver prodded the donkey with the handle of his lash; the cart rolled forward. Stevan grabbed Joko by the armpits and held him as the cart rolled away. Alarmed, the women pulling at Joko lost their grip so that two fell backward and one forward, all landing in the dusty street. They began screeching in anger. Then it seemed that every denizen of the district screamed and chased after the cart, Joko still dragging his booted feet behind.

Out of character, the driver—the claimed descendent of Alexander the Great—became concerned as he glanced at the actions in the street. He swore. He lashed his donkey, lashed and shouted. The donkey picked up to a fast trot. Gawhar grabbed the back of Joko's jacket to help Stevan pull Joko into the cart, even as the Cairo Chariot rolled faster, bumping and clattering over the cobble. They escaped, the driver using all his skill at the reins and all his vast knowledge of the area's twisting streets.

When the driver thought he was safe, he allowed the exhausted donkey to slow to a plod; that his passengers were also safe was due, not to his concern but to their simultaneous occupation of his wagon. Joko sprawled, hiccupping in the back of the bumping cart, Gawhar and Stevan on either side.

Stevan glanced at Joko and laughed. Joko glared back at him. He glared at Gawhar, at the driver, at the buildings around him, then finally, at the moon above him, matching glare for glow but it failed to make him feel better.

"Lost my knife too," he muttered.

"No. It was here on the floor of the cart," Stevan said, holding it up for Joko.

Joko brightened considerably as he took the knife and inserted it under his belt. Then he gave the acrimonious grin of a half-drunken man wronged. He said, "We are family! You are more like a brother to me than a nephew. Through many trials we have ridden together. Tonight, you wished to celebrate! Tonight, our moods were light—we drank! We celebrated! Then at once you are shouting, 'Get in the cart! Do this! Do that!' How quickly your mind turns pleasure into pain! If you weren't my nephew, one who I am sworn to look after—" Joko withdrew his knife and slammed it into a floorboard, which split from the blow. Gawhar jumped in his seat and fell against the driver.

"Come now, Joko," Stevan replied, "in the end, you saved us all from the evil eye." Joko didn't know what Stevan was talking about, but both Gawhar and the cart driver laughed.

Chapter iiii   -5-

T HE DRIVER DIRECTED THE cart up a switchback lane which climbed toward a cliff above the Nile. The moon hung low in the heavens now, near Cairo's western skyline; as her light began to flow west, darkness swept in around the passengers to corrupt eyesight and subvert the city with hues of grey and black.

As they rounded a curve, Gawhar pointed. He whispered, "The Persian Fortress."

In the remaining dim moonlight, Stevan and Joko saw several towers looming into the sky, but others were half-collapsed and wrecked. A wall, perhaps forty-feet high, faced the river. They could just make out gaps, where sections had crumbled. The cart had now reached the top, and the driver let the donkey rest.

Gawhar said, "This is the ruin I told you about. Now we go back."

Stevan climbed out of the cart. Gawhar reached over and grabbed his arm, "We should not stay here. You do not wish to enter now!"

"Yes," Steven answered.

Gawhar whispered, "Not safe! Bad jinn, no one goes there." He paused and then added, "And never, never, never at night!"

"I have a message that I intend to deliver to Festus Griveaux, and I intend to deliver it tonight!" Stevan pointed at the eerie redoubt. "He thinks he's safe in his rack and ruin, stalking there like a ghoul! He was in league with Hitler, did you know that? Now he hobnobs with Stalin. Two of the world's notorious mass murderers! He offers them and men like them occult means to enhance their power over the miserable masses, as Dick puts it."

Gawhar replied, "Can't fix tonight. We go!"

"Gawhar, you give me a headache," Joko said as he climbed out of the cart.

"What? You too? Out of the cart? I'm with crazy men."

"Tell the driver to wait, Gawhar, until we come back."

The driver shook his head after he understood the order. Stevan walked toward the driver holding out money in his fist, but the driver lashed the donkey, and the cart rolled away.

As the cart rolled, Gawhar jumped out. He said, "You see? Never pay money in advance."

"Let him go," Joko said, "his miserable cart and his miserable donkey."

"How do we get in?" Stevan asked Gawhar.

"Not through main gate, may be watched, may it not?"

Stevan grunted agreement.

Gawhar led them down a path around an east tower to a pile of rubble standing against a high parapet. Climbing the rubble to a kind of loophole, pieces crumbled out, that halfway up, cut though the wall, Stevan squeezed through to a wall walk inside. From there, he gingerly stepped onto the roof of a squat building and jumped down into the huge bailey, or courtyard, of the Persian Fortress. He could just see what must have been a once-magnificent arcade now half-ruined inside the courtyard walls. As he observed the grounds, Joko and Gawhar, following his route, leapt down beside him.

Hearing the wind groan through the arches, Gawhar had further misgivings. "Perhaps we should have told your friend, Thoth."

"Thoth would approve, we have a plan."

Tapping Stevan's arm, Joko pointed to the tower near them, then walked to it, leading the other two. As they neared the entrance, which had no door, they heard sounds of bat haunt but nothing more. The interior was as dark as the primal void.

Joko found a candle in the doorway and lit it, but Gawhar, already haggard, gasped, "He'll see us!"

Ignoring Gawhar, Joko and Stevan ducked inside, crouching beneath the swoop of bats. Dust, thick, covered all interior surface area except that contaminated with fresh bat dung.

"No one's been here," Stevan noted, and they quickly returned to the night air outside. When they emerged, Gawhar pointed to the southeast, toward dark shapes of ruined arcade arches.

"There is a chamber by the vault. Perhaps . . ."

Joko said, "Gawhar, how do you know these things?"

"As children, we came here on a dare, more than once. We learned a few things. But never at night!"

Through the masonry-littered bailey they walked, Stevan at times thinking he heard the fee, fie, foe, fum of spectral giants. He wondered if Gawhar's misgivings were influencing his mindset. In response, he concentrated on his mantra, the oath he would deliver to Festus. As they neared the chamber, they glimpsed a dim light within. Joko withdrew his knife from his belt and crept near the entrance, the others following. Hearing no sounds, the three men rushed into the room to surprise any occupants. Someone had furnished the chamber with pillows and drapes of grey and black, but no one was inside.

"I wonder at this game," Stevan said.

Joko fingered his knife.

"Only one place left," said Gawhar. "The north tower. It is only one not broken."

Quickly now, they walked alongside the Persian wall to the north tower. Nearing it, they saw light issuing from overlapping arrow loops and above them, a window.

"Remember, he has men with machine guns," Joko noted.

"And we have a message and your knife," Stevan answered.

"We come back," said Gawhar, "tomorrow we bring many men."

Stevan and Joko turned toward Gawhar. All remaining effect of the champagne had worn off, and under such circumstance, the Arab made sense. In fact, he had been making sense all along, since their arrival at the cliff top.

"But he might not be here tomorrow," Stevan argued. He was not sure of himself, but he said, "Festus has many lairs in many countries, which makes it hard to track him down. This is our best chance! If we scale the tower to the window, we'll take him by surprise. I know it."

Gawhar shook his head and said, "How are you sure he's here now?"

Stevan replied, "I can feel it. I know it."

Joko said nothing. He could barely see his nephew's face in the dim light from the tower. "OK. That's your word, isn't it?" he said. "OK. I'll go first, as I have the knife." Without hesitation, he began to climb, finding numerous handholds in the ancient masonry, until he reached an extended lintel over the twenty-foot-high entry.

Stevan allowed Gawhar to go next while he kept watch and was halfway up himself when he felt something pierce his side, and he realized—he'd been shot with an arrow. His mouth felt dry and his shirt grew wet. His hands burned against the wall as he fell to the ground.

Chapter iiiii i   -6-

Aving heard Stevan fall, Joko glanced down to see four dark shapes pick him up and carry him inside the dreadful tower.

Furious, Joko wanted to scream obscenities. He berated himself: Why did I go first? Why did it work this way? He grabbed Gawhar's shoulder to steady himself. He said, "Fly, Gawhar, the Suebi Order has Stevan."

Gawhar's mouth gaped open; he had been unaware of Stevan's fall. He whispered, "I bring help, you see!" Taking care, he descended and was off.

Joko wondered why they hadn't also been attacked. It's true he and Gawhar were wearing dark clothes. Had the henchmen not seen them? Certainly, the fortress was moonless now and dungeon dark. He let it go and decided to continued up the wall to the window, which he climbed through to an interior balcony. Entering, he heard Festus in midsentence, browbeating Stevan.

"—so, it was lovely of you to turn up! I have willed it, you know, this recent colliding of our lives. And where is your beautiful wife? I remember her name: Marian! I would like to have a little talk with her! I think I'll send several of these musketeers to bring her here!"

Joko, hidden and silent on the balcony, looked down to see Stevan tied to a chair, encircled by Festus and four of his henchmen.

Steven replied simply, "That would be most difficult."

"Oh, not for me!" Festus replied, "I have resources."

Stevan said, "Festus, you damn fool."

"Now, Stevan, don't be unkind. After all, we were pals!"

"You killed her."

"I killed who? Whom? I've killed many who vexed me."

"Festus, you fucking idiot. You killed Marian."

"What? I did no such thing! I adored the woman."

"She thought less of you."

"Well, I'm sure we would have been friends . . . if you hadn't disrupted my principality!"

"Is that what you call it now?"

"My colleagues don't want association with anything, past or present, hinting at a democracy." Festus paused, then smirked and said, "Even a fallacious one like mine was! But I think Marian could have understood the reason for my methods, eventually."

"She understood you alright. That's why she dropped a fin-bomb through your piazza. She was so disappointed it failed to explode."

"Well, a little tiff between friends. I certainly wouldn't have killed her for it. A little torture would be all. If she is dead, it is because of you."

At that comment, Stevan felt a catch in his throat but said, "Why were you in the Nag Hammadi region?"

"Why were you?" Festus replied.

"We found a codex. I was keeping it from you."

Festus flared his nostrils. He said, "A codex?"

"We found them all. We took them all."

This had the desired effect on Festus. He'd had no idea the codices had been found and taken away. He said, "You lie!"

Stevan was beginning to feel faint. He was still bleeding from the arrow that had been shot into his side. He said, "I had a chance to read part of one. I found words, words of . . ."

"Words of what?" Festus said, exasperated.

"Words beyond your understanding."

Festus replied, "You took my sword."

"You killed Marian."

"How so? I say you did it."

"You confined us to be interrogated by your Nazi cronies. We escaped. You shot Marian."

Festus actually looked shocked. "I . . . That was not supposed to happen! A mistake! We were returning fire on the aeroplane. If only I had done what that Irishman wanted—let you go!" Festus mused for a moment. "I think we killed that Irishman back on the Nile, and, at the same time, your flying boat was supposed to explode and exterminate you all . . . but now, I know why it did not. The codices! You had them on board? They would have been lost forever!"

"No, they weren't on board at that time. You just lost out. And now we have the library. You lose again."

Joko still remained on the balcony, waiting for any of the henchmen to be sent away on some errand or other. He figured he could deal with three, but not four of them. He saw that Stevan looked weak and exhausted. A plan, Joko thought, I need a plan!

Festus said, "Ah, yes, let's circle back to the Library, as you call it. You mentioned that you read in a codex *words*. You said you read words of . . ."

Stevan said, "I need medical attention."

Festus replied, "Are you ignoring me? Oh, you think your friends are going to come and save you. We'll find them. In the meantime, allow me to show you the view from the top of the tower." Festus clapped his hands, causing his "musketeers" to untie Stevan and drag him to the vice—a spiral staircase that wound up to the tower battlement.

Joko saw his chance. He worked his way off the balcony to a passageway accessing the same staircase. Because the vice wound clockwise upward, it was to his advantage; he would have room to swing his large knife in his right hand, but the wall would limit a henchman's right-hand strikes. If Festus came first, Joko would sink the knife into his chest. But two henchmen came first, followed by two more dragging Stevan up the stairs. Joko was on them like a whirlwind, separating them, and casting them about.

Stevan, lying on the stairs, looked up and said, "Joko! You are an august fire!"

It seemed for a time that Joko would grasp victory. But even as he throttled a henchman, smashed him to the stone stairs, the others flew at him, oblivious of their bloody, gaping wounds, attacking again. The four henchmen of the material are not easily defeated. They are Masters of Matter in this world. You cannot fight matter in hand-to-hand combat! As Joko grew exhausted, Festus appeared around a lower corner; he fired a machine gun burst, sending lethal ricochets up the vice.

"Enough," Festus shouted, "Bind him! We'll deal with this ignorant Slav later! But he has made a mess of you, my musketeers!" He commanded several henchmen to drag Stevan up to the battlement that overlooked the Nile.

Once there, Festus noticed Stevan wore a ring on his right ring finger. "Musketeers! Remove his ring," Festus ordered. Two henchmen grabbed Stevan's right arm and one of them removed the ring from Stevan's finger. "Ah, yes, I know your tricks," Festus said. The henchman gave Festus the ring. He glanced at it. "The serpent sigil designed to protect the wearer from the malign influence of the astral genie. My genie! My world!" He lowered his voice, "Now you will be subject to the fates of this world. No Gnostic escape for you!"

Below, bound and lying on the stairs, Joko could easily hear Festus. "We shall see," Joko muttered.

Festus continued, "You shall be torn asunder according to the dictates of harmony, astrological harmony, you see—fate governed by the stars, my stars!"

Joko thought, *They aren't your stars, Festus, they are but Sophia's gentle laughter.*

Festus went on, "But you don't have to go to the place of suffering. Just tell me, what words of . . . power? Yes, I know you discovered words of power. You will now tell me those words."

Stevan coughed, he could hardly speak now. At last he said, "It is Gnosis from beyond your cosmos, hidden within your world."

Festus cried, "That's exactly why I need to know it! Musketeers! Bring him over to the battlement. He can look down and see the Nile flowing to the sea, a thousand feet below!"

Though bound, Joko climbed the stairs on his elbows and knees, rubbing them raw on the harsh stone. He saw flickering torchlight as he climbed. He noticed shadows cross the wall; one looked like a fierce cat, another like a bird of prey. He saw shadows of flowers. He heard Festus go on.

"If you tell me, I may not toss you into the Nile, and we all can have a convivial dram of baijiu instead. What do you say? Otherwise, you'll have lots of time to think about your mistake on your way down."

Stevan croaked, "So this is your command? You order me to tell you? Then we have a dram?"

Festus insisted, "Yes! I command you to tell me the words of power!"

Stevan gasped, *"When you meet the Lion, and the Eagle, in consort with the Queen of Spring, you will meet that which destroys you."*

"What?" shouted Festus.

"An oath from beyond the cosmos. You commanded it into your world," Stevan whispered. "It will haunt you to your death!"

At once Festus understood. "You tricked me!" he shouted. "You are a haunter of misty hollows, you are a fool, you are nothing! Musketeers! Get ready to see if he can fly without his infamous aeroplane!"

Joko reached the top of the stairs. Dawn was breaking. He heard shouts in the courtyard. Gawhar had returned with many men.

Festus still raged, "You are nothing!"

Joko distinctly heard Stevan say in a calm voice, "You give me glad tidings."

"What?" Festus shouted.

"If I am nothing, then, I am not here. And if I am not here, you are mocking yourself."

Festus yelled, "Throw him over the wall!"

Joko struggled to his feet, but still bound, that was all he could do, except cry, "No! Stop!" He saw the four Masters of Matter grab Stevan by the arms and feet.

They swung Stevan back and forth once, twice, but the third time they threw him over the wall for a one-thousand-foot plunge; yet, at the very moment Stevan hung in the air before gravity could take him, Joko saw Stevan transfigure into a blinding shimmer of light, the purest light Joko had ever known. At once, he thought of Lazo and Yasoda, and of Marian. He heard Stevan laugh. Then he fainted at the top of the stairs.

◆　◆　◆

At that point Thoth stopped his narrative. He seemed to be fighting some strong emotion, and Anastasia, sitting right next to me, was openly sobbing. I turned my head so Dr. Moe, if he were to glance in my direction, couldn't see my face because, I confess, I'm always a basket case when a person close to me is having an emotional meltdown. Or were tears in my eyes because of the story Thoth told about death of Anastasia's father, a record of folly, bravery, and sacrifice? What about that tale reminded me of my Great Uncle MacRobbin?

Before I could think about it, Thoth said, "So ends that part of the story. Now I'll leave Egypt and take you back to Montenegro."

He continued, "Storm clouds rolled around Mt. Lovćen and rumbled toward Njeguši. Dick and Joko and I stood by as Anastasija withdrew a heavy leather case from the vault beneath Vojvoda Lodge. Placing the case on a dusty table while Joko held a lamp close, she unfastened the straps to confirm the case held hundreds of thousands of pounds of British currency. Also enclosed was a timeworn letter from Anastasija's father, saying the money represented the Romanov legacy. Anastasija knew she must flee to America with the baby Anastasia. She would rely on help from me, Joko, and Dick. I told her to contact a man named Pyotr Ouspensky, who would help her resettle in New Jersey. I gave her methods of contacting Ouspensky as well as methods of escaping Montenegro with the money. Lazo's letter warned that Festus Griveaux and his Suebi Order would find ways to penetrate Njeguši; it warned of his ruthlessness. The letter closed, 'Safeguard the insights which our ways have given you. Those with pure heart will congregate around you because of the word which you will reveal. And remember the evil will wax and wane but will not cease.'"

Chapter iiiii ii   -7-

WE ALL SAT SILENT for a time—Anastasia fussing with a Kleenex, while I finished off my double whiskey.

Dr. Moe was the first to speak, "Excuse me, Mr. Thoth—"

"Please, Dr. Littlejohn, call me Olympia."

"Thank you, Olympia, most kind of you. Now, in this account, why didn't Stevan bring his . . . 'scientific sword' when he confronted this . . . dangerous enemy? He must have known he would encounter the Suebi Order at some point. And again, who in the world is Festus? What are the four 'Masters of Matter' who cannot be defeated in combat? Don't misunderstand me, I really enjoyed the story. It is a story, is it not, a Gnostic metaphor perhaps?"

Thoth seemed to be delighted with Dr. Moe's questions. He said, "Good of you to inquire, Dr. Littlejohn, I have noted that you have a keen, skeptical intellect.

"Firstly, recall that Stevan did not go to the Persian Fortress to attack or defeat Festus, he went there to trick Festus, to bring him an oath, an imprecation that would lead to his demise. So, even if the sword had been available to Stevan, it would not have helped but rather have hindered his plan.

"Secondly, as it turned out, Stevan had previously left the sword with Anastasija at Vojvoda, but yes, it would certainly have been a useful weapon against the four Masters of the Material: Phloxopha, Ororotohos, Erimacho, and Athuro, who rule over heat, cold, dryness, and wetness, respectively."

I said, "I thought Phloxopha was female."

"Yes, usually she is a feminine spirit, but remember also, a master of matter. She can change form," Thoth noted.

Dr. Moe, flabbergasted, said, "What? These beings are described in the Apocryphon of John in the Nag Hammadi Library!"

Thoth shrugged.

"But these are books! Myth! Story! You are asserting these entities are running about spreading their mischief even as we speak."

"And have been doing so for centuries, Dr. Littlejohn. Before Festus and his minions settled in the Balkan Peninsula, causing all manner of conflict and strife, he resided in the Near East, advising rulers of each succeeding empire. Also, it was Festus who planted the poison, the destructive suspicions in the minds of the electorate of the Greek and later, Roman democracies, which in time led to their dissolutions. In their place came the reestablishment of autocratic authority in those regions. In our present era, Festus is still interested in returning to his previous model of global autocratic rule, as when Alexander III reigned over almost the entire known world."

Dr. Moe inquired, "For the sake of argument then, why does he seek this supremacy?"

Thoth replied, "He wants to keep humankind in its place: He views all the human advances in social, technical, and scientific endeavors, the endless curiosity, the willingness to strive, to at times risk the present for the sake of the future, as a direct threat to his desire for hegemony. Existence for him is a matter of hierarchy. He is at the top. All others shall serve him. That's why he favors the autocratic political model."

"I see," Dr. Moe replied.

I sought further clarification, "Exactly who or what is he?"

"The enemy," Thoth said, surprising me with a terse reply.

Then, Thoth mused for a moment and went on. "*Festus Griveaux* is not his real name. He simply adopted it early in the century in order to fit in with modern times and likely stole the surname and surnom from a grave. His real name? Only a being such as Phloxopha can pronounce it, and it cannot be written down. This is as close as I can come to it." Thoth wrote something on a scrap and handed it to me.

I took it in my hand and read: "*Thrmcplx*, the verisimilar name of the demiurge."

Thoth said, "The name existed before the emergence of language, and the names of his Masters of Matter comprise these consonant sounds."

Dr. Moe and I exchanged a glance. Thoth was beginning to creep me out, and Dr. Moe looked like he wanted another pour of Powers.

"But it is the resistance of the few," Thoth went on, "imbued with oral traditions and the science of sound—I told you about such science earlier—who have succeeded in muting his 'symphonies of chaos,' and yet we have never completely brought the curtain down on his cacophonous stage production. Excuse me my metaphor, but after all, what did the great playwright say? 'All the world's a stage!'"

Thoth continued, "Although we have baffled him at times, in fact, he has often thrown us into disarray, so that at length, we inscribed our Gnosis on papyrus pages and combined the pages into books. We hacked into cliff faces these codices, buried them in valleys, hid them in subterranean caverns and amongst shifting sands, in order that our knowledge would survive even if he overcame us. Our informal circle, or our clan if you insist, hinders Festus from obtaining these writings as they are discovered, because they would reveal the methods we use to thwart him, and perhaps inform him where our objects of power are concealed, objects like the Saxon broadsword, or Stele of Fate."

At this I commented, "Well, then, what of our Coptic Gnostic Library at the Institute of Antiquity?"

"Ah, yes," Thoth replied, "These Coptic writings are mostly already known to Festus. It is the Greek texts we possess which he now seeks, and this is why Anastasia is in danger, but also why she and you may be the answer."

This was as far as I wished the conversation to go, especially with Dr. Moe perched next to me wide-eyed like an owl. He knows I have had esoteric proclivities in my past, and probably thinks I am waiting for some rabbit of wisdom to pop out of an enchanted hat, if there were a hat. Thoth immediately discerned my reluctance to pursue this line of discussion; so did Anastasia. In fact, she yawned, almost as a damsel in a turn-of-the-century melodrama, an expansive display of stretching, arms over her head, accompanied by a sort of tuneful sonance, I must confess, then stood up and announced that it was time to go.

Dr. Moe, however, was in no hurry. He said, "Well, but, one more for the road, as they say?"

She said, "Oh, come on, Dr. Moe! If I have another drink, I'll be in bed before six, and we have a reservation for dinner at eight."

Thoth, amused, said, "I would love to, Dr. Littlejohn—"

"Please, Olympia, call me Dr. Moe. Everybody does."

"Thank you, Dr. Moe. But as I was saying, I'm afraid . . ."

Well, from there it all went to "blah, blah, blah," "appointments," "obligations," "must be somewhere," etc., everything you say when it's time to get rid of the guests. Dr. Moe, finally, like a recalcitrant child and with furrowed brow, gave in. I know he was afraid he'd never get the scoop on why I, along with Anastasia, might be THE ANSWER! I'm pretty sure Dr. Moe thinks it more likely that I am a question. Actually, I would have been perfectly happy to join him in one for the road, but—I'm not turning into an alcoholic, am I?

CODEX V
Jockey Hollow
CRNA GORA (Return To The Black Mountain)
Anagryph—the anagogic image

Chapter Jedno   *-1-*

Bᴀᴄᴋ ᴀᴛ ᴛʜᴇ Cᴀʀʟʏʟᴇ, Anastasia put on a front of taking Thoth's chronicle in stride, but I knew her emotions were raw. I could feel her melancholy. I ordered us a room service dinner, and we moped around for a while. Eventually, she informed me that she wished to introduce me to her aunt. Preoccupied creature that I am, I forgot Aunt Anastasija lives across the Hudson River somewhere in the hinterlands. I agreed that perhaps a visit would be good for all of us.

So, I decided that tomorrow, I would need a car. The concierge could have arranged for a driver, but I like to take the wheel myself, if we are going to the country. I have a friend who sells classic cars in Lower Manhattan near the Village, and he will rent me one for a week or so. Because he knows I adhere to the credo *No boring cars*, he will allow me to pick an automobile, perhaps interesting, like an old Bentley, or fun, like an XKE—anyway, something that Anastasia would like.

When I say *going to the country*, in this case it means driving to north central New Jersey, where the aunt resides. Well, I guess at what you're thinking, but don't worry, most mob hits are buried in the Jersey Meadows across the river from Manhattan, not in the woodlands of north central. And all the highways you encounter, after emerging from the Lincoln Tunnel, continue to snake mostly south, leaving our northwest destination horse country, farmland, and forest. "It's not called the Garden State for nothing," Anastasia would inform me.

I was curious to meet this formidable aunt. The things she'd been through! Loss of family and the resulting grief, the escape from Yugoslavia, the responsibilities of raising a precious orphan child, all the while balancing the child's training as an adept against her need for the trappings of a "normal" American upbringing. I expected that Aunt Anastasija would be quite careworn when I finally met her.

I called my old high school friend the next morning to reserve something automotive, old, and wonderful, but the only car he could loan me—yes, he insisted it would be a loan—was a modified 1950 Ford Custom Convertible. Was I worried about the efficacy of a twenty-three-year-old car? Well, I've learned that with Eli, you just let him be your guide.

Late that morning, the front desk informed me my car had arrived, so I called for the bell captain to prepare some poor sap to go three rounds with Anastasia's Great Huge, and to please include my sensible duffel. Then I switched to the front desk and said we would be staying overnight in New Jersey, but we would keep our suite. Meanwhile, Dr. Moe intended to remain in Manhattan. He had set meetings with colleagues from Columbia and NYU to keep him busy.

Told that a driver had parked the car in front of the hotel entrance on Seventy-Sixth Street, we strolled outside to find a Matador Red, tan-top convertible. It had a retro split windshield and a two-tone, maroon-and-brown interior. The Ford looked to be brand new, as if it had just rolled off a 1950 showroom floor. I guess that accounts for the hotel staff making sure the auto was parked up front in a spot usually reserved for JFK or the Beatles. The porter, a hero in my view, wrestled Great Huge into the cavernous trunk of the Ford and plopped my duffel in the back seat.

I spread tips all around as the staff helped Anastasia, a little too much, I noted, into the car. I climbed in, found the key in the ignition and a Hurst three-speed manual shifter mounted on the floor—with a cue ball shift-nob on top. A pair of fuzzy dice dangled from the mirror. When I fired up the Holley four-barrel-carburetor engine, the motor's low frequency burble sounded like something being emitted from a powerful and expensive mahogany Chris-Craft. The staff nodded approval. I had to hand it to Eli. The man would surely make it in New York.

We drove over to Ninth Avenue, then down to Thirty-Fourth and through the Lincoln Tunnel to New Jersey. Anastasia directed me to the turnpike and on to an exit that skirted the new buildings at Newark Airport. Eventually we ended up in a burg named Summit. It looked like a factory town, with a pharmaceutical firm called CIBA looming over the place. Since it was about 75 degrees, with intermittent clouds, I pulled over in the driveway of something designated Kent Place School—maybe they teach the local children drug compounding, although the expertise probably goes in the other direction—and put the top down. We proceeded down a road called the Shunpike, a term which means side or backroad; that is to say we would be heading deeper into the boonies. Anastasia directed me along a quaint lane that paralleled a babbling brook; I thought I saw a snake wiggling in the water. She had me turn left at another road by a waterfall. Gigantic hardwoods created a leafy canopy-tunnel over the two-lane blacktops, and this made the top-down motoring most pleasant.

On we went, twisting through farm and forest, until at length she had me turn into a gravel drive that continued two hundred yards to an East Coast style house, rambling, with white painted siding, divided glass windows framed by black storm shutters, and a roof of gray slate. That was all I could take in because an attractive older woman (who, by the way, didn't look careworn at all), long gray hair tied in a bun, emerged immediately from the front door to greet us.

With the 1950 Ford Custom still rolling to a stop, Anastasia popped her door, jumped out, and hair flying behind her, ran like an eight year old to hug her aunt. It was kind of touching. What is it about women? They seem, at times, to transform themselves into any age, from eight to eighty. I pulled the handbrake, put the Hurst in first gear, and climbed out into the New Jersey countryside. Although I was again wearing my blue hopsack blazer over a polo shirt, I felt like I needed my safari jacket, boots, etc. (which still hadn't arrived from Claremont), because after all, Aunt Anastasija might need me to chop wood for the stove.

As I walked toward them, the Anastasias turned, watching me, smiling. When I put out a hand to shake, saying, "Hi, I'm Griffin," Aunt Anastasija reached out, hugged me, and whispered in my ear, "Oh, I know who you are."

Have you ever heard the song by Bob Dylan, about Mr. Jones: Something is happening here—but Mister Jones is clueless as to what?" Was I Mr. Jones?

My Anastasia grabbed my hand and pulled me through the front door, which stood open under a fan window, and into the front hall. Entering, the first thing I saw was a sable collie lying upside down on a love seat. She didn't seem to feel there was any reason to move.

I said, "Hello good dog!"

Aunt Anastasija, who had come in behind us, shut the door and said, "This is our darling Alta."

Hearing her name mentioned by her mistress, Alta flipped off the couch, landing smartly on her feet, and came over to us, wagging her tail. After seeing what Aunt Anastasija needed, the collie decided she was supposed to check me out.

"Well, come on," I said, patting my thigh. Alta came to me and leaned in for a good petting of her side. Satisfied with me, she turned back to her loveseat, jumped back up and lay down as if to say, "Don't try to sit here."

"Anna, why don't you and Griffin bring in your luggage? I have a room for you upstairs. I'm sorry, but I have been doing a bit of remodeling, and as a result your bedroom is on the third floor."

Upstairs, Anastasia, looking around, said, "Aunt Anastasia has moved all my things up here. It looks exactly like my old room! How sweet of her to take the trouble!"

I could tell this trip had lifted Anastasia's spirits. I glanced here and there to satisfy my curiosity, this sudden peek behind the door to her past. But before I could think further about the things in her room, she wrapped her arms around me, and we . . . lost track of time for a while.

Chapter Dva   -2-

LATER IN THE EVENING, after dinner, Aunt Anastasija led us into her library. She poured us each a glass of port. She and her niece sat on a couch near a fireplace, but I wanted to peruse the library shelves.

Although the books in her library wore masks of age, leather covers cracked, pages yellow and brittle, they were not dusty; indeed, Aunt Anastasija had cared for them with ritual attention and love, I think because they represented, more than any other symbol, her Romanov legacy of mysticism, myth, mystery, and story—a life of the imagination, which, in turn, shaped the material world around her.

Having observed my critical viewing, she said, "The books belonged to my father, Lazo. When I was a girl in Montenegro, he would take me into his stone-walled library, where the fire burned and the oil lamps flickered, Rade, the wind, whining through the pines outside. He would tell me things like, 'The imagination makes the world, child, you must try to hear its murmurings and use them to shape your life. But beware! There is danger! Risk! There is always opposition!'"

Fascinated, I walked over and sat down on a nearby chair. I sipped my port and glanced at Anastasia.

She said, "Go on, Aunt."

"Well, I don't want to bore him."

This must have been strictly theater, because the aunt is a woman who knows it is impossible for anything boring to come out of her mouth.

I said, "Please, I'd love to hear more."

Aunt Anastasija smiled, took a sip of port and continued. "I would flounce into a chair and not know his meaning. He would recognize my confusion, yet continue, 'Understand, child, your essence is a river flowing from a self-regeneration fount, coursing through misty gorges and nearly impenetrable mountains, through harsh deserts, across deep canyons, each obstacle threatening the waters, threatening to dam them, drain them, dry them up. But the river in its wisdom seeks the low ground, or when it must, rises to overcome that which would defeat it. There are always obstacles, child, but answering them is the imagination of the creative river, whichever finds a way to flow onward.'"

"Well," she continued, "as I grew older, Lazo's words did have an impact. I chose a book from his shelf one day and so began a deep study of esoteric knowledge, my family's legacy. When they determined I was ready, my mother and father, Yasoda and Lazo, taught me their secret oral tradition, Gnosis so profound it could not be solidified on the pages of a book. At length, they warned me: as my consciousness reached higher levels, forces in the cosmos would take notice and try to misdirect my thoughts away from the true path of knowledge.

"'First come subtle attempts,' counseled my mother, 'each by itself nothing. But pressures, one after another, push you toward consciousness with pain: you become constantly aware of the anguish of material existence. Such anguish leads to madness, and in madness there is no liberation.'

"My father would say, 'Heed the waters and you cannot fail.'

"My mother would say, 'Dim your eyes, sit quietly until you hear the silence, wherein flow the waters. You will know.'

"Then my father warned, 'When it is found the subtle things cannot sway you, terrible forces may be sent against you. The one now known as Festus Griveaux is such a force. But not as you might expect. At times he is crafty, yes, but mostly he is ignorant and clumsy. Seek the low ground, he cannot find you there. If he catches you elsewhere, use the power of our way to overcome him.'

"My mother told me, 'When I birthed Stevan, a plan was set in motion to defeat this entity, for though he is unable to overwhelm our clan of knowledge, he can cause us trouble, and he causes great suffering in the world among the common folk. He is constantly setting one ethnic group against another and can even create regions of geo-political strife.'"

Aunt Anastasija paused and took a sip of port. I might have been stunned by this . . . far-ranging, almost chimerical soliloquy, if I hadn't already experienced a loosening of my synapses during our visit with Thoth in his wonderful and somehow disturbing office in the netherworld of the Met.

Aunt Anastasija continued, "When my Uncle Joko told me the details of Stevan's death in Egypt, I knew my brother had sacrificed himself, had confronted the malevolent power, had suffered under it in order that esoteric constructions could be set in motion to defeat it. So, I escaped Montenegro carrying my niece and a suitcase full of money. I had already been told that we, the baby and I, were involved in the plan to defeat Festus, and I should raise my niece with all the care and attention our tradition afforded us. Thoth would help. The child would be taught ways of power, but gently, so that she would hardly realize she knew them. Her upbringing would be as normal as could be permitted. Until it became unavoidable, she would not be told of Festus and the Order of the Suebi's hovering presence."

Anastasia, leaning back on the couch, turned to look at her aunt. She said, "I knew a lot more than you think!"

Ignoring the comment, the aunt rolled on, "Now, with Anastasia arriving home, saying that all had been revealed to her by Thoth, the time has come to continue the plan to defeat the entity, Festus. And I agree with Thoth's conclusion that Stevan's texts must be recovered from their concealment in Montenegro." The aunt turned to look back at Anastasia and declared, "It is my niece's fate to seek the texts."

Aunt Anastasija poured us another glass of Graham's 20. After she put the decanter down, she looked directly at me, smiled, and said, "But what of this oddly compatible man she has in tow? Griffin? You are an outsider, are you not?" She took one more sip of port, put her glass down, and said, "Excuse me, please, I have something I must attend to." At once, she arose and disappeared into another part of the house.

That might have worked on a younger man, but I didn't just fall off yesterday's turnip truck. I've encountered this female ploy more than a few times, when they deliver a direct and personal non sequitur and then either stay and watch what happens, or they head for the hills to give their ploy time to fester.

My inamorata said, "I do think you are compatible, even though you're not particularly odd."

I grinned and said, "This is fun."

We regarded each other, contemplating. Then I lifted my glass of port, this sweet, thick wine fortified with brandy—drink sherry before dinner, wine with dinner, have port and cigars after— assured to give you the gout after years of heavy consumption (I take a drink), but it is a warming liquid (I drink again) . . . It's Anastasia in bed under quilts of down, rain on the windowpanes; a fire crackling on the eighteenth-century hearthstone is this liquid (I drain the glass). First light of dawn on the lacy curtains, feminine knick-knacks covering tabletops, a silver brush, comb and hand mirror, amethyst stones, various flasks, jars, phials and vials, a golden unicorn, ribbons, a diary, letters, books: *Green Mansions, Quo Vadis, Mansfield Park*; on the wall are ribbons from horse shows, a pen-and-ink drawing of the Left Bank, muted tapestries, a mummer's mask. In the canopied bed, her black (but with a hint of chestnut) hair on the pillow, pale skin warm beneath sheer gown, she turns to me, I see her face, the dark-green eyes, but there, on her nose, are freckles . . . I pour another glass, hold it up to the light to see browning-rose luminance. "I remember you, Anastasia."

"He remembers you, Anastasia," crooned Aunt Anastasija, who just reappeared in the library doorway.

Seeing her, I stood up.

"Remembers . . ." she said again as she crossed the room. Taking my arm, she led me to the bookshelves. She asked, "What else do you remember?"

I ran my hand over the book spines. "I love your library and this rambling house . . . I remember leaving Claremont with Anastasia, arriving in New York, our meeting with Thoth, but then driving from Manhattan, Anastasia directing me over a twisted mass of highways, finally leaving them behind, driving down a narrow road through a land she called Jockey Hollow, saying, 'We're almost home!' The trees thick, bending over our heads, cool green shadow, dense woods where possibilities still hide—anything could live beyond those trees, unlike desert scrub where you see for miles. I remember the heavy air that makes sweat on your body and flora on the earth. Approaching your driveway, post-and-rail fences weathered gray, fitted together in imperfect, artful construction. I saw dirt paths bending uphill through fields. Where do they lead? An enormous barn, old, stood as part of the land, against it a wheel turned rusty, long spokes like rusting rays of sun, a barrow of yellow straw standing dripping with dew, two great horse vans parked under an oak of a thousand branches, a pitchfork stuck in a steaming pile of horse manure, dogs yapping, a horse whinnying, birds all around us. I remember thinking, 'What journey is this?' I look at Anastasia, whom I hardly know, yet slowly I remember her. And I recall this house. Have I said this before to you? Will it ever be right?"

Aunt Anastasija didn't reply at first, but I observed she exchanged a glance with her niece. Then the woman turned and took my arm again. We strolled along some further bookshelves. She said, "Do you know, ah, Griffin, that even though my hair is gray it still reaches below my shoulders? I keep it wrapped in a bun during the day because many think it unseemly for an older lady to wear her hair down—it is a small way to conform—and during the day I see myself in a glass and I wonder, who is this woman? At nightfall I let my hair down, again before a mirror, and I wonder, who is THIS woman? A new set of memories whirls through my mind. Oh, it seems I have long-hair memories and short-hair memories, that's what I call them. Often, they don't intermesh but are separate, as though I've lived separate lives. Then there are moments when my thoughts come together all at once. At such instants I can see forward and backward beyond time, so it seems. Perhaps I do recall talking to you this way, Griffin, perhaps I do." She stopped and pulled a book from a shelf and opened it. I could see the pages were hand-stitched and bound and covered with mysterious, black, hand-printed Cyrillic lettering. Across the room, Anastasia knelt before the fireplace, stabbing wood and kindling together with an iron fire poker. She lit a match.

Aunt Anastasija remarked, "This book is called *The Esoteric Metaphysica of Love and Marriage*, Griffin." She turned the pages. "It tells how souls find their mates, the characteristics of attachments between souls, of the desire for union of opposites in the higher and lower bodies . . . how casual promiscuous relations are dangerous because they create connections which are more easily made than broken, connections that create traps for the soul in future lives . . . yet how for any form of creation the two opposite forces are necessary. So, this book discusses the desire for sex, but it's not limited to the physical level, but rather the mating of our seven bodies."

"Would that I could read Russian," I said.

"It really should be translated. However, only a few would ever read it anyway. Just as well, it is only meant for the few. You could understand it."

Anastasia, finished lighting the fire, came over and stole me away from her aunt. We settled on the couch. Alta wandered into the library, walked directly over to us and jumped up on the unoccupied third seat and lay down, snuggling up next to me.

"Well, she's made up her mind about knowing you, Griffin, and, I feel the same way! Good night, dears. See you tomorrow." Aunt Anastasija withdrew for the night.

The next morning after breakfast, I packed up the car and felt almost sad to be leaving. I know Anastasia did too. Alta, standing on the top of the steps, wagged her tail, trying to welcome us back inside and seemed disappointed when we didn't give in to her furry wonderfulness. And Aunt Anastasija had that look of sad acceptance, the countenance of one who had encountered things in life, both momentous and sundry, that she either could not control or considered she should not try to, such as saying goodbye to us that very morning.

And then it occurred to me: none of us knew if we would ever see each other again, and we realized it. It may be always true, whenever you say goodbye to someone, for whatever reason it may be for the last time, but usually with family and good friends, you assume you will get together again soon. Not this time. Perhaps not ever again.

I'd heard from Dr. Moe, or rather, I phoned him that morning to tell him our air destination would be Belgrade and to have Byah book us a first-class international flight, and yes, put it on my private card. He told me he had learned something interesting from his colleagues during a get together at the 21 Club. That's as far as the conversation went. We both knew that there are things you don't discuss over the phone. I put the top down on the Ford so that we could wave as we motored down the driveway, tires crunching on the gravel, bugs and birds singing in the trees, the smell of honeysuckle in the air. Anastasia turned in her seat to look back and wave to her aunt, who, as I saw in the mirror, was waving back at us, and behind her Alta wagged and barked.

Anastasia directed me along indecipherable country roads, something called Glen Alpine, another called Village Road, which, indeed, went through a tiny village. I saw a woman in a field directing three or four collies over fences and ramps for agility training. I could tell in an instant she knew what she was doing, and, if I wasn't on my way to confront the prince of disruption, I'd turn in, ask her if she were a breeder and if she would be kind enough to sell me a puppy.

I turned on the AM radio, the only wireless option available in a 1950 Ford. It worked! Someone named Cousin Brucie was making himself annoying, so I turned it off. We again passed the CIBA pharmaceutical factory. The building reminded me of something I had noticed yesterday when I had driven past an industrial complex west of the city, but what? It was a factory with a logo similar in font to the one we had just passed, but not the same. I'd scan for it on the way back.

As we waited in a line of traffic for the turnpike tollbooth, I could feel a change in the East Coast weather: a tsunami of hot, muggy air rolled over us. I started extoling the virtues of the temperate West Coast, but Anastasia didn't want to hear it and gave me an eye roll.

Traffic moved not an inch—some obstruction, some problem, some delay. My back began to stick to the vinyl seat. I put my hands on the windshield surround and pulled myself up into a standing position. Anastasia thought it was a good idea and did the same. Cars behind us honked, so Anastasia turned and gave them a friendly wave. I could see over adjacent cars now, and as I looked around, there it was: a series of buildings that could well have been an industrial complex. Printed on a cylindrical tank in large font was:

SUBI BIOCOM

For A Better Tomorrow

Back at the hotel, Dr. Moe told us that our overseas international flight would leave Kennedy at 6:00 P.M. I guessed our happy stay at the Carlyle had come to an end.

Chapter Tri   -3-

FOR AN INTERNATIONAL FLIGHT in today's world of 1973, you have to arrive at the airport an hour and a half in advance of takeoff; obsessives insist on at least two hours, but many of those types like to kill time in the airport bars.

We boarded the Pan Am airliner. Ah, first class, with the curving staircase up to the stars. We were soon to discover Boeing had constructed more than a bar up there; in preference, they had created an exclusive restaurant for expense-account types, where a uniformed waiter carves a slice of roast beef for you at your table. And yes, a full bar is included. Plus, there is the added intrigue that if the plane hits turbulence during the carving, the waiter might mistakenly slice your jugular instead. Byah, the wizard, booked us reservations that included dinner in that lordly dining den. So, by 8:00 P.M. New York time, winging thirty thousand feet above the Atlantic Ocean, where below us were probably one-hundred-foot rogue waves, Beluga whales, dismasted yachts, etc., we settled into our comfortable overstuffed chairs next to a table adorned with a starched white tablecloth and set with linen napkins and actual silverware.

Are you shocked at how the other half lives? So was Dr. Moe. I was going to have to pillage my retirement account to pay for all this—however, I say, when you are possibly going to your doom, you might as well stop and smell the roses, as they say, otherwise you will never have memories of "Days of Wine and Roses." Were those good memories? I forget. Meanwhile, I observed that Anastasia was familiar with this upper-class setup. I sometimes fail to remember that in addition to her weighty responsibilities of saving mankind, she is also an heiress.

I ordered the roast beef because I really wanted to see the waiter do his thing with the carving knife at our thirty-thousand-foot table, but it turned out the knife was electric! An electric knife similar, in miniature, to what you clip the hedges with. What a disappointment, a decided lack of swashbuckling. The bottle of Barolo made up for it though. Anastasia ordered filet of sole and a half-bottle of Vouvray, and Dr. Moe ordered steak-and-kidney pie with peas, mashed potatoes, and gravy. What a maniac!

Anastasia said, "Dr. Moe, Griffin tells me that while we were out of town, you met with several colleagues at the 21 Club. Years ago, my aunt took me there for dinner on my twenty-first birthday."

"Did she?" Dr. Moe replied. "It was my nephew, Tuck's, twenty-first birthday, so four of us old professors took Tuck and three of his friends there to celebrate. We had a grand time. But now you've reminded me of what I learned during dinner that evening."

I butted in, "OK, let's hear it, Dr. Moe."

He grinned at me. Evidently, he thought he possessed pearls of inside information. He confided, "A nascent yet rapacious industrial concern has been headhunting top talent from universities, labs, corporations, and government—in fields such as computer technology, statistical analysis, communication science, biochemistry, biomedical engineering, genome research, electronic miniaturization and naturalization, particle physics, etc. They are also seeking theorists in the mathematics of sound and wavelength. In addition, one of Tuck's friends insisted, the concern's HR department is hunting for borderline-autistic geniuses who may be cobbling together god-knows-what in dank basements or dusty garages. The multinational enterprise pays well above the standard wage and bonus compensation, and the rumor is they are backed by Sino-Soviet investment. So, it seems, this is a state-sponsored monstrosity."

While Dr. Moe related this information, I glanced at the other three tables nearby. I made a hand signal to remind my friend and colleague to keep his voice down because, despite the noise, vibration, and harshness of the Pratt and Whitney jet engines, their din could only do so much to mask his pie-fueled voice. I mean, for all I knew, the four Asian gentlemen two tables over were executives of the very enterprise we were discussing.

I said, even though I thought I already knew, "And what is the name of this mega Corp? No, don't tell me, I'll tell you!"

But before I could speak, Anastasia butted in and said with a grin, "Subi Biocom."

So, I piped up: "For a Better Tomorrow." At that, I swear the Asian table glanced in our direction, but I ignored them. It was more fun to observe Dr. Moe being impressed with our deductive reasoning.

"That's it, Anastasia!" he exclaimed, paying no attention to me. I think he was starting to like her.

She asked, "How did your friends learn that much detailed information about Subi Biocom?"

Reflecting, Dr. Moe said, "Well, let's see, we had Professor Glen Fleischer, the head of the Columbia University School of Strategic Communication; Professor Dan Bowers, director of the MIT School of Bioengineering; and Professor Matt Martinez, from NYU, the foremost expert in the application of mathematics to sound. Believe me, these men know what is going on in the realm of hiring and fir-ing in the private sector and the poaching of their faculty and grad students by industry. The poaching is so extensive, all the kids are aware of it, and said so."

We were four hours into the six-hour flight—4:00 A.M. Belgrade time, 10:00 P.M. New York time, 7:00 P.M. California time—talk about a spacetime continuum. What a lark! We would pay the piper for our profligacy, via jet lag.

That's why Byah had reserved a car for when we landed at 6:00 A.M. or so to take us directly to the Belgrade City Hotel. There we could crash in a room for a few hours and then board our connection to Tivat at 5:00 P.M. From there, we would hire a boat to take us down to Sveti Stefan, where we would stay and meet up with the one and only Joko.

Well! It was almost like we were on vacation instead of seeking eerie, spellbound, myth-laden codices. But we believed these codices could be the key to preventing international disasters invoked by the Suebi Order, perhaps to be implemented through their new enterprise, Subi Biocom. I had to admit, if this so-called Festus Griveaux was behind Subi Biocom, he had a way with autocratic despots, somehow manipulating them to fund his corrupt, damnable war on free, creative, self-governing people wherever they could be found.

Chapter Cetiri   -4-

S OON WE WERE WALKING down a wharf, pulling Great Huge
the way one might try to rule a reluctant mule.

"Ovim parobrod ima može se putovati duž čitave obale," said
a man's voice. We looked down toward the water to see an old man
standing in a small but seaworthy-looking wooden fishing boat. He
was addressing us.

Anastasia said, "Kazi!" and the man spoke again.

I nudged Anastasia with my elbow.

"He says it is possible to travel right down the coast by those
steamers," Anastasia explained, and pointed at the commercial boats
resting along the pier. "But he can take us, too, and will leave now. He
says he will take us anywhere."

"Well, just Sveti Stefan."

The boatman nodded his head and pointed down the coast when
he heard Sveti Stefan. I thought, What the hell, this might be a gypsy
boat-cab, but I sort of liked the guy, so I gave Anastasia's suitcase a
swift kick. Anastasia smiled, then struck a bargain over the fee, and
shortly we were chugging out of the harbor, with, by the way, Dr. Moe,

who had showed up in the nick of time from God knows where (we would have waited).

As we sat around the cockpit, the boatman, speaking in the local language, said to Anastasia, "Do you know the tale of Sveti Stefan Islet?"

She translated his question for Dr. Moe and me. I looked up and appraised the boatman. He was tall, dressed in brown wool pants that would make most men itch, a brownish-yellow shirt and a dark-gray wool coat. A peaked captain's cap, also dark, balanced out his appearance against his heavy jowls. Between the jowls, the corners of his mouth bent downward in the stoical expression of a man who has faced down the wind for years at the sea.

I said, "Tell us."

Anastasia nodded and the boatman narrated as though he'd been telling the story all along, Anastasia translating every few sentences.

"The Ottoman climbed the rock wall amidst sound of gun and cannon fire. Thirty feet below him, big fish gobbled little ones, undisturbed by the human struggle above. His scimitar dangled behind him as he scaled the wall. A comrade on his left took a salvo in the face and was unable to scream as he fell to the water—a white circle of foam, then nothing. The Ottoman climbed and climbed until he grabbed the top of the cliff. In a moment he would vault over and begin chopping Montenegrin heads, but instead, he was flying through the air looking at a stump on his left wrist where his hand used to be. In shock, he drowned at the foot of the seaward cliffs.

"The islet was not always inhabited back in those old days, and it was a wild, lonely place. But a full moon after the Ottoman drowned, a nun, who said her name was Stefan, a man's name, began to live at the cliff's summit right where the Ottoman's hand still lay, black and withered but, strangely, not decayed. In the years after, Stefan became known to both Montenegrin and Ottoman as a woman of healing and mercy. But strangest of all, legend says the nun, in symmetry with the Ottoman, had a stump on her right wrist where her hand should have been. When she died, we Montenegrins erected a chapel on the cliff, the chapel of Sveti Stefan, and the rock islet became known by the same name." As the boatman finished his tale, he observed us, gauging its effect, I guess.

"I've never heard that story!" Anastasia exclaimed.

The boatman looked out across the gray sea where dark ripples formed patterns, the whole seascape alive with movement. Speaking English for the first time he said, "There are few of us left who know the female origin of the name."

"The name?" questioned Anastasia, alert.

As the boatman gazed at her, his gnarly face bent into a smile, a genuine, loving smile. "The holy, unspeakable name. A little story about a nun with a man's name reminds us that many holy names have been changed by careful scribes from female to male."

Dr. Moe, sticking to his own exegesis, remarked, "Many researchers claim the brain is divided in half. The left brain or analytic, prosaic side controls the right half of the body. The right brain or intuitive, poetic side controls the left half of the body. The Turk lost his left hand, perhaps symbolic of his renunciation of the creative goddess. The nun has no right hand, indicating female disuse of the analytic left brain, yet she has a man's name. That indicates a combining of male and female, and thus she was a merciful healer! Together she and the Ottoman have no hands or both hands. I love these old folktales!"

Ignoring Dr. Moe's analysis and instead glaring at the boatman, I exclaimed, "You speak English."

The boatman nodded.

I said, "You've been putting us on for the last half hour."

The boatman shrugged.

"All right!" barked Anastasia, "quit rocking the boat, both of you."

"But the man speaks English! He's been playing the role."

The boatman grinned at us and laughed.

Anastasia snapped a question at him, "Does the word Yasoda mean anything to you?"

"Yasoda means everything to me," the boatman replied.

She questioned, "If you saw a woman with one egg, a willow rod with three leaves, a bouquet of nine flowers . . . "

"I might tremble with fear or delight."

"How so?"

"A woman who wields such objects, if I hear her speak, will become my guide. If I am weak and try to bend her to my image, she will abandon me."

Anastasia, excited, said, "I should know you, shouldn't I?"

"I don't know why. You were just a baby," answered the boatman.

"Yes, but some things I should know. You are Joko."

Replied Joko with a grin, "Who else?"

Anastasia turned to me. "He is Joko, the uncle of my father and Aunt Anastasija, the very Joko whose older brother was Lazo. He is my Granduncle! He knew Yasoda and also Herak."

She was veritably beaming, but I was still annoyed. I said, "Well, why the hell didn't he identify himself? He knew who we were!"

Joko replied, "We have to be a bit more careful than that. We don't want to act like the biggest idiots on earth."

Paying attention, Dr. Moe exclaimed, "Now, see here! We will not be spoken to that way!"

I don't need Dr. Moe to defend me, but sometimes he goes off like a firecracker.

As if seeing Dr. Moe for the first time, Joko glanced down and, sizing up the little man, he decided there was something to him, so he said, "OK. I apologize. But I had to be sure of you. I am still afraid of Festus and his Masters of Matter."

I remembered what Thoth had told us about Joko's encounter with those beings at the Persian Fortress back in 1946, and I understood his caution with us. I said, "Yes, Joko, Thoth told us what happened. I'm very sorry."

"Was a long time ago."

Dr. Moe said, "Time doesn't always work like that, though, does it?"

Joko said nothing. He looked off to the horizon, a response to the memory I'm sure he had borne often over the years. The boat crashed through a little rogue wave, showering us with spray. "No," Joko finally replied. "Could have been yesterday."

As Joko stood at the helm, Anastasia arose, walked up to him, and threw her arms around him. I think I heard her whisper, "I know . . . I know."

The fishing boat rolled and bounded toward the south. I looked to the coast, where dark peaks at least a thousand feet high dropped steeply to the shoreline—a wall guarding the interior against invasion from sea people. Soon, jutting out into the azure water, came the rocks of the Sveti Stefan islet.

Joko and Anastasia exchanged a glance, and she returned to the seat beside me. She said, "Aunt Anastasija has reserved several lodges for us tonight."

Hearing the mention of his niece, Anastasija, Joko brightened. He said he had, at times, spoken with her via overseas cable, but had not seen her in many years. He said, "My niece is a wonder! Look what she has done with you!"

Anastasia replied, "And she has told me things. Tomorrow you take us to Herak's caves. That is where you hid Father's codices, isn't it, Joko?"

"Yes," Joko conceded, "but that was thirty years ago. Ten years ago, a quake caused the earth to cover the only entrance I know. We go to Njeguši. From there, perhaps we find a direction to take."

It turned out Joko no longer lived in Njeguši, that it had been a dying village for a number of years. He'd been living in Budva since 1955, working as an independent fisherman and sometime guide for Montenegrotourist. He said, "I've arranged for your stay at Sveti Stefan to be free. It is off-season. I have friends, found you all good rooms."

"Joko!" Anastasia said softly, "It's such a relief that you're with us."

Joko stretched his mouth into a smile, then turned to me and said, "You are either very brave or very stupid to be here. I think it may be a lot of one and a little of the other. Do you know what you are getting into?"

I replied, "You have a way with words, Joko. All I can say is that I'm following my intuition."

"Ahhh," said Joko. "She is very beautiful."

Chapter Pet   -5-

A HUGE, MUSCULAR MAN WALKS the Adriatic Highway to Budva. We passed him while driving north on the narrow road in Joko's Yugoslavian Fiat.

"Potres-Čovjek," Dr. Moe said, attempting to repeat the Serbo-Croat phrase just intoned by Joko.

"It means Earthquake Man," Joko explained. "He haunts earthquake ruins like a ghost. His job is to pile aside rubble, stone atop stone. The task is endless. When he finishes one job, it seems the earth yawns and stretches like a restless beast and somewhere another village tumbles to the ground.

"We will climb a very old road, narrow and dangerous. It rises above the Bay of Kotor, writhing like a python. It is called the Serpentine."

Anastasia remarked, "Twenty-five reverse bends in the Serpentine."

I noted, "Five times five."

Joko applied the brakes and pulled over to the side of the road; a large truck roared past, almost scraping the Fiat's faded paint job. Joko muttered, "Not so ignorant after all. Therefore, Griffin, you drive. Can you drive?"

Anastasia noted, "Like a maniac."

"Good," Joko said, "he will fit these roads perfectly. Everybody's a maniac! Nobody has a license! Do you know the best drivers in Yugoslavia come from Montenegro? It is true, because all the bad ones are dead! Since I am of seventy-eight years, perhaps your reactions are a little faster than mine."

Joko and I changed seats and I began to steer the little Fiat up the Serpentine. As it twisted and turned, I caught glimpses of the coast in my rearview mirror. Ahead, little green lizards ran across the potholed blacktop. On one side of the road grew small blue flowers, white flowers, yellow flowers, purple flowers; on the other side, nothing but empty space.

Anastasia exclaimed, "I celebrate these vertical mountains! It is like I'm climbing them in a dream or . . . a prophecy."

From the backseat Dr. Moe commented, "If you are acting in a prophecy then we all are, but what does that mean for our free will? Are we just destined to behave according to a cosmic plan?"

Joko suggested, "You are the deep thinker, Dr. Moe, are you not? I say, we all do what we must."

Anastasia said, "The philosopher, Ouspensky, declared that if you would like to go back in time and relive your life, making better choices, it wouldn't work, you would just do everything the same because you would be no different than you were in the past. The only way to become better is to start where you are right now, change how you do things now! And that's when you express free will."

Joko said, "Oh, yes, Ouspensky! One of us! He lived just long enough to help my sister, and you as a child, to settle in New Jersey near his complex, Franklin Farms."

"Ahhh, there's a god loving bus! Time to ditch!" Steering with both hands, I jerked the Fiat to the right until it bumped to a halt in a small cut by the roadside. The bus, not even slowing, scraped past us and continued down the road.

"It just appeared around the corner," Joko said, shaken, looking over the sheer drop into the Bay of Kotor.

"Joko! I was given to believe things like this don't upset you," Anastasia said.

"Heights do. I don't like aeroplanes either."

I drove on until Joko said, "Observe! The twenty-fifth bend. Soon we will reach Njeguši."

We passed a smokehouse advertising famous Njeguši ham, then the road curved ninety degrees to the left. On the outside edge stood a sign attached to rusted metal poles. It said "NJEGUŠI." I could see a valley surrounded by gray stone mountains specked with pines and low shrubs, thickets and brambles.

I gazed at the area: churches, graveyards, apple orchards . . . women in black working the fields, and chickens pecking in the open doorways of stone huts . . . and there, a white-faced calf peeked from the window of a cabin. A small car screamed past us as though it had taken a few wrong turns off the track at Le Mans.

"The women dressed in black are in mourning," Joko explained. "They wear it five years for a father, two for a brother, one year for a husband."

Anastasia said, "The men don't wear black. They just go down to the tavern and drink themselves silly when someone dies."

I drove further along the road until the recent Le Mans car, having turned around, careened back toward us in the wrong lane, our lane; it slued back and forth into both lanes. I honked the Fiat's feeble boo-pa-boopa horn, but it had no effect on the blind and deaf driver, his unguided missile of a car coming at us, Anastasia saying, "My God!" Dr. Moe and Joko shouting something less genteel from the back seat. My only option was to dive off the road to the right where the drop-off looked to be about a meter. I needed to avoid rolling the car when we landed in the adjacent loamy field—a potato field? I launched us off the road at a forty-five-degree angle as the oncoming car shot by us. Once in the air, by my returning the steering wheel to straight ahead, our Fiat did a rather nice four-wheel landing, bounced up into the air, landed again, and slid to a stop opposite a nameless little café.

Joko pointed to it and said, as if he were still with Montenegrotourist, "Here we are! This is where we'll stay."

I restarted the Fiat's engine, which had stalled, and we bumped through the field to park on loose gravel next to an old, beat-up Land Rover. Joko and Dr. Moe, happy to be out of the car, I guess, entered the building, but Anastasia and I paused to reflect on our good fortune of still being alive. Above us, great clouds spilled upward into the sky—moisture from the Adriatic.

When we entered the café, we were greeted with another cloud—thick, choking, the room was crammed with workmen sitting on benches at long tables smoking cigarettes as they watched a football match on a black-and-white television mounted over the unstained wooden bar. Almost all of them turned when we entered, well, when Anastasia entered, as though her presence changed the room's ion count, as though she emitted a phantom negative charge, as from lightning, which split the fetid air. Heads turned toward her; I could see the orange glow of cigarettes in the dim light.

We stepped over outstretched legs and crossed the room to the bar, where Joko was introducing Dr. Moe to a plump, gray-haired woman. The exchange amused me as it consisted of Dr. Moe's wordless nodding and smiling and pantomiming—doing his congenial goofball act. I didn't think it was working on the proprietress, who perhaps wondered what this man was smiling about (Perhaps he's a moron?). But when Joko presented Anastasia, the woman commoved back and forth, shouted into the kitchen, presumably to the cook, and trotted into the main room to order a tableful of workmen to clear out.

Joko said in a low voice, "I told her who Anastasia is."

She returned to Anastasia and said something in Serbo-Croat and then looked at me. Anastasia replied and then said, "I told her you are my husband. Otherwise, we must stay in separate rooms."

The wonder of this day. I nodded.

The woman took Anastasia by the arm and directed the four of us to sit at the just-vacated table while the workmen looked on in sardonic amusement. She related a bit more café information to Anastasia and Joko and withdrew. Anastasia told of what she had just learned of the honey-wine . . . in the whole world, made only at this café by old family recipe, and of the Njeguši ham, and the goat cheese, and the homemade bread.

I couldn't suppress a smile. Joko noticed and said, "Is a good place, is it not? You will like what she brings us."

I replied, "I think I'm hungry."

A workman strolled by, the first of many of them doing this, stopped, and offered Anastasia a cigarette. She shook her head, no. He had a black eye and his nose was wrapped in a bandage. I pointed at the wrappings and shrugged my shoulders. The workman grinned, held his hands in front of him, and mimed driving a car until it crashed. We all exchanged a glance and then burst out laughing.

The proprietress brought a large carafe and we ignored the workmen's smoke by trying to get looped on the esoteric honey-wine (Dr. Moe's suggestion).

Joko explained the workmen were not from Njeguši but were repairing the main road through the valley.

"They are in the café to see the football match but are housed at the other end of town," Joko said and added, "We have three rooms upstairs. There is one other guest, a German or a Swiss, the woman isn't sure."

The match came to its conclusion. The workmen filed out and strolled down the road. According to Joko, they had yammered about their team's strategy and the skill or clumsiness of the players, and he added, he had heard them discuss us, the strangers. "They wondered at their lack of success with you, Anastasia, saying, 'The girl! She doesn't smoke! Why, at least ten of us offered her a cigarette!'"

I heard their laughter fade in the distance. Anastasia finished her last morsel of goat cheese, her last drop of honey-wine. She took my hand and said, "We are going to explore Njeguši, Joko, we'll be back for dinner."

"Vojvoda is just a shadow now," Joko said. "If you wish to see it, look for the large ruin at the valley's upper end."

She noted that should be our destination, and so we hiked a faded path along the rise of the valley away from the road. The warm evening carried the scent of wildflowers. Through oblique fields to steeper ground we climbed, where we slipped past briers and scrub. In the still air, I heard nightbirds calling from somewhere down below.

A bit before Vojvoda, we entered a grove that looked down over the vale. Here lay a rounded, grassy glade "in the luxuriant earth which is in the midst of stones. And desire is in the midst of the trees since they are beautiful and tall." Yes, that is what entered my mind, as it did in Claremont under Anastasia's great leafy tree:

She knows this. She throws off her blouse. Her shoulders almost glow beneath the black-mocha waves of her hair, and her eyes hold me . . . such a dark green they are, like a jungle cat at midnight in the year of the rain.

She whispers to me, "Love is in our hearts, Griffin," and she steps barefoot across the light-green grass called fairy grass and before I know it, we are lying together in this soft secluded garden under the trees. Anastasia whispers, "You've heard of Tantra?"

I can hardly think. She is referring to the dance of the divine, merging the visible world with the spirit world . . . or something.

She whispers, "We are going to use our sexual energy to be born onto a different plane. We will approach orgasm. If we can hold each time and avoid passing through those open doors, we will fly free in meta-space."

Perhaps I'm a good lover . . . or, somehow, she made it happen. Seven times we shudder together, energy rising, until the eighth and the ninth power reaches our heads and we are soaring, our bodies the same, but no, there is a difference; it has to do with light . . . There is a heavy rumbling coming from above, electric snaps of lightning, then a sound like a swarm of bees.

There is a sound of heartbeats. There is a sentiment inside my head and I realize it conveys Anastasia thoughts: "Language is not able to reveal this, because I am there but also here."

I think, "Yes, I can see you. We are mind or . . ."

We cross a wide valley, see swirling clouds, spiral-shaped like Bogomil symbols; we lurch in and out of black space, then begin a climb toward steep cliffs which rise majestically in the northwest.

Ahead looms a forest, thick with oak, beech, and lime trees. Over the greenwood rises a high cliff, and a sheer drop. Worried, we think, *There above an abyss, a shepherd child plays too near the edge.*

A shout breaches the pastoral setting. A priest runs across the rock shouting, "Nijedan! Nijedan!" The child looks at the father, stands, wobbles backward, and falls over the edge. The priest said, "Isao Je Prema Svjetlu!" (He went toward the light.)

Anastasia and Griffin are thinking as one mind now, Anagryph as it were, an anagogic image which is rushing forward to repair, in some way, the child; but even as Anagryph starts forward, a wave of thick, binding MATTER rolls into the Anagryph image, carrying it backward. Through snaps, flashes, and clangs of grossness merging, a voice moans, "From fear comes the wave…"

With a startling electric snap, Anagryph fades into Anastasia and Griffin, who realize they are still lying in the fairy grass together. Griffin raises his head.

"Be still," says Anastasia, This can't be happening, she thinks, and suddenly it isn't.

Instead, once again, Anagryph is rushing toward the cliff, the wave nullified. Anagryph wonders, Where is the child?

The Anagryph image ducks under a stone archway and stands looking at an uprearing white wall. From a lower doorway, out pops a monk. Stocky in appearance (enormous, bearded head and fiery eye) he isn't comely but strikes a noble pose, full of gesture and life.

"Child!" he speaks with a gravelly voice, "Twas a roundabout way here but now you've arrived. The fertility of woman is on both planes, visible and spiritual." He raises his black eyebrows.

"The child!" says Anagryph

"You are," replies the monk.

"The one that fell, landed just here." Anagryph points to the ground.

"And so HERE YOU ARE!" says the monk, a hot twinkle in his eye.

At once, Anagryph understands that the child is the merged soul of Anastasia and Griffin—the child that fell over the edge was Anagryph all along. It was if *they* had been observing *themselves* from outside *their* Tantric vision.

Before Anagryph self-examines further, the monk informs, "We established this monastery, Ostrog, because this is an enchanted place!"

"Enchanted?" questions Anagryph. "You are a monk!"

"And a lazy monk, so I've been accused! But a monk of this mystery cave I am. You had no need to fear it. When the child falls toward the light it lands in the lap of the Goddess unhurt. We built this monastery as a shrine to the lap of the Goddess. On August twenty-eighth pilgrims come, Serbian Orthodox, Moslem, Atheist . . . all come to her. Do you know it is the day of Our Mother in the Orthodox Church? Yes! We admit it!"

At once Anagryph can hear the surrounding woods alive with birdsong, further in the distance are children's voices and a rooster crowing.

The monk shakes with laughter. "Yes, yes," he says. He pulls out a book and a pen and says, "Sign the book." He places it on a wooden bench and gestures to Anagryph, who sits, turns to a blank page and writes "*We, Anagryph,* Spring 19 . . . " But as Anagryph scribes, the book wavers, and a scene comes into view on the page. It is the monastery at Cetinje. The scene carries inside the building, down steps, to a ditch at the end of which is a small cave opening.

"It's a tight squeeze for the body but after one hundred heartbeats it widens considerably," says the monk. "Inside, always take the first opening to the left. You will find Herak's den!"

Anagryph lurches in and out of black space specked with stars. There is a faint roll of thunder that stops short, and the monk comes into view. He appears as an image drawn on the book's page, as does the forest around him.

"Take that path," he says quickly, pointing to a break in the trees. "Goodbye."

"Wait!" Anagryph says, "are the codices—"

But the monk is gone. The book seems to envelop Anagryph, and at once *they* are on a stone path only wide enough for one; no matter, *they* are *one.* Luminescing gold, the path winds through the bower and ends at the beginning of a deeper forest. From Anagryph, *they* separate back into Anna and Gryphon, but they are not yet home. Animistic white boulders haunt the forest floor; uncanny faces peer from their pitted masses. The faces' miens reflect any emotion a wayfarer might carry when sucked into the antiylem, the nonsubstance of the supernatural wood.

They hear a rustling amongst the trees to their right: *No, tis not gentle fingerlings of Notus stirring the porridge of leaves above, nor is it cloudburst droplets splashing the treetops, it's a shadow . . . no, it's Tom O'Bedlam, dressed as he is, in a heavy black loincloth stitched with a cross, a fishnet hosiery over hair-matted legs, gauntlets of gold binding his fingers, a turban too small and jackboots too big. Why, he's moving erratically but still it seems he'll cross the gold-blaze path where Anna and Gryphon tread. He speaks in strange tongue, why, these been his thoughts! He is the third person—he watches him walk:* "He am King Tarquin," *he announces through foam, on his lips, on his chin, now his eyes start to roam round the visage of Anna and Gryphon it seems, they have somehow quite rudely encroached on his dreams . . . He shall creep to the female on the curve of the path, he shall whisper to him, he him thinks he is daft:* "Whatsoever man thinketh the moon should be called of the feminine gender then to her he's thralled, a slave unto women, his life till the end, till it comes back round'n he tries 'er again; but he holds a moon as a male deity shall rule o'er his wife . . . and be secured, against, all female treachery!" *Now! He'll grab charmer's long hair and pull it like Hell (for women with hair cut can't perform magic spells!), he'll grab it and yank it and spellbind it tight and . . .*

He's wild! A wild thing! Though it may sound quite trite, the slightest of noises would make him take flight . . .

A weasel darts out from behind a root, scurries through dry, fallen leaves and draws up behind Tom O'Bedlam; it rises on his hind legs and mimics exactly Tom O'Bedlam's fitful parade through the woods . . .

"Look at the weasel follow that strange man!" whispers Anna to Gryphon. "Why, it mimes him exactly." At that moment the weasel deliberately falls toward a steep ditch, taking care not to land too near the edge. King Tarquin (who hasn't seen the weasel) falls sympathetically in the exact same manner, but tumbles over the bank and out of sight. The weasel laughs and scurries ahead. The two hear King Tarquin screech as he falls, *"I will be the guide . . ."*

Along the path the two are confronted by a woman standing near a rivulet, brushing her flaxen hair. "There shall be an end of ends," she says.

"Yes, fatalism is just spiritual arrogance," replies Anna, picking the conversation right up.

There's a rustling in the forest. The woman says, "I shall speak to those to whom it is right to do so. Shut your ears, profane ones! My name is Erin. I give gifts of culture to help defeat the bestial above and below. The shrine of poetry is the shrine of Brigid . . . remember . ."

The woman disappears, and in her place stand three Muses: Meditation, Memory, and Song. The Muses are joined by Agape and Irene. All five of them bid Anna and Gryphon to follow. They are led through the tangled wood, past circling wolves, past gushing founts, past crystal skulls on shaggy mounds, through a temple hung with hoary age to an aqua-blue river, gentle and cool. Anna and Gryphon are told to enter the river and float downstream . . . they do so.

Anna floats on her back, looks up and sees the moonrise. She turns over, looks down and feels her head on Gryphon's chest; he is breathing softly. She notices her arms now hug his ribs. She lies there happily until, at last, she stretches her legs out.

Something is bringing me out of . . . wherever I was. It's Anna . . . Anastasia moving against me. I love the feel of her. She lifts her head and peers into my eyes. Her hair falls around me. I don't know what to say, so I kiss her. We lie there for a minute more and then get up. She takes my hand as we step from the grass circle, moonlight shining through the trees casting shadows on the ground. The darkened land is magical; what creatures roam these wild hills?

Once dressed, Anna takes my hand again and we start back down the path.

Chapter Sest   -6-

WE REACHED THE BOULDERS where perhaps serpents cowered from the evening chill. As we descended toward the café, I felt overwhelmed and I couldn't think much, my emotions a jumble, and even though we walked in affectionate silence, somewhere in my mind . . . I felt disgruntled, my ego, my sense of self . . . had been unhinged a bit by the experience.

Incandescent light defined rectangular windows of the café and splashed out into the yard as we approached. We climbed up the concrete steps and across the board floor of the main room, almost empty but for a bearded man in a black cape sipping red wine while gazing into the dark through an open window.

We crossed over to the bar. Anna asked the woman for our room key, a room we would find to be small but clean and furnished with a double bed and a chest of drawers. Entering, I saw my duffel, which also carried some of Anastasia's things (Great Huge in Joko's Fiat? No.) set in a corner. I killed the only light, a harsh overhead bulb, then lay on the bed, gazing through the window at moonlight in the hills, but soon clouds came, and the moonlight dimmed and went out.

Anastasia walked down the hall to the bathroom, an extremely unattractive tiled box, but it was clean and featured a huge clawfoot bathtub. Stretch out in hot water up to the ears. Hot water? Anna returned to the bedroom and smiled. Soon we were reclining at opposite ends of the tub, grinning at each other.

I said, "Tom O'Bedlam?"

Anastasia thought for a moment and replied, "Yes, or King Tarquin, along that gold path . . ."

I said, "Women, goddesses, muses, guided us through the woods."

She said, "Remember the weasel?"

"Anastasia, do you mean we had the selfsame dream?"

"That was the idea. We were one being, Griffin."

"Well, I usually don't dream other people's dreams! Even if they're yours."

"Not exactly a dream, my love."

"Hm?"

"What else do you remember?"

"Anastasia, I will try to remember—tell me, though, how did you learn such a practice?" This question was burning a hole through the pocket of my mind.

But she kept to her question. "Think . . . what else do you remember?"

That I wished to know more about her training (Was I shocked? Scandalized? Jealous?) was a given, but the mystery of what I had experienced also intrigued me. I said, "I kept giving you a nickname. I called you Anna. I have done so before, but it seemed as if that was your only name. What do you remember?"

"I recall your calling me Anna. But I also recall . . . Anagryph!"

Now it came back to me. I said, "Anagryph! What can you tell me about that?"

She said, "When you were young, did you have a friend, that when you were together, you both acted differently than you did when you were alone? Together, it was as if you had created a third mind, you would come up with ideas and perhaps mischief that neither of you would have imagined by yourself?"

"Well, yes . . ."

"We created a third being. However, on a very different level— a combining of our very souls: Anagryph! We did this to navigate the world that lives above our world."

When I heard her say this, I suppose I should have been awed and grateful for the esoteric experience of being enveloped by mystical, cosmic love. Was it love that made the tantra possible, as she says, or was I just a convenient, physical tool? Well . . . I don't think I can be turned—without warning or explanation—into a different being, a whole new entity, and not be discomposed. I mean, how about the feeling of not exactly being me! Yes, I recalled our merging was not an entirely unpleasant feeling; it was actually a sensational feeling (get it?), and yet . . .

Emotions did a kind of round dance in my psyche. Feelings welled up in me, elation, confusion, sorrow, fear . . . and then anger, up from somewhere. Yes, my ego. Was I cross and cranky because I, the wunderkind professor, had become the student of my student?

I replied with uncharacteristic churlishness, "You! You came to the Institute of Antiquity more able than any of us to translate Gnostic text, but you pretended you were just a mere graduate student. You! You knew the codices in a way none of us could imagine! You! You had already walked me down your path of Knowledge at the Claremont Conservatory and in your house garden with the monstrous leafy tree, then, you increased the stakes by waltzing me off to this strange land, Montenegro, with your Joko taking me up the Serpentine to the valley of your ancestors . . . You have—"

"Griffin . . . don't you see? I love you. I have always loved you!"

Still annoyed, I thought, Always loved me? We've only known each other for ten minutes! But then I knew better; I recalled the revelation at Aunt Anastasija's house, when I understood I had known Anastasia before, a remembrance of things past, as the poet said.

I thought I could see tears welling in her eyes and naturally, that meant I'd be a goner in about seventy-two seconds, so I decided I must escape the tub.

But she said, "I know this has been a rapid collection of experiences that would overwhelm a novice, but Griffin, you are far from being a novice. You know many things about antiquity, about esoteric practices, about the spirit and the middle ground between body and soul. You are a learned man, who will be able to assimilate our knowledge."

During this conversation my heartbeat had increased, and I was sort of huffing, so I climbed out of the tub and grabbed a towel before looking back at her. "I will think about this, about what you have said. I need some time." I escaped to the bedroom to get dressed. And the emotion storm I was experiencing? I wondered: Is this what it's like for souls who visit the higher planes of existence?

Downstairs at the empty bar—wondering where Dr. Moe and Joko had gone—I ordered vodka, which was the only hard liquor they seemed to have, other than raki. I don't like vodka, or raki for that matter, but well, how do I know? Maybe Anagryph likes it. I choked down half the double shot and noticed the bearded man still ensconced like a bat under the beamed window, still wearing his black cape. Very medieval, I thought.

He was observing me. He said, "I recommend drinking the house vodka as a martini—using a decent dose of vermouth and whatever else she can throw in there."

I grabbed my glass and walked over to his table. He got up, shook my hand, and said, "Hello, Griffin MacRobbin, I am Rudolf von Konigswald, explorer and speleologist."

Every time I turn around, something strange is happening. It's like being back at the Institute trying to navigate my way around all our patrons' crazy requests. Well, but not. Stranger. More strange. Increasing strange. Odd.

I said, "The famous spelunker. Certainly, I've heard of you. But you have me at a disadvantage. How do you know of me?"

"Dr Moe! I ran into him in Manhattan. Didn't he tell you?"

I replied, "Poor Dr. Moe had a lot going on in his mind at the time. We all did. And still do."

"Yes, the codices, their whereabouts—someplace under the earth. And now I've learned the cave access to where they had been secreted has been lost! Collapsed in an earthquake, shafts broken and displaced, the object itself maybe torn from its original location, thrown into a subterranean river to be carried by fearsome currents for many kilometers, ending who knows where?"

I said, "So, have you seen Dr. Moe this afternoon?"

"Ah, yes; he and Joko went off to Cetinje to search museum records and perhaps the old embassy for any information on underground caverns in the karst. They asked me to join them, but a futile quest isn't to my liking. I only pursue futile quests that I think aren't futile."

I knew of what he spoke. He held up two fingers and ordered, in the native language, drinks from the barwoman.

Turning to me he commented, "Ever since the football obsessed finally stumbled out of this establishment, I have been enjoying the quiet of this window table, happily sipping my red wine . . . which I brought with me. Now! I would love some company! And, in addition to this excellent Côte du Rhône, I also brought along some very nice vermouth. We are going to have a martini together! We can drink to the subterranean wonders of the earth!"

Well! How convivial. I decided I liked the man. What a self-promoter! No wonder he is the world's most famous caveman, he knows how to maximize the mystery. I mean, even inside this empty café, he still wears the cape.

I was starting to feel more like myself again, in that my emotions were no longer overwhelming me. Firm footing. Terra firma. That's the ticket, as my grandfather would say. So of course, at that moment, having come down the stairs, she appeared in the doorway. Anastasia. She was wearing jeans and a blue Brooks Brothers boyfriend shirt, my shirt, with a few naughty buttons undone. That would have been enough, but no. She had cut her hair! No longer falling below the shoulders, her hair now only reached to just below her chin. Did I do that? With my unjust, tirade in the bathtub? I'm sorry! I didn't mean it. I wasn't even me! She remained there, in the doorway, gazing at us, well, at me. I got up and crossed over to her. There was so much going on between us, our experiences rolling through us like the *City of New Orleans* train.

Reaching her, I said, "As soon as I left you, I heard myself, my words. Please forgive me, Anastasia."

"No, Griffin, no. It was my fault. I had never done this before, this Tantric mystery. I didn't really know what I was doing."

"You had never done it? Then how . . ."

"I'd been instructed on the method. But in all the world, it could only have been with you, don't you see? And only on that consecrated ground. And perhaps, never again."

I gazed at her, drank her in, but I said, "And your presence at the Institute—"

Cutting me off, she said, "As I told you, Griffin. You are the reason I became a grad student there." Then she smiled and added, "We had a journey waiting for us."

I said, just as Joko and Dr. Moe banged through the café door, "So we did. And let's see what tomorrow brings."

Observing us from his lair the whole time and probably waiting for his chance to give us the third degree about our romance, Von Konigswald must have been frustrated when Dr. Moe shouted, "Rudolfo! You should have come with us! Look at this book cover we found at the museum. They let me—well, Joko—borrow it to show you."

But von Konigswald was nothing if not adaptable. He got up grinning and said, "Come, join us, you two explorers. We are having martinis!"

I saw Joko mouth to the proprietress, "Raki," and then he sat down at the table with Dr. Moe and von Konigswald (Do I know the spelunker well enough to call him Rudolfo?).

I saw von Konigswald nod his head toward us and heard him whisper, too-loudly-on-purpose, "They're having a lovers' spat. They will join us in a minute."

We did join them in a minute. Observing us, Joko, with a theatrical raise of the eyebrows, asked, "And what have each of you been up to? I hope you did something together."

What is it with Joko? He always seems to know too much and reveal too little. Anastasia said, "We may have discovered information that will help us, but we need time to understand what we learned."

The proprietress-barmaid-waitress brought over our martinis and Joko's raki along with some snacks. Dr. Moe reached into his coat and produced the treasure, the cover of a book by Jacques Gaffarel (1601-81) called *Le Monde Sousterrein,* a book thought lost except for fragments.

Von Konigswald spluttered, "Gaffarel! But only the cover remains, I see. I can do better!" He reached inside his cape and withdrew a leather pouch. Undoing the thong, he opened the flap and removed an ancient (Morocco-bound, perhaps?) volume. He exclaimed, "Here is the real thing! Gaffarel's book! This very book has been in our family library for centuries! Now, I always carry it with me. This is a book of considerable value to me, and I speak of psychic worth. It always remains in my care for safekeeping."

He said, "See here! This book drove me to become an explorer, a speleologist. Does everyone read French? No? Allow me to translate the subtitle:

THE UNDERGROUND WORLD or historical and philosophical DESCRIPTION, of all the most beautiful CAVES, and all the rarest GROTTOS on earth: Vaults, Holes, Cellars, hidden Lairs, and secret Dens of various animals, and unknown peoples: Abysses, Hollows, and marvelous Openings in the Mountains, memorable Pits, and famous Mines of all kinds: Underground Towns: Crypts: Catacombs: Temples cut in the Rock: Wells, and wonderful Fountains: Rock Overhangs: Cisterns, and hollow Baths: and generally of all the most celebrated CAVERNS, POTHOLES, and CAVITIES in the world; and of everything most curious about them.'"

"Rudolfo!" Dr. Moe exclaimed. "Please allow me to examine this rarest of books! I must hold it in my hands." He added, "I will stay here while you four go caving tomorrow. I am not a caver, and I must set up an overseas cable call to the Institute to check on things there. I could keep the book safe with me while you are underground."

In an act of trust, the spelunker handed Dr. Moe the volume. Then, von Konigswald told us, "This book has descriptions of the subterrane that a speleologist needs to fire his imagination, which burns away fear."

✦   ✦   ✦

Outside, further up the valley, Rade, the wind, whipped and wailed against the foothills and then soared to strike against Lovćen itself, the high mountain where it is said Rade was born. Gusts hurdled up into the sky to conceive Adriatic storm clouds, which charged the atmosphere. Soon, driving rain flooded the highlands, causing torrents to flow down the valley, some streaming near the inn's foundation. The proprietress, unconcerned, lit a fire, took additional food orders and disappeared into the kitchen.

As described in a Brioschi advertising jingle, we ate too much, drank too much. We discussed the spelunking book and the wonders each of us had seen: caverns, codices, pyramids, antiquities, cultures, countries, etc.

At length, von Konigswald announced, "The time has come for entertainment! I will go first, then you will entertain me!"

Having imbibed several martinis, raki, etc., the four of us clapped our hands, encouraging the spelunker. When he arose and walked to the middle of the room, I was impressed by how large he was. The black cape only accentuated his size, and I wondered at how the man could wiggle down a cave chimney. It turned out that von Konigswald was a Wagnerian. Singing in English, for our benefit, Rudolfo took a theatrical stroll, turned, and in a decent baritone launched into lines from *Parsifal*.

> "Now today, we have the most dangerous to meet;
> he is shielded by his foolishness.
> But, ah!
> An evil curse drove me about
> In trackless wandering,
> Never to find the way to healing.
> Numberless dangers,
> Battles and conflicts
> Forced me from my path
> Even when I thought I knew it.

Then, I was forced to despair
Of holding unsullied, the treasure."

Finished, he took a bow. We clapped and cheered as if he were Rudolph the Red Nosed Reindeer.

Now, it was Joko's turn. He stood at the table, raki in hand, and sang a seemingly moving folk ballad which neither I nor Dr. Moe could understand, because Joko sang it in Serbo-Croat. Both Anastasia and Rudolf got it and said they would translate later, if Joko didn't. Anyway, we clapped and cheered again.

Next, it was my turn. I only had one act that I could do, something Dr. Moe and I had cooked up to deal with the faculty/grad-student talent contest. Don't ask. Mine was a talent that always required a certain on-the-edge inebriation and the assistance of Dr. Moe. I guess we were primed and ready. Out to the floor we went and sang in passible harmony:

> "We went to the animal fair!
> The birds and the beasts were there,
> The big baboon by the light of the moon,
> Was combing his auburn hair.
> The monkey, he got drunk
> And sat on the elephant's trunk,
> The elephant sneezed
> And fell on his knees,
> And that was the end of
> The monk, the monk the monk!"

More wild clapping. Dr. Moe and I bowed and shook hands as if we were Bob Hope and Bing Crosby in one of the Road To Dorothy Lamour movies.

The best came last. Anastasia walked out on the floor, turned, and gazed at us. She appeared so pale and vulnerable—her cut hair looked to me like an open wound.

She said, "Have you ever heard voiced, this ancient invocation of 'Sarapis?'" Then, she sang in an almost husky mezzo-soprano:

> "From stary heavens, I have flown,
> My wings—the earth surround;
> The water of the seas: my blood!
> My glance of lightning-flash astound;
> Hear my voice of rolling thunder
> Echo in the hills and vales,
> And beware, O foolish hunter . . .

The storm suddenly roared above us—interrupting her performance. The charged air rolling down the valley brought a blast of lightning, a blinding flash and an instant explosion of thunder. At once, heavy rain, while beating against the side of the café, flew in through the open window. But she had taken us from my cheap, forgettable vaudeville to a place of wonder: the timbre of her voice, her phrasing, the lyrics, the melodic intervals of the song. These things, when mated—well, it's a kind of alchemy, isn't it? A process which transforms our lead hearts into gold. And so, we sat in awe—no boisterous clapping, cheering etc., no, instead just reflecting on what we had heard.

It was then I looked around the table and began clapping. The table took up the rhythm and all of us rose to our feet clapping and shouting "Brava! Brava!"

Still standing in the middle of the room, Anastasia gazed back at us. Finally, she smiled, but said, "Well, it wasn't that good."

Joko replied, "Oh, yes, it was. You even brought the wind, Rade, and the storm, just as Yasoda would have."

Dr. Moe and von Konigswald, worried about rain striking *Le Monde Sousterrein*, reached out into the storm to pull the window closed. Anastasia and I said goodnight and went upstairs.

✦ ✦ ✦

Lying under the quilt with rain on the roof, its pitter-patter punctuated by occasional rolls of thunder, I felt caught in a current I couldn't control. Was I out of my depth? Probably, I thought, a hard admission for me, as usually I was the one deepening the waters. Anastasia, exceedingly quiet, waited for me, I guess, to speak my mind.

At length I said, "Sorry about my ridiculous song. I don't think I elevated the evening. Thank you for your performance and bringing the house down." Did I sound a little rocky, a little barren?

She stirred and replied, "Is that what you think? Griffin! *Your* song was the important song of the night."

"Ha," I said in reply.

She gave a dismissive laugh and said, "When are you going to again trust your intuition? You always used to, as I understand."

"I'm kayaking down a torrent, trying to reach shore, but the banks are steep, rocky, and unforgiving."

She said, "What is the last line of your song, "Animal Fair?"

I decided to play along. "The elephant sneezed and fell on his knees and that was the end of the monk, the monk, the mo—" I got it. The monk!

She laughed when she knew it had dawned on me. She said, "Yes, the monk, the monastery. When you kept saying *monk* at the end of your funny song, I remembered everything we needed."

I said, "Children laughing, rooster crowing: a shrine to the lap of the Goddess. The monk asked us to sign a book."

She said, "And the page began to waver, until another monastery came into view. I recognized it, the monastery of Cetinje. We learned there is a cave entrance inside. According to our journey as Anagryph, that is our way into Herak's caverns, where the codices are hidden. We may have never remembered but for your campy vaudeville."

Chapter Sedam   -7-

Von Konigswald's Land Rover rolled through the Njeguši valley as light began to turn the sky from gray to blue. Last night's storm clouds: gone. The morning air felt clean and cool. Joko sat beside von Konigswald, the driver, while I crouched in back with Anastasia, with mounds of caving gear: four coils of 165-foot Edelrid Perlon dynamic braid rope, brake bars and locking carabiners, pulleys, slings, Premier brass carbide lamps that can be mounted on foam-lined hard hats, steel cable ladders packed in bags, packs filled with spare carbide in waterproof plastic bottles, water for drinking and for the lamps, flashlights and batteries, spare bulbs, candles, butane lighters, spare lamp parts, containers of food and first aid kits.

We had overslept, and Anastasia didn't have time for her morning bath. I could see she felt frazzled—what was left of her hair was wild about her head. She had dressed as we all had, in heavy overalls, wool sweater, wool socks, and climbing boots. Because we had rolled back the top and sides of the Land Rover, we saw the workmen as we passed, lugging equipment to their new worksite. One of them recognized Anastasia and waved.

We listened to Rudolfo going on about his battered truck, "Once, driving from Lake Victoria into Sudan, I broke an axle mount. My God! We were miles and centuries away from manufactured parts. We tied it with a rope. It held for fourteen hundred miles!"

We drove past the house where the prince-bishop and poet, Njegoš, or Bishop Rade, was born. Above us I saw thirteen black ravens glide overhead, riding a zephyr, wings outstretched, silent, like souls that have risen from the valley floor. The old Land Rover passed a stone farmhouse, its roof a red-tiled pyramid, its window frames white-washed and ringed by leafy tree branches, and on the surrounding grounds, broken stone walls.

The road climbed sharply; the Land Rover groaned. Von Konigswald down-shifted. In an hour we entered Cetinje. Rudolfo took us past former embassies, built when Montenegro was an independent nation and this inaccessible city was its capital.

"Observe," said Joko, "the French embassy. It looks as though it belongs in Cairo, doesn't it? That's because it does. The plans were inadvertently shuffled, and the building intended for this city was constructed in Cairo, whilst the Cairo embassy was built here."

Von Konigswald finally slowed and parked the Land Rover before the black, rusting iron grillwork of the monastery entrance. He peered through the intricate meshing, and I heard him mutter something about his grandmother's lace wedding handkerchief. A monk descended the heavy stone stairs and opened the gate, hinges creaking. Joko, out the door, stepped forward to exchange witticisms in Serbo-Croat, while Anastasia and I moved into the bleak courtyard.

Joko told the monk we knew of a cave entrance hidden in the monastery and we wanted access. At first the monk shook his head, claiming there was no such portal within. But then, Anastasia joined the negotiation. When the monk learned who she was, his manner changed from resistance and obstruction to one of welcome. She,

Joko, and the monk talked some more, and just before turning to go, Anastasia pressed a large sum of dinar into the monk's hand.

Von Konigswald, loaded with assorted caving gear, headed into the monastery, and taking the hint, we grabbed armfuls of the stuff to bring along. Inside, the monk led us though halls that wound and burrowed into the hillside. Although I felt a cool draft, I also smelled musty air. We came to a ditch running to a small hole in the earth.

The monk pulled Anastasia aside for a conference. When he finished, she said, "The monk confides no one has ever been down this hole because it's too narrow."

Von Konigswald held up a pick and shovel. Joko nodded. We began to unpack the caving gear, filled the lamps with water and carbide, checked the flashlights, and uncoiled one of the ropes.

Von Konigswald grabbed his tools and said, "Stand aside, amateurs!" He climbed into the ditch and began to enlarge the narrow cave entrance. Soon he disappeared around a zig-zag, then reappeared an hour later.

"The cave widens suddenly. We're free to begin." Von Konigswald lit a lamp and attached it to his helmet, then dredged through a large canvass duffel until he yanked out a cassette player with a belt attachment. He inserted a cassette into the player, strapped it on, and then attached a rope to the belt. He asked, "Griffin, do you know how to belay?"

"Remind me."

"And Joko too, it will take the two of you to hold me if I fall into an unexpected fissure! Griffin, sit here. Joko, sit there behind him." Von Konigswald slung a strap around my waist and gave the ends to Joko. He continued. "No, you both must face the cave entrance directly. Griffin, pass this climbing rope around your back, low, like this—coil it there on your right. Never allow your right hand to leave the rope, guide it out on your left. Wear these gloves." He gave Joko and me sturdy grips. "Now, if the rope should play out suddenly, that would mean I took a fall. Joko, you anchor Griffin. Griffin, you plant your feet, hold fast! I don't know if there is a gap but, as Nietzsche says, our destiny exercises its influence over us even when, as yet, we have not learned its nature! When I want one of you to enter after me, two whistles mean you needn't belay again."

The large man reached down and switched on the cassette device. Out came the first notes of *Parsifal*. He confided, "The celebration of the pure fool helps me enter this dark belly."

Into the slanting cave shaft Von K went as I played out line, Wagner's somber music echoing in the tunnel.

Joko asked, "What is this celebration of the pure fool?"

I said, "*Parsifal* means fool, or innocent."

Joko replied with a laugh, "Well, I don't know anybody like that."

Two faint, high-pitched whistles rose from the depths of the cave. Now it was Joko's turn. I pulled the climbing rope back out of the way, and off Joko went, dragging a canvas bag of gear behind him.

A quarter of an hour later, the whistles came again. It was Anastasia's time to enter the cave. She lit her lamp, already attached to her helmet, and crowned her head with the whole contraption, a flame against a mirror. She gave me a kiss and started into the cave, dragging a bag as Joko did.

✦   ✦   ✦

She can feel the cool cave wind in her face. Shadows cavort with her lamp. The passageway becomes quite low and narrow and, as a result, she must hook the bag handle around her ankle and squirm forward on her belly, keeping arms in front of her to avoid pinning them to her side. She wonders how von Konigswald wedged through. The cave becomes wider again and slopes downward at an eighteen-degree pitch. The soft dirt has given way to limestone. She can hear Von Konigswald's recording of Parsifal:

"See there the wild rider!

How the mane of her devil's mare is flying!

"She must bring momentous news.

The mare is staggering . . . she has flown

through the air! She is crawling over the ground."

Now she can see Joko, light emanating from the center of his forehead. Crawling closer, she sees a giant cavern of purple ice, splendid silver slivers, leaping shadow forms, Joko standing with the lamp on his head.

"Oh, Joko! Ice! It's beautiful."

"Von Konigswald has strapped on crampons and is exploring for a further passageway. I'll whistle for Griffin."

Parsifal echoes from the distance:

"Now today we have the most dangerous to meet he is shielded by his foolishness."

Anastasia turns and turns, casts her beam about her, wants to remember this extraordinary world that lurks unseen below the surface.

✦ ✦ ✦

Feeling awkward, I worked my way through the passage, also towing a bag of caving goodies. I hate entering black holes, but I didn't find it as difficult as racing the downhill on the "Course of Fear" at Innsbruck. And my God, I was impressed by the grotto I entered. Anastasia and Joko were shining their lamps about, and mine made three marvelous points of illumination. Then there were four.

Von Konigswald, out of breath, crunched up to us on crampons and said, "A slippery place, heretics! No passageway out."

Anastasia disagreed. "The way should be on the left."

I asked, "How can there be ice down here?"

With a chuckle, von Konigswald said, "These caverns were, at one time, nothing but solid ice! Over the centuries as the ice slowly melted, the caverns remained. In another hundred years, this ice will also melt away."

Joko remarked, "Meanwhile, it makes climbing difficult."

Von Konigswald shrugged. "Put on crampons. We must rope together. We'll climb that ice barrier to see if there's a way."

He led. With each step, he jammed an axe into the ice; one by one, in a line, we surmounted the gleaming tower. On the other side, I saw the ice fall away toward chutes that disappeared into several different black holes.

"Anastasia," von Konigswald cried, "you are magnificent! There is our route! Let's be off."

Anastasia said, "Wait! This knot is unraveling."

All three men, us idiots, clambered toward her to help with the knot. Anastasia had unfastened the rope and was beginning to knot it again. Joko and I arrived at the same time by her side, but von Konigswald, rushing now, ice chips spraying from his gouging crampons, shouted, "I will tie the knot! Amateurs!" Four feet from us, he tripped when a crampon point caught his opposite pant leg. He slid forward into us, and like pins in an alley we all went down, then over the edge. Anastasia and I were still roped up, as were von Konigswald and Joko. We slid through one opening while von K and Joko slid through a different one, *Parsifal* still booming from his player.

So sudden. No time to dig crampons into the ice. Too much whirling, a crazy bobsled run with no bobsled, banking through twists in the limestone. Fear of being splattered, the same fear I had after catching an edge in a downhill race. I slid on the seat of my overalls while trying to keep the rope from tangling around my neck. I yelled to Anastasia to keep the rope off her. The chute went on and on, seeming to have no end, and as I rounded a sharp turn at speed, I scraped my helmet against the chimney wall. I bounced, and my crampons scraped the opposite wall, showering sparks, but my descent didn't slow. More turns, more bumps, more sparks. Just as I heard an echo—Anastasia swearing in Serbo-Croat—the ice simply ran out, and we bumped together in a heap somewhere in the darkness. The lamps had snuffed. I could hear the roar of flowing water.

"Anastasia?"

"Griffin?"

"What a rush!"

"Still in one piece?"

"If my butt is."

"It definitely is a piece!"

"Ha ha. Have a match?" I'd been fumbling in my pockets but couldn't find one.

Anastasia produced a match and struck it. In the small light, we could only see each other's faces. She relit her lamp, burned her finger, swore in Serbo-Croat again, then, with another match relit my lamp also. The increased illumination revealed we were sitting in an extensive rectangular cavern, a magnificent cataract at the far end plunging into a deep pool, surging forth, water flowing along a channel the hall length to submerge underground.

Anastasia screwed up her face and said, "Déjà vu!"

"What?"

"We should climb up behind the waterfall."

"I'll call the others." I shouted and whistled but no reply came. I said, "We ought to climb back up, they might need our help."

"You're right," she said, "let's try it."

At the chute, I stepped onto the sloping ice and immediately fell down.

"Griffin, your crampons . . ."

I knew both my ice-climbing tools had torn off my boots during the descent. So, what the hell was I doing? Well, I had thought I could kick steps in the ice with my boots alone. Wrong. Anastasia had only one crampon remaining, its prongs bent. We didn't have an ice axe, so we were not able to return the way we came. I shouted up the dark tunnel, waited.

A reply came echoing back through the waterfall din, "Gufffrffwed!" or something.

I looked at Anastasia. "What did he say?"

She shrugged and looked at me. "It sounded like *gufford*." Then, "Go forward?"

I looked at Anastasia. "Go forward. No kidding."

"Right!" I yelled back at them, doubting they would understand me.

We approached the thundering waterfall.

She said, "Look, a narrow path."

We followed it behind the flow of the waterfall and came to a gap in the rock. When I poked my head through, I saw a swing bridge spanning a void in another voluminous cavern, the far wall forming a structure of some kind, balconies and windows cut into the cliff. I said, "This is bizarre! Have a look at this, Anna."

As soon as she saw the cavern structures she exclaimed, "I think we've found Herak's grotto!"

"How can this exist, underground, unknown?"

She said, "Griffin, do you think that old bridge is safe to cross?"

I replied, "If not, it's a one-way trip to . . ."

"We still have our rope."

"Brave girl."

"We can't stop now!"

"I'll go first."

"No," Anastasia replied. "I'm lighter. And you're stronger. If something happens, you can pull me up."

Men always like it when women appeal to our egos, but I didn't say anything.

"It's just logic, Griffin."

Now she was instructing me again. The problem? She was right. "Alright, but I will check your knots."

She allowed this concession, so, I sat in the manner shown by von Konigswald and belayed Anastasia as she crossed the bridge. She started slowly, but picked up the pace until she was striding across the slightly swaying span. She called out, "It's fine! Like it was built yesterday."

Masking my lingering doubts, I replied, "Sure!"

With the rope coiled and slung over my shoulder, I crossed also, and by my having survived the rickety thing, which I guarantee was built nearer to the dark ages than to yesterday, we continued, following running slabs of rock before the high structure. We entered a fissure in the rock to find a winding staircase to a domed hall, where light reflected from crystals in the ceiling. It was then we heard Joko's voice calling out, echoing, followed by von Konigswald's baritone reverberating with lines from *Parsifal*,

"Now listen, shifty one! Keep your word!

Where have you been roving?"

Only in the depths is there tenderness and truth:

false and faint-hearted are those who revel above!"

Anastasia called out, "Very funny! We are up here, reveling above! Find your way."

After we reunited and told of our experiences following our different slides down the ice shafts, Joko said, "I know where I am. I will lead you."

✦　✦　✦

We climbed to the ninth archway, following Joko's torch light.

He stopped, allowing us to catch up and then shouted, "The time has come. The time has come! I wish Stevan were here, but"—he grabbed Anastasia's arm—"here is his daughter, granddaughter of

Yasoda and Lazo, here in the grotto of Herak!" His voice echoed around us.

Anastasia said, "You're sure the books are here, Joko, you're sure?"

"I wouldn't have you climb this high, Anastasia, and not be sure." He led us through an opening onto a long, narrow balcony—it must have been three hundred feet in length— overlooking the grotto.

The torch threw faint light to the far walls, and below, I could just see the swing bridge, now but a thread spanning the fabric of darkness. He proceeded along the narrow balcony under hundreds of fissures creasing the rock above us, seemingly absorbed in thought. He stopped.

He said, "Give me a boost, Rudolf, I'm too old for this now." I took the torch while von Konigswald lifted Joko up to a fissure, and Joko wriggled inside. I could hear him rustling. He poked his head out and called, "Anastasia! Catch." Leaning, he dropped a cypress case into her outstretched hands and then, with a bit of difficulty, climbed back down to join us. The case was carved with spirals and a figure with a hand, palm outward. He announced, "Inside are the Greek books, once a part of your Nag Hammadi Library."

I said, "How did you remember where you hid it?"

"The seventy-second fissure! What else?"

I said, "What made you think anyone would find Herak's grotto anyway?"

He replied, "Who knows what time brings? War? Progress? An entity, Festus? But man and beast could have searched here forever and never found the books! And all these nights I've slept without worry."

Anastasia set the box on flat limestone and released the clasp. She lifted the lid slowly. She hesitated. "The wood is wet. I hope the books are . . . "

Joko grabbed the torch from me and held it close. Von Konigswald and I bent near. She pulled the lid completely open to reveal an oil-slick bag.

"They'll be as dry as an Englishman's wit," Joko said, "I wrapped them myself. Leave them in the bag, Anastasia, until we find our way out."

"Are you kidding? I'll have a look at these!"

"And I," the cheeky professor said.

Joko glanced at me. Was that a dirty look?

"And I," added von Konigswald.

Joko gave von K the same look and said, "So, all of you are like Parsifal."

She ripped open the sewed seam. Inside, surrounded by uncooked rice, the leather-bound codices lay dry. She pulled one out to show us a rose emblem adorning the leather cover. Inside, the pages looked in good condition, dry and whole. She examined the other book, and found it undamaged.

"These are very old codices," Anastasia commented, "but very similar to the ones in the Nag Hammadi Library."

"Which means," I added, "they likely are volumes that were buried with the Coptic-Gnostic Library, as your father and"—I nodded toward Joko—"this brave man have said."

✦　✦　✦

By the time we had returned to Njeguši and the café, we had been up for twenty-seven hours. Exiting von Konigswald's Range Rover and climbing up the café steps, we ran directly into Dr. Moe, who was sitting at a rustic table on the porch, sipping coffee and reading the *International Herald Tribune*.

He spied Anastasia's cypress case at once—she was carrying it as if it were a precious child—and he said, "Here. Place it on the table, here!"

Anastasia squinted, hooded her eyes, ignored him. I think her instinct was to retire to the bedroom and evaluate the codices alone at her leisure. Wishing to enter the café, she continued to the door but then relented, turned, and crossed the porch to place the box on the table before Dr. Moe.

She said, "You can have a peek now, Dr. Moe, but that's all. We must immediately make plans to leave this isolated place and go to a teeming city, where we will be hard to find."

Joko said, "We need some sleep. A few hours. Then I'll take you up the coast to Dubrovnik, make shore a little before dusk. You'll find a zimmer to stay in."

We bid goodbye to von Konigswald, in case we didn't see him when we left Njeguši, thanking him with affection for his assistance, in fact for his getting us out of the cave as well as his getting us in! You see, he had kept his feet and crampons out of the fray during his ice tunnel plunge, so he was able to use them later to climb back up, kick steps in the ice, and set ropes for us to climb out.

We shared phone contact numbers and addresses, but I said, "Before you go, I wanted to ask you, how did you become fascinated with Wagner's music?"

Von Konigswald replied, "Well, as Wagner says, to be German means to carry on a matter for its own sake."

I laughed and said, "Well, you can tell me about it next time. Goodbye, von Konigswald!"

He said, "You know, by now you should just call me Rudolf!"

Chapter Osam   -8-

APPROACHING DUBROVNIK ON THE water from the southeast, a voyager is taken with the diagonal slant of the city's west wall, before which rise steeples and towers, and above, high flags flap in the wind. Red-tile roofs and gray stone arches sit happily surrounded by glinting sea, all of it spread beneath the 412-meter rise of lush Mount Srđ, green with subtropical vegetation, almonds and olives, palms and citrus, cypress and laurel and black pine.

The voyager was me, standing beside Anastasia in the cockpit of Joko's fishing boat. Behind us, Dr. Moe and Joko were arguing about fishing or garbage or raki or something.

Observing the ancient city, Anastasia commented, "I wonder if Dubrovnik is another geographical vortex like Herak's grotto, like Stonehenge, or Notre-Dame de Paris, a place where ley lines converge."

I replied, "It looks like a locale where anything is possible."

Joko landed at a wharf, tied up, and helped me extract Great Huge from the deck. We said goodbye again but vowed to be back next year.

Joko said, "Maybe I'll come to California to visit!"

Dr. Moe said, "And you can stay at my place. I have an extra room."

A porter on the dock heard Joko's comment and said, "Oooooo, Kalifornije! Kowboje! L.A. Ha ha ha."

I said to the porter: "Here, help with this suitcase."

Joko said something in Serbo-Croat, and the man became very cooperative. We waved as Joko untied and pulled away from the wharf, then we continued up the dock past a stone café fronted with open arches, viewing the harbor. Inside, tourists sat sipping cappuccino or wine spritzers.

We reached the city gates at Ploče on the east wall and walked through the portal, blending in with the German, French, English, Italian, and Yugoslav travelers; wandering hordes amassed in the city because the summer festival would start early this year.

This was where Dr. Moe said goodbye. While we had been caving, my deputy director had heard from Byah that our illustrious grad student, Karl, had been causing problems at the Institute. Karl had been demanding to talk to me, or second best, Dr. Moe. Something about THOOTS! Poor Dr. Moe; he wasn't even going to get the dining room flight on the return trip from Dubrovnik Airport and then would have to deal with Karl and the Suebi by himself.

Was I worried for Dr. Moe? Not yet. THOOTS probably had stopped paying Karl's tuition or something. At any rate, THOOTS was not going to risk attacking Dr. Moe at the Institute. That could go wrong a thousand ways and would risk bounce-back on their nascent enterprise, Subi Biocom.

Dr. Moe shouldered his perfect little backpack-suitcase and headed for the cab stand while we shouted encouragement and waved ciao.

The porter, meanwhile, said he could go no further, so I tipped him and began pulling the portmanteau myself, rolling it behind me on its four substantial wheels, with my bag sitting on top. Soon, Anastasia grabbed the strap from me and lugged it along behind her for a while. She had a vague plan to rent a zimmer, that is, a bed and breakfast in a private home, for an indefinite time, long enough for us to translate the codices.

I mused: the esoteric, mystical, cryptic writings within those two books might unlock her destiny, perhaps shatter fate's wheel or reveal a magical formula that would send Festus and his Suebi cult to the center of emptiness where they could sit in wonder.

As we walked past the Rector's Palace and its arches of weathered stone, I heard ethereal music, a beautiful soprano voice accompanied by a chamber orchestra, performing Vivaldi's "Laudate Pueri," a musical offering of the 113th Psalm. But the secret of the music is that it's written for solo soprano and orchestra in nine movements and six keys. It's the wily priest's homage to the Triple Goddess, hidden in the music of the Christian liturgy. He set the 113th Psalm to music because of the Gnostic line, "Light rises in the darkness for the upright."

"Griffin! We must enter here. I have a feeling . . ."

"Sure," I said, "but ask those boys if they will watch our cases for cash."

Anastasia cajoled several boys into guarding the cases and then gave each fifty dinars. She informed them there will be more when we return. They seemed to be ecstatic at the news.

Still carrying a canvas bag holding the cypress box of codices, Anastasia entered the Rector's Palace with me, but a guard stopped us at the courtyard entrance. Anastasia bent his will with a few chosen words, and after entering, we found discreet seats in the center back to hear movements three through nine. The program notes identified the soprano as Lili Sandor.

Anastasia whispered, "She sings the 'Laudate Pueri.' I must speak with her."

At the conclusion of the performance, the mustachioed director came on stage to give the soprano a beautiful lotus flower, and then two large men escorted her directly down the center aisle, the whole effect being rather over the top, I thought, yet theatrical.

As soon as Anastasia realized Lili Sandor would be exiting nearby, she left the codices with me and positioned herself by the door. Walking by, the soprano cast a sharp eye directly at Anastasia, who, in turn, said something in Serbo-Croat.

Lili Sandor came to an abrupt halt, turned, and walked over to Anastasia. Lili made some reply, and before you could say Jumpin' Jack Flash these two women were laughing together.

Then they turned toward me, and Ms. Sandor invited me, in excellent British inflected English, "Won't you join us?"

Approaching, I observed her blue eyes—not of the shallow, brittle quality you sometimes see, but eyes that have taken in both magnificence and tragedy through the years, eyes of understanding. Her red hair was short, gathered, rimming her roundish face, which was dominated by her cherub mouth. I estimated her age to be about fifty-two. I smiled and complimented her on the performance.

She said, "Won't you both join me for the reception? You are my guests. After, we will have dinner and can talk."

We continued conversing as we departed the palace, the two bodyguards following discreetly behind. On the street, the urchins guarding the suitcases spotted Anastasia and rushed up to her happily, explaining the numerous battles they'd fought to protect the obviously very expensive items inside the bags—at least, if I were them, that's what I would have said—and she gave them an additional fifty dinars. The bodyguards came forward and began to disperse the ragamuffins, but I intervened.

I said, "They were guarding our bags."

Anastasia repeated it in Serbo-Croat.

"They should guard their heads," a bodyguard replied in passible English.

Lili Sandor, observing the luggage, said, "If you haven't found lodging, you must stay with me. I have the run of a large house up on Mt. Srđ. I'd enjoy your company."

✦ ✦ ✦

After dinner at Lili's house on the mountain, we sat on a balcony overlooking the lights of Dubrovnik and the moonlit bay. She told us a little about herself.

"I was born in Bohemia, as were my parents and grandparents and all my forebears stretching back to the Boii Tribe, who were Celts. The Boii are the origin of the name *Bohemia*, and the Celts are the origin of my song. My father said it was because we are Celts that we lived alternately in Paris and London, he following the trail of the Druids and orders of adepts. He would take us to visit friends in the British countryside who were interested in such things, the Graves. My mother recognized my musical talent when I was six, and I began solfeggio study in Paris under the tutelage of a friend of Father's, a most passionate young opera star, Maria Felicita."

She stopped her narration and refilled our glasses with the local white wine we were drinking. She said, "Do you Americans like opera? I know some do in New York. I have sung at the Metropolitan Opera House."

I said, "We just spent a bit of time with a passionate Wagnerian."

She replied, "Oh, Wagner! Great art from an awful man!"

I said, "Our Wagnerian, von Konigswald, is a famous spelunker. He uses Wagner's operas to gain the courage to descend into the depths of the earth."

"Oh, yes," she said, "No doubt he sometimes uses *The Ring* cycle."

I replied, "Next time we meet, I intend to quiz him about his fascination." We talked a bit more, but since we really hadn't gotten much sleep lately, we soon said goodnight and retired to our room.

The following morning, I awoke alone, with an idea. Through the window, I could see Anastasia already up, sitting on last night's balcony with Greek codices and blank notebooks spread out before her. I wrapped myself in my Christian Dior silk robe, which squishes down to the size of a Wilson Match Play tennis ball for easy packing, at least the way I do it, and marched to Lili Sandor's bedroom, where she sat in bed, drinking tea and reading a newspaper.

"You are not the first man ever to storm my boudoir, but I'm a bit old for that now."

I smiled and said, "Oh, I think not, but you know, I was reflecting on what you said last night concerning Maria Felicita and your family's travels. You mentioned a British family called the Graves. Did you know them well?"

She replied, "We often stayed with them when we were in England. They were kind to us. My parents knew them as an enlightened couple."

"Did you by chance know their daughter Marian?"

"Yes! When I visited the Graves, Marian and I behaved like sisters. She was a charming girl and curious about everything."

"In later years, did you ever meet her husband, Stevan Romanov?"

She said, "I knew him before they were married, he being from Montenegro, I from Bohemia, both of us Eastern Europeans moving in the same circles in England—Stevan Romanov; King Peter II of Montenegro, who back then was still a schoolboy; Maria Felicita; my family . . . I remember an Irishman named Dick, who was Charles Graves's friend and master mechanic; he had saved Charlie's life in the Great War. There were others I don't remember but we would meet at Graves's mansion, Cismontane, to create a harmonious group mind, merge physics and metaphysics."

I said, "Anna and I are Americans, but she was born in Montenegro. Her mother and father were Stevan and Marian Romanov, and Marian was Charles Graves's daughter. Anna is Graves's granddaughter."

Lili, silent, stared at me so long that I began to feel uncomfortable.

Then she exclaimed, "Oh! The Queen of Spring!"

"What?" was all I could say in reply to her exclamation.

"Where is she?" Lili set her teacup on the bedside table and leaped from the bed, grabbed a robe, and marched out, calling for Anastasia.

"I'm here, on the balcony," Anastasia replied.

I followed Lili onto the balcony.

She said, "I knew your parents, Anna Fearina Romanov."

"My parents? What did you call me?"

"I knew them in England, and I knew Charles and Catherine Graves, at Cismontane!"

Anastasia threw her pencil down, looked at Lili, then me, then Lili again.

Lili said, "Both your parents and your grandparents were friends of Maria Felicita's, and then as I grew older they befriended me. I know your affiliations, Anastasia, so you will believe me when I say they came to me one day, your future parents, with a prophecy." Lili took a theatrical pose and recited:

"Our unborn Anna

Soon nimbus of life

With winter and summer

She'll be bride and wife.

But you shall bestow her

With the title of Queen

Anna Fearina: Tsarina of Spring!

"Fearina is your middle name, and, as you know, Anna Fearina is the Queen of Spring."

"My name is Anastasia."

"But your man calls you Anna!"

A smile slowly crossed Anastasia's face. She peered at me and said, "So he does." She didn't resist this information. She probably recalled the experience: *Anagryph.* I know I did.

Was this how pivotal events happened in her life? She knew of the Nag Hammadi Library but not of its connection to her family until Thoth finally piped up; but the older Romanovs planned it that way. She met me by accident? Well, no, she knew of my work before she applied to the Institute. Did the older Romanovs orchestrate that too? We met Joko at the wharf by accident . . . or maybe not, since the old man probably planned it. And now, this chance meeting with Lili Sandor? Was it chance? As I worked through it, I started having doubts.

"So, my parents declared their unborn child would be the Queen of Spring!"

Lili said, "Back in September 1940, I had just arrived with Maria Felicita for a visit at Cismontane. There, I discovered your parents had recently been married, somewhat to Charlie's chagrin, I soon found out. The evening of our arrival, after dinner, Stevan and Marian took me aside to tell me that when they had a child, a girl, they would name their daughter after Stevan's sister, Anastasija, yet that would not be all to her name. They said that one day I would meet their daughter and when I did, I was to tell her the rest of her name. Then they gave me the prophecy."

Anastasia remarked, "My mother's firstborn was a boy, but she experienced the tragedy of a miscarriage."

Lili said, "It grieves me to hear that! I didn't know . . . I don't think Marian was even pregnant when I last saw her before they flew off in that antique aeroplane. Yet, she and Stevan were sure they would have a girl one day, that you would be here someday, Anastasia!"

Anastasia said, "My grandparents, Lazo and Yasoda, took care as to the character of their firstborn—my father, Stevan. They made careful readings of alchemical formulas. They took to drinking rosehip juice from a golden flask, and they constructed a magical circle of nine: twelve signs of the Zodiac divided into four sections superimposed on a sacred triangle—the lower corners representing three and six, the apex nine, or the months of gestation. If they followed the dictates of the circle, Yasoda would birth any one of four male beings, one with a tendency toward the physical, vital, mental, or spiritual."

Hearing this, I realized I was now getting a further glimpse into the esoteric training Anastasia acquired as an adept.

She continued, "I know my grandparents journeyed to the deep karst for consultation with Gospodar-wizard Herak, to ensure they followed the natural order—that their son would be of the mental. And so, it came to pass, he was a savant."

Lili commented, "He was indeed."

Anastasia added, "Thus, I don't doubt Stevan and Marian had a plan of Gnosis for me as well."

Lili mused, "It could be that Thoth was involved with the nomen. You know Thoth? I'll bet you do! But actually, I wonder if Thoth knew of the prophecy. If he didn't know, perhaps that's why I was to be the fail-safe, the secret godmother holding the key to everything, as the Romanovs insisted. Oh! They should have chosen someone less forgetful! Anyway, the next morning, the Romanovs and Dick flew away in that wonderful antique flying boat and I never saw any of them again. It's been so long, I almost forgot about it. Then I saw you at the Rector's Palace, and you said, 'Light rises in the darkness for the upright,' and I knew I should pay attention, but I couldn't think why. So I asked you to stay here. I hoped it would come to me."

Lili and I observed Anastasia, her white robe falling loose around her shoulders as she sat framed by olive branches and five-petal mallows, behind her the sun rising between clouds, casting shafts of light upon the Adriatic.

Lili smiled at Anna and whispered, "You look to me like one who nurtures seeds."

Chapter Devet   -9-

Sitting beside me, Anastasia, relaxed yet focused, worked on translating a page from one of the codices while I attended to the following page. We had been working on the translation project for about a week. She said, "Look at this. What do you think?"

I read her new translation, as I had her others in previous days, checking back to the original at times. "O my father, yesterday you brought me through the gate of oblivion and afterwards the cave of birth, then beyond the dark tunnel of ignorance, you said this is the order of the tradition, and so led me onto the hill of learning.

"O my son, indeed this is the order, for I told you, If you hold in the mind each one of the steps, I set forth the action for you. Indeed, the understanding dwells in you so it is here we come to the parting.

"O my father, you said despair is in this land . . ."

I congratulated Anastasia on her fine translation. Then I showed her my work: "And death, my son. It is now you must cross the (fem.) sea to this world's ungoverned regions (H . . . .) There mind will surely bring you through the wilderness to that which is called beauty: under perpetual fire, the shrine of poetry. O my son, take this tract written on a stele of turquoise in hieroglyphic characters, bury it beneath the fire on the edge of the world. Eight guardians guard it with the fire of the sun, the males on the right are frog faces, the females on the left are cat faces.

"O my father, everything you say I will do eagerly.

"And write an oath in the book, lest those who read the stele bring the language into abuse and use it not to oppose the acts of fate."

Anastasia dropped her pencil, picked up the translation and read it through again and again. She said, "Use it to oppose the acts of fate! This is it! It tells of the hidden tablet or stele, the Stele of Fate! It is the magic, or science as Thoth would say, that can end the power of Festus and the Suebi! All these years! Written on a stele of turquoise . . . Griffin! Remember Stevan's story, the story Thoth told us of my father's death. What did my father say, the oath?"

I was sure she remembered; she was just looking for confirmation. I said, "The incantation is: *When you meet the Lion and the Eagle in consort with the Queen of Spring, you meet that which destroys you.*"

She nodded and called to Lili, who was reading a score in the music room. "You said my parents told you we would meet one day. You were to entitle me, Anna Fearina—the Queen of Spring!"

Lili sang out, "It's true, Anna Fearina . . . Anastasia."

Anastasia said, "But Thoth didn't mention that my father knew his own daughter was destined to be the Queen of Spring."

Lili said, "Well, I never mentioned it to Thoth. I guess the Romanovs didn't either. They were sometimes circumspect about their Gnosis, and Thoth can be that way too. You will have to ask Thoth if he knew what your father realized when he learned of the incantation to oppose Festus."

"Um. But now I am so named by the Western Esoteric Tradition."

Lili replied with a steady voice, "Yes, the task is carried out."

"My lover's name is Griffin."

"So it is." Lili replied, probably wondering what Anastasia was going on about.

Anastasia said, "A Griffin, or, let's use an older spelling, Gryphon, is a creature with a lion's body and an eagle's head and wings."

Lili paused but finally said, "Good lord, how is it that we could not see? Griffin's the lion and the eagle in consort with you, the Queen of Spring!"

"According to the oath spoken by my father, Griffin and I together are the instruments of Festus's demise, and we are the ones who will find the Stele of Fate."

Lili looked away; now her voice wavered. "Anastasia, Griffin, I'm so deeply sorry. I grieve for you, for surely as I hate Festus and the Suebi, your task is a heavy one."

Anastasia replied, "Yet, when we find the Stele, all possibilities are open. Now look, Griffin has translated words which mention a geographical location. This is not a metaphor."

Lili read the translation. She said, "Buried at the edge of the world but born somewhere else. Where? When?"

I may have had some ideas about that, but I was still back with this whole lion-eagle-gryphon thing. My name, Griffin, goes back in time to the misty green isle and into its misty, dim pagan past. However, it's just my name, the name I've always had. You grow up with a name—it's you! It's your family. What else do you need to know? You certainly don't need to know that your head is wrong, that it should have beady eyes and a beak, there should be wings spouting from your shoulder blades, and you should sport an enormous lion butt. Even metaphorically, who needs it?

Anastasia, apparently. Her clan. This Thoth character. Where the hell is Dr. Moe when I need him? Oh, yes. I sent him back to Claremont. I noticed the two women looking at me, wondering, I guess, when I was going to return from my mental walkabout. Well, under stress, I can still concentrate, focus my mental acuity to the task! That skill helped me in the past to win ski races. It would assist me now.

I said, "The codices which make up the known Nag Hammadi Library were translated from Greek into Coptic in Upper Egypt during the last half of the fourth century, perhaps at the Basilica of St. Pachomius. But where the original texts were written, of which these two survive,"—I spread my hands over them—"well, that is open to speculation." In other words, I didn't know. So much for my concentration.

Lili said, "Written in Egypt also? The edge of the known world would have been the Sinai desert."

No. That suggestion seemed wrong. I thought. I thought some more. Then, I rallied! I said, "It's likely the Greek texts were written by Alexandrian Gnostics close to the time of Christ. They were under siege, as we know. The heretic monks would often flee over the edge of the known world . . . I think that meant —to the British Isles!"

Anastasia said, "The Isles of the standing stones."

Lili said, "To the adept it would make perfect sense. We must travel at once to England. No one knows ancient sites better than Charlie Graves."

"Charles Graves?" Anastasia exclaimed. "My grandfather is still alive?"

"Didn't you know?" Lili replied.

"Why would I know? My grandfather is unaware of my existence, as I have been unaware of his!"

I said, "I'll call Dr. Moe. We are going to need him to help with the search (I was going to need him to help me retain my sanity). I'll have him meet us in London."

Lili said, "Have him go directly to Cismontane. I'll call Charlie and explain the situation."

Anastasia shook her head. She said, "My family has had no contact with Charles Graves since Stevan and Marian flew away in 1940. He didn't even attend my mother's funeral—his own daughter's funeral—because he had banished forever both Stevan and Dick, who were both pallbearers. He refused any contact, word, or information from them or anyone representing them. My grandfather expunged them from his existence. That's all I know. I don't think I'll be staying there."

Lili exclaimed, "Oh, posh! I'll straighten this out once and for all! This will not continue! Leave it to me! How can he go on like this? His own granddaughter! He must learn of you!"

Anastasia said, "I will not go there. Aunt Anastasija has tried with him. Joko too. Dick many times. Even Thoth! My grandfather is intractable and insufferable!"

Lili replied, almost to herself, "Though I have not spoken to Charlie in years, I will fix this. People like us are few, but the world needs us whether it knows it or not. We cannot let darkness and error destroy us!"

CODEX VI

The Stele of Fate

Chapter Aon   -1-

We ENDED UP AT Cismontane. I could go into agonizing detail about the machinations and negotiations, the tearful casting of opprobrium and eventual chilly amnesty settled upon by all sides, a grace accepted for the sake of the greater good. I could, but then I would be trying to write *Middlemarch II* or *Little Women XVI* or something. I'm not doing that. I'm just trying to describe what happened to me after I fell in love with my graduate student. Remember? It was never my intention. It just happened, almost by accident. Or did it?

Yes, I opened the door to all this years ago. I think my present life path started when someone, probably Uncle MacRobbin, left a Ouija board around the house when I was nine, and with it, I and my friends conducted scary experiments in the candlelit dark.

It went further in grade school with my delving into the geography of foreign lands and strange places. Later, my senior year in prep school, I met Aldous Huxley—no need to go into that! Then, at the university came my occult ski-racing experiments, and finally, as a grad student, my delving into antiquities, my travels to those strange lands I'd read about as a boy, where strange things happen. And most recently, came my being menaced by the Suebi society and, as a result, my being waltzed down the garden path by the Romanov clan. Members of the clan think my involvement is ordained; meanwhile, Dr. Moe wants to know what that assertion implies about free will. And here I am, tap-dancing in the middle with you, as they say.

When I arrived at Cismontane, I encountered an imposing mansion with vast landholdings, all of which had gone a bit ramshackle. Too bad, because I observed that the materials originally used for the mansion's construction had been of the finest quality. But as with anything in life, maintenance is the key. The fields needed haying, the forests needed limbing, the barn and garages needed painting, the pavers needed resetting, shutters here and there needed rehanging where they had lost a hinge and were akimbo; the mansion gave off a sort of "The Fall of the House of Usher" feel, except that I saw one small, well-tended meadow near the house, adorned with spring daffodils.

Before we came to the great house, Anastasia, Lili, and I had stayed in London at the Savoy, because Lili said she always likes the Irish Coffee and the after-dinner floor show. After the dinner hour, the circular center floor rises up to make a stage in the round. Stepping on to it the other night for our entertainment, the performer, a strongman, ripped a giant London telephone book in half in one try, and then bent a hefty steel bar into a circumflex. After that, the singer, Dusty Springfield, took over. She was accompanied by John Renbourn, a good acoustic guitarist. The quality of Dusty's voice? Dusty and seductive.

The next morning, riding in one of those annoying London cabs with one of those execrable cabbies who try to make you pay fast when you're jet-lagged from your west-to-east flight, hoping to make you flustered as you try to convert dollars to pounds, I went to Heathrow to pick up Dr. Moe. I didn't want him to experience cab-driver hassle.

But, when I met him at the gate, it wasn't just him! He had the abominable Karl in tow!

On the cab ride back, I learned why. It seemed Karl had been attempting to exit from the Suebi Order. He had become frightened of the two Suebi "secretaries," Loxo and Roto, who, he claimed, had caught him researching Subi Biocom. He had told them he didn't mean anything by it, he was just curious. According to Karl, the two women overcame him by chanting in unknown tongues and then threw him into the trunk of a car for twenty-four hours. After he'd peed all over himself, he was released and told to report to an address they gave him.

Instead, Karl found his way to Anastasia's house and hid under her porch. He would sneak out at night and use a pay phone to contact Byah. When he found out Dr. Moe was back in town, he convinced Dr. Moe to help him. Karl ended up with a shower and a ticket to London. Now we were graced with Karl's presence. Well, not really. I put him up at a B and B in Bury Saint Edmunds. We had enough going on at Cismontane without Karl lurking around.

I had to admit, though, what Karl had found out disturbed me, as it did Dr. Moe. Evidently, all divisions of Subi Biocom worked independently of each other, doing research and development in far-flung buildings on campus, each division barred from communicating with other divisions, but they all reported to a central command.

On the surface they were developing a pocket communication device about the size of a pager. By speaking into the invention's little microphone, users could send each other a one-word text, like "Hi!" "Dinner?" "Dance?" "Money?" The device would save a few transmitted words, which you could view at your leisure. Pretty hot stuff, but after all, it was 1973, not the 1950s. The test group found this communication activity to be fun and addictive.

Subi Biocom's advertising, even before the rollout, asserted that the single-word text feature would be the latest social trend: Distill your desires into just one word! In fact, the company called the device "ONEWORD," and printed that name on it in the same font as the Subi Biocom logo, but miniaturized.

The hardware engineers had designed the device to fit easily in a pocket or purse, with smooth curves and an integrated dot-matrix screen, and it came in a variety of bold colors. The hip, those in the know, were already greeting each other by just saying, "Word," as in "What's the word?"

Well at that point, it sounded to me like ONEWORD would be a worthy gadget, one that would connect people in a positive way by engendering creativity and fun. In addition, it could be used for business activities, for weather warnings, and . . . I suppose, for criminal activities too.

The messaging capability had been designed by a team of game-theory psychologists in order to "steer" the user in a predetermined direction. The gadget did this by sometimes "accidentally" mishearing owners' one-word commands. If they said "Dinner," it might print "thinner;" instead of "Hi," it might print, "Bye." These "mistakes" might redirect a conversation, for good or for ill, in an entirely different direction and gave the appearance that the device was alive and participating in the conversation. This behavior of the device anthropomorphized it as did the stylized eyes and mouth integrated into the design. The "mistakes" the device made would be random, resulting in classic random reinforcement, which would actually increase the user's bonding to it.

Over time, say a year, the cumulative effect of this steering would be one that would create a vague annoyance in the mind of the user, nothing that anyone would really notice, just a dissatisfaction in the back of the mind. That would be the "set." Remember how a psychedelic experience is affected by set, and set is what occupies your mind over a given period of time? Once the nagging little negative set brought on by steering was infecting a large part of the population, the next step, the bioactive component, would come. And this was the crux of Festus's criminal design. Here is, more or less, what Karl told us:

When enough customers are using the device in a given region, a negative tipping point will have been established. Then Subi Biocom will send out its own message, a message not to the device owners, but rather to the device itself. The message will instruct the device to release its nano biologic component which will pass hallucinogenic molecules through the skin, into the blood stream of the owner. Soon, with the already established negative set, and the hallucinogen coursing through the user's brain, the user will experience a vast surge of distressing emotions, transforming a vague feeling of dissatisfaction into an all-consuming sense of hopelessness and anger.

As Karl revealed this plot, I realized such a widespread mindset could create a perfect atmosphere for the rise of a populist politician, one with an autocratic style who could emerge from either the political left or the right. And from what I'd learned over the last few weeks, this Festus character wouldn't care which side he coopted, he'd just pick the one with the most potential for assisting his rise to power.

The Cold War intentions of the Suebi Order, the Soviet Union, and Maoist China were clear. Their objective was to disrupt and weaken the world's existing republics and democracies, perhaps even rid the world of them, so that their wealth and resources could be divided, plundered, and ruled, by—they would assert—a more natural system of government: autocracy! Democracies fail, the thinking goes, because self-governance is unnatural and will be undone by reversion to tribalism, where people pursue the goals of their own group at the expense of other rival groups. The only thing to fix it? The ascent of a Great Leader who asserts ultimate rule over the tribes.

Thank goodness Dr. Moe had finally arrived in the British Isles. We could soon be discussing my analysis over a dram and look for failure of logic. Hopefully, things aren't as bad as they seem. At any rate, until I knew more, I wouldn't bother the group about the ONEWORD device.

However, "Time's a wasting, Earl," as R. Crumb put it (my Boomer grad students left a *Zap Comix* lying around the conference room), so, as I said, we were headquartered at the great house, Cismontane. There, Dr. Moe and I discovered there was nothing in the way of aqua vitae to drink; but the ancient retainer, Smythe, descended into the bowels and tunnels of the house to find us a bottle of vintage Armagnac. I tried to tip Smythe for his effort, but he just looked at me with disdain. I'm sure he was right to do so, after all, most of the time in England, we Americans haven't got a clue.

Speaking of being clueless, Dr. Moe had never attended a séance. Well, a séance was to take place in the gallery this very evening at nine, in order to ask the spirits to reveal the location of the Stele of Fate . . . or something. I explained to Dr. Moe how I had held a séance, at age nine, with the assistance of my uncle's Ouija board; my pal Murph and I had descended into a crypt to ask the Ouija board to draw down the spirits of old. I still don't know if anything happened. We spooked ourselves and ran out of the basement as if our pants were on fire.

It was already seven, with dinner to be served at seven-thirty. Anastasia had been aloof all day. I'm sure her mind was a jumble after meeting her estranged grandfather, Charles Graves, for the first time, followed by the viewing of her dead mother's room, a room, incidentally, where she and I were to spend the night.

Anna came down from that chamber, heavy of heart. I could see it on her face as she entered the sitting room where Dr. Moe and I had been discussing the drawing down of the spirits. She went directly to the bar tray and poured herself a glass of Armagnac.

"This is from the Wolly's vast cellar."

I questioned, "The Wolly?"

"An ancestor. Don't ask."

"OK."

From the doorway, we heard a voice: "Dinner is served." Smythe keeping us informed.

I'm not going to talk about dinner. It was very good, much better, I'm sure, than you'd get at the House of Usher. But after a glass of postprandial port, which the ladies took with us men, we moved into the huge expanse called the Long Gallery, which, as I looked about, was guarded by the busts of philosophers and a statue of Diana the Huntress. A round table of burled walnut stood near the far end, and as we walked closer to it, I could see a spiral of rosewood radiating from the center to the outer edge, which created a whirling vortex effect. Nearby, French doors stood open on the left, bringing in the night air.

Anastasia's grandfather, Graves, nodded his old head, white hair falling in his eyes, long chin jutting forward, and said, "Come. It's time to sit at the spiral table."

We all chose a chair. I sat between Anastasia and Dr. Moe. Lili sat between Anastasia and Graves. Yet still stood four empty chairs. I looked at my watch. It was ten to ten, Greenwich. Smythe walked to the end of the gallery to raise a shade, which was obscuring a round window high on the outer wall. He then lit five standing candelabra, each with three branches. They stood in a twenty-five-foot radius outside the perimeter of the table.

Graves removed a daffodil from a wicker basket he'd pulled out from under his chair and carefully placed it at the center of the rosewood vortex.

He said, "We must perform a ceremony, a ritual to calm the little orator within us so that a greater voice may speak over him . . . hmm? But timing is everything." He looked at his watch.

Just then, I could hear through the open French doors the sound of a motorcar crunching to a stop in the driveway. Car doors slammed. Footsteps. Through the doors entered Joko, his niece whom I knew as Aunt Anastasija, and von Konigswald! With little greeting or preamble, they immediately occupied chairs, von Konigswald next to Dr. Moe, then Joko, then Aunt Anastasija. Between her and Graves was the last empty seat. Time was of the essence.

"Smythe!" bellowed Graves. "Smythe, you blackguard, get in here! Time! Time!"

Smythe, who could be quite silent, I'd noted, had been standing three feet in a direct line behind Graves's seat. He replied softly, "I thought you'd never ask," and then without fuss occupied the last seat, completing the circle of nine.

Graves pulled more foliage from his basket. He strewed willow and oak branches around the daffodil to the north and south, a halved apple to the east, and whitethorn to the west. This task accomplished, we waited. As I watched, a sliver of moonlight slowly crossed the table, growing larger, until a perfectly round shaft, a soft spotlight, illuminated the daffodil at the center of the table. Moonlight streamed through the high window Smythe had uncovered.

Then Graves said, "Arise. Pull your chair outside the circle of light."

I took this to mean beyond the circle of the candelabra, which seemed to be correct, since everyone drew their chairs to the far side. Then, as we stood around the table, Graves turned his back and held out his left hand for Lili, who also turned her back to the table and held out her left hand for Anastasia, who also did the same, holding out her left hand for me. This was the first physical contact she and I had experienced in twenty-four hours, and she gave my hand an affectionate squeeze, which filled me with joy, and then I had to turn and was supposed to hold hands with Dr. Moe. We looked at each other.

I said, "Remember my Ouija board séance? Same thing."

So, Dr. Moe complied (I found his hand to be dry and whiskey pickled . . . or was that me?) and then he had to hold hands with the Wagnerian— but that was OK, since on the Balkan karst they had already discussed opera. Next came Joko, Aunt Anastasija, Smythe, and Graves again, closing the Circle of the Nine.

Graves intoned, "Graces pace the round. I will blow the pipe. Dance the round all."

Well, this was familiar to me. Maybe my conflation with these people *was* ordained. What do I know? Without effort, without a starting point, the Circle of the Nine began to move slowly around the table clockwise, me being dragged along, trying not to trip over Dr. Moe's clumpy feet.

Lili chanted:

> "She wore a robe that was brighter
> than a fire flash, and she had on spiral
> ringlets, and bright ornaments,
> and necklaces around her delicate neck
> that were beautiful and lovely and
> the moon on her delicate breasts and
> astonishing."

Graves intoned, "The nine of the numbers paces the round aloft. To each and all it is given to dance. He who joins not in the dance mistakes the event. I will flee and I will stay. I will adorn and I will be adorned. I will be understood and I will understand. A mansion have I not and mansions have I. I will be saved and I will save. I will be free and I will free. I will be wounded and I will wound. I will hear and I will be heard. A way I am to thee who passeth."

The circle moved faster. Someone whistled three times. Distant bagpipes and harp sounded.

Aunt Anastasija said:

> "Lovely maiden of the moon
> and lovely daughter of the sun
> in their hands hold the weaving comb
> lifting up the weaving shuttle,
> weaving the golden fabric,
> rustling move the silver threads,
> at the edge of the crimson cloud,
> at the border of the wide horizon
> Golden garment for the moon,
> shimmering veil for the youthful sun."

We danced to the bagpipe and harp, all in a circle we danced and became giddy with the movement and the setting— the candlelight flicker in the streaming darkness and outside, shining through the great round window of the gallery, the full moon rising higher in the sky. Then Anna gave my hand another squeeze and said:

> "Hear me, you hearers,
> and learn of my words, you who know me.
> I am the hearing that is attainable to the everything;
> I am the speech that cannot be grasped.
> I am the name of the sound
> and the sound of the name.
> I rise from the earth to gather the light
> and the earth and light will gather in round

to be whole again!"

Joining the distant bagpipes, I heard the addition of a drum, and, echoing from the far corners, infectious music haunted the great gallery.

As the music stopped, echoed, and faded away, we dancers ceased movement in the same organic manner in which we had begun, yet we were panting and grinning at each other. Before anyone could speak, Graves said, "Retrieve your chair, return to the table, and sit!"

Graves was good at ordering people around, as if he had done it in the military, which I guess he had. Returning to the table with our chairs, I saw a wonder had occurred. The branches and the apple were all whirled together at the table's center, on top of which sat the single daffodil. How had this happened? I suppose any of the adepts, Graves, Lili, Joko, Aunt Anastasija, Smythe, could have done it . . . except we had all joined hands with our backs to the table. Our hands had been joined the whole time. Impossible! None of us could have done it. In addition, Graves had retrieved his chair at the same time as the rest of us. It wasn't he. I dropped my glasses case to the floor so that I could peek under the table to check for a motor-gear assembly—I saw no sign of one.

Graves turned directly to Dr. Moe and demanded sternly, "Dr. Littlejohn, what did you see?"

Dr. Moe, flustered for the first time in his life, no doubt, scratched his nose and said, "Nothing. I don't—"

Graves, gently now, said, "You are more than your garments and your degrees, Dr. Moe, much, much more." Graves paused and looked around the table. "As each of you danced, your minds went effortlessly toward the music and the movement, you reeled and laughed and thought of nothing in particular, except for a fleeting moment when you had a vision or an impression of something." Graves shifted his gaze back to Dr. Moe. "Now, with concise description, tell me what you saw, Dr. Littlejohn."

Dr. Moe sighed, trying to decide if he was being talked down to, something he'd occasionally contended with because of his small stature, his race, or both—until of course, he used his vast intellect to squash the offender like a bug. But I think, with eight of the Circle of the Nine staring at him, he succumbed to peer pressure.

He said, "I had the impression that a woman . . . stood alone."

Graves pressed, "Any other impression, Dr. Moe?"

"Trees in the wind."

Graves turned to von Konigswald, who answered, "A great loamy field is what I saw."

Graves turned to me. "Dr. MacRobbin?"

I said, "Stones, standing upright, comes to mind."

Lili said, "Dancers I saw, under the stormy sky."

Smythe said, "This is strange, but I saw a ring in gray mist."

Graves said, "Not so strange, my friend, I saw two sentinels in gray mist. Anna?"

Anastasia replied, "I saw . . . no, I smelled the ocean."

"I saw a man, a tinner it was! On a narrow lane," Joko said, and added, "I could have sworn that for an instant Dick stood there . . . on a wall."

At the mention of Dick, Charles Graves's estranged friend and colleague, I think the man went a little pale. He turned to Aunt Anastasija, who had been sitting both near, and away from, Graves, if you see what I mean, projecting an air of distance between them.

Graves plowed on and asked her, "And what did you see, Anastasija?"

Anastasija, who had been writing on a notepad during our interrogation (is that characterization a little harsh?), I mean, during our gentle questioning by Graves, said, "I heard a strange voice, words I couldn't understand."

Graves asked, "Could you discern the gender of that voice?"

"Female."

Hearing this, I glanced at Anastasia.

Noticing, Graves addressed me, "Dr. MacRobbin?"

I looked at Graves and said, "It was Anna."

"So, he saw you, Anastasia. Did you see anything else?"

She looked at Graves, fixing him in her eyes, and said, "At my feet was a flash of green and I thought of the turquoise . . ."

"Good! Good!" exclaimed Graves, "I think we are getting along here. Anastasija? What are you writing?"

"A poem"—she glanced at Graves—"about what's been said."

Graves looked around the table, raised his eyebrows. None of us made any comment, so, deciding the interrogation, um, the questioning was at its conclusion, he addressed Aunt Anastasija in a gentle manner, in fact, diffidently, and asked, "Would you read it for us?"

Aunt Anastasija crossed something out, wrote another line, and said, "Yes, Charles, I've got it." She read,

> "A woman sings to swaying trees,
>   the ground is loamy, I see great stones,
>   dancers, a ring, two sentinels,
>   all in gray mist by the sea.
>   Walks a tinner down narrow lane,
>   stands a friend on sarsen wall;
>   primeval storm fill the sky again:
>   She roams the fields chanting strange tongues,
>   She rules o'er the garden of spells."

From Graves: "Oh! Very beautiful, read it again!"

She did so.

"Now," Graves said, "let us examine with our scribe what we have wrought with our hearts! I will begin. If we are looking for a place, we know it's on loamy ground by the sea, near a grove, where there are tinners, narrow lanes, and stone walls—and that, dear friends, sounds to me like Cornwall!"

Smythe noted, ""Why, indeed, it does, sir, except there are hardly any trees down there."

"Yes, we must think about that. But dammit, that's where the tinners mined, near the roaring sea, the standing stones, the mist. Most of the description fits."

"Then here's something that doesn't fit," Dr. Moe commented.

"Go on, Dr. Littlejohn."

"The poem refers to a lone woman and then says there are dancers and two sentinels. Not so lonely. A contradiction, I would say."

Lili spoke up, "It would seem so, Dr. Littlejohn, but I believe it can be answered thus: In Cornwall, there are many Bronze Age, perhaps even pre-Bronze Age stone circles, not as imposing as Stonehenge and not as celebrated. Instead, they stand hidden in farmers' loamy fields, difficult to find unless you know the way. Near Tregeseal are stones called Dancing Stones, or Merry Maidens, and I believe these are the dancers with the lone woman."

"And the two sentinels," Joko asked, "what of them?"

Leaning toward Graves, Smythe whispered something to him.

Graves replied out loud, "Yes, good! I think you should."

Smythe arose, walked over to the large doors under the demilune, pulled them open to vanish through them and then returned a minute later carrying a large book. He set it on the table and flipped through the pages until, finding what he wanted, he pointed at a photograph and said, "The Men-an-tol! The stone of the ring." He passed the book to Aunt Anastasija and it made its way around the table. Smythe said, "A ring, two sentinels, all in gray mist by the sea."

Receiving the book, Anastasia and I gazed at the donut-shaped stone with a standing stone, each like a sentinel, on either side of the aperture. We looked at each other and nodded.

Von Konigswald, his voice filled with wonderment, said, "And do you think the mystic Stele is buried there at the Men-an-tol or the Dancing Stones?"

"Not at all," replied Lili.

"Not a bit of it," Graves said, "but the message is as plain to me as if 'twere written in a letter. Anastasia . . . Anna must journey alone to the oracle of Merlin, who is the friend on the sarsen wall—a wall of Druid stone. She must see into a primeval storm, that is, see things which we in our rational minds don't see, and she will reign in the Garden of Spells, that is, become the Goddess, the Queen of Spring, and learn where the turquoise lies."

Everyone at the table was silent. Dr. Moe, who only an hour ago thought he was being put on, now had nothing to say. Nor did I or anybody else. Swirling mysticism formed a structure that the uninitiated never would believe existed.

In fact, Dr. Moe, still hanging on to his rational mind, broke the silence and remarked, "Just a moment. You said there are few trees in Cornwall."

"The answer to that has come to me, Dr. Moe."

We all looked over at Lili, who continued, "The people of the standing stones always built their circles near sacred groves. Cornwall during that age was covered with forestland. Our mystic vision isn't limited to the twentieth century."

I said, "Then Anna and I will leave tomorrow."

"Oh. no, Dr. MacRobbin," replied Graves. "The message is clear. My granddaughter must go alone!"

I thought, Your granddaughter! You hardly have a claim on her. I replied, "Land's End is three hundred and fifty miles from here. I won't let Anastasia travel down there alone."

"She must seek the Oracle alone!"

I noticed everyone else around the table was staying on the sidelines. I said, "And who is seeking her? Festus, the Suebi, the Masters of Matter!"

Anastasia ran her fingers through her thick but chopped-up hair. She turned and smiled at me, melting my heart. She said, "I must go alone, Griffin."

Chapter Do   -2-

ANASTASIA DROVE DOWN THE A30 towards Land's End, trying to recall a poem she'd heard:

Land's End isn't
the antediluvian
paradise O
it's a bit more tumbled than that:
ultramarine winds, rude brambles,
clod earth, and granite cliffs wave-ridden.
On the moor stand circle stones
where Druids danced for
waning waxing moons
a shiver ago . . .
like friends I once knew
in the maw of time,
said lost . . .

Yes, Griffin, she thought, I do wish you were here with me.

She had started early from Cismontane, taking a nondescript Land Rover from Graves's garage. She wondered what Griffin, Dr. Moe, von Konigswald, and Joko might do while she was gone. Perhaps they'd go fishing in the Lark or the Linnet. Or they could drive Graves's 1931 Bentley around the country roads near Bury St. Edmunds, where Hopkins had persecuted witches.

She was feeling a bit morose, she realized, and she glanced at her watch: four in the afternoon; she'd been driving since eight that morning, stopping only to buy petrol and lunch in a village on the way. The Tregiffian Hotel was her destination, near Sennen, the westernmost village in England, where legend holds King Arthur and Cornish forces defeated the Danes.

Lili had told her about the village and the hotel. She loves her places of refuge, mused Anastasia, glancing at the directions Lili had written the night before: proceed through Crows-an-Wra (Witches Cross) a village, and about one-and-three-quarter miles beyond, turn right and keep to the right-hand forks.

She switched off the radio, a rabid French station, and soon turned down a lane to reach an old Cornish farmhouse, which stood on cliffs overlooking the Atlantic. She parked the Rover, grabbed her small bag, which was Griffin's, and entered the farmhouse.

"Hello! Anybody home?"

Apparently not. Setting her bag down and walking out around the house to the oceanside, she gazed down to the breakers crashing against the granite cliffs, the salt smell inviting. A seabird rose above the cliff directly in front of her. Without hesitation she spoke to the bird: "I am the daughter of Marian and Stevan, granddaughter of Yasoda and Lazo. Though my center is in Crna Gòra, my mother connects me to the British Isles. My task is to find the turquoise Stele of Fate."

The seabird drifted out over the waters. Anastasia cried into the wind, "Will you help me?"

The bird dove below the cliff, reappeared to Anastasia's left, swooped around her, and flew away to the east. Turning, Anastasia hiked back to the inn, where a man working in a garden greeted her.

"I didn't think anyone was around," Anastasia replied to the greeting.

"There's a bit of it to do if we are to serve garden fresh vegetables. You must be Miss Romanov."

" I am."

"Come for a holiday? Clearly, you have! That is why we've visitors. You're a friend of Lili's."

"Yes."

"She's a rollicking songstress!"

"Yes."

"You, ah, seem preoccupied, Miss Romanov. Allow me to show you to your room. You can relax before dinner."

"I want to see the Men-an-Tol."

"You want to see . . . The stones! Plenty of time for that tomorrow, stones all about down here on the Land's End."

"I want to see the Men-an-Tol now. Is it far?"

"Now?"

She nodded.

"But it's late."

She smiled slightly.

"Well, come. I'll make you a map."

✦   ✦   ✦

Driving east on the Mandron-Penzance road, Anastasia spied an old woman at a lone farmhouse taking in the laundry from a drying line. The innkeeper's cartography was accurate to this point, but he said she'd have to walk a long way down a muddy cart track to find the holed stone, and without being there he wasn't sure which track it was. Anastasia pulled into the driveway.

"Excuse me. I'm trying to find—"

The woman turned, clothespins in her hands, smiled, and giggled. "The Men-an-Tol! Carry on,"—she pointed down the road—"the next track on your left."

"Why, thank you."

After driving to the cart track, Anastasia parked on the edge of the gravel and started on foot up the dirt lane, hedges on either side, rough farmland spreading to the horizon. In the dimming light of the early evening, she could see a distant farmer gliding away on his tractor. She continued up the muddy track, deeper into the land: a rolling scape almost naked but for a covering of low gorse beyond untended walls. Blackbirds reeled through the sky. At last, through a gap she saw, rooted into the ground, the Men-an-Tol, a holed stone with a standing stone on either side, or the ring and two sentinels of the poem.

Pausing at the gap to peer at the stones, she tried to center herself and calm her mind. She climbed up and over the broken wall to follow a narrow path to the stones. Standing against the darkening skyline, mist rolling in from the sea, her red skirt billowing, she untied her heavy blue Aran sweater from around her neck and pulled it on to keep warm.

She circled the stones clockwise, not knowing what to expect, but she moved her hands around her like a tai chi form, feeling the spatial energy, a pressure against her hands. She stopped and removed a silver crescent from around her neck to place it atop the holed stone. Now circling the ancient menhirs widdershins, passing outside the sentinels, she happened to glance at her hands and discovered they mimicked the Men-an-Tol! Her thumb touched her ring and middle finger, forming a circle, while her first and pinky fingers stood upright on either side of the ring. Her hands tingled with energy. Amazed, she sat cross-legged on the ground facing the stones "against the sun," her hands still in the form, resting on her knees. She calmed herself. Finally she chanted:

"I am partial and I am whole,
I am unknown and I am of this land.
I am between the eternal earth
and the limitless sky.
I see the black bird of earth
climb to the clouds,
the white mist of sky
descend to earth,
each seeking union with the Stranger:
their lost selves.
Confounding this union is Festus Griveaux
who would rule the world
with Heimarmene,
fate of the stars;
Years follow years
a new age comes!
Show me the Stele
which I may shelter from
(he the shadow)
so that earth and sky
may be one again
and no longer
strangers to themselves."

The land is dark now, yet Anastasia can still see the Men-an-tol; rooted deep are the stones. Closing her eyes, she feels the cold mist against her face and hands, yet she is warm. Time signifies a mechanical division, but there are no engines on the moor. Slowly she feels herself being pulled by energy, the same energy she had touched with her hands. She fights the desire to open her eyes, fights the emotion of fear. At a sensation of flying from the ground, she opens her eyes to see the holed stone rushing towards her or she towards it. In a blink she's through the hole and coursing through blackness.

✦ ✦ ✦

A fire blazed in the hearth of the Tregiffian Inn while guests prattled convivially in the bar, some drinking whisky, others sherry.

The proprietress called out to her husband, "Didn't you mention the new guest arrived this afternoon?"

"The Andersons are right here, dear, I'm telling them old Cornish legends."

"No, not the Andersons, dear, the woman . . . Miss Romanov."

"Oh, right. Well, she had a bee in her bonnet, had to forge ahead to see the dancing stones . . . or was it the stone of the hole? One of them, dear."

"And how could you allow her to go? Now it's late and stormy. Are you sure she wasn't to take supper elsewhere tonight?"

"Why, no, I'm not sure! That must be what happened, dear, and I forgot."

The proprietress entered the bar carrying a plate of hors d'oeuvres; glancing at her husband, she said, "This man's insufferable, is he not?"

"Oh, no, Mrs. Greenwood," replied Mrs. Anderson, smoothing her new, sturdy tweed skirt, "Mr. Greenwood's telling us tales of the countryside."

"Yep," added Mr. Anderson, "a fine tall tale teller. Now, Greenie," Anderson continued, taking a draught of whisky, "tell us about the Howling Cairn. And from now on you can just call me Swede."

"Fine, Mr. Anderson. The Howling Cairn is north of Madron-on-the-Moor, a great hillside of tormented rock thrown at monstrous

386

angles, time gobbled under countless moonlit nights, bleached bone white by the ever-born sun. Spirits of the ancients dwell amidst those musty masses. 'Neath the shadow of that hill, the land is worn and rotten, with frazzled clumps of brown grass and tangled brambles where a shriveled naggie may struggle for a mouthful."

"Mr. Greenwood! Why, you're giving me the shivers!" exclaimed Mrs. Anderson, looking through the window into the darkness.

"Come on, Mary, it's just a little tall tale," said Anderson. "Go on with the story, there, Greenie, and don't mind her, cause she gets a little excited sometimes." He lightly clapped Greenwood on the back.

"Right, Mr. Anderson." The proprietor bent down, grabbed a whisky from the tabletop and drank deeply, emptying the glass.

"By God! I like the way you do that, Greenie!" exclaimed Anderson. "I'll buy you another . . . and from now on, call me Swede like I told you."

"Oh, my, I drank your—"

"I respect a drinkin' man, Greenie, come on, set us up with the whole damn bottle . . . right here! I'm buyin'!"

Several of the other guests who had been talking, not in whispers exactly, but using polite modulation, looked up and smiled at the tall, skinny man from Houston.

Anderson noticed and said, "Hey! Y'all kin have some too!"

Ignoring him, the others turned back to their various conversations.

Anderson, who couldn't have cared less, said, "Now that we're all oiled and greased, go on with your tall tale there, Greenie!"

"Well," began Greenwood again, feeling the alcohol warmth in his gut, "well, you wouldn't want to wander about there at midnight, the boundary between days, because it is then the archfiend pursues the lost across the empty moor, where lie the barrows of the dead, the supernatural circles and ring stones, the crude antiquities, henges, and altars that still, it is said, carry unfathomed powers!"

Anderson took another long pull of whisky, glanced at Greenwood and said, "You know, Greenie, I think you're gettin' t'me too! When's dinner?"

"The superstitions," continued Greenwood without missing a beat, "surrounding the various prehistoric monuments are many, so I'll simply mention a few. Now then, Mrs. Swede, to become a witch you simply touch a Logan Stone nine times at midnight."

Anderson, who was taking another swig, choked, coughing into his glass. Mrs. Anderson said, "A Logan Stone, Mr. Greenwood?"

"A great stone that is set in such a way, by unknown forces, that it rocks about madly when given the slightest pressure upon one side or the other."

"Go about into the haunted scrubland at midnight? No, I don't think so, Mr. Greenwood. It'd be madness!"

"What about a stroll across Burn Downs on Midsummer's Eve, when all the witches in the West meet? The Downs is a tract much like that 'neath the Howling Cairn, hulking monoliths strewn erratically across storm-ravaged land, mounds, cromlechs, rock basins, and cairns everywhere." Greenwood paused, took a modest sip of his whiskey and with lowered voice, as one does when providing clandestine information, said, "On Midsummer's Eve every ancient construction and natural temple is wild with flame of the oak fires that are lit to strengthen the sun that has reached the height of its summer apex and must fall back in the journey toward winter. It is boundary time, the midnight of summer, when shadows and spirits are a fly, and there is a high festival of the little people . . ."

By now, Anderson was sitting back in his chair sipping his whisky and grabbing an occasional hors d'oeuvre, spilling crumbs down his shirt. The other guests had also quieted to listen to Greenwood's mythology.

Greenwood continued, "Mrs. Swede—"

"You can call me Mrs. Anderson, dear."

"Right! Mrs. Anderson, let us not forget the Men-an-tol! How the holed stone came to its construction is a matter of conjecture, some saying it was used as a doorway to limit access to a great burial mound that has since sunk into the earth, others insisting it is clearly a . . . how to put this delicately . . . a symbol of womanhood."

Anderson questioned, "Womanhood! Now, why is that, Greenie?"

"Well, the hole . . ."

"Yes, the hole?"

"Is comparable to the female organ."

"Oh, my goodness! There's women present! Hush your mouth!"

"Gracious, Sidney, don't be so embarrassing!" exclaimed Mrs. Anderson, "We're having an intellectual conversation here. Now, be quiet!"

Anderson's mouth dropped open, he frowned, and poured himself another whisky.

Mrs. Anderson reiterated, "So the holed stone is a kind of mystic vagina, is that correct, Mr. Greenwood?"

Anderson cupped his hands over his ears in exaggerated gesture, got up and paced about.

Greenwood, pouring himself another whisky said, "Why yes, Mrs. Anderson."

"Call me Mary."

"Yes, Mary, and the implication is that if one crawls through it at the magic time of year, or at evening-fall, really any boundary time, which as we've seen are magic times, one will be birth'd into the fairy world. To return, the person must find the stone again and be birth'd in the opposite direction. This is symbolized by the phallic standing stones on either side of the hole."

"Yes, of course, the rigid phallus."

"Now, Mary, some researchers claim that great mystical sites are connected right through the earth by forces of energy called ley lines, not only in these British Isles but throughout the world, the pyramids, the Tibetan temples, certain Western cathedrals, sacred wells . . . along with mystic sites of Cornwall. Perhaps the Men-an-Tol is one of those sites."

✦　✦　✦

Anastasia has experience with the unseen world, having been born at nine minutes past midnight. She can see things in the dark that others, born past daybreak, can't see. She's been on a tantric journey with her love, Griffin. If only such a journey would provide her with insight now, but the elements of her existence aren't gathered in the British Isles as they were in the magical circle of her Montenegrin ancestors. She must work with forces present on this island, so she may ride them as she would a powerful steed, her mother's ties forming the reins.

When she feels herself birth'd through the mystical portal into the fairy world, involuntarily opening her eyes to see herself plunge into blackness, she experiences both exaltation and fear, but the murkiness alters to a shimmery rainbow light akin to the aurora borealis, and she grows fascinated with the shapes and colors of the ether. Because of this, she comes to a slow realization she has alighted on a grassy knoll, mushrooms and clover around her. No moon shines, but above her, stars glimmer.

The air smells like sweet countryside, thinks Anastasia, arising and stretching before rambling down the hill. In the dark, she almost steps over a stone ledge. Kneeling to look over the edge, she touches the stone with her hand, feeling a raised pattern. It's a heliced stone, she thinks, running her fingers over it. Walking down to the left, wary of stepping off another slab, she reaches a gap where she can leave the cliff and descend to the ground below. When she emerges from the gap, she sees oak trees bordering a path that runs from the wide horizon to a narrow opening, a portal leading into a prehistoric mound.

It's the majesty of the geography that's confusing, she thinks; this mound is often called by archaeologists a "burial mound," yet intuition tells me this is no such thing. Reaching it, she feels the inscription over the doorway, a sinuous line with nineteen troughs or ridges running beneath eight curves and spirals. She realizes the mound is a moon temple, the crescents, and circles obvious to her: they represent moon phases. And then there is the familiar number: nineteen, the number of years it takes for the moon to rise in the same place and phase on the horizon.

Wondering what to do about her discovery, she becomes aware of an ethereal presence, a light between the towering trees, a silver glow . . . the moon is rising! She looks at the narrow doorway, then back at the far glow. That's why I'm here. It's the nineteen-year cycle. The moon temple's aligned so that moonlight will flow down the passageway into the chamber.

Without further thought she enters the black doorway, feeling her way slowly as she goes, standing stones on either side. She's aware of possible pitfalls, but they're not common to this type of construction . . . unlike the pyramids. A minute later, looking behind her, she sees a quarter of the moon peeking over the edge of the world, aligned as it should be, she thinks, and the passageway is straight. Crawling further, she feels the way widen, enters the chamber and sits as a meditation, observing the moonrise.

Slowly, a stone luminesces at the far end of the chamber opposite the entrance. Only once every nineteen years! The polarized moonlight doesn't diffuse throughout the chamber as sunlight would. Only the stone is alight now. Crawling close, she detects an inscription hewn by hand.

✦　✦　✦

Later that same evening, at the time Anastasia stood before the moon temple, midnight, the bar of the Tregiffian Inn prospered with after-dinner merriment and storytelling. Greenwood was remarking to Mary Anderson, "Modern witches claim the craft is what remains of a pre-Christian fertility cult . . ."

Entering the bar, a worried frown crossing her face, Mrs. Greenwood said, "Robbie Greenwood! I'm concerned about Miss Romanov. Restaurants and pubs have been closed for an hour. There's a terrible storm tonight. Try to remember where she went, what she said."

"Oh? Well, yes, dear. She came up behind me as I worked in the garden. She must have been by the cliffs. She said hello. I remember. She insisted on seeing the Men-an-tol. Why, I drew her a map."

"I can't believe it. I asked you this hours ago! Following your map, she's probably lost. Or her car broke down, or she fell and hurt her ankle. We'd best drive beneath the Howling Cairn to look for her."

"The Howling Cairn at the witching hour?" exclaimed Mary Anderson.

"Oh, come on!" snorted Mrs. Greenwood, pulling her husband's arm.

"I'll come along," Mary Anderson announced.

"By God, so will I," cried Anderson, perking up from a slight doze. "You'll need a man out there."

The four of them piled into Greenwood's van and rode through the driving rain. After several bumpy, soggy miles, while turning down a narrow lane, the rain diminished . . . a lucky break in the storm.

"There's an automobile," observed Mrs. Greenwood, "Is that her automobile?"

"I—I don't think so. They're all alike to me."

"Sure, that's her car," declared Anderson. "I looked out the window 'safternoon and saw it in the lot."

"The lot?"

"The driveway. Less talk and more walk! Let's get up there while the rain's stopped." Anderson bulled ahead while the other three followed.

Mrs. Greenwood called out, "Mr. Anderson! Wait for our torch! You may stumble in the dark."

"I hear ya, little lady," replied Anderson, who looked about himself, now feeling skittish. He decided to wait for the others to catch up. "I saw something over there."

"Where, Mr. Anderson?"

"Didn't I tell ya? Call me Swede!"

"Where, Mr. Swede?"

"No mister. Just Swede . . . Never mind. There!" He pointed into the darkness and Mrs. Greenwood directed the light. A drenched owl peered back at them from a stile in the wall.

"Hoot! Hoot!" Anderson shouted, but the owl sat peering at them.

"It's best to be a bit more subtle on this moor," suggested Greenwood.

"What's that, Greenie? Oh!" Anderson lowered his voice. "Ya mean we might disturb the ghosts?" Then he laughed.

Mrs. Greenwood hissed, "Hush now! Look around you," and snapped off the light. As the moon glimmered between storm clouds, they saw rolling scrublands and plowed fields, some with standing stones, or mounds, amongst stumpy twisted willows and dark thickets. They proceeded more quietly along the muddy cart track until, at last, they found a stile that set them on a Men-an-Tol path. Approaching, they could see the holed stone and the two uprights, damp and eerie in the moonlight.

"It's beautiful," said Mrs. Greenwood.

"Yes, it is," breathed Mary Anderson.

"I don't see anyone, except look," said Anderson. "Is light shimmering around that thing?"

There did seem to be an aura around the stones; the others noticed it too. The four of them didn't continue their approach, but Mary Anderson called out, "Miss Romanov!"

✦   ✦   ✦

The moon mound, or temple, is an artistic and scientific achievement, thinks Anastasia. The beauty of this experience! As she assesses the figures carved into the moonlit stone, she feels a force pulling her back. It makes her angry. She fights it. Female images mark the stone; she counts them, nineteen. There is a structure housing a flame. Over the structure, three women ride a swan; there are other symbols, but Anastasia is pulled backwards up the passageway by a force she can't control. She finds herself flying into the shimmery ether. She hears shouting, hears her name . . . There is an opening in the aurora: the Men-an-tol. Flying through the hole, she discovers she sits on the ground in the shadow cast by the western stone in the moonlight.

✦ ✦ ✦

"She's not here," whispered Anderson. "Let's get off this spooky plain."

"Wait," sang Mary, "I saw something." She picked her way along the path to the stones.

"Mary! Don't go over there! Don't touch it nine times!" shouted Anderson.

As Mary drew near, she observed Anastasia sitting on the ground, legs crossed, hands on knees forming replicas of the Men-an-tol. Mary noted the woman on the ground looked completely dry, as if the rain hadn't touched her.

"Miss Romanov? Miss Romanov? Are you alright?"

Anastasia smiled up at Mary and observed, "You, don't need to touch a Logan stone nine times."

Chapter Tri   -3-

AT THREE A.M. I was sitting with Dr. Moe, on the couch in the library with the rope. No, that's *Clue*. I mean with the Armagnac bottle. But I was conversing with Dr. Moe in the Cismontane library: leather couch and chairs, green-shade lamps, rolling bookcase ladders, Aubusson rug. I surmised this was where Anastasia's mother, Marian, had spent much of her time growing up. From what I've heard, she knew about horticulture and animal husbandry, airplane mechanics and Lewis machine gun workings. And she was a pilot. In addition, according to Lili, Marian had read English and European literature and could hold her own with any of the university snobs who occasionally haunted the halls of Cismontane.

Anastasia never knew her mother, who by all accounts was a bright light in the darkness, and she hardly knew her father, said to be a man of honor. The person, the being, the entity, (the fiend?) responsible for Anastasia's very intimate loss of her parents: Festus Griveaux.

No wonder Anastasia has a touch of contumacy in her character, as when she had announced the subject of her dissertation during our gone-by midsummer's day in Claremont, proposing that Gnosticism had attempted to unite the God religion with the Goddess religion, and all the professors and grad students dropped their pencils or spilled their water glasses. Easy to say. Hard to prove.

But now, all that takes a back seat to her real quest and the focus of her clansmen, to defeat once and for all their enemy, who they say is the enemy of free people everywhere: Festus Griveaux and his Order of Suebi. Musing, I mentioned Festus to Dr. Moe. As I said, he was also up at three in the morning drinking vintage Armagnac with me. Perhaps the time change was keeping us up, plus the twenty-seven hours of caving in Montenegro for me, and the retrieving Karl from California for Dr. Moe. Our biorhythms must have been out of whack.

Dr. Moe looked at me and said, "Who is this Festus Griveaux? I've never met him. I've just heard the tales of his wickedness from the point of view of the Romanov clan. One example: the account Thoth told us of Stevan, Joko, and Dick when they encountered Festus and his Suebi Order in Egypt."

Dr. Moe continued: "In addition, I agree that one, his Suebi secretaries are abrasive and annoying; two, Interpol doesn't think much of him and keeps tabs on the Honorable Order of the Suebi; and three, now Karl is waxing ill of his former THOOTS colleagues and claiming some crazy stuff about their kidnapping him by way of speaking in tongues."

After his list (he loves lists), Dr. Moe added, "And meanwhile, these people, Anastasia's family, let's consider them. Charles Graves: What a bizarre old fellow, living on this vast estate, his primary concern to defeat an enemy he and his occult group have been warring with for generations! How does it work? It seems to me the responsibility has been handed down from mother to son, father to daughter, Yasoda to Stevan, Graves to Marian, Stevan to Anastasia. Have I got that right?"

I replied, "Well, yes. Except Graves had quite a falling out with the Romanov clan after he had welcomed in Stevan while the lad was at Cambridge and the boy ended up seducing Graves's only daughter Marian. Stevan spirited away Marian and they married but she died after birthing Anastasia, the result of a wound caused by Festus."

Dr. Moe said, "A tragedy for Stevan for sure . . . yet, I somewhat understand Graves's feeling of guilt, his sorrow at his only daughter's death, and his churlish response. But thinking about this line of succession—we don't know who came before Graves. Who was his mother?"

I said, "No idea. I've heard of someone called the Wolly, but he wouldn't fit your proposed pattern of occult succession."

Dr. Moe said, "Well, what in confoundation are we doing in the middle of it? One teardrop from Anastasia and you follow her straight into a private war, fought mostly on the higher levels of the nervous system, the invisible world so to speak. OK, I confess, I had a taste of that last night, at the séance or round dance or whatever, but . . ."

With Dr. Moe, you just have to butt in sometimes, as when he's on a roll. I replied, "Perhaps I should not have dragged you into this, however, there's an integrity about Anastasia that draws me to her. As far as I'm concerned, everything she's avowed has been proven out."

At this, Dr. Moe shook his head.

I said, "Remember, I've been to the caves, whose entrance she and I discovered —I won't tell you how—and we found the 'alleged' Greek codices in the grotto. Furthermore, those books reference the Stele of Fate, just as she said they would. So, I believe her concerning Festus and the Suebi, because I know her knowledge of higher consciousness is profound."

Dr. Moe replied, "If that's the case, how is *your* knowledge on the supernal level? I don't think you know what you are doing. And don't cite your ski racing mumbo-jumbo."

I replied, "When she and I are together, our combined mind is joyous and seeking." Well, mostly. I decided to leave it at that and turned to the discussion of her clan. I said, "Then there is Joko, Aunt Anastasija, Lili, Graves, von Konigswald, Smythe, and Thoth, although he's not been here, I can feel his presence—the old guard. I sense they're passing something on to us, a knowledge so subtle that it cannot be approached straight on."

Dr. Moe replied, "Ah, yes. That's the carrot for you. You want to pursue and acquire secret, occult, esoteric knowledge. It's not enough for you to be a renowned archaeologist, head of an august institute, a scholar of ancient languages—no, you want more. But I will remind you that the knowledge you seek comes with great responsibility and usually brings danger and madness. I think you'd best contemplate your options very carefully. You seek immense and overcharged pieces of mystery. But you might remember, Gnosticism is a mirror—it will reflect anything put before it."

Well, this was quite a diatribe from Dr. Moe. I would not be able to dismiss what he said out of hand. But I decided I'd give *him* something to think about. I replied as a man of learning, as any scholar might reply, because the pursuit of knowledge is our destiny. I said, "As to your warnings, the secret may be less important than the fact it is kept secret."

But Dr. Moe is not easily put off. He replied, "I wonder how Anastasia and her Romanov clan would react to that statement."

He had remembered Anastasia's dismissal of any suggestion of our publishing the magical formulas of the sacred books of her clan, the Greek codices. Yes, if we could publish the entirety of those two Gnostic codices, it would be a tremendous boost for the Institute and for both Dr. Moe and me personally. However, I had become quite convinced such a publication would bring danger to the Romanovs, the Institute, and to the world in general. I daresay there are esoteric secrets that should never be illuminated by the light of scholarship.

I replied, "Anastasia has agreed to allow us to publish sections of those codices, but we are not to violate the passages that, for her, are fraught with meaning."

Dr. Moe again shook his head in negation, but at length he said, "We'll see."

And that's the last thing I remember because the next thing I knew, I woke up lying on the library couch with a cashmere blanket tossed over me and Anastasia sitting in the chair opposite.

When she saw my eyes crank open, she said, "Have a nice night?"

I looked at her. I couldn't believe she was sitting there and wondered if it was some sort of trick of the mind. I finally said, "Anna? You must have been driving all night."

"I left at two. Now it's ten."

"You better join me on the couch."

She stepped out of her shoes and climbed in next to me under the blanket. She said, "It's raining. I'm cold."

"Then you've come to the right place."

I woke up again at noon, Anastasia still asleep beside me. I had to pee. I wondered where everybody was. The house was as quiet as if it had been abandoned and shut up tight, perhaps to ward off the ravages of a pandemic, as if outside, raging across the countryside, came the black plague, and only when the danger had passed could the house again be unshuttered and life resume. But it was only closed down against the driving rain of a proper blustering tempest. When Anastasia woke up—OK, I woke her up—she told me the storm had followed her up the A5, all the way back from Cornwall, flashes of lightning, thunder, washouts, running rivulets. She said nothing was going to stop her, and the Land Rover Defender had been up to the job.

I excused myself to visit the WC, and on the way I mused: Were we in that early stage of infatuation, when you long for your beloved the moment she or he walks out of the room, and like a timekeeper, you count the seconds until the reunion? She drove all night. To be back with me! And I would have done the same just to feel her breathing next to me. If time wasn't a mighty river, washing away everything you could see, then perhaps we'd love forever, you know, that'd be alright with me . . . Lyrics. Sometimes they waft through my head.

I had just returned to the library when, marching through the door came Graves, Lili, Joko, von Konigswald, Aunt Anastasija, and Smythe.

Aunt Anastasija said, "Darling, I believe you have news."

Anastasia turned to her aunt. "Come to the spiral table. I shall speak my mystery."

As we proceeded to the far end of the great hall I said, "You're giving this the formal approach."

She replied, "We must be in the proper frame of mind, Griffin. I drew down the moon! She speaks with me in this matter."

The eight gathered around the spiral table, the six old ones facing the two younger ones. Where was Dr. Moe? Sleeping late? Or, babysitting Karl?

While the storm yet raged outside, rain beating hysterically against the large, round moon window above us, Anastasia described what had occurred on her pilgrimage and then with pencil and paper sketched the symbols of the illumined stone: nineteen priestesses, a shelter housing a fire, three goddesses riding a swan, each carrying a branch with bells attached, also various spirals and moon symbols. When she finished, she was quiet. No one spoke.

Finally, Lili declared, "This is familiar to me. We have a moon goddess of triple aspect. She has a shrine with a perpetual fire attended by nineteen priestesses. The branch with bells, the swan . . . it will come to me." She arose, and the old ones, following her lead, left the table, passed the statue of Diana and disappeared through the double doors.

The two of us, Anastasia and I, remained at the table grinning at each other. She said, "It will come to me too."

I said, "Me, also. What do you think happened to Dr. Moe? And Karl, for that matter?"

Anastasia shrugged. How would she know? She'd fallen asleep next to me a few minutes after she'd returned to Cismontane.

✦　✦　✦

The next day, Graves approached Anastasia and me after break-fast. He said that we should walk down to the boathouse on the lake, since the storm had finally spent itself in its fury or had renewed itself and gone on to give mainland Europe something to think about. He assured us that the lake path is always beautiful after a storm.

He was right. The Cismontane grounds glimmered in the dewy air, green and wet, yet the gravel path seemed to be dry as it wound down through field and forest to the lake.

"I'd like to see the lake in the moonlight."

I would too. I replied, "We'll come back tonight."

"I hear frogs."

"Frogs?"

She said, "On the shore," and started jogging down the path.

I caught up and we continued through wet grass to the bank. As we approached, several frogs jumped into the water—a splash, then nothing. We saw a rock outcropping and climbed up to where it jutted out into the lake as a peninsula. There, looking down into the still, black water we could see the light of the sky with intermittent clouds passing above us, and our images looking back up at us, images so clear that I felt like we stood on the edge of infinity itself.

Looking down she said, "I'm getting dizzy."

"Anna, the illusion! I feel like a god."

She replied, "It's not an illusion, Griffin, it's a reflection."

♦ ♦ ♦

We decided to explore the boathouse, which lay on shore about a quarter of a mile to the east. It didn't take long to reach it. We found a door, and inside, a light switch. Switching it on, I saw the crisscrossed wings of various aircraft.

Without delay, Anastasia walked up to an aeroplane, one that attracted her, and touched its wing. She said, "It's odd, this biwinged boat fits the description of . . . " Moving to the right she noticed a faded painting of a bouquet of daffodils on the plane's fuselage and the script, *Daffodil.* I saw it at the same time she did. She exclaimed, "An exact replica!"

I shook my head. Like an idiot I said, "The exact craft."

"What?"

"That's your father's plane. Look at the weathering, the fading. It would be impossible to duplicate."

Anastasia stared at me wide-eyed, then turned back to the aircraft. She said, "I thought it was destroyed, or just gone with age." She found foot and hand holds and climbed onto the pilot's cockpit, sat at the controls, moved the levers. Then she crawled back through the fuselage to the aft cockpit to where her mother, Marian, was shot by Festus's henchmen as the flying boat attempted its escape. An old stain marred the seat, a bloodstain.

"My mother's blood!" she shouted. It echoed in the hanger. She reached out, touched the stain, pulled her hand back, looking at her fingers.

"Anna?" I breathed. She didn't answer. I stepped back for a better look at her, but her face was in shadow, and I couldn't read her. I thought I heard a sob. I said again, "Anna?"

Slowly, she stretched her arm over the side, spreading her fingers. She wailed, "See this blood?" (There was no blood on her fingers)

"This blood . . . is prime!" The cry echoed through the hanger. She was looking past me into shadow. "Replace her! Give me her! Can you? Can you, you horror-eyed specter?"

I didn't move, but peered at her, my face knotted. At last, I heard her rustling. She climbed down and stood opposite me. Neither of us could speak, but I took her hand and pulled her out into the light of the afternoon, where we walked silently across the grounds of Cismontane.

✦ ✦ ✦

Two days later, Anastasia and I were up early, only to find the six elders already in the garden sipping Earl Grey tea in the warm, dewy air humming with the melodious din of nature.

Lili was saying, "I've examined the alternatives, Charlie,"—no more Charles, it seems they've made up—"and when you hear my conclusion, I wonder if you'll feel surprise, for the answer is surprising. Yet,"—she chuckled and shook her head—"we mystics should know it is typical of the way things work. The unseen has a sense of humor!"

Von Konigswald blustered, "You think I don't learn that lesson sometimes in the darkness of a cavern? Twist and turn for miles only to end up where I started."

Joko, sticking to the job, said, "Enough of this jabber. What do you say, Lili?"

Anastasia and I pulled up metal chairs. As we sat down I said, "Well, yes, although I've some ideas, I'd love to hear yours first, Lili."

Lili smiled at me, dabbed honey on her spoon and stirred it into her tea.

Joko looked like a pot ready to boil over. He reminded me of Dr. Moe and I wondered, What has happened to Dr. Moe? And Karl? I hadn't seen either of them in three days.

Lili said, "The swan appears in myths of many cultures—the Greek legend of Zeus turning into a swan to impregnate Leda; Aphrodite is often pictured riding a swan; the Finnish Kalevala legend tells of a mythical swan. There are swan legends in Norse mythology, and throughout France, Germany, and Slavic lands."

Joko muttered, "Ahhh, I haven't thought of that in years."

Graves said, "What is it, Joko?"

"Lazo's story. Once, when I was a young boy on my first trip to Herak's grotto, while camping on a high plateau one night, I asked Lazo for a tale. He told about a swan who turned into a magical woman. When Lazo tried to rule her, she shapeshifted into an old hag and gave him his first wound. But in her presence he discovered how to heal himself. He couldn't rule her, yet he could be free."

I said, "What? That's my Uncle MacRobbin's story!"

Aunt Anastasija put down her cup and peered at me. She said, "Sometimes it's a small world."

I didn't know what to say, so I said, "Yes, I've heard that," and everyone laughed as if the joke was on me.

Lili continued, "The goddess represented in Anastasia's moon temple is a healer. I will show you. There are three women riding a swan. That bird, able to fly high in the air or move well on land or water, is a creature of all worlds and can even cross over supernatural boundaries, thus it is a gatherer, not a divider. The three women on a single swan indicate a triple goddess such as worshipped by the Celts. The spirals and moon symbols are also Celtic."

Joko interrupted, saying, "The Bogomils also held the spiral as emblem."

"Yes," agreed Lili, "and I imagine your Herak was partial to them. But there are too many hints here indicating a goddess of Celtic origin. The threefold goddess is carrying a branch with bells, a bard's symbol of poetry. She has a shrine housing a perpetual fire attended to by nineteen priestesses. In Celtic lands there is such a place!"

"All right, Lili," cried von Konigswald, "what is your conclusion?"

Lili smiled at the drama she'd created. "There is a saint whose shrine was once attended by nineteen nuns, who kept a perpetual fire burning for her. The swan was her emblem. She was known as the patron saint of fertility, childbirth, and healing. There stands a cathedral now where her firehouse once resided in Kildare, Ireland. Saint Brigid's Cathedral!"

Joko, von Konigswald, and Graves gasped. Smythe, who had been quiet the whole time, smiled. And Anastasia, Aunt Anastasija, and I weren't surprised at all because we had come to the same conclusion.

Anastasia said, "Before she was called Saint Brigid, she was known as the goddess Brigid. She's the goddess of poetry and carries branch and bells for the poet."

Lili observed, "I know you know this, Charlie, that your friend, whom you have long banished and abandoned, our good friend and occult colleague, Dick McBride, is now resident bishop of that very cathedral."

Joko, astonished, said, "What? How?"

Graves said, "Ah, you didn't know this, Joko? He never told you? Typical. Between the wars, when he wasn't with me, he taught theology at Trinity College in Ireland. He had already been ordained as a priest in the Church of Ireland. After the second war, Dick returned to the ministry and eventually became Bishop of Kildare."

Joko, who had been pursing his lips and muttering, burst out, "You say that insufferable limper, that round little leprechaun, our own Dick has been sitting oblivious all these years on the mystic stele?"

"Yes, Joko, it appears to be true," replied Aunt Anastasija.

Anastasia turned to Joko and confided, "The two Greek codices you, Father, Thoth, and Dick obtained in Egypt at the expense of

Festus and the Masters of Matter tell of the Stele's hidden location but, until reflecting on my visit to the moon temple, I didn't know what the words meant. Now it's clear."

Extracting a page of the translated text from a notebook, she read: "'It is now you must cross the sea to this world's ungoverned borders'—the text is damaged; however there is an image of the letter *H*, which indicates Hibernia, the Latin name for Ireland. The text continues: 'there the mind will surely bring you through the wilderness to that which is called beauty, the shrine of poetry. Under the ever-burning fire, O my son, take this book written on a Stele of turquoise in hieroglyphic characters, bury it there on the edge of the world.'" Anastasia stopped reading.

"So it's true," Joko said.

Chapter Ceathair   -4-

THE ANCIENT STONE WALLS of Saint Brigid's Cathedral in County Kildare are solid gray and vine covered, making them seem more a part of the vegetal earth mysteries than of the suprasensory Christian milieu. Inside, Bishop Dick MacBride sat wrestling with problems of humankind, that singular species which seems descended from the two: matter and spirit.

Cessair, the parish secretary and member of the laity, entered the office to read a list: "Now. We've sent the money to Mother Teresa in India because of your Yugoslav affiliations."

"Aye, I'm not lookin' forward to explainin' sendin' alms to a Yugoslav nun in India."

"Well, now, feeding the poor 'n' miserable is all the same anywhere, but we do have our own problems right here," commented Cessair, brushing back her auburn hair. Seeing Bishop MacBride's usually bright round face gloom a bit, she added, "But ya couldn't be ignoring her letter now, could ya."

The short, round bishop looked more like a part of the fairy race than a member of the clergy as he sat behind an enormous desk of fifth-century Irish ash. Legend avers St. Patrick formed ash logs into crosses to chase the snakes from Ireland, and Christian wisdom assures the wood even keeps the devil at bay. Mostly.

The bishop replied, "Many things I try to ignore, Cessair, but either God or the Devil knocks me on the head, vyin' for my attention."

"They're afraid your attention's with the Great Lady rather than with them, Bishop MacBride, son of Brigid of the Holy Fire!"

"Now, I'm ignorin' that little bit there, Cessair—"

"Oh, don't be ignoring the following information, Bishop, because the Arab girl is coming Thursday next week and we need t—"

"All right, Cessair, please, you disembark before reachin' land. What is it? The Arab girl?"

"Yes, Bishop, and you remember the talk with Cardinal Eiseley only a fortnight ago concerning the pregnant, unwed Arab girls who must flee home, with nowhere to go, all to escape being slaughtered at the hands of their own brothers, or fathers or even their own mothers, burned they are, or stoned, or strangled, with the babes growing in their wombs, so-called honor killings."

The bishop replied, "I'm rememberin' the conversation now, Cessair, an' about the Swiss human rights organization with the Jewish doctor and the Catholic woman helpin' the girls escape the West Bank of the Jordan, and the Quakers helpin' too and the Cardinal objectin' t' the abortions, but offerin' parish help throughout Europe so the unfortunate girls can have their babes in peace . . . and such help we're providin' by takin' in one of these girls Thursday next." The bishop rubbed his eyes with the heels of his hands. "O Great Day! Well, we'll have to clean out the back room. And what about the orphans of St. Columcille, who at the very least need indoor plumbin' and someone to donate 'em a peat burnin' oven?"

The telephone rang. Bishop MacBride answered it.

"Dick?" said the interrogative and demanding voice of Charles Graves, a call from England. It was a voice Dick MacBride hadn't heard in thirty-some years.

"Ya sound like the Red Queen, Charlie, or like a black bear carryin' off the honey with the bees awakin' up."

A grunt at the other end of the line, then, "Red Queen? Black bear? I wish you were sitting across from me now, so I could observe the subtle hues on your face as I relate the following information."

"Well, now, Charlie, that we haven't seen each other in a score and ten? Whose obstinate, miserable fault is that?"

Silence on the line. Finally, Graves said, "I know. I couldn't get my head above it, Dick, I just could not."

"Well, ya better start relatin' for I've a wake to attend to in"—he looked at Cessair, she held up nine fingers—"in . . . the crane must, aye, take nine steps before she flies . . . nine minutes."

"The Irishman is incapable of doing anything in nine minutes but saying good morning."

"And if it wasn't for the Irishman there'd be a dearth of eloquence upon the craggy earth, no majesty of exposition, no flowin', graceful, or graphic, vivid, meaningful and passionate expression—"

"What?"

"NO CONVERSATION!"

"Are we having one?"

"Ah, get on wi' it then, ya miserable Sassenach!"

"I can only hint on the wire, you understand."

"Hint away, for you make no sense by any manner or means."

"I'm coming to visit you, Dick."

A pause on the line. Then, "Right. I guess you're owin' me a visit."

"We're all coming, including my granddaughter."

"All? And you've finally learned you have a granddaughter? Finally? Well, just bring Anastasia, for I've yet to set eyes on her grown self!"

"You'll need to go no further than your Cathedral of Saint Brigid to find a mystery."

"Your tongue's a mystery."

"We'll arrive tomorrow afternoon."

"Well, don't make a fuss as you come. We don't appreciate promotion or publicity! We prefer lettin' the world 'Hear so it cannot hear an' see so it cannot see.' We don't want to be a fleein' before all those who haven't the knowledge to interpret the wisdom."

Graves sighed. "True words, Bishop, and I hope Festus is not on to us, with the object we seek so near."

"The object? The Stele?" cut in Dick, forgetting subtlety himself.

"A boil is coming to a head, Bishop Dick MacBride."

Dick paused, then said, "That's what Festus wants now, isn't it? Always the carnage increases when heads are a boil."

"We need to harvest the object before he does."

"You are a sphinx, Charlie, rhyming and riddlin'."

"Goodbye, Bishop."

Dick rang off the telephone. "Cessair."

"Right here, Bishop," Cessair replied from the account desk, where, with her long legs tucked under the chair, she sat doing the ledger.

"Ah, sorry, Cessair, heads are comin' to a boil."

"The better the stew," she replied.

✦   ✦   ✦

To pilot the flying boat called the *Daffodil*, Graves recruited RAF Flight Lieutenant Chris Leigh. To my eyes the *Daffodil* looked decrepit and neither fit for air nor water, but Flt. Lt Leigh assured us it had, in fact, been restored to and remained in "Bristol flying condition." Leigh was a rangy, handsome guy who exuded and air of competence, which was a relief, because Graves had wanted to pilot the aeroplane himself. None of us would have it since the man was in his eighties.

Instead, Graves would still be the copilot, so he'd sit up there with Flt. Lt. Leigh, while the rest of us would stuff into various flying boat compartments. Anastasia and I would occupy the aft gunner's cockpit. This she insisted on, and no one would deny her that, to experience some of what her mother had plunged into all those years ago.

So, Joko and von Konigswald sat in the forward cockpit; Aunt Anastasija and Lili remained happily out of the wind in the forward cabin, and Smythe stayed behind at Cismontane to keep an eye on things. I told Smythe to keep a lookout for Dr. Moe and Karl.

Upon saying goodbye to England, we crossed the Irish Sea under cloudy skies and cold drizzle. Anna and I sat in the open cockpit all the way to the Irish coast and beyond, she fingering the unloaded Lewis machine gun and peering over the side at the cold gray sea two thousand feet below. Upon reaching Ireland, we crossed over the Wicklow Mountains, the sprawling Poulaphouca Reservoir, the towns of Ballymore Eustace and Kilcullen and the Curragh Plain, to land in a field near Kildare—Graves having installed, at some point in the past, retractable landing gear to the belly of the flying boat.

The bishop and a young woman named Cessair, his secretary as it turned out, had been waiting by the landing field in the church van when the faded, sky-blue biwinged antique half-rolled into the west wind and landed. I think that was Anastasia's favorite part of the flight. A half roll!

She whooped, "Yaahhha!" and a huge grin crossed her face. I had to laugh. What a character she can be!

The bishop and Cessair rushed onto the field, the bishop limping madly, Cessair striding beside him, he calling out, "Anastasia! Anastasia!"

But we sat trapped in the aft cockpit until Leigh and Graves climbed down from their pilot's seat; with Graves, that took a while.

In the meantime, Anastasia waved and called out, "Dick? Bishop MacBride? Dick!"

He, upon viewing the dark-haired beauty in the gunner's cockpit, where Marian took an evil bullet through her gut, seemed for a moment struck speechless until he finally managed, "Why, why, child!"

"You'll never know the whys and wherefores, you mad old limper, even if they lie under your very feet!"

Hearing the familiar voice from his past, Dick turned to the bow of the flying boat, where Joko grinned down at him.

"Joko! Ye indestructible bandit! Even the earthquakes haven't harmed ya. And now ya've finally made it to a land where there's drink t' put yer miserable plum juice t' shame."

Sometimes Joko can beam. This was one of those times. He replied, "It's good to see a Round Man."

Still viewing from the aft cockpit, I saw Graves—who was finally standing on solid ground—and Bishop Dick MacBride approach each other. Each paused for a good look at the old friend standing opposite and perhaps seeing through a glass darkly, gazing through years of misunderstanding, accusation, guilt, error, lost time, just loss, they stared, shook hands . . . and then hugged. Auld lang syne. Auld lang syne! It brought a tear to my eye.

Then Anastasia climbed down. The bishop walked up, held her hands in both of his, gazed into her face. He said, "I knew you in that Montenegrin keep that you and your father and Aunt Anastasija lived in all those years ago, but you were just a baby. Your mother was a great friend of mine. Really, like a daughter she was. And you! You have so much of her in you! To see you, finally! The joy! The wonder!"

Anastasia, teary now, said, "I feel that I know you, Dick, all the stories I've been told about Father and you and Joko. To finally meet you . . . I'm at a loss for words."

But as they walked arm in arm across the field, Anastasia found her words, and the two of them began talking as if they were old friends. I imagine this is how normal life should be. The rest of us threw down our travel bags, climbed down, introductions and helloes all around, and we were soon bumping along in the church van down a narrow Irish lane. Now that Graves and the bishop were friends again, so to speak, Graves, with unconcealed amusement, told MacBride about the Stele.

The bishop said, "So, what yer sayin' t' me is—"

Joko blurted, "What he's saying to you, you sleepy round limper, is that you've napped for years and years over the mystic Stele of Fate, which is buried under your silly Irish nose!"

MacBride coughed. "And thank you for that, Joko, for assurin' me by yer mockery that ya haven't changed a bit, even though yer old enough t' be buried yourself! And don't worry. If ya knock off tomorrow, there's plenty of room to plant ya in the loam of this beautiful Emerald Isle."

"OK," Joko replied, "but with a jug of raki at my head and feet!"

At that Cessair, who had been quiet while steering the van down the lane, mused almost to herself, "Oh, no, they don't sell that here."

First, the bishop took us to his residence. Cessair showed us our rooms, etc., but soon impatient, we made it clear we needed to see the cathedral, its grounds, its environs, its secrets.

At Saint Brigid's Cathedral the bishop showed us the hidden crypts, holes, keeps and cashes of the stone building, then we went on to the surrounding grounds. We viewed a doorway into the earth which led to a root cellar, and behind the church, a twelfth-century, hundred-foot high round tower.

"We've seen everything but the shrine where Saint Brigid's perpetual fire was kept," Anastasia complained.

"Why, yes, indeed, 'tis true child, but there's nothin' left o' the shrine."

"You know the site, though, don't you?"

"To be sure, I do."

He led us clockwise around the cathedral, past rooted gravestones, Celtic crosses, a carved abbot with bell and crozier, looming angels, and common markers, until we came to a depression in the earth some twenty feet square, bordered by rocks. Inside the border, grass grew in wanton, thick, and tall clumps, nothing like the mild lawn of the churchyard. This site, between the cathedral and the ancient round tower, was the place that once held Brigid's shrine.

I entered the enclosure, knelt down, dipped my fingers into the long grass, and at length whispered, "My name is Erin. I give gifts of culture to help defeat the bestial above and below. The shrine of poetry is the shrine of Brigid . . . remember . . ."

Anastasia knelt beside me. She said, "Anagryph! We met Erin on the path."

"Under perpetual fire, the shrine of poetry," I said as I quoted Erin. "The Stele isn't buried somewhere on the grounds. Not somewhere, but exactly here."

Graves, Lili, Aunt Anastasija, Joko, von Konigswald, and MacBride observed us working together, and I heard Graves whisper, "We're never complete, are we? The new generation always brings more to bear."

"This is it!" Anastasia declared. "The Stele of Fate is buried here."

Lili warned, "Now to uncover it before Festus and the Suebi gain knowledge of our action."

I noted, and Lili and Graves agreed, that without a doubt, the first-century monks would have constructed an underground crypt for the Stele of Fate's resting place. Hearing this, von Konigswald said the excavation of an underground structure would be no small task and would likely take at least a week, because the site would need to be dug out by hand, no machinery allowed. We all agreed, damage to the Stele must be avoided at all cost.

Chapter Cuig   -5-

THE NEXT DAY, AFTER persuading Cessair to be our guide, von Konigswald borrowed the bishop's van to explore the town of Kildare in search of a wheel sledge, which von Konigswald claimed would be necessary for the excavation of the shrine.

As we bumped down a lane, Von Konigswald said, "Cessair! What a beautiful name. Is it a family name?"

"In a way, yes."

"How so?"

"I took it from the first woman of Ireland, Cessair the outcast, who occupied this island before the flood."

"The outcast?" Von Konigswald nodded his head. He asked, "And why do you take on such a stigma?"

She didn't answer, but now I wanted to know too.

So did Anastasia, I think, but she said, "He doesn't mean to pry."

Cessair, brown eyes, looked over at von Konigswald and said, "You are German, and although you can speak a form of our language, you know nothing about this country, or you wouldn't ask such a question. I don't think you know of the women whose husbands are taken with the drinking and the debt, who come home from pubs to beat their thin wives, and when the children scream, beat them too and teach them the violence. You wouldn't ask that, in a land where there's no divorce allowed, and you just take your beatings and bitterness with the rain and the poverty.

"I've formed a women's group for all of Ireland called by my name: CESSAIR, an acronym for Catholic Erinyes Sisters-in-Servitude Aiming for Independence or Rage! Isn't it easy to understand why I take the proud name of the outcast?"

I felt the weight of her passion, her life so different than the one I've led.

Anastasia said, "Oh, Cessair . . . tell me more."

Cessair continued, "They say to me, 'Things could be worse, Cessair, ya could live in Belfast, live in a war zone if ya want to see sufferin,' as if they weren't bringin' it down here anyway, and then they turn back to their bottles and dreams of Banba the Queen of elegance and wealth and grandness unattainable.

"I don't ask for much. Freedom or Rage. I'll not take another punch from a cynical man. And I don't want his bitter wit. I've loved him and left him and I'm never comin' back."

Silence in the van. Von Konigswald drove slowly. He said, "Cessair? How is it that you work in a Catholic church? Isn't the Catholic church your enemy?"

"Well, you misunderstand. You see, Saint Brigid's is in the Diocese of Kildare, a diocese in the Church of Ireland. So, Catholic after the Reformation, not Roman Catholic.

"But I am Catholic! I am. My mother, too, and father, three sisters and four brothers. We all are what we are. And I . . . I am not a destroyer. And Brigid with her perpetual fire, if only in my mind, still stands her ground by the round tower, and the bishop is a magical man, though he'd blanch to hear me say so."

✦   ✦   ✦

The next morning, Anastasia and I left the bishop's rectory early; we passed von Konigswald still snoring on the rug by last night's embers, the downstairs room gloomy, the windowpanes damp with mist. Out the door and into the cold dampness we crept. We sought privacy. I know our urgency should have been on the dig, but my mind had been smoldering, causing sweats in the night. Below the surface, disturbing thoughts like embers glimmered but needed more rarified air before they'd deign to flame into consciousness. I had to get away, if just for a few hours. Cessair had allowed us to borrow her Mini, and with the benefit of the hand choke I fired it up, and we drove into the dawn.

I said, "We'll go to Glendalough, and like the hermits hiding among the lakes and streams, we'll sit on Kevin's bed."

"Will Kevin mind?"

"Only his sixth-century bones. It's a cave he carved in a cliff above the upper lake. He lived there after renouncing human love."

"A good place to perform a heresy," Anastasia commented. "And how do you know all this?"

"I've been here before," I replied. I drove us through the Wicklow Gap, past the Vale of Glendasan and Thonelagee to the glen shadowed by mountains: Lugduff and Camaderry. I rolled up to a primitive church in the glen.

"What's this?" Anastasia asked, and I could tell she was enjoying the drive.

I replied, "I've something to show you."

We extracted ourselves from the Mini, and I pulled Anastasia, who was gaping at the landscape, to the Irish church of the hermits. She was wearing her blue Aran sweater and wool skirt, her black hair tinged so slightly with chestnut sheen . . . she looked Irish today. We entered the church.

"This is a musty compartment right here," she noted.

I said, "It smells like a cell."

"A cell for your soul, Griffin, if you don't watch it."

"Don't be so sure. See here." I led her to a holed stone standing in the church.

She exclaimed, "I don't believe it!"

I said, "Yes, you do. This glen is another . . . place. It's like Saint Brigid's Cathedral; like the monastery at Ostrog; the Rector's Palace in Dubrovnik; the Men-an-Tol and dancing stones." I walked around to the other side, and we gazed at each other through the hole.

"There's something about the Stele," I said.

Anastasia raised her eyebrows.

"Or the oath," I added.

"I can almost touch it," she agreed, "An objection. Something's wrong about the Stele."

"Come on, Anna," I said, and we returned to the Mini.

I drove us to the lake path, where we got out of the car and walked up through pine, heather, dwarf furze, and bracken. I swung a picnic basket in my right hand. Anastasia walking on my left carrying her own bag. She shoved her right hand into the left pocket of my jacket, keeping it there as we walked. Intermittent sun glimmered through clouds, but it wasn't warm in these heights.

"Look at the cliffs! Though it's not like Montenegro, it, too, is a mountain fastness. Griffin! I hear a waterfall."

We stopped at the lake house to rent a rowboat. Once aboard, with her bag and the picnic basket stowed, I shoved off and we glided out onto the deserted water. Each of us took an oar. We wanted to head to the far cliff.

She said, "Rowboats are insane! We're going in a circle. Griffin! you're pulling too hard. Relax."

I replied, "You're too weak for this, Anna, why not just sprawl in the bow on a blanket?"

Backhanded, she punched me in the stomach. I grunted. "Oof! OK, OK, you pull softly, I'll pull hardly."

"Ha ha."

With thin sunlight here and there on the water, jumping like a sprite from place to place, near and far, we crossed the lake. Steps hacked out of the rock led to the hermit's cave long ago hollowed out in the cliff.

I tied up to a small dock and we climbed to the shallow cave. The silence. Only wavelets gently slapped the rowboat's wooden slats. A breeze sighed through the crags; a single crow crossed the lake, cawed twice . . . then once more. We sat at the entrance to look out over the water. At length, I offered Anna morsels from the picnic basket, but she wasn't hungry. I didn't open the wine bottle. Out on the lake, fragile sunlight still crossed here and there, Irish light so delicate as to be an illusion.

"We've got to find out what has happened to Dr. Moe."

She glanced at me.

"I can feel it. Something's not right. I fear Festus has grabbed Dr. Moe and perhaps Karl. Or Karl facilitated the grab, because, although Dr. Moe is Mr. Self-Reliance and will often go off on his own, I think by now he would have checked in."

Anastasia looked at her feet dangling over the edge, her cut hair tumbling forward. She said, "If that is the case—and Griffin, there's absolutely no proof that anything has happened to Dr. Moe—but if you are right, then we will rescue both of them when we uncover the Stele of Fate."

"Is there a Stele of Fate? I don't know, Anna. We could wait forever for the Stele to turn up. The Stele of Godot. I've got to look into this when we return this afternoon."

"Now you've also got me concerned about Dr. Moe and Karl. But the Stele is at hand. You know this! With it, we will deliver the Oath and destroy Festus, dismantle his Suebi Order, and rescue Dr. Moe and Karl. How's that for a day's work?"

I turned, as in a dream, to Anastasia and said, "That's it! That's what haunts me. That damn Oath we must say to Festus: 'When you meet the Lion and the Eagle in consort with the Queen of Spring *you will meet that which will destroy you.*' It's as though fate declares I am a destroyer! My whole life . . . I've been gathering. What have I destroyed? Now I realize it was Cessair who got me thinking about it when she said of herself, 'And I . . . I am not a destroyer.'"

Anastasia whispered softly, "Do you think that's the foundation of our love? Destruction?"

"Our love? I wonder. Or were we thrown together to fulfill a mystery?" I didn't actually believe that, yet I said it, the idiot professor exploring all possibilities. Try to remember, Griffin: Words can hurt.

Anastasia had been holding a rock. She dropped it; it clattered down the cliff and splashed into the water. She grabbed my hand and whispered, "No, Griffin, no! We've existed longer than the Oath. It didn't throw us together. It exists because we are . . . we have always been together. Don't you remember, Griffin? You said you did!"

I turned, and leaning on one hand, bent close to her ear and whispered back, "When you remind me . . . I remember."

I said, "And because I remember, I know we are not masters of the great void. We aren't ones who massacre and annihilate."

"Festus is a murderer!" Anastasia cried.

I said, "So what are we to do? Become like Festus to defeat him?"

"Ah, Griffin! I want revenge! Revenge for my mother and father! For my clan!"

I replied, "But we'll use our knowledge. There's an answer, Anastasia."

"The text decrees we will destroy Festus."

"The text!" I climbed down to the rowboat, retrieved Anastasia's bag, the one she always carries with her, and brought it back with me to the cave. I said, "I'm glad you bring this wherever you go."

She looked at me, apparently wondering about my next move.

I pulled out one of the Greek texts, the one Thoth had translated. I said, "Did you decipher the Oath yourself or did you just take Thoth's word for it?"

"Griffin!"

"Well, really. Thoth quoted an oath he said was written in the chapter called Hypsiphrone, but check it. See if it really exists."

It was early afternoon. Clouds rolled over the glen, dimming the light.

It took Anastasia a few minutes to locate the Oath; I didn't interfere.

"Here now, I have it," she exclaimed.

I crouched beside her. She held the codex up, so that soft light fell on the pages. She translated: "As it is ordered into the world, one should say: when you meet the Lion, and the Eagle, in consort with the Queen of Spring, you will meet that which will destroy you. There,"—she looked up at me—"you see!"

"Anna, that's Thoth's exact translation. You're being influenced by it. Imagine you've never heard Thoth's version, that you're translating it for the first time."

She glared at me but then softened and regarded the page again, reading, "The moment it is ordered into the world, one should announce: when you meet the Lion, and Eagle, together with the Queen of Spring, you will meet that which shall . . . ahhh . . . the closest

English word is *revise*. Revise you! Griffin, the word isn't *destroy*, it's *revise* or *transform*!"

I examined the tract. Finally, I said, "Revise and transform. We are not destroyers. And now we know the answer: not destruction, but transformation is necessary for creation!"

Chapter Se   -6-

WHEN ANASTASIA AND I returned from the Wicklow Mountains in the late afternoon, I called overseas and across the North American continent to reach Byah, hoping Dr. Moe, for some reason, had returned to Claremont, California. But no. Byah had not heard from him, which she noted, was unusual. I called Smythe at Cismontane. Neither Dr. Moe nor Karl had been about, he said. I called the local Kildare county council and the Chamber of Commerce to find out if the Subi enterprise had built any facilities in Ireland or Great Britain. They didn't know but suggested that I should check with the COC of Northern Ireland. I called them but just got the runaround, a result of dealing with the complex sociopolitical, socioeconomic aspects of that province. There was always someone else to call, and I just ended up calling in circles.

So, I wondered: What would be my answer as to the whereabouts of Dr. Moe? No doubt the Honorable Order of the Suebi was holding him somewhere, perhaps at one of their Subi industrial facilities. Could a more sinister place exist in which to sequester Dr. Moe, a Subi factory built in a war zone crammed with checkpoints, combatants, spies, backstabbers, paramilitary militias . . . in short, a THOOTS facility built in a land occupied by warring destroyers. It seemed likely to me. I just had to locate the Subi setup.

Do you remember, I confided that I am not Sam Spade, nor am I Mike Hammer or Bogie, those fellows who would have driven up north and crashed through checkpoints, avoided the militias, blasted a few henchmen on the way, snuck into the putative Subi headquarters, pulled Dr. Moe out of there, and brought him back to Claremont for a steak and a whiskey? No, that's not me, but we academics have our own way of doing things that prove to be just as effective: Research, Discovery, Application, Result.

So first I had to discover if such a place existed in Northern Ireland, but my research wasn't paying off. I had left messages with colleagues at Trinity College in Dublin to see what they knew; however, I had hit a dead end. Meanwhile, the Stele of Fate was at hand, I hoped. As Anastasia had insisted, perhaps the Stele would be Dr. Moe's means of rescue.

✦　✦　✦

With the help of a couple of strong local lads whom Dick knew, we had been digging for a week, sledging dirt across the church grounds, shoring up the pit's sides as it grew deeper, until the auspicious morning when von Konigswald had uncovered the entrance to a horizontal shaft thirty feet down. At that, he sent the local lads home, since they were working on a need-to-know basis, and we did not wish to explain our quest for the Stele of Fate. We told them we were looking for church relics that had been buried long ago.

Von Konigswald told us that in the past, there likely had been an easier access to this entry tunnel, but he didn't know how or where. The balance of the day was spent digging out and supporting collapsed sections of the shaft until the master spelunker broke through to an underground chamber, letting us know with, "A vault! Come, spelunkers!"

Responding to von Konigswald's voice, Anastasia, who had been standing next to me in the muddy pit, tossed her shovel and plunged into the passageway; she had both implored and insisted that she would be the next person to enter the chamber. With that, I couldn't really argue. It was more her show than mine. But since it was my show, too, I went in after her, and then Graves followed me. Above ground, though drizzle had emerged from the darkness, the bishop, Joko, Aunt Anastasija, and Lili remained, holding lanterns amidst the dirt piles, scaffolding, and tools.

When I followed Anastasia into the chamber, I saw an eight-sided polygonal vault at least fifteen feet around, with a corbeled ceiling about twelve feet high at the center.

Anastasia said, "Look, corbelling, like the moon mound of my Men-an-Tol journey. And Griffin, look here! Did you see these when you entered?" She had turned back to show me carvings on the stone archway we had passed through.

I moved closer for a look.

She said, "Women with cat faces."

That got von Konigswald's attention. He moved from the center of the vault, where he had been standing, watching us enter, and pressed near for a look.

Then, having also entered, Graves crowded the other side near the portal. He said, "See here, men with frog faces." He shined his light on an entry stone.

We all were rather excited to have found this underground vault. After I had examined the images on both sides I said, "They are fine carvings, perhaps first century."

Something caught Anastasia's attention, a kind of green luminance emitting from across the vault. While the others continued to examine the entrance stones, she approached the faint light. She whispered, "Griffin. An altar."

As I crossed over to her side, the domical ceiling curved lower, to about five-and-a-half feet, and I had to duck my five-foot-eleven frame until I reached a place where the monks had carved out a kind of dormer over an altar and I could stand up again.

I saw a flat stone a foot wide, two feet long, resting atop five small upright stones, the slab about four feet off the floor. Anastasia brushed away dirt and dust with her sleeve, revealing a glint of green turquoise. She blew on the slab to clear the remaining dust. I bent closer. I saw carvings on the stone, hieroglyphs, ringed with cat and frog faces.

"The Stele of Fate," she whispered.

◆　◆　◆

A shapely but muddy backside emerged backwards from the underground passage.

I heard Lili say, "Persephone arises from the underworld!"

And Aunt Anastasija say, "Here comes Hades too."

I could hear them as I followed Anastasia out of the tunnel, each of us holding an end of the Stele. Since the access tunnel had only about five feet of clearance, we had found it easier to each carry an end of the Stele, with Anastasia walking backwards.

The bishop looked over the edge of the access pit and said, "Well, now, what have ya got there?"

"We've found it!" Anastasia announced.

"So," Lili said, looking over also, "your augury was fruitful. But what is that green glow?"

"It must be an illusion caused by lantern light," said von Konigswald as he emerged from the shaft behind me, Graves following.

"Well," the bishop said, "put it in the basket, and we'll haul it up, then climb out of there, and we'll take it to the rectory for proper examination.

✦ ✦ ✦

Anew, Cessair's fire blazed at the bishop's house, and with gentle care we set the Stele on a table cleared and placed before the flames. Then, Anastasia and I stepped back to allow the others to gather around for a look. As they did so, they noticed a change in the Stele's color.

Joko said, "The tablet isn't green. It's sky blue."

I stepped forward again for a closer look at the Stele; it was crisscrossed by orange lines, and as noted, covered with finely carved hieroglyphics, ringed by cat and frog faces, but instead of green turquoise, the stone was emitting a blue aura.

"Is that a glow or a reflection?" Cessair wondered.

"The thing was green out of the tunnel," Joko said, and Graves agreed. So did I, and I had an idea why. I thought of what Thoth had revealed about Anastasia's autogenetic capacity to interact with the leptons of ancient objects in relation to the Higgs field.

Lili said, "We're seeing it in a new light, so to speak. The color seems to depend on the quality of the light around it."

"No," I said, "It reacts when Anastasia gets near it."

At that, Anna glanced at me and then walked up to the Stele again and reached out towards it; as she did so, the blue turquoise transformed to green.

We all watched in utter fascination, but Graves was the first to speak.

He said, "So, it is confirmed. Anastasia, you are the keeper of the Stele of Fate."

"It's a most amazin' relic," the bishop commented, and then asked, "Now what do we do with it?"

"Back to Cismontane," Graves snapped. "We'll collect ourselves tonight and be off Friday."

I saw Aunt Anastasija shake her head, and then fix Graves with what could only have been an exasperated stare. She said, a chill in her voice, "Yes! She's the keeper of the Stele, Charles! Where have YOU been for the last twenty-nine years? Because of your unrelenting, unrepentant, misanthropic antics, enclosed and cut off for years on end at Cismontane, ignoring all attempts for reconciliation between our families, you know nothing of the training she has accomplished, the extent of her work, and the sacrifices of our Romanov family! YOU don't declare her the keeper. She IS the keeper!" Aunt Anastasija glowered at Graves. She added, "And back to Cismontane? It's hardly your call, Charles!"

"Well!" said Lili. "Charles, you needed to hear that! I'd wager we all agreed with every word. What do you say?"

Graves, chagrined, replied, "Well, yes, naturally. I was just offering a plan." He paused, fighting an upheaval of emotion, and attempted to cobble together some half-dignified response, I think. At last he explained, "But, I am deeply ashamed and sorry for my past behavior. I wish I had been able to overcome my grief at the loss of my only daughter, my beloved Marian, and I had allowed you to grieve with me, but I did not. I would go back and change that if I could! But I was not completely in the dark about you Anastasija, and about my granddaughter. One of Smythe's important duties was to keep me informed about you. And I sent funds to Thoth to be used on your behalf."

I considered her grandfather. From my point of view, Charles Graves had been generous and knowledgeable concerning our present endeavor.

I think Anna realized that, because she said, "Thank you, Aunt Anastasija, I love you so much! It's fine, Aunt. I believe my grandfather is looking out for our safety. But I also think we cannot move the Stele of Fate until Griffin and I have translated the hieroglyphs and discerned their meaning. In fact, moving the Stele from its location near the shrine, where it has resided for centuries, might weaken or damage it. Right now, we just don't know, we must try to learn more about its behavior."

Aunt Anastasija smiled at her niece. She said, "If you think it's for the best, darling." She glanced at Graves, who, in turn, looked away, and then she looked back at Anastasia and said, "I love you so!"

With Graves having been put in his place, Bishop MacBride, lightening the mood, said, "I'm imaginin' I can put up with all a' ya for one more night, and it'll take ya that long t' draw seven tubs o' hot water t' wash the mire from all of ya. But then, while Anastasia and Griffin remain here . . . the bulk of ya back to Cismontane! Because the diocese has a visitor from the Orient coming to stay with us any day now, and she doesn't need to contend with an overstuffed house full of strangers when she's new here and feeling lost in our faraway land."

Then Graves did a most astonishing thing. He said, "I'll contact Flight Lieutenant Leigh to let him know we are to leave tomorrow," and he pulled a gadget from his jacket pocket, a small, modern, transistor device.

I almost grabbed the device from him because, although I'd never seen one, I'd only heard it described, I was sure it was a communication gadget that had been manufactured, and very recently, by Subi Biocom. At that point, I knew I should have already told the group about the danger of the ONEWORD device, but initially my information had come from Karl, and Karl is the classic unreliable witness, and, therefore, I hadn't felt confident that I could explain the source of my information. I could just see myself talking to Lili, for example: *"How did I learn of this? Oh, not to worry, the ridiculous Karl told me."*

I have since, through a few well-placed academic connections, heard additional rumors that expand upon what Karl had discovered about Subi Biotech and Subi Biocom.

I drew Graves aside, into the study, and said, "What are you doing with that gadget?"

Graves smiled and said, "Oh, this!" He held the thing up. "Flight Lieutenant Leigh gave this to me so that I could communicate with him at any instance. I can only send him one word at a time. But! That's all I need. He can answer me the same way. Isn't it marvelous? Neither of us are ever near the telephone, and I no longer have military communication clearance, so this works better. Brand new! Cutting edge!"

I could see the man was already taken with the thing and excited about it. I said, "May I have a look?"

As soon as I asked for it, I wondered if I should be wearing gloves. Yes, I remembered that Subi Biotech had interfused in its case a nano-biologic component, a molecular alteration to the device exterior which would, any day now, release a subtle but long-lasting hallucinogen into the blood stream of every user. Why? In order to foment social disruption, anarchy and chaos. Subi Biocom intended to spread disinformation through universal random messaging to all the in-service devices, and combined with the hallucinogen, the strategy was intended to bring about a political earthquake, an undermining and destabilizing of western democracies.

Randomly, it will send a message based on fact, but more often, plant disinformation instead. Used this way, over and over, a single word might be more effective than a complete sentence in disquieting the mind of the user, because the user would fill in the rest of the story with their imagination, here skewed towards their own distressed emotions.

After a year or so of this "steering," Subi Biocom intended to release their hallucinogen to cause the user to imprint a negative mindset. The escalation of a general feeling of dissatisfaction among the populous, into an all-consuming sense of hopelessness, mistrust, and anger, might cause governmental, financial, and cultural institutions to unravel. When anarchy finally loomed, the only solution: the ascent of the great leader. Festus! And coming down the pike, the new order, the autocratic hegemony of Festus and his friends!

Taking it in my bare hand, I found the gadget to be compact and comfortable to hold; it fit well in a pocket. In fact, this ONEWORD device was just as my unreliable witness, Karl, had described it. I had to concede, if it wasn't about to emit disinformation and, eventually, hallucinogens, it would have been a desirable device to own.

Graves said, "The RAF has, in just the last few weeks, acquired a pallet of these devices to hand out to the pilots and ground crew. Very useful. Saves them lots of time, according to Leigh. Very secure. And when the device is within thirty yards of a friend's ONEWORD, the screens turn from white to orange to let you know your mates are nearby. Great for friends when they're out on the town. Easier for the lads to keep track of each other. And as for civilians, great for a hunting party, for example."

His description alarmed me. I said, "Do you know from where they are shipped?"

"I'm sure I could find out. Flight Lieutenant Leigh likely knows . . . from somewhere in Northern Ireland, I believe."

I tried to explain the situation to Graves, the threat his new gadget posed. He responded with disbelief, and it was evident he didn't want to give up his little communication toy.

Changing the subject, I brought up the missing Dr. Moe, but Graves thought I was being ridiculous. He said, "Dr. Moe isn't missing—"

I interrupted, "Yes he is! Dr. Moe has been missing for days!'

Graves replied, "No, he's not. He left a note." Graves dug around in the various pockets of his Norfolk jacket until he pulled out a wrinkled piece of fine Cismontane stationery and handed it to me. He said, "Here it is. With all that's been occurring, I forgot about it."

I took the note, smoothed it out, and saw, written in hasty script:

Gone with Festus, Karl in tow

Ink smeared the rest of the line, something the meticulous Dr. Moe would never have ignored. He would have thrown this note away and started over, if he could have.

I knew one thing. You don't go with Festus; Festus grabs you by agency of his Masters of Matter. I glared at Graves and shook my head. But there was no point in vilifying the man, who, although in his eighties, was doing everything he could to help us. So, Graves forgot. It happens, especially to octogenarians.

I sought out Anastasia, filled her in, and gave her Dr. Moe's note.

As she read it, she turned ashen, as when she had learned that Festus Griveaux and the Subi had infiltrated our institute back in Claremont. She whispered, "You were right! I . . . "

She hugged me, but I was already formulating my next moves. I said, "At least, we know. Now, we need a plan to rescue Dr. Moe. First we must identify locations where he could have been taken." I realized I'd have to wait to find out more about possible Suebi locations in Northern Ireland, wait until Chris Leigh returned with the *Daffodil* and I could quiz him.

Anastasia thought the Stele of Fate would be the answer, the means to rescue Dr. Moe, once we learned of its powers. She carefully wrapped the Stele in burlap and placed it in a canvas pack provided by the bishop. She said we'd need to translate the Stele's hieroglyphics to understand the subtle behavior of the aura and the extent of the Stele's power.

I said, "Look, Anastasia, our friend is imprisoned in some Subi Biocom facility, and if Flight Lieutenant Leigh has information of such an installation, I first would need to find a way to get Dr. Moe out. The translation project will have to wait."

Anastasia stared at me. She insisted, "We will need to use the Stele to overcome Festus."

I stared back at Anastasia and replied, "Anna, learning to use the Stele of Fate will take time, time Dr. Moe might not have."

She held my gaze and said, "You're being reckless. You know the danger Festus and his Masters of Matter pose—no human being can go up against them for long, certainly not alone. It takes the teachings of our clan, our hard-won knowledge. What do you think you are doing?"

"OK," I said. "Think? I've thought about it. Would the authorities assist us? Not likely, considering our lack of palpable evidence. For proof, I can only provide the note Dr. Moe had scribbled, and although its meaning is clear to us, to the authorities it would appear ambiguous at best. I have to put together a plan on my own, and there is no opportunity now for a translation project that would take time, since we will need assistance with the hieroglyphics."

Anastasia replied, "Put together a plan on *our* own, one that must involve the Stele of Fate."

I said, "Anna, let's wait to talk to Flight Lieutenant Leigh, find out if there is a Subi location up north."

Chapter Seacht   -7-

Tʜᴇ ɴᴇxᴛ ᴍᴏʀɴɪɴɢ, Fʟɪɢʜᴛ Lieutenant Leigh returned to the landing field with the *Daffodil*. Cessair picked him up in the church van and brought him back to the rectory, and we all shook hands and had tea.

I took Flight Lieutenant Leigh aside to ask him about the Subi Biocom device and possible factory locations or other facilities up north. As I described to Flight Lieutenant Leigh the more sinister workings of the ONEWORD device, he looked at me with an increasing mirthful smile, as if to say, "This is a good joke you're telling me, and any second now, I know you'll get it too!"

So, I abandoned that tack. I instead explained that my friend and colleague, Dr. Moe, had been kidnapped by operatives of Subi Biocom and was probably being held at a Subi facility in Northern Ireland. After I gave Dr. Moe's note to Leigh, it was enough for him to at least consider that my assertion might have a basis in fact. I asked him if he knew of a Subi Biocom location up north.

He replied, "I know of a Subi Biotech location, and that is public information, although such information is a little hard to find these

435

days . . . but if you really think illegal activity has taken place, I should call the authorities."

I said, "Flight Lieutenant Leigh, have you heard of Festus Griveaux? Dr. Moe's kidnapper?"

He said, "Call me Chris. Who are you, again?"

"I am Dr. Griffin MacRobbin, Director of the Institute for Antiquity in Claremont, California. Call me Griffin."

"So, who is this Festus? You say he kidnapped someone?"

"Festus is the founder of a cult called the Honorable Order of the Suebi," I replied, and added, "I refer to the order as THOOTS—a disrespectful acronym, as I view them with contempt."

Chris said, "The Suebi? That group Interpol has been monitoring? You think they are up north?"

"That's what I've been trying to confirm—if or where a Subi Biocom facility or a THOOTS facility has been established. And yes, THOOTS is behind Subi Biocom, Subi Biotech, and the ONEWORD device. I believe it is very dangerous for the RAF to adopt that device for operations. How do you know Interpol monitors THOOTS?"

Chris replied, "Since Interpol occasionally asks for our assistance, they like to keep us informed about certain fringe groups they've identified as dangerous. But I hadn't been told the Suebi Organization controls Subi Biocom, a respected international corporation with deep-pocket state sponsors. I'm not sure, just because the names are similar, of the connection. These devices, though, aren't only for the military, they are all over Northern Ireland! Civilians have been using them for over a year. I haven't noticed a downside."

I had to smile. I said, "Our research"—and here I'm afraid I meant Karl's research, which had gained more credibility with me with his accurate ONEWORD device description—"suggests these devices foster misunderstanding, division, mistrust, and chaos. Anything like that going on up there?"

He looked at me, assessing. After a minute he said, "I do know of buildings that were built on one of the northern islands about a year or so ago belonging to Subi Biotech." He added, "I am on leave for the rest of the week. I love flying this contraption." He turned his head, directing his gaze towards the *Daffodil*'s landing field and added, "Why don't we fly up to the island? It lies up in the North Channel. Great view, wild, except for the complex they built up there. I don't know what to think. But whatever's going on, it won't be boring. And if it is, I'll bring my fishing pole. There's some top-notch fishing in the North Channel. I know because my family used to spend the summers up there not so long ago."

While I had discussed the Suebi problem with Chris, Graves and the others had wandered to the library and heard the end of our talk. Graves frowned at Flight Lieutenant Leigh but Aunt Anastasija took Graves by the arm and collected him for a little stroll. She seemed to be the only one who could talk sense into the man.

Meanwhile, the bishop had heard all *he* needed. He said, "You'll be needin' a crew member with some experience. I'll be climbin' aboard."

Chris glanced at the bishop. We all did.

The bishop said, "I crewed on that craft from England to Montenegro during World War II. On the way, we took out a Nazi sub and a Focke-Wulf transport to boot. We also escaped in this aeroplane from the erstwhile Autocratic Republic of Suebi, dropped a bomb on the Suebi redoubt, which must have been a jinxed fin-bomb since it didn't go off, and then a few years later, I crewed and flew this aeroplane from Montenegro to Egypt and back. And the modifications you have observed on this flyin' boat? I designed and installed most of them."

Chris whistled. He said, "OK! Glad to have you aboard, Bishop."

"On this flyin' boat, just call me Dick."

Chris replied, "Aye, aye, Dick!"

I said, "I'm the rest of the crew."

Anastasia interrupted, "No he's not! You get me too!"

Chris gave her a quizzical glance.

I turned to Anastasia, took her aside, and said, "You need to stay here and translate the glyphs on the Stele of Fate. We need to know something of its behavior, how to wield it."

She replied, "Griffin! What if Festus is on that island? Then what?"

"Then you won't get captured, and the Stele won't fall into the wrong hands."

Anastasia was adamant that she accompany me to look for Dr. Moe, but I felt Dr. Moe was my responsibility alone, not hers.

I said, "Remember when you had to go to Cornwall to seek the Men-an-Tol and the Moon Temple? You had to go alone? Now, I must do this without you. Please, Anna, I know you haven't been able to locate Thoth, but I'll give you the names of trusted colleagues at the British Museum to help you with the translation project on the Stele. That's the important work you need to do now."

She looked at me as if she would never see me again.

✦   ✦   ✦

Cessair drove Chris, Dick and me to the makeshift airfield. Since plans had changed, everyone else chose to stay at the rectory rather than return to Cismontane. Besides, we had borrowed Graves's aeroplane. We climbed aboard the flying boat and Chris fired up the engines. He flew us up through intermittent clouds, heading northeast.

After about forty-five minutes, he said we were going to land "for my fishing pole." And so we landed at what I took to be an airbase. Chris climbed down, ran inside a Quonset hut, and reappeared a moment later with a surf-casting fishing pole that he lashed to several struts, tight to the fuselage.

Before we took off again, I asked, "Can we put the plane down on the island without landing on the airstrip? I would like our visit to be clandestine. If Dr. Moe is being held there, our stealth would be in his best interest."

Chris replied, "When we approach the island, since you don't want to land on the airstrip, we can put down on the water. Then we can motor to a cove I know of that will be calm, where we can safely moor. I doubt anyone will see us there."

Chris took us north by northeast over the Irish sea, heading for the North Channel. As we approached our landing site, I saw a horseshoe-shaped island with the ends facing south, or down—a classic symbol of bad luck. Bad luck, because an upside-down horseshoe doesn't hold luck, it spills it out. So, bad luck for Festus and Subi Biotech. I could see buildings and an airstrip on the inside of the west leg of the U shape; the west leg faced the Irish side of the channel. The U formed the island's harbor, with a hefty breakwater built across the open end to ward off storm surge. A cargo ship was docked by a wharf.

Dick said, "It's lookin' like a serious industrial operation."

Chris banked the flying boat away from the island, toward Scotland, which lay just six or seven miles to the northeast, then after running far enough north, banked west to head toward the top of the U shape.

We landed in the channel behind the island. It was a little rough, with a bit of chop, but since the ocean swell rolled up from the south, the sea calmed the nearer Chris motored to the shelter behind the horseshoe. There, he found the cove he had talked about. It had a keyhole entrance, just wide enough for the *Daffodil*'s wings, and as we entered the inlet, I saw a flat beach ahead, with the surrounding land rising at a thirty-degree angle from the water.

I said, "How do you know of this island, Chris?"

He replied, "My brother Stu and my pal Tim used to fish here with me when we were boys. We fished all these islands. Our family's summer house was on Rathlin, the only inhabited rock out here." He directed the flying boat to the beach to nose up on the sand.

From the front cockpit Dick said, "Well, now, this looks familiar. I remember another Festus cove where we cast up on a beach like this! You'll want t' be watchin' out for Festus's assistants, Phloxopha and Ororotohos, because those two can put ya into a swoon." He threw a rope ladder over the side and climbed down to the beach. I crawled forward to the ladder and climbed down too.

Chris unfastened his fishing pole and handed it down to me before also descending the ladder. He said, "I'll be here, casting into the cove. It's amazing what swims into these waters."

Dick grinned and said, "Well, it is now, isn't it?"

Chris said, "Just give a whoop, and I'll climb back up and start the engines."

With Chris heading for a good casting spot, we turned and ascended the rocky slope. I reached the top well ahead of Dick, and I thought—*He's really too old to be doing this, it's not Dick's burden.* The bishop limped up the hill, panting and mopping his brow, until he stood with me at the top, out of the wind in the lee of large boulders.

When the bishop had recovered somewhat from the climb I said, "Dick, I'm worried about leaving Chris alone with our only means of escape from this isolate. Just the two of you know how to handle the flying boat. I think the best plan is to have you help guard it. Chris, obviously, is very capable . . . but he has no idea of what he would be up against, if the Suebi discovered the plane moored here on their island. But you do."

The bishop looked at me, and I felt he was sizing me up, trying to determine if I was worthy of being alone on this task. Could I stand up to the kind of unfathomable horror that he had once encountered and fought against in the past? Against Festus, Dick had won, but at high cost.

The bishop and I regarded each other. Below us lay more boulders and wind-swept trees and scrub. It looked to me like, at minimum, it would be a three-mile trek to the Subi Biotech buildings.

"Can I ask ya what is your plan?" Dick said.

"Just to locate Dr. Moe. If I can confirm he is here, I will attempt to get him out, but if that is impossible, I'll come back to the aeroplane and perhaps we can inform the authorities. "

Dick nodded. He said, "I'll keep an eye out and guard against anything other than you comin' to the cove."

Chapter Ocht   -8-

I TOOK MY TIME DESCENDING the three miles of rocky slope, because I was trying to take advantage of all available cover. I moved toward a line of large, domed stone buildings clustered below in the distance. As I came nearer, I saw that each building was connected by a windowless, enclosed stone passage. It looked like the builders had quarried the material from the island itself. Narrow windows about eight feet off the ground encircled each dome, and at the top sat HVAC systems.

I crept to the exterior of the nearest dome and climbed up a series of boulders to look through a window. The dome seemed to be empty, but I couldn't view the whole of the inside, so I supposed the building might have been occupied. I did observe what I thought to be part of a maze constructed within the building. The maze sides climbed to at least seven feet tall, almost as high as the windows. The construction looked like something scientists might build for testing rats, but more complex and, I would say, sized for humans.

At the second dome, I saw a lab, or a medical facility, with stainless-steel tables, stools, and chairs forming workstations, and various chemistry supplies arranged on shelves.

At the third dome, the one closest to the main buildings, I boosted myself up by scaling the rough stonework to again look through a window. I saw movie theater seats attached to a turntable in the middle of the room, with curved screens all around the perimeter.

I made my way to a section of the third dome's exterior curve, where I could view other infrastructure of the complex. Nearby, I saw a large warehouse. Through its extended open door, I noted various sizes of stainless-steel tanks, from portable to those needing a forklift to be moved. I heard the hum of a motor, and a workman on a power stacker came into view. When he jumped off, I ducked back behind the curve of the dome. I guess he hit a switch to close the exterior doors, which began to clang and squeal as they rolled together. I peeked around the curve of the dome again and noticed a large sign hanging near the door. It said:

SUBI BIOTECH - NORTHERN FACILITY
WARNING
Hazardous Chemical Zone
Monitor For Aerosol Emissions

Beyond the warehouse, two runways intersected at a forty-five-degree angle to account for various wind patterns on the island. This gave aircraft a choice of direction to take off and land. The longer runway passed the warehouse to the west and ran south along a modern-looking structure: housing for workers? More lab space?

Could Festus be holding Dr. Moe somewhere on this island? That's what I intended to find out. If I had no luck sighting Dr. Moe here, at least I might get a lead on other Subi locations in the British

Isles or Northern Europe where Festus might sequester him. But because this facility was the only Subi facility Flight Lieutenant Leigh knew about, and because Leigh's job required knowledge of local industrial infrastructure, I thought there was a good chance Festus had stashed Dr. Moe on this island. The status of Karl—kidnapper or kidnapped—still needed to be determined.

I had to discover the goings-on here, on this sinister rock. I thought the operation looked like a chemical manufacturing plant, but of what? Likely, an unhealthy aerosol agent as the sign indicated, at least, something dangerous, which would require the isolation afforded by this windswept, sea-ravaged erstwhile refuge of seabirds.

Above the sound of the constant wind, I thought I heard an aircraft approaching from the northwest. Sure enough, what looked to be a four-engine turboprop passenger aircraft lined up to land into the south wind. I looked at my watch. Seven minutes to noon.

The plane taxied to the midpoint of the building, where it stopped. The engines shut down and the propellers wound down. Then workers wheeled stairs to a forward door, and passengers exited the aircraft.

As the arrivals milled on the tarmac, I decided to join and try to enter the Subi building with this group. I didn't hesitate. I worked my way down around the northwest side of the complex to insinuate myself. There must have been fifty passengers, many wearing lab coats but some, a dozen, were dressed in street clothes like me. Some of them looked cold, and bundled up against the wind. Everyone carried a bag, or a pack, or a purse; I saw several men in lab coats up front, who were hanging on to their briefcases as if concealed inside were state secrets. They looked to be the executives in charge.

I tried to fit in with the line of passengers by hanging back with the group wearing everyday street clothes. I was wearing a canvas shirt, safari jacket, cargo pants, and the Asolo hiking boots I'd worn on every excavation and dig for the last ten years, so I thought I could blend.

I said, "Hi, I'm Titotanovich."

I don't know why I said that. I guess I was trying to hide my identity, as if that would now make a difference.

Two or three of the group glanced at me; they were young, college age, and at once seemed to decide that I was a clueless old guy, not worth their trouble.

I felt, however, they were the clueless ones, unaware I'd arrived on a different aircraft, now hidden in a cove at the far end of the island. Ha, you take your pleasures where you can.

It wasn't until I was inside that I noticed all and sundry wore nametags. Near us, various Suebi officials had begun to greet the bigwigs with the briefcases, while lesser staff handed out keys and began to escort the lab techs to their rooms. Us people in street clothes were told we would shortly be taken to the cafeteria for lunch so we could digest before the experiments started at two o'clock. I wondered, Experiments? As I glanced at our group, I realized not just the rude three, but everyone in the circle was of college age. Except me.

A Suebi secretary approached me. The first thing she said was, "Where is your name tag? Even volunteers must wear one! Did it fall off on the plane?"

I immediately decided to act like a clueless newbie in this hubbub of checking in. I said something in Serbo-Croat, a little something I'd learned from Anastasia, indicating that I did not speak English and what did the woman want anyway?

The secretary looked at me. I shrugged and shook my head.

"Come with me," the secretary ordered. "I'll fill out a new tag." I stood there clueless until the woman shooed me to her desk.

At the desk, she asked for my name.

I pretended I did not understand what the woman was asking me.

The secretary pointed to her own name tag and then pointed at me.

I said, "Joko Titotanovich," trying to mimic Joko's accent. He'd get a laugh that I'd incorporated Tito into a fake Yugoslav name.

The secretary handed me a pen and paper and made me write my fake name down. Was it too much? So many letters! We Yugoslavs are crazy. She filled out a name tag, handed it to me and gestured that I should pin it on. I did so, and she actually gave it a tug to see if I'd done a good job attaching it. I wondered if that made us friends until she pointed back to the circle of college kids, indicating that I should return to the group. Then she addressed a man wearing a blue blazer and clown pants outfit with which I am familiar, since we professors often wear the same. Clown pants. The balloon-like bellbottoms that have taken over menswear in the seventies. She gave the fellow instructions that he should take us to the cafeteria, and so he told our group to follow him.

It was useful to follow the blue blazer; it gave me a chance to look around the complex. Specifically, I was trying to find a door to a basement dungeon, if there were a basement dungeon—I had no proof that there was or wasn't, but if Dr. Moe were here, wouldn't they be keeping him in a cell?

On top of that, I really didn't know if the Honorable Order of the Suebi, THOOTS, had hauled Dr. Moe off to this site or some other one. I wished Dr. Moe had just been an inconsiderate so-and-so—had been influenced by Cismontane's stash of vintage Armagnac—and had gone off to the South of France for a vacation without telling us. Well, if wishes were fine horses, I'd run one in the Kentucky Derby.

At the first likely basement doorway, I tried the knob. Locked. This might be harder than I thought. Meanwhile, where was Festus and his four Masters of Matter, his Ororotohos and Phloxopha, Athuro and Erimacho, as Dick called them? Not here, I hoped.

In the cafeteria, carrying my tray of questionable vittles, I approached a table already occupied by two of the college-age newbies:

a woman, who seemed grumpy, and a fellow, who might have been the cause of her bad mood. Was he an unsatisfactory boyfriend? Were they having a fight? I wondered, because they glared at me as I sat down, as if I were interrupting something.

I stuck out a hand and said, "Titotanovich," and then laughed and said, "I speak English."

Neither of them took my hand. The grumpy girl said, "Good for you."

I asked, "So, what brings you here?"

The boyfriend replied, "Are you a narc?"

I grinned and replied with my Yugo accent, "Oh, yes. Titotanovich. We are all narcs. Every one of us!"

The grumpy girl laughed.

The boyfriend gave her a look of disapproval. Sam Spade would have called it a "dirty look."

She said, "Aren't you too old to be a volunteer?"

I didn't mind being called old. In fact, I felt I had earned the status. I didn't know what she was talking about, but that was what I was trying to glean. The word *volunteer* was a start.

I said, "Well, what did they tell you the requirements were?"

"Oh," she said, "you just had to be adventurous and fun loving, in other words, wild and crazy!" She considered me and added, "I don't know if that's the definition of an old guy."

I replied, "Well, it depends on what you call adventurous and fun loving. We all have our parameters. What do you think of the task ahead?"

The boyfriend butted in. "Gittin' high is the fun part."

She said, "I hear there is a maze puzzle to walk through . . . high! That's the crazy part!"

I questioned, "They are testing something?"

"LSD, man. Get with it. Sure you don't want yer momma?"

I may have grinned back at them, but I realized Subi Biocom was using these kids as guinea pigs to refine the hallucinogenic component of the ONEWORD device.

As a ploy to look around, I got up to go to the bathroom. At the refectory door, I said "Loo," to the guard and he let me out.

What a place. I tried many doors along the way, using my clueless act, but all were locked, so I made my way back to the cafeteria, where I had to pound on the door to get back in.

After our lunch, the Subi Biotech execs led us into a long hall and told us to stand before an expanse of windows open towards the airstrip. No sooner was everyone rooted than a corporate jet performed a touch down and takeoff maneuver over the airstrip, and then, climbing with deafening jet-engine whine, made an elaborate smoke-trail bank to the west, came around again and landed on the runway to taxi to a stop in front of the windows. Very theatrical. As it rolled to a stop, I noticed beyond it an identical jet identified as *SUBI No.2* parked off-runway nearby.

The company had decorated both jets with their flaming sword logo, but the arriving one had *SUBI No.1* scripted underneath. Of further interest was the Soviet CCCP lettering on the tail section. Since the aircraft looked similar to a Gates Learjet 25, which you often see on LA airport runways, the Soviet markings indicated the jet had probably been reverse engineered.

After the door opened and stairs descended, two people and five malevolent beings disembarked. Yes! First came none other than Dr. Mortimer Littlejohn. The Suebi had dressed him in some sort of ancient Egyptian robe outfit. He almost tripped on the vestment while going down the stairs.

Following him came the awful Karl, who had been dressed up as a schoolboy but with a pointed, black dunce cap topping his head. *Dunce* was scripted in gold lettering on the cap's front. Next came the four Masters of Matter, and, although I had the good luck of having never encountered them, I had no doubt it was they, having heard descriptions of the creatures from Joko and Dick.

And last, looking like an overly groomed politician, ridiculous in an oversized, big-shouldered Armani suit, came Festus. At that point the newbies clapped and cheered, although some of us (me) had to be told to do so.

Next, we volunteers left the window hall and, as instructed, found assigned seats in the auditorium for orientation. Since there wasn't a seat assigned to me, the interloper, I improvised. While we waited, the lab techs drifted in, to cluster together on our left.

Nothing happened for about an hour, until someone began to play a record over the PA, something cribbed from James Brown's band, and eight dancers in hackneyed go-go outfits came on stage to do some choreography, I guess to wake us up.

Then came the four Masters of Matter. I noted that the four of them simply appeared to be unattractive humans well-dressed, which disguised their true natures: that of elemental creatures bound in service to Festus. If you knew of their provenance, you would detect that something about them was a bit off, as I did. For example, I could track a subtle, odd sheen dancing around them as if light near them became ever-so-slightly refracted, as if each of them retained their own atmosphere.

Festus walked onstage. Above him an applause sign flashed, and he beckoned the three briefcase executives to join him on the boards. When they were settled next to him, Festus didn't identify any of the execs by name but rather just referred to them as "my rockstars." This was unintentionally funny, since, while emerging from backstage, they had tangled themselves in the big black upstage curtain, as if they'd been taking lessons from Dr. Moe. Once the "rock-star execs" had shed the curtain encumbrance, and their briefcases, each was free to give Festus an unctuous two-handed handshake.

As I observed them, I thought the execs looked to be "citizens of the world" types—but where in the world? Since Festus didn't invite them to speak, I couldn't place their provenance.

Festus approached the mike and shouted, with an emotional delivery, "Subi Biocom! Subi Biocom! Subi Biocom!" He turned towards the group of lab techs on the left and spread his arms, allowed the PA system echo die down, and continued, "You people are here because you are my most trusted employees. Subi Biocom needs your dedication and your expertise. We are in the endgame of our market strategy—domination through superior technology. We are pioneers! We are the first industrial entity to develop a product which infuses technical machinery with a biologic interface! I refer to ONEWORD. Each of you look under your seat. Yes, that's right! Remove it from under . . . That shall be your very own device to keep, take home, show it off to your friends! All I ask is each and every one of you to do your job here to your utmost ability!"

I wondered why any of the techs would want one. They already knew of ONEWORDs biochemical interface and the purpose of the device itself. They already knew the device was designed to inculcate a negative mindset and then release a hallucinogen.

Festus continued, as if reading my mind, "Naturally, these particular ONEWORDs I give you are simply for your individual communication needs. They do not include the bio-interface! You, my best people, don't need the thought steering that's necessary for the hoi polloi in order to be receptive to my ideas for world governance."

Then he turned to us volunteers. He said, "Volunteers! Thank you for offering your help with the psychological component of our design. I think you'll have fun! Have you heard of our Logic Maze? The Maze has rules! When you enter, you are not alone! A hunter is waiting for you, and the hunter gets two steps for every one of yours. Not only must you escape the maze, you must keep the hunter from catching you. You can't win. The logic maze is unsolvable. The question is how long will you last?"

I heard uncomfortable shifting in theater seats around me.

Noticing this, Festus said, "Oh! Don't worry. The hunter, whose job it is to tag you, will be"—he motioned to someone off stage, and out came dunce-capped . . .

"Karl!" Festus said with a delighted inflection.

My adjacent volunteers laughed, and the unsatisfactory boyfriend from the cafeteria blurted, "What about the best part, the LSD?"

With a little frown, Festus gazed in our direction but said, "Yes, a hallucinogen is part of the test. We wish to ascertain how much the drug will affect your ability to think logically in the maze. So, without further ado, I give you"—he made a gesture to bring his next trick pony out— "Dr. Mortimer Littlejohn!"

Dr. Moe advanced from backstage, and even though he looked comfortable enough in the Egyptian pharaoh getup, I could tell he couldn't wait for some Festus payback.

Festus approached Dr. Moe, put his hand on the doctor's shoulder, and said, "This man. This man lasted in the Logic Maze for five hours straight, without food or water. Finally, Phloxopha, our master hunter, got bored and gave up! Impossible! Yet it happened. And now he has been elevated to the Honorable Order of the Pharaoh! Be like him, volunteers! What an opportunity for you! If any of you volunteers can last more than ten minutes—a mere ten minutes in the Maze, against Karl—you will be paid a bonus and be given the option of being admitted to the Subi Biotech Training Program, all expenses paid! However, if you can't last ten minutes against our dunce, well, I would call that a washout."

With that astonishing preamble, Festus turned the stage over to Dr. Moe.

Dr. Moe lumbered up to the mike without tripping on his Egyptian finery and said to the audience: "If I squint, I can see you in your respective groups—the technicians already wearing their white lab coats, sitting together in comradery and fellowship on the left, as we wished, and the volunteers who have signed up for the experiment, gathered together . . . " He paused, and almost seemed bemused for a moment, but then continued, "Over here on the right."

I thought, Yes, I have turned myself into a "volunteer," something involving taking a hallucinogen and walking a maze. But I would palm the dose, just pretend to take it, and if the ploy got me close to Dr. Moe, my being a "volunteer" would be useful. I wondered if Dr. Moe might see me sitting there in the dark, but I surmised the spotlight shining on him would prevent that.

Dr. Moe continued, "Volunteers! I'll give you a little preamble about the proper mindset when experimenting with a hallucinogen, and our tech friends over here"—Dr. Moe pointed to the left—"will be carefully observing, monitoring and recording your behavior as they accompany you on your journey. It's nice to have friends, isn't it? I would remind you of the most important thing to remember: Whoever you are, whatever you bring with you, your hopes, passions, fears, guilts, secrets, determine how you will explain to yourself what you are experiencing during a hallucinogenic session. Please realize: Whatever you see or experience will be an illusion that wells up from your own psyche. You may see beautiful things, or you may be confronted by monsters! Remain calm. Nothing you might encounter will be real, other than you will be learning about yourself, about things you didn't know about yourself. Remember that, and you will keep your balance . . . even in the maze, as I did!"

I thought that sounded like pretty good advice! His sagacity on the subject caused me to wonder if Dr. Moe had, back at the Institute, been imbibing more than good old Powers Irish whisky.

Festus had heard enough. Apparently, Dr. Moe wasn't supposed to be giving out this much good advice to the soon-to-be hapless volunteers. Festus motioned for Athuro and Erimacho to escort Dr. Moe from the stage.

Then, addressing us hapless volunteers, Festus said, "Well! We can't give away all our secrets yet, can we? What fun would that be for you?" He motioned to stage left and said, "Karl! Join Phloxopha and Ororotohos in escorting our volunteers to the Domes."

Karl, still in his dunce hat, walked over to the stage steps while keeping a wary eye on the two Suebi "secretaries," the female Masters of Matter who had thrown him into a car trunk in Claremont.

Addressing the audience, Festus said, "Karl still has a bit of penance to perform until I can fully take him back into the fold, people. Don't worry! I'm sure you won't behave the way he did. He must wear the cap. Now, I won't tell you about his transgressions because, you see, around here, we try to keep it fun!"

Coming down from the stage, sandwiched between Phloxopha and Ororotohos, Karl didn't look like he was having fun. The three of them walked over to our section of the auditorium and ushered us out into the hall. They lined us up. Twelve volunteers—whoops, thirteen? A baker's dozen? Karl looked at his list, then looked back at us. And then he saw me.

I'd known it was just a matter of time. Maybe I should have dodged the situation; however, by then, it was too late. When Karl saw me, I thought he was going to have a stroke, yet he managed to tamp down his surprise—alarm?—and wonder of wonders, he did not give me away! At first. Instead, he consulted his list again.

Phloxopha stepped up to glance over Karl's shoulder. She seemed dissatisfied. Then she raised her odd, fiery eyes to look directly at me. I returned her gaze. Ouch, too close: The glowing eyes stared out of a stone-age face framed by artless ashen hair. And as I took in her faint, somatic diffraction pattern, the barely discernable dark and light bands at the edge of her shadow, the whole package of her made me want to back up. In fact, the dozen college kids had retreated several steps, distancing themselves from her . . . and me.

Phloxopha approached me. She put a hand on my shoulder. When she did, I felt a chill, as if she had just emerged from a six-foot deep grave.

Karl said, "Ah, sir, you are not on the list." He looked up from his list consultation and said, "Why, hello, Dr. MacRobbin. How nice of you to join us. Did you sneak aboard the volunteer's airplane?"

Was Karl caught between a rock and a Phloxopha, yet still trying to help me? I replied, "Very astute of you, Karl. How did you know?"

"Oh, I'm in training here. Phloxopha is such a good teacher."

The Master of Matter finally took her rimy hand off my shoulder, but even though she did so, I felt a little faint. She turned to Karl, whispered something in his ear and then walked away and vanished around a corner.

That's when I noticed Ororotohos, the other female Master of Matter, still with us, standing off to the side as an observer. Now she came to the front of the group.

She said, "Come," and began walking down the corridor, expecting the volunteers to follow immediately.

After Phloxopha's intimidating display, everyone did. As I followed at the end of the group, like a cowboy riding drag, Karl fell in beside me.

I said, "When I see my chance, I'm going to ditch."

Karl said, "Don't." He lifted his chin towards the front of the line. "She'll know and cause you great harm. Look, we haven't much time. Phloxopha said she will be the hunter when you go into the maze."

"How did Dr. Moe win?"

"I don't know, other than his innate abilities."

I said, "Karl, where do your loyalties lie?"

"With you and Dr. Moe and the Institute! But we, both Dr. Moe and I, are on a . . . What do you say? A shoestring? A tight string?

"A short leash."

"Yes, a short string. We are like pets to Festus. He likes to see what he can make us do. Jump through hoops. Maybe Phloxopha won't kill you in the maze. Festus might wish to also make you a pet."

Our group came to an exterior door on the north side of the building. Ororotohos ordered us outside and told everyone to follow the path to the Subi Biocom testing domes, the ones that I had scoped earlier.

Hurrying, Karl said, "If you can make it through the maze, it will exit to a hall leading to recovery rooms. The hall has a door on the left. Go out. I'll try to help you, and I'll try to get word to Dr. Moe, but he's being watched by Athuro and Erimacho. You do have an exit plan, don't you, Dr. MacRobbin?"

We stopped talking, because standing outside the door, Ororotohos was watching us volunteers as we went by. Karl was now trailing me as if he were on guard duty, which I guess he was.

Chapter Naoi -9-

A T THE LOWER DOME, we were met at the entryway by the three briefcase executives—the PhDs? Like Goldilocks's three bears, one was tall, one was medium, and one was fat. Right? I'm sure the three of them were Subi psyops goons. They told us to settle in the theater seats that outfitted the interior.

The stocky one said, "We shall now show you on screen everyday scenes from your television news, clips of the"—here he gave himself away when he made a dismissive snarky sound that only a Russian can do well—"free world. Pay attention. This will remind you of what it's like in your daily life. Now, because the turntable is going to rotate, you must fasten your seatbelt. We don't want anybody getting hurt!"

So now I knew at least one of the three bears was a Soviet operative. The other two still remained quiet. I couldn't place them simply by observing their features; however, I swear, an odor of formaldehyde hung about them.

The college kids laughed. One said, "Is it a tilt-a-whirl? Awesome!" They all became quite boisterous, making fun of the situation.

The theater itself was impressive. Our seats had been fastened to a turntable which at first didn't move, but around us, the movie screens formed a complete circle. I thought if the screens worked, they had outfitted the dome with innovative audio-video technology.

As the lights went down I realized, judging from the comment of the snarky Russian, the psyops team was going to try to create a negative narrative of western culture in our minds.

The team promptly began showing us images from television news clips. As the screening proceeded, we were assailed by reports of murders, bombings, heists, beatings, war, strife, governmental misdeeds, massive stock market disruption, oppression, race riots, false imprisonment, also, cuts from movie thrillers and slasher fests.

After about ten minutes, the turntable began a slow counterclockwise spin, so that our view of the screen was always moving. Every ten minutes or so, the rotating platform would pick up speed. After an hour, some of the kids tried to unfasten their seatbelts to leave the platform but were unable to release the buckles.

A few began yelling, "Hey, turn this thing off! Let us out of here!"

I tried to release my buckle, but I found it to be electronically fastened. There was no getting out. This experience went on for two-and-a-half hours, and by the end, the turntable rotated a complete circle every thirty seconds, a very disorienting thirty seconds. One of the college kids threw up.

The rotation stopped, the screens went blank, the lights came on, the seatbelts released. Near the door, I saw the three PhDs shake hands, congratulating each other for their sick piece of work. What psyops now had was, I guess, what they wanted: disoriented, pissed off, and disturbed volunteers. Since the screening had created a negative set and setting for the volunteers, it was time to dose them with a Subi Biocom hallucinogen.

So far, their psyops procedure wasn't working on me because I was pretty sure I could discern their antisocial plan. I surmised the three doctors were confident they had created, in two-and-a-half hours of screen time, a microcosm of western culture. But their program was designed to exaggerate and focus exclusively on the free world's supposed decadence and decay.

In the next dome, the volunteers would be dosed with Subi Biotech's lab-developed hallucinogen to imprint in the minds of these kids this myopic view of western culture. This was to be done before the kids had taken time to critically evaluate the one-sided show.

The psyops PhDs must have been hypothesizing that if the hallucinogen worked within this experiment, it would work when the ONEWORD devices released a similar dose to the early adaptors in the general population. Subi Biocom had been planting random disinformation on those devices in test markets for over a year. It was all set up. The right drug would turn many of the ONEWORD users into culture disrupters, the kind who would be unable to build on society's advances and could only tear down and destroy the good with the bad, as if both were equal.

The stocky lab-coat PhD ushered the discombobulated, irritated volunteers into a passageway opposite from where we had entered, to dome number two. Again, I fell in behind them. But before I had made any progress, coming through the ingress walked none other than the demiurge himself, Festus.

"Well," Festus said, wasting no time, "I seem to have the entire brain trust of the Institute for Antiquity visiting me right here on my own little island! Bring the whole Institute! You are invited. You should all come! Bring your graduate students. Perhaps we could recruit them for our experiments. Free room and board!"

Geeze. Such a sarcastic entity. I can be sarcastic too. I said, "Nice suit."

Festus pretended he didn't get me. He said, "Thank you. Giorgio designed it just for me."

I said, "Oh. That Giorgio must have a good sense of humor!"

Festus took offense, I could tell. He dipped his head and his salt-and-pepper hair flopped down over his eyes . . . to hide his hurt feelings? I decided to push my advantage.

I said, "I just saw a ridiculous and distorted take on western culture. Can't you do a better job than that?"

In response, Festus perked up. "Yes, we can! We forgot to feature the American diplomatic debacle and military massacre in Southeast Asia. I'll have my team make a correction, and when I do, I'll note that your government is in need of an autocratic transfusion."

I couldn't help but observe that Festus had a thing for aggravating alliteration. I ignored his wordplay and said, "Unlike you, we believe in the egalitarian rights of the individual in politics, economics and the rule of law."

Festus scoffed, "Ooo, very noble. How's it working?"

I replied, "That idea was meant to be the lifeblood of our Republic, but I admit, we don't always live up to it."

Festus asserted, "Well, that's because that idea is all wrong. For all of previous human history, no one thought all men had rights or all were created equal! Slaves equal to pharaohs? Peasants equal to kings? The proletariat equal to the members of the Politburo? Never! Preposterous!"

I felt a twinge in my spine. Anger. But, then I realized that losing my cool would be disadvantageous for me. I decided to move on. I said, "I think it's time for you to fly Dr. Moe, Karl, and me back to Ireland."

Festus laughed. "Oh, no. I think not. First of all, Karl would wish to stay here. He enjoys our little dunce game. That's why we allowed him to be a hunter in the maze. Secondly, Dr. Littlejohn? Really? Well, I must inform you, he's not going anywhere. He is our permanent guest. And you, Dr. MacRobbin? Let's see, Mac in Gaelic gibberish means *son of*. That makes you son of Robin. And here you are, trying to meet up with your pal Little John. Now I wonder, did you hie from the Greenwood, son of Robin Hood? Where are the rest of the Merry Men? I refer to the Romanov clan and their ilk. Where are the Greek texts from Nag Hammadi that were stolen from me? You know, don't you!"

Hearing him, I realized Festus didn't fathom the existence of the Stele of Fate and was probably not even sure we'd found the Greek codices. I wanted to keep it that way.

I replied, "Those codices would certainly be a feather in our cap at the Institute. If we already had them, we would have announced it to the world. Think of the additional funding that would come our way."

"Yes," Festus said, "think of all the funding the Honorable Order of the Suebi has sent you. What have we got to show for it?"

I observed, "The path of scholarship is a long and winding road, as the poet and others, have said. Exhaustive research is required, then peer review, followed by reevaluation and revision.

Festus snorted. He said, "You're obfuscating. But I have a solution for that. Soon we will test you in the maze. Oh? Not worried? You think you will be better even than Dr. Littlejohn? Well, for you, Karl is not the hunter. For you I send Phloxopha, and unlike with Dr. Littlejohn, she will be free to use all her powers against you. Imagine all the things you will tell us after she's through with you!"

I replied, "So! Dr. Moe wasn't tested against all of Phloxopha's powers. Moe merely met a muzzled maternal Master of Matter." Why did I say that? I wondered what was going on with me, I was getting giddy as a gaffer.

Festus revealed the shadow of a grin. He said, "Are you mocking me? Mocking my alliterative affinity?"

I replied, "Why don't we both sit down, have a whisky, talk about it."

The thought of Phloxopha had spooked me; I could still see her glowing coal eyes and feel her icy hand on my shoulder. In the cove, Dick had told me she was supposed to be the hot one, as her eyes would indicate, but I had experienced her hand on my shoulder as icy. I guess she can go either hot or cold. Ugh. If I had to go up against all of Phloxopha's powers, well, I could use a double whiskey.

He regarded me. He said, "You know, I would! But I'm on a tight schedule. Problems with manufacturing at our New Jersey plant. We might, instead, move the plant to China if Nixon lets us." Here Festus exhibited a jack-o-lantern grin and added, "He'll let us." He continued, "Meanwhile, I've had to make contingent plans. We've even brought a hallucinogenic aerosol product here for safekeeping in the event my ONEWORDs fail to release their drug. In that case we will release hallucinogenic aerosol chemtrails over the cities! So, my responsibilities take me away now. I will leave you in good hands. Phloxopha! Come. Escort Robin Hood to the dome of doom!" Festus then actually cackled, delighted at his inane wordplay.

Chapter Deich   -10-

INSIDE THE SECOND DOME, lab techs were already fussing with beakers, small vials, and smaller phials, wetting sugar lumps, drawing potions into syringes, getting things ready. I glimpsed Karl just before he proceeded down the passageway to the third dome. Phloxopha and Ororotohos remained with us volunteers.

One by one, at ten-minute intervals, a Nurse Rachet-type gave each of us a lump of sugar to ingest. The additional lab techs watched us closely. I couldn't even palm the sugar lump, and instead had to put it on my tongue.

The techs monitored our blood pressure and temperature as we sat on folding metal chairs for thirty minutes—I guess the time it took for the drug to take effect.

The first volunteer, already hallucinating, was taken down the passageway to the second dome and likely shoved inside the maze. Five minutes later I heard horrible and disturbing cries and screams echoing down the stone passage from the second dome. A tech ran down the passageway holding a syringe in his left hand. Soon the screaming stopped.

No one wanted to go next, but the die had already been cast, and the grumpy woman from lunch was next to go. Similar results, with the tech again racing down the hall with the syringe in his left hand.

I saw Phloxopha get up and proceed down the passage to the third dome. My hunter.

Where was Dr. Moe? If he were here, he wouldn't approve of this setting for an LSD trip, a lab full of sharps, stainless-steel furniture, chemical jars, odd beakers, weird odors, all of it overseen by an angry nurse and hovering, creepy lab techs, along with, emanating from Dome Three, the anguished cries of the damned. Really, what in the world was going on with Dr. Moe?

And Karl? The lad was a puzzle to me. Was he inclined to assist me? Assist Dr. Moe? The risk to him would be immense.

My watch looked funny; the thing glowed like Phloxopha's eye. A half hour had passed since I'd been dosed, and I was losing my moorings. Looking through the eight-foot-high window, I thought I saw, bathed in green aura, the round tower that stands next to St. Brigid's Cathedral in Kildare. I wanted to observe the tower illusion longer, because it almost triggered a memory of something important, I was sure of it, but two techs came up on each side of me and walked me down the passageway to the entry of the third dome, and the memory, whatever it was, faded.

One of them barked, "Pay attention! You see a grid on the floor. You get to move one square each time, but the hunter gets to move two squares. That is the hunter's advantage. You can, however, move diagonally where there is room, the hunter cannot. That is your advantage. If you cheat and move more than a space at a time, well, that will be bad for you. Bonne chance!" And he gave me a little shove into the maze.

Is it fair to give one instruction when one is beginning to hallucinate? I understand Timothy Leary does it, but he airs instruction of a more important nature, such as how to approach the second Bardo as described in the *Tibetan Book of the Dead.*

I knew the hunter would be Phloxopha, trying to make up for Dr. Moe's defeat of her when he conquered this puzzle-maze. I intended to make it two for two for antiquity scholars.

And then I saw it, a thing, a black swirl of something like diesel exhaust flowing around a maze divider. I went diagonal, one square. Phloxopha stepped around a corner into view, advancing two squares. She was now three spaces away. I took a diagonal step, which brought me to a corner. Phloxopha fell behind by a space, but her black fog roiled towards me. She was both following the rules by waiting for her turn and cheating by sending out her fog.

With her fog rose unintelligible babble! And, when I heard it, I became confused. I thought I stood in a peat bog, with brackish muck up to my knees, and things, invisible things, wiggled in the bog all around me. The wiggling things reached out of the bog; they were fingers, attached to hands, attached to arms, climbing up my legs, and I felt their weight pulling me down. I tore a hand off me. It—the hand—screamed and was replaced by two more hands. I sensed a fear I had never experienced, and I began frantically ripping fingers off me, yanking arms away, but there were always new ones bubbling up from the dreadful bog, and I felt I was sinking.

It was then I heard, "Oooooooooooo ooo osoahsahahhh." The voice enabled me to see the form of the sound, and the sound transported me, at once, to a circle of calm:

"Oh, there you are!"

"Yes, I can see you. We are mind, or—"

"Anagryph!"

And with the Anagryph transformation came a kind of Dionysian power: The voice informed, "We sent Tom O'Bedlam to visit Phloxopha."

A flash of none other than Tom O'Bedlam, aka King Tarquin, rounded the corner and disappeared into a dead end where Phloxopha had wasted a move.

The swamp vanished and I stood back in the logic maze . . . yet, I was lost. I had to get a grip. I'd always heard: keep making left turns in a maze until you get out, but when there is a hunter that doesn't work.

Then, I swear I heard Tom O'Bedlam say to Phloxopha, *"But he who holds the moon as a male deity shall rule o'er women and be secured against all female treachery! Now! He'll grab charmer's long hair and pull it like Hell—for women with hair cut can't perform magic spells!—he'll grab it and yank it and spellbind it tight and—"*

Phloxopha screamed in fury, and a fight ensued, rustling and slapping sounds echoing in the maze.

I wondered if I could take my turn anyway. Were the rules still in effect?

Phloxopha appeared around the maze divider. It didn't look to me like she was keeping to the rules of the maze. She tried to wrap O'Bedlam in her fog, but he was erratic, like a moth, and she couldn't catch him.

I thought, The hell with it, and tried to find my way out but I kept trapping myself in dead ends.

The commotion across the maze was riotous. I now observed on the scene the weasel magician who had previously vexed King Tarquin. Here, the weasel magician pursued the Master of Matter called Athuro, mimicking him and making him trip every three feet or so. What wonderful, perverse magic!

I heard tinkling of bells. A gentle voice addressed me. I turned toward the voice and saw a woman.

She said, *"I shall speak to those to whom it is right to do so. Shut your ears, profane ones!"*

I thought, Well, she's just being polite. Profane ones can dish it out, but they can't take it. They always shut their ears.

She said, *"My name is Erin. I give gifts of culture to help defeat the bestial above and below. The shrine of poetry is the shrine of Brigid . . . remember."*

I did remember! Before, as Anagryph, I'd already met Erin.

Erin disappeared, and in her place stood the three Muses: Meditation, Memory, and Song. The Muses were joined by Agape and Irene. I recognized all of them also.

All five of them bid me to follow. They led me through a tangled wood, past circling wolves, past gushing founts, past crystal skulls on shaggy mounds, through a temple hung with hoary age to the aqua-blue river, gentle and cool, all so familiar to me. I had been in this dream before. They told me to enter the river and float downstream. I did so; I followed the watercourse way.

✦ ✦ ✦

I'd heard an LSD trip can last from eight to ten hours. How long had I been on the island? Where was I now? I looked at my watch. 7:00 P.M. I should still be hallucinating, but I was not. Short-timed doses for the first experiment? Over in four or five hours? I hoped so.

I took stock of myself. I was lying on the floor of a camo backpacking tent. I rolled over onto my hands and knees and crawled out into the early evening. Then I climbed a rock to discover I was well away from the Subi Biotech complex. When I turned and glanced back at the tent to get my bearings, I could barely see it; the tent looked like a boulder. Good camouflage! Then I heard a familiar voice.

"Pleasant dreams?"

Well! On a flat boulder, ten feet to the right of me, sipping something—tea? whisky?—from a thermos cap, a Cheshire Cat grin on his face, sat Dr. Moe. He was no longer wearing the pharaoh getup,

466

but instead was dressed in the dark-green corduroy suit he'd probably been kidnapped in.

I said, "You don't write, you don't call. What kind of friend are you?"

"I'm the kind that would like to accompany you as we escape from this godawful island."

I took a minute to try to remember what the hell I was doing. Dr. Moe remained patient as I stitched my mind back together. I said, "How is it you are here? What is this location . . . with a tent?"

I'm sure I still didn't sound very coherent, but Dr. Moe let it go and said, "I am here because my keepers for the day, Athuro and Erimacho, were given an urgent assist call to the logic maze. Evidently some miscreant had turned the place ass over teacup. That gave me a chance to ditch the robes and dress for departure. I figured you were the source of the commotion. Yes, I thought I saw you in the auditorium when I was trying to give some tips to the poor volunteers."

I said, "I attended your helpful little speech about set and setting—"

"Yes," Dr. Moe interrupted, "you were in the auditorium. I knew that was you."

"You did? I wondered if you might see me, but I didn't think you could, dazzled by the spotlight, no doubt."

Dr. Moe thought I was being sarcastic and muttered, "Very funny."

I continued, "Later, Karl was forced to capture me and make sure I ended up hallucinating in the maze."

"Some maze! Some hallucination! After you had ravaged the maze experiment, the freaked-out volunteers bolted and made a run for it, helter-skelter, shouting and howling. Most raced towards the airstrip, towards the airplane they had arrived on, but a few dashed down to the docked cargo ship, God knows why. While the lab techs, also frantic, chased after them, I hurried in the opposite direction, past the domes, and happened to run smack into Karl, who had been waiting for you outside the door of the third dome. That door is usually locked, but he had unlocked it in case you would get that far. I guess he had faith that you could prevail in the maze. Karl has been most helpful to me and to you. When I walked right into him, he suggested I continue to this spot and wait. He assured me he would bring you along if he could, and true to his word, he led you hither while carrying this tent, brought it up into these rocks for you to come down in . . . down from the clouds. He told me there had been just enough time to make these arrangements because he had been dismissed by Phloxopha from being a hunter in the maze."

Although I sardonically reflected on Dr. Moe's employment of the verb-particle combination *freaked-out,* I didn't mock him for it, and I only noted about Karl, "That was good of him." A second later, I muttered to myself, "Clouds!"

Dr. Moe gave me a look, perhaps afraid I was now having cloud visions, but, you see, it was all coming back to me. I remembered the *Daffodil,* nose up on the beach down in the cove, Dick and Chris waiting for word of success.

I asked, "Where is Karl now? I have pilots lying low, waiting to fly us out of here. Dick is one of them."

"Karl said he was going to blast open one of those air-gas bottles, a large one from the warehouse, to cause a crisis that will occupy Phloxopha and her pals while we get away."

Alarmed, I said, "What? That doesn't sound like a good plan. According to the sign, the stuff is dangerous."

"It is a beta-grade experimental hallucinogen. It is meant to be dispersed as an aerosol, but it will cling to surfaces it comes in contact with. The hallucinogen can be inhaled or absorbed."

I said, "If it gets into the air, this whole island will be compromised."

Dr. Moe replied, "We can escape before the vapor drops on us. We'll be several miles away from the discharge. Karl is right about one thing. It will keep everyone busy."

The sound of an explosive blast pounded our ears at 331 meters per second, a deafening vibrational disturbance.

I looked down the hill towards the complex and saw two things: One, a gossamer, shimmering plume of mist rising and spreading, mushroom-style, into the air over the island; and two, Karl making pretty good time uphill towards us. He must have set a timer for the blast, because he'd already covered over two miles in our direction. We waved to Karl, motioning for him to follow us, and then climbed toward the cliffs overlooking the cove. We had a rocky, half-mile slope to cover. It took us twelve minutes.

I kept looking over my shoulder, expecting to see Phloxopha's tendrils of mad molecules coming after us, but I saw nothing of the sort and only heard sounds of panic and confusion, a kind of din, erupting from the complex. I wanted to get the hell out of there. I didn't relish having another "trip," and if the gas overtook us, there was no telling what kind of dose of hallucinogen the vapor would give us.

I thought Karl had been reckless. He had endangered unworldly innocents below, the college kid volunteers who, I'm sure, didn't understand the underlying plans of Subi Biocom and the Suebi Organization. It was the kind of behavior that had always bothered me about Karl, his frequent failure to think things through. Karl! Brains, not explosions, get things done! Please learn the academic code!

Ah, well, at least Karl had been trying to help. He had helped, so I shall keep attempting to teach him the Way of the Scholar.

After all, how did I get out of the maze? Through the fruits of research, not applications of explosions. We didn't find Herak's grotto, retrieve the Greek codices, translate their scripture, discover the Shrine of Brigid, and uncover the Stele of Fate by employing explosions. We didn't coalesce Anagryph by means of explosions. You see, academic research isn't just sitting, reading in a library; it requires imagination, along with diligent, focused, extensive investigation of facts and theories. But, unless you are an academic in a specific field, nuclear physics for example, it doesn't require explosions.

I didn't know how we could assist the college kids now. No doubt the Masters of Matter were already searching for us, and we could not confront them on our own. My connection to the Stele of Fate, Tom O'Bedlam–King Tarquin, and the weasel magician had been broken as I had cleared from the hallucinogen, and redosing myself would be a fool's errand. Our best option would be to notify the authorities as soon as possible, to tell them a dozen college kids needed rescue from this island.

We reached the overlook where, below us, lay the flying boat and a campfire setup, with Dick and Flt. Lt. Leigh—Chris—frying up something in a pan.

I gave a couple of loud whistles. The two of them looked up the cliff towards us, and I waved. Dr. Moe waved. Karl waved. Dick and Chris kicked out the fire as we descended to the cove. By the time we got there, Chris was in the process of tying an enormous North Atlantic salmon into the bomb bay for transport.

Chris said, "I fought this monster for twenty minutes on twenty-pound test. He must weigh at least seventy pounds! I don't intend to give him up!"

Dick said, "It was an amazin' display of anglin,' it was. Can't leave that fish behind!"

I noted, "We're not safe yet, by any means. You know this, Dick, and now I've seen Phloxopha's fog. I don't wish to see it again."

Dick agreed. "Nor I, lad!"

We pushed the *Daffodil* off the beach and began turning it, floating it, to face the keyhole, the passageway to the North Channel. Both Chris and Dick had already climbed up the bow rope ladder and had worked their way aft. We waded into the shallow water, and I asked Dr. Moe to ascend the ladder, with Karl next, then me. While I climbed to the bow cockpit, Chris ignited the engines and we slipped out into the cove. Dick sat in the copilot's seat, while Karl ducked into the forward cabin, but Dr. Moe and I remained in the forward gunner's cockpit. No ammo available, though. Since we didn't have ordnance, I hoped we wouldn't need it. Anyway, escape is all about navigation, I thought. Chris will be smart, evade, and disappear.

As the *Daffodil* cleared the keyhole, Chris opened the throttles to both engines and at the same time turned into the south wind. We were forced to fly south for takeoff, but at least we were paralleling the eastern leg of the horseshoe, not the western, where the Subi Biotech complex had been built.

As we gained altitude, I trained binoculars on the complex. It looked as though Phloxopha and Ororotohos were trying to use their powers to shield the complex from the aerosol dispersion. They employed roiling molecules in the form of a black fog to swirl the atmosphere and prevent the hallucinogenic droplets from descending onto the grounds, buildings, and people; but were they going to let the plume drift over the North Channel?

Chris banked us sharply to the west. As we crossed over Rathlin Island, he pointed to a house overlooking the Channel, his family summerhouse I guessed, and then we headed toward the North Irish coast.

Just when I felt we had made it, our rescue a success, a jet aircraft buzzed us, causing considerable backwash turbulence, buffeting the flying boat the way a wind shear might. I saw the jet bank east to come around for another pass.

Chris said over the com, "My ONEWORD device beeped. Its message: Die! I think the pilot of that jet sent the message, but I don't know how, because I have a security code."

I replied, "I told you, Subi Biocom can't be trusted. They probably have a way to defeat the security code and track us, too, some sort of backdoor into the device."

Chris said, "Maybe, because the ONEWORD proximity indicator has turned orange."

As I looked back at Chris in the pilot's cockpit, I saw him toss the device over the side. Too late, I thought.

The jet came around again, the flaming sword logo visible on its fuselage, this time trailing acrobatic smoke, like a skywriter, intending to envelop us in it, confuse us and crash us. But then I realized what the smoke really was.

So did Dick. He said to Chris, "Um, this, this is not smoke in the usual sense, Chris, this is what I was tellin' ya about . . ."

The roiling black smoke morphed into tendrils, which reached out towards the *Daffodil*. Chris banked right and up, but the sinister coil wound its way to the propellers, fouling them and slowing their rotation, causing the aeroplane to lose speed and maneuverability. The coil was now detached from the jet, but it continued to harry us. It was obvious to me that a Master of Matter controlled the Subi Biocom jet.

Alarmed, Chris said, "What in the hell is that? That's what you were telling me about, Dick?"

Dick said to Chris, "Allow me to take the controls, I know all the quirks of this machine."

Chris said, "Take it," and ducked through to the aft cockpit just as the jet came fast from directly behind and flew under us, causing nasty upwash turbulence, destabilizing the aeroplane and scaring the hell out of the landlubbers.

But Dick said, "No worse than the storm we encountered off Portugal in '40."

I didn't believe him. The flying boat rocked back and forth and seemed ready to plunge into a spin. I latched my seatbelt. Dr. Moe already had. But Dick brought the aeroplane back level.

Chris fussed in the bomb bay—why? I didn't know. Resecuring the giant fish, perhaps? I wasn't sure this was the time to worry about it.

As the jet came up behind us for a third pass, Dr. Moe and I held on to a gunwale with our knuckles white; Karl poked his head out of the cabin, yelling something in patois that we didn't understand, and then Chris barked, "Bombs away!"

He pulled the release lever. The giant salmon plunged from the belly of the *Daffodil*, somersaulted, tumbling with momentum as it dropped, and dove into a yawning engine opening of the attacking Subi Biocom business jet.

I first surmised the jet engine had sucked it in, but I've realized since, the jet literally ran into the tumbling fish.

Dick instinctively banked left and was just able to stay level, the slightly unweighted *Daffodil* managing follow his inputs on the controls.

The mechanical mayhem caused by the now-sashimi salmon to the engine and the jet itself caused the Subi Biocom aircraft to do an immediate, terminal dive into the sea. The gaseous tendrils that had menaced us dispersed and disappeared, and our props regained their efficiency.

Chris said, "Put us down, Dick, perhaps there are survivors, though I doubt it." He radioed to the RAF, the Sea Rescue command, and the Coast Guard.

Dick landed the *Daffodil* in the chop of the Irish Sea, and we motored toward the wreckage.

I saw no survivors, but there was an awful lot of fish chum. Back at the pilot's controls, Chris carefully motored the flying boat near the wreckage, but none of us saw a hint of life. And if we had, what would we have seen? I didn't want to think about it.

Before all the possible agencies arrived on scene, we decided we didn't wish to get caught up in Northern Ireland red tape. Who knew where that would lead? How could we explain the attack by a Subi business jet, the menacing fog tendrils, the whole surreal experience? Chris had thrown his ONEWORD device into the ocean, the message gone with it. So, we just kept to the essential truth: We said we were flying south and had observed the business jet flying erratically, as if there were something wrong with the pilot. The jet went into a spin and crashed. We landed to help but observed no survivors. We advised the authorities that the business jet had markings identifying it as a Subi Biocom aircraft.

Chapter Aon Deag   -11-

WE NIGHT-LANDED ON THE field near St. Brigid's Cathedral at about eleven, all of us emotionally spent, wrung out, exhausted. But it was good to be back.

Chris had radioed the regional RAF hangar to forward a message to Graves that we were to land in Kildare in three quarters of an hour. I guess Graves received the message, because he had sent Cessair to park the church van at the near end of the field to illuminate the landing zone with the van's headlights. Cessair had sat waiting in the van with Anastasia until the *Daffodil* flew over to follow the lights and land in the field.

The *Daffodil* turned and taxied towards the van, bumping across the alfalfa until Chris shut down her engines.

When I hit the ground, Anastasia was on me, and I on her in an instant, embracing. It was such a relief for me to be back with her in what I thought of as reality.

Dr. Moe made it down the ladder, and Anastasia gave him a hug, too, although not the same kind of hug. But she was relieved, ecstatic

(I saw a tear run down her cheek), to see him safe once again. Then Karl climbed down.

She said, "Karl! You're safe too. I'm so happy for you, for all of us!"

Dr. Moe testified, "Karl was a great help to me and to Griffin. Also kidnapped, like me, he held up under dire circumstances against supernatural beings by being clever, by biding his time until he could see an advantage. Festus just thought of him as a dunce to be exploited."

I could tell that while they were held in captivity, Dr. Moe had been teaching Karl how to deal with the adverse circumstances they had encountered. Now my distinguished friend and colleague was praising his pupil. I just wished Dr. Moe hadn't turned Karl into a bomb-tossing mercenary to boot.

Karl replied, "Both Dr. Moe and Dr. MacRobbin beat the logic maze. It was a big deal! Against all odds!"

Cessair said, "The logic maze? Well, now, whatever is that?"

Both Dr. Moe and I replied in unison, "Don't ask!"

Anastasia looked at me and grinned; she had taken in some of the logic maze experience as Anagryph. We would talk about that later.

Chris Leigh and Dick, having secured the aeroplane, climbed down and joined the group. We piled into the van to run back to the vicarage, where we would spend the night. It was soon midnight, and when we entered the abode, everyone there had already retired. Cessair showed each of us to our previous rooms and found a place for Karl and then for Chris too. Did I detect a bit of chemistry between the rangy, freckle-faced, Flight Lieutenant Leigh and the winsome Cessair?

✦ ✦ ✦

The next morning, I tuned in to the BBC news. It seems an industrial accident had ravaged a Subi Biotech site in Northern Ireland, and the complex required worker evacuation and facility abandonment.

The Coast Guards from Northern Ireland, the Irish Republic, and Scotland jointly assisted in the rescue of college kids and workers.

In addition, a Subi Biocom aircraft had crashed in the North Channel, leaving no survivors, and no bodies had been recovered. Goodness. Not a happy day for Festus-The-Kidnapper. Was it he, piloting the Subi jet? Unlikely, as he is an old-fashioned kind of guy, well over three thousand years old, according to Thoth, and I doubt he knew how. He'd be more likely to fly without an aircraft, on a broom.

Anastasia and I sat in the rose garden sipping black tea and munching scones snatched from the kitchen counter. Above us, thick cloud cover bathed the Irish morning in twilight, and the rose petals lay heavy with dew.

I said, "Now, tell me about the Stele of Fate."

She ignored my inquiry; she wanted her own questions answered. She asked, "Why did the Subi industry location have so many dangerous casks of hallucinogen stored there? And what were the volunteer experiments for?"

I replied, "This is conjecture, but I think the Northern Facility of Subi Biotech was built in the safest location to hold the experiments, which at some point, would involve the use of aerosols."

Anastasia asked, "Safe? Safe how? You think Festus cares about safety?"

"I imagine he cares about the wrong kind of publicity. If there were an accidental release of aerosols, the remote location would be an advantage, because any fumes would be dispersed over the water by the local sea breezes, and no one the wiser. But I think Karl's sabotage was more than they bargained for."

"OK," she said. "What else did you learn?"

"Dr. Moe told me he overheard Festus complaining one night that the hallucinogen project, the fusing of psychoactive elements to the ONEWORD device, was not going well, and his Sino-Soviet investors were becoming impatient. So, to speed things up, the investors foisted a psyops team on Festus. They encouraged him to transfer his best techs to the island. The techs were to run questionable experiments to identify a drug that would work with the ONEWORD gadget. If they still had no success, they planned to use chemtrail aerosols over cities instead."

Anastasia sighed. "What a misuse of psychoactive substances. Psychedelics have always existed in nature and have been used from time to time by various cultures."

I agreed, "Peyote, mescaline, certain fungi."

She added, "Leave it to modern man to isolate a hallucinogen and manufacture it as a chemical but fail to learn from ancient teachings when, where, how, and why to use it."

I said, "Doctors Leary, Metzner, and Alpert have been trying to persuade people to understand both the possible benefit and also the sure dangers of experimenting with such a substance without proper instruction, but they have been vilified for their efforts."

Anastasia glanced at me. She said, "Cutting-edge professors are always at risk."

I let that soak in. Then I questioned, "The Stele of Fate?"

She replied, "I guess it is my turn, now that you've told me some of what went on after you landed on the Subi Biotech island. I had a lovely conversation with Professor Drinkwater at the British Museum. By consulting the Rosetta Stone, he was able to help me translate some, but not all the glyphs. So, when he was flummoxed by certain pictographs, guess whom he consulted."

I replied, "Well, I know it wasn't Dr. Moe."

"Ollie. He and Professor Drinkwater are old friends. I might have known, what with the connection to the British Museum and all."

"We should have contacted Olympia Thoth in the first place."

"Oh, remember, I tried," Anastasia noted, "but neither Aunt Anastasija nor I could get ahold of Ollie. Infuriating!"

Thinking about something Dr. Moe had mentioned, I mused, "If Festus is a demiurge, his power is beyond the breadth of human knowledge. I wonder why he would kowtow to Mao's CCP and the Soviets."

Anastasia said, "According to Thoth, Festus is the ultimate autocrat. To that end, he has been studying human behavior for centuries, trying to discern why civilizations rise and fall. His continuing experiments involve totalitarianism—the subordination of the individual to the state—and now, with the two distinct projects he has carefully nurtured, I imagine he wishes to work with these regimes because they might speed him towards his fundamental goal: total human acceptance of his 'magnificent' rule on earth."

I replied, "That makes some sense. However, after my encounter with Festus, I think he would not allow any 'investor' impertinence."

Anastasia said, "There is another reason."

I raised my eyebrows.

She gazed at me, deciding. What would she reveal?

At length she allowed, "For centuries, the Gnosis of our coterie has attenuated Festus's power, so he actually needs human assistance to achieve his grand schemes."

I interrupted, "Your coterie?"

In reply, she just looked at me, sans expression.

So I added, "Dr. Moe and I have already determined you come from an Eastern European Gnostic clan, Anastasia."

A shadow skipped across her face. She whispered, "Not a clan. A loose affiliation—as Thoth has told me—from the time of the pharaohs, reaching all the way to the here and now."

I questioned, "From the time of the pharaohs? What do you mean?"

Her dark hair fell forward, caught by gravity as she made a sudden downward glance. Then she slowly raised her head and said one word: "Immortality."

I shook my head and repeated, "Immortality?"

She asked, "Do you believe in reincarnation?"

I didn't reply. I mean, what was she talking about? Buddhism?

Anastasia whispered, "Thoth, Herak, Yasoda, Lazo, Joko, Aunt Anastasija, Graves, Dick, Lili, Stevan, Marian, Smyth, me . . . you. We have been here before."

Not Buddhism. Pop culture—something about, we've already been here, roaming around the planet in a previous life. But, whenever I have dismissed Anastasia's assertions out of hand, I have been wrong. Still, I thought for a minute about everything going off the rails, so I kept my mouth shut.

"Don't you remember? I told you: you and I have always been together. You said, 'When you tell me, I remember.' You said so, sitting on Kevin's bed at the lake, and recall what you learned from Aunt Anastasija on our visit to Jockey Hollow."

I remembered when, over tumblers of whiskey, Dr. Moe and I considered that Anastasia might be nuts. I thought of the bluegrass song "Whiskey 'fore Breakfast." I felt like having a breakfast whisky now. I said, "These tidings, that I'm a part of your immortal coterie, you couldn't have presented sooner? Back in Claremont for example?" *Dr. Moe would have had her committed.*

She squinted at me. "In Claremont, this information had just come to me from Thoth, when he told me about Festus, the Suebi Order, and about my murdered parents. I was hardly ready for it—even with all my training as an adept. Were you prepared, then, to learn such information?"

I, the professor, replied, "And on this exegesis from Thoth, this fugue of mythography, suddenly, your critical thinking takes a holiday?"

Anastasia looked at me and laughed, not a mirthful laugh. More ironic, I would say. She insisted, "No. You weren't ready. Neither was Dr. Moe. That's why Thoth has kept this mystery from you ever as he did in New York."

I had considered Thoth was a trickster. Photons, leptons, et cetera, be damned.

She said, "What do you think happened with my father when he confronted Festus on the tower of the Persian Fortress in Cairo?"

I shrugged.

She said, "What do you think happened in the sacred circle below Mt. Lovćen in Montenegro? Remember Anagryph? What about the Round Dance at Cismontane? The Subi island Logic Maze experience? The Stele of Fate?"

I had to admit to myself: These things of which she spoke—they all had happened. And during the Cismontane Round Dance, I did have déjà vu. Déjà vu, like the first time Anastasia and I crossed eyes in my seminar so many months ago, when I had scanned the class and immediately identified Anastasia Romanov, as if I already knew her. I allowed her words to churn around in my head. I heard a door slam in the rectory. It began to rain, but we were still sheltered by the tree. I finally asked, "Do you think you are a Goddess? Actually, the Queen of Spring?"

She glanced up at the rolling clouds. I saw tears well in her eyes. She said, "It has all come before me, and as you know, I am now the keeper of the Stele of Fate."

The Stele of Fate. I pictured the altar in the crypt under St. Brigid's perpetual fire shrine, pictured it as it had lain unknown, concealed for centuries. The Stele exists. It wields power on Earth. I stared at Anastasia. Until now, I hadn't realized, I hadn't understood the burden, the weight of centuries, of what my esteemed colleague, Dr. Moe, had called "immense and overcharged pieces of mystery," the

All. The All had sought her out: the overburden had landed on her. How could I be so dim? So self-centered, with everything we'd been through? You'd think after my experience on the Subi island complex I would have fully grasped the cosmogonic implications of Anastasia's duress. I took her hand in mine.

We sat together but alone in our thoughts, gazing out at the dampened roses. Birds fluttered in the trees above and a raindrop landed on the stones at our feet.

Still looking out at the garden, Anastasia forced out, through a husky voice, "Come with me."

We borrowed Cessair's Mini for a trip to St. Brigid's Cathedral. After parking on the gravel, we extracted ourselves from the little car, and the rain stopped as we made our way to the round tower. There, we mounted the staircase to the entrance that stood about fifteen feet off the ground. Anastasia unlocked the door so we could climb (and climb and climb) ladder-like stairs to finally reach the top, which I might note, through the battlements presented an expansive view of the countryside. But I saw nothing in the tower but a low shelter, open on the sides, with a rustic roof. If it rained again, maybe we could creep under it.

Anastasia knelt there and muttered something, an incantation. The Stele of Fate shimmered into view.

I observed the slab sat on five upright stones, like the ones on which it had originally been placed, and it occupied the little shelter. The Stele radiated the green-turquoise aura I was familiar with.

Before I could comment, Anastasia said, "The incantations revealed by the hieroglyphs allow me to hide the Stele from view, by manipulating the Stele's photon vibrations."

I stepped to the battlement edge to observe the Stele's aura, which now radiated brightly, like spokes on a prone wheel, by shining through the crenellations, the battlement openings, in all directions, both over the town and the surrounding countryside. The long rays occasionally bounced and scattered off low-hanging clouds, creating an astonishing light show against the dreary morning. Anastasia joined me, and we stood for a time, marveling at the mysterious luminosity of the ancient stone.

Eventually she said, "The Stele enabled me to meld with you so that we could again form Anagryph. By using incantations instructed by the hieroglyphs, I understood you needed me, needed Anagryph again. I brought the Stele to the tower—I thought the height might help the Stele reach you, and when I felt what you felt, I became frantic but focused."

"You sent me Tom O'Bedlam! And the Russian magician-weasel! That turned out to be inspired."

"Gnostic knowledge is poetic knowledge. I sent a wild man and beast to confront a wild woman, because sometimes a Dionysian poetic approach is required."

"And then Erin and the muses led me out of the maze." Just then, I thought I heard a noise from below echo up the inside of the round tower. I said, "Did you hear that?"

Anastasia replied, "This tower is ancient, it creaks and moans."

I said, "Did I tell you, when I was in the Subi Biotech dome, out its window I saw this tower bathed in green aura."

"That was the Stele of Fate reaching out to you."

We heard a creaking on the ladder nearby and a voice said, "Reaching out to us too! When you used the Stele of Fate to attack our island, Anastasia, its existence, presence, and location were revealed to us."

Climbing up through the opening came Festus Griveaux followed by Athuro, one of the Masters-of-Matter. I did a doubletake at Athuro, because half his head was a fish head! Specifically, part of his head had combined with that of a large Atlantic salmon such as the one

Chris Leigh had caught but had to utilize as a *bloquer le passage* to disable the attacking Subi jet.

If I had not recently been experiencing hallucinogenic visions and had not learned how to assimilate them, the sudden appearance of a man-fish horror might have caused me to jump off the tower. But, in fact, as Director of the Institute for Antiquity, I'm quite comfortable with mythopoeic constructions and their manifestations.

Oops! I began to realize: it was exactly Chris Leigh's salmon that had combined with Athuro to turn him into a chimera. He must have been piloting the Subi jet, and after his aircraft collided with the salmon, the jet's ensuing plunge into the sea had scattered bits and pieces of Athuro throughout the crash site. When he reconstituted, as Masters-of-Matter are supposed to be able to do, his matter became comingled with Chris's sashimi salmon chum, which was also floating at the site. Disgusting! I also noted that Athuro had a tailfin where his right arm should have been . . . probably would have made him an Olympic swim champ.

I thought: *This is ironic; a Gryphon is a chimera too.* Yet, I was merely a symbolic chimera, I believe.

Anastasia looked at me as if she knew what I was musing, and I think she felt I wasn't grasping the seriousness of the situation.

She said, "What do you want, Festus?"

"I want the Stele of Fate, Anastasia."

She replied, cool as an Irish breeze, "You may ask. I shall deny."

Athuro took a menacing step toward her. I cut him off and said, "Uh-uh." I was crazy to think I could contend with a creature such as he, but I thought maybe I could keep circling toward his right (fin) arm, leaving him only with a left-hand jab to rely on.

Festus said, "Come now. Please. We are all gentlemen here, and of course, a lady. I always hate it when you humans insist on making things unpleasant. Dr. MacRobbin, we had such a stimulating conversation on my island, but I understand you didn't like our logic maze. So disappointing!"

I asked, "Why do you want the Stele, Festus?"

"I want it so that it is no longer a threat to me," he replied matter-of-factly.

Anastasia said, "And if there were no threats to you, what would you do?"

"Oh, I've had this discussion at length with your parents, Anastasia, long ago now, but I haven't changed."

Provoked by his comment, his reference to her murdered parents, Anastasia decided the time had come. She said, "You've been calling me by my improper name."

Festus questioned, seeming to enjoy this little cat-and-mouse exchange, "So what is your proper name, Anastasia?"

"Anna. Anna Fearina."

The smile wavered on Festus's face. He seemed to be remembering something.

Anastasia said, "I'd like to introduce you to my . . . consort, Gryphon."

Festus mused, "Gryphon? Gryphon whom?"

Anna said, "Why, your friendly conversationalist, Doctor Gryphon MacRobbin."

I didn't have to say anything as I watched the smile disappear from his face.

He said, "Anna Fearina, the Queen of Spring?"

"And Gryphon MacRobbin," she reminded him, "A Lion and an Eagle."

Festus lunged toward the Stele of Fate, but as he did so Anna said, "Mercurius!" and a force halted Festus as if he had hit an invisible wall. Now I knew. Anastasia had chosen: Transformation! You see, Mercurius is the giver of life, as well as the revisor of the old form.

I said, "We are not set on destruction, but the Stele of Fate will transform you."

With a smirk Festus replied, "Transform me? Into what exactly?"

I didn't know precisely into what or whom the Stele would transform Festus, however, Anna's knowledge of *Mysteria* well surpassed mine. Her reply was a dish served cold. She said, "Transform you into an entity that is enveloped by your past history, and you will forever grieve as memories of your transgressions enshroud you!" At this remark, the stele shimmered brighter.

But Festus laughed. "What hubris!"

The turquoise aura of the Stele of Fate had been emanating from the top of the round tower to such a degree that it had been visible at the rectory, not to mention the surrounding countryside, and we could hear a crowd, attracted, gathering below. It was then we learned Festus still had a last trick of his own. He had sensed the gathering on the cathedral grounds. He whispered an incantation, and I soon heard shouts of alarm. Festus grinned.

Avoiding Athuro, who was starting to reek of spoiled fish, Anastasia and I looked over the battlement to see Phloxopha and Ororotohos weaving their black coils around the perimeter of the churchyard, trapping the men, women, and children who had converged there. We could see Dr. Moe, Bishop MacBride, Aunt Anastasija, Joko, Lili, Graves, von Konigswald, standing amongst the townsfolk, and country citizens.

Festus barked, "Now, Anastasia, Gryphon! What do you say? Shall I kill them? Do you want them to die?" He made a gesture, and I could hear more cries of alarm below the tower. Festus said, "I'm growing impatient, Anastasia, so is Athuro. It's time for his swim. What will it be?"

"I told you, Festus, my name is Anna Fearina!"

The Stele pulsed, emitting new, short bursts of radiant photons.

"Oh!" he said, unconcerned, "The living Goddess . . . but she can't choose!" He laughed. "Give me the Stele of Fate and I will rule mankind as I was meant to do. If you do not, we will go on as before, but with dead citizens on your hands, Anna Fearina!"

Anastasia, wordless, glared at Festus.

Festus folded his arms and grinned at her, and the Stele's light show seemed to bounce off his teeth.

Suddenly, Anastasia declared, "I'm not a goddess! I'm a woman!"

Oddly stunned by Anna's reversal, Festus stepped back.

Where will this lead, this abdication? I began to sweat.

From the depths of what could only have been her true heart she cried, "We want our friends. You shall have the stele!"

Festus gasped. "What? You wish to make the exchange?"

We all stood, unmoving, the sounds of alarm continuing below.

Anastasia, now calm, and cold as ice, said, "Give us what does not belong to you."

Whatever would happen now, she had chosen. So, squinting against the flare and flash, I crouched, lifted the Stele of Fate, turned, and gave the stone slab to Festus. Although the Stele wasn't fiery hot, I was glad to get rid of it!

Festus took the Stele in hand. When he did, the turquoise emitted an enveloping radiance, and below Saint Brigid's tower, the menacing coils of Phloxopha's and Ororotohos's dark matter began to recede from the terrified crowd huddled on the cathedral grounds.

Festus said, "You would enable me to rule all of mankind to save this little town? Holding the Stele high, he whirled around. "What has been banished from the heart of humankind?" I thought he was going to dance a jig. He sang, "Is the human race ready to take on responsibility for itself? No more scapegoats? God?" He shouted, "Fate? Fortune? Luck? The Queen of Spring? Aha . . . I don't feel the lust for slaughter anymore!"

I considered that his antics were part of an elaborate trick. But then I realized—the oath that Festus had mistakenly ordered into his world many years ago, delivered at the crumbling Cairo Persian Fortress by Anastasia's father, Stevan, had reached its conclusion: The Stele of Fate gleamed with the prophecy constructed from Gnosis that lives beyond the cosmos, transubstantiating Festus, changing him into something . . . other. As I watched this enigma unfolding, I wondered if Festus realized what was happening to him. I knew one thing for certain: Festus Griveaux's time, his centuries on Earth, had come to an end.

Festus held up the shimmering Stele—which flashed brighter and brighter. His voice was fire. "I recognize those who came before me! I recognize the divine that lives beyond the stars!"

The glow, caused by the disintegrating leptons and nucleons of the Stele of Fate itself, ran up Festus's arms and over his body, consuming him, even as the process of transubstantiation also consumed the Stele. The chimera, Athuro, disappeared, and below, the other Masters-of-Matter faded into the land. Only Festus Griveaux's final words echoed, before they, too, were no more:

"HUMANKIND!"—his shout cannoned across the country-side—"You are free from me at last. THIS DAY ON, DO WHAT YOU WILL!"

-End-

THE MOON AND THE GRYPHON

Acknowledgements

I met James Robinson (1924–2016) who was the director of The Coptic Gnostic Library Project of the Institute for Antiquity and Christianity, after the publication of the project's initial volume of *The Nag Hammadi Library in English*. I was and am grateful for Dr. Robinson's generosity with his time in speaking with me and for pointing me in fertile directions for my research—concerning my novel inspired by the codices and the translation project. It was his inspiration to photograph the papyrus pages so that any scholar could access them for research. Thanks to my permissions editor, Diane Kraut, and to HarperCollins Publishers, New York, NY, and to E. J. Brill, Leiden, The Netherlands, for allowing me to use a few of the translations for the novel. But otherwise, and assuredly, *The Moon and The Gryphon* is a work of imagination—a work of fiction with no resemblance to the actual translation project, or to the learned scholars who did the translation work.

I thank my copy editor Christopher Hoffmann of Copy Write Consultants, for his sharp eye for error, and for his knowledge of my subject matter. Any remaining errors are purely my own. Thank you

Rosemi Mederos—America's Editor, for manuscript evaluation, and for noting that after starting the book, she couldn't put it down, yet had cogent suggestions to make the story even better. Thanks to one of my first readers, Dan Bowers, retired Prentis Hall field editor, who remarked that if I could get a fiction publisher to read it, they'd publish it. He also pointed out that a phrase I had written, "soft susurrations," was redundant. Thanks, Dan! Thanks to Scott Herron, my erstwhile short story editor. He's a former newspaper editor, and is retired from Radio Free Europe, Voice of America, and CNN International. He remarked my novel is not the kind of book he normally reads but was dismayed that I killed off Marian, as she was a favorite character. I took that as encouragement. Thanks to Gale Herron who informed Scott that Marian's daughter, Anastasia, admirably carries the book forward—further encouragement! I'm grateful for the time, years ago, I spent in County Kildare, Ireland, fox hunting with the master of the Kildare Hounds, my father. Most of all, I thank my lucky stars that I'm married to a knowledgeable, patient, and insightful developmental editor, Deborah, whom I love for countless unrelated reasons, who would not allow me to stop halfway through the manuscript.

Permissions

Excerpts from pp. 126-127, 168-169, 277, 296-297 from The Nag Hammadi Library, James M Robinson, General Editor, Copyright © 1978, 1988 by E.J. Brill, Leiden, The Netherlands. Used by permission of HarperCollins Publishers; and by permission of E.J Brill, Leiden, The Netherlands.

Notes To: The Moon and The Gryphon

—Pomegranates were often carved at mystical sites; they symbolize eternity because "It's the only fruit worms do not corrupt." Graves, *TWG*.

Khalifah and Muhammad Ali are the actual discoverers of The Nag Hammadi Library, and said they found the texts while sifting for "sebakh," a fertile soil for their garden. For an historical account of the discovery, and its significance, see *The Gnostic Gospels* by Elaine Pagels.

The idea of spirits, of magic, was very real to Egyptian peasants in 1946, according to several books which discuss that locale and era.

According to Paul Schmitt and Otto Kern, "Heraclitus (refers to) the mysteries of night ramblers, magicians, bacchants, maenads, mystics, wizards and the haunters of misty hollows." *The Mysteries, Papers From The ERANOS Yearbooks*. Bollingen Series XXX * 2, Princeton University Press Copyright 1955; Second printing 1971.

"Whose garments were sky colored . . ." etc. This description and the poem: "This day, this day, this this, The Royal Wedding is . . ." etc. are adapted from the alchemical romance of 1616 by Christian Rosencreutz: *The Hermetic Romance or the Chymical Wedding*, a Rosicrucian tract.

The mysterious disappearances and difficulties in carrying out the translation project are basically true. *The Laughing Savior*, by John Dart discusses this.

Thoth: Egyptian god of wisdom, learning and magic, the inventor of numbers and letters. The Greeks called him Hermes, hence I call him Olympia Thoth to combine Egyptian, Greek, and goddess aspects.

The Indian Bo Tree—Buddha was enlightened after sitting for forty-nine days under the Indian Bo tree.

The Hypsiphrone tractate is, according to John D. Turner, translator, in such a fragmentary state, it "prevents a clear understanding of the nature and contents of the discourse." However, *Hypsiphrone* means "She of High Mind." Hence, one of the original "Greek texts" is Hypsiphrone in this novel. The Babylon Fortress is an ancient, fortified city, which presently stands in what is now called Coptic Cairo. But it is thought the original Babylon Fortress, or Persian Fortress, stood on cliffs overlooking the Nile.

The Nag Hammadi Library mentions "steles of turquoise" on which are written hieroglyphic characters, in the Hermetic tractate, "The Discourse on The Eighth and Ninth."

The Round Dance was a Gnostic mystical dance. Lines are reworked from "The Acts of St. John." Max Pulver, *The Mysteries, Papers From The ERANOS Yearbooks.* Bollingen Series XXX * 2, Princeton University Press Copyright 1955; Second printing 1971.

"She wore a robe that was brighter than a fire-flash . . ." etc. An ancient Greek poem, Anonymous.

"Lovely maiden of the moon . . ." etc. 41st rune of the *Kalevala*, Finnish 19th century work of epic poetry.

Excerpt from p. 179 *The Mysteries, Papers From The ERANOS Yearbooks.* Bollingen Series XXX * 2, Princeton University Press Copyright 1955; Second printing 1971.

Excerpts from pp. 272, 215 From *The Nag Hammadi Library in English* Translated by members of the Coptic Gnostic Library Project Of The Institute For Antiquity And Christianity, James M. Robinson, Director Copyright 1977 by E.J Brill, Leiden, The Netherlands.

"I, Eve, sad mother . . . Miserable Eve!" Christina Rossetti – *Eve*

"A thousand handicraftsmen wore the maskOf Poesy, Ill-fated, impious race!"
"A drainless shower Of light is poesy; 'tis the supreme of power . . ."
"Then let us clear away the choking thorns . . . overgrown With simple flowers . . ." John Keats—*Sleep and Poetry*.

"Beneath yon Birch with silver bark . . . find the Knight that wears The Griffin for his crest." Samuel Taylor Coleridge from *The Ballad of The Dark Ladie. A Fragment.* "When a man refers to inward feelings and experiences, of which mankind at large are not conscious . . . I name Mysticism." Samuel Taylor Coleridge—*Aids to Reflection.* "a savage place! As holy and enchanted as e'er beneath a waning moon was haunted by woman wailing for her demon-lover!" Samuel Taylor Coleridge—*Kubla Khan*

THE MOON and THE GRYPHON is divided into six Codex sections:
Codex I chapter numbers are in *English*: Chapter One, Chapter Two . . . etc.
Codex II chapter numbers are in *Coptic*: Chapter Owway, Chapter Esnav . . . etc.
Codex III chapter numbers are in *Latin*: Chapter Unus, Duo, Tres . . . etc.
Codex IV chapter numbers are in *Egyptian numerals*: Chapter i, ii, iii, iiii, iiiii, iiiii i .
Codex V chapter numbers are in *Serbo-Croat*: Jedno, Dva, Tri . . . etc.
Codex VI chapter numbers are in *Irish Gaelic*: Chapter Aon, do, tri . . . etc.

About the Author

T.F. Long is a writer from Colorado, USA.

T. F. Long worked in advertising before transitioning to journalism as a police reporter, and as a feature writer for various daily newspapers. Long has traveled extensively throughout Europe, including visits to Britain, Ireland, France, Germany, Italy, Croatia, Slavonia, and Montenegro, all of which served as inspiration for this novel.

www.ingramcontent.com/pod-product-compliance
Lightning Source LLC
Chambersburg PA
CBHW021329310726
48971CB00001B/45